Reborn

Reborn

Book Two of the Cartographer

Craig Gaydas

Published 2014 by Creativia

Book design by Creativia (www.creativia.org)

Cover art by http://www.thecovercollection.com/

"Some fight for honor. Some fight for glory. Others fight for riches. No matter the cause, it only matters that you fight."
- Vanth the Adjudicator

"The cycle of life knows only one ending. Death."
- Mortem the Destructor

"Appear weak when you are strong, and strong when you are weak."
- Sun Tzu

"Sometimes you have to start a war in order to have peace."
- Calypso

"We have witnessed the beginning of the universe. I fear we will live to witness its end."
- Ibune the Progenitor

"And I saw a new heaven and a new earth, for the first heaven and the first earth had passed away, and there was no more sea."
- Revelations 21:1

"My universal discombobulator-recombobulator must be on the fritz again."
- Grillick the Artificer

Contents

PROLOGUE

"I see a court-martial in our future." Embeth frowned and shoved a grenade into the bandolier before reaching over and grabbing the last neutralizer. A cartridge for the weapon lay on a nearby table. He scowled at it before grabbing it, loading it into the gun and slipping it into an ankle holster.

"Let's worry about that later," I muttered.

Kedge slipped his staff into the sling strapped to his back and fixed me with a hard look. I felt his monocled eye boring into me. He continued staring until finally I threw up my hands in exasperation.

"What?" I asked, mildly irritated.

He offered a weak smile before reaching into the folds of his robe. His closed fist emerged and he held it out. "Open your hand."

I opened it reluctantly, realizing it remained difficult for me to trust him. He had been the former leader of our enemy, the Lumagom. No matter how many times he attempted to make amends for past misdeeds he was still responsible, in part, for the mess we found ourselves in. He hesitated before dropping a small, metallic object into my open hand. Despite the dirt and grime which had accumulated around the object I managed to observe small glimmers of gold. When I rubbed the grime away I saw it was a small, golden ankh.

"Is this what I think it is?" I asked, irritation giving way to surprise.

"Yes," he replied. "I kept it safe for centuries in order to preserve the memory of Mars. This trinket is enchanted with good fortune. It has kept me safe up to this point. I pass it to you in the hope that its luck will transfer over to you."

I was about to offer my thanks but Wraith interrupted us. He shoved several golf ball-sized objects into my hand. Instead of dimples, several tiny metallic diamonds were embedded in its surface.

"What are these?"

"Stun grenades, in order to keep the casualties to a minimum," he explained.

"Thanks," I replied, letting the cold metal tickle the palm of my hand as I turned them over and inspected them. "Good idea."

"Of course it's a good idea. It was my idea," he quipped.

Lianne clipped her sword to her belt and moved to my side. "We are ready." She frowned at my apprehension. "Perhaps I should ask if you are."

I shoved the grenades into my pocket and shrugged. "I guess so." My reply did not satisfy her. Her scowl became annoying. "What do you expect me to say? Last month I was a teenager worrying about math grades, now I'm trying to save the world. It's a pretty difficult transition."

Her frown faded and her features softened. "Sorry, Nathan. I seemed to have forgotten you are still young, and have a lot to learn."

"I'm not much older than you, Lianne." My reply, dryer than intended, caused a pained look to cross her face.

Before she could respond, Gard interrupted. "*Sir, Earth's satellites have moved out of position. We are cleared to launch.*"

"Thank you, Gard." Satou turned to us and called out over his shoulder. "Get ready and strap yourselves in, folks. We are ready to take off!"

Wraith hopped in the co-pilot chair while the rest of us did as Satou instructed. We launched from Docking Bay 5 into the emptiness of space. I chuckled nervously when I glanced at our "crew". Two Council members, an emotionless robot, a Defense Fleet Captain, an ornery weapons specialist and a human teenager whose greatest accomplishment up to this point was getting an A on his Advanced Physics exam. We were an odd group about to do something that only a short time ago I would have never in my wildest dreams thought possible.

We were about to invade Earth.

TROUBLE

"I gave you explicit instructions to remain on the Argus until we arrived!" Meta's face grew darker with each word. His enraged face filled the screen.

Embeth remained resolute and matched the High Prince's scowl with one of his own. "I refuse to leave my men behind. It was a judgment call, plain and simple." Embeth tapped the control panel impatiently.

"Embeth, you should know better! Your men wouldn't have been left behind. Helios Protocol is a proactive defense measure," Meta explained. "They would have been recovered."

"What have you done?" Enraged, I stepped between Embeth and the screen.

Meta's face turned crimson when he saw me. "You," he spat. "I am beginning to think we made a mistake integrating you into the Explorer's League. Humans are nothing but trouble."

"What the hell is that supposed to mean?" I roared.

Meta leaned back and took a deep breath. Behind him, the remaining members of the council whispered to each other. They seemed oblivious to the exchange going on in front of them, as if they had something more important to work on. Their indifference only served to aggravate me more.

"Your barbaric history," Meta replied. "Mankind, throughout history, has shown that their only desires are money, power and bloodshed. For eons we have waited patiently, yet they failed time and time again to evolve into a species more focused on knowledge and self-improvement. Despite all of the technological advancements afforded them, they regress morally, ethically and in most cases, mentally."

"Now wait a minute—" Kedge interrupted.

Meta held up his hand to stop him. "There is nothing more to say on the matter. This debate is pointless." He leaned back and whispered something in Hark-Kalech's ear.

"Are you sure that is a wise course?" he asked with uncertainty.

"Of course I am," Meta roared. "Just do it!"

Hark-Kalech glanced uneasily at us before leaving. Varooq and Kale followed him out the door.

"There are many things you do not know regarding recent events." Meta returned his attention to the screen. His initial anger seemed to have ebbed. "This is more than just simple treachery by Calypso."

"What do you mean?" Embeth inquired.

"Charr is not being destroyed by natural phenomena, as he claims. I admit there had been some unusually high volcanic activity which threatened the planet's crust, but it had stopped a while ago. Members of the Science Cooperative had developed a way to repair any damage done and are currently based on the planet, conducting field tests."

"What?" I scratched my head. "But Calypso told us—"

Meta dismissed me with a wave of his hand. "I know what he told you. It was just a lie to help cover his true intentions."

Lianne brought her fist down violently on the control panel. "All of these riddles and no answers. What is his true motivation?"

"We are not sure. But we are going to find out."

I suspected the High Prince wasn't telling us everything. *What are you hiding? Why are you hiding it?* I held my tongue since he was angry enough and we did not have the time to conduct a verbal war. We had more important battles to fight.

"I refuse to go back until we are done," I insisted. As soon as the words fell from my lips, everyone turned to me. I swallowed hard and cleared my throat under the weight of their stares. "I refuse!" I continued defiantly. "Mankind doesn't need a second relocation. We have a responsibility to stop this."

"*We* have a responsibility?" Meta scoffed. His demeaning tone cut me more than any weapon ever could. "It is not your decision to make."

"No, it's not," Embeth interrupted. "But as commander of the Defense Fleet it is mine. I made the decision to recover my soldiers and stop Calypso."

Meta narrowed his eyes. "Your decision lingers dangerously close to treachery, Embeth. You could be stripped of your seat on the Council." When Meta saw that he would not back down he waved his hand dismissively and turned toward the Council members. "We do this with or without you."

Satou turned and whispered to Embeth. "We will be landing in the East River in five minutes. So far everything looks clear."

Embeth turned toward the screen and shrugged. "Take my seat then. It seems this Council is broken."

Meta folded his arms across his chest with a look of disappointment. "Open a channel to the Swallowtail, Sergeant."

"Channel is open, sir."

"Captain Daranan, this is the High Prince. Continue with Helios Protocol."

"*Yes sir.*"

"I'm sorry, Embeth. You made your decision." A weary look came over him. "I had to make mine."

The screen went black. Wide-eyed, I turned to them. "What now?"

"We finish the job," Embeth responded.

Surrounded by the approvals of the others, I felt a sense of relief. Ahead, the East River appeared in the distance and Satou worked on slowing our descent. As we approached the water he eased the shuttle gently upon the murky depths of the river. Instead of descending into the water like last time, he guided the craft toward a wall adjacent to the United Nations building. Stealth mode allowed us to appear as nothing more than a breeze on a cloudless day.

"What are you doing?" I asked. "Aren't you worried we will be seen once we exit?"

"There is no time for covert tactics," Satou replied grimly. He pulled open his tunic and reached inside. He produced an object that looked like a cell phone and handed it to Gard. "This alarm is programmed to sound in twenty minutes. If we are not back by then, you are to take off and return to the Argus."

"*Acknowledged.*"

We left the shuttle via a side exit. Once I stepped foot outside, the crisp New York air filled my lungs. During our first trip to Earth, I felt a subdued sense of excitement. This time, however, the task laid out before us seemed much more solemn. Excitement escaped me.

"Well, here we go again," I muttered.

"What did you say?" Wraith slipped soundlessly behind me.

"Never mind."

We quickly crossed the ramp and dropped to a nearby window. Gard closed the ramp behind us which masked the ship once again. Everyone huddled outside the window while Satou pulled out an object that looked like a pen.

"What are you going to do with that?" I asked.

He ignored the question and instead pressed a button located on the handle. A yellowish light sprang from the tip and fell on the window. With the light, he carved a large O into the glass. A huge chunk of glass fell inward with a crash. "Get us inside," he responded.

We entered the building and found ourselves inside a large office. Judging from the film of dust on the mahogany desk and lack of decor it appeared to be empty. Satou traced a finger across the surface of the desk. Tiny flakes of dust fell from his fingertip like brown snow.

Kedge removed his staff from the sling and gripped it fiercely. Wraith and Satou unholstered their neutralizers. Lianne clutched her sword and searched the room. Embeth, neutralizer in hand, turned toward us. As he did, the grenades in his bandolier clanged together dangerously. I cringed, expecting an explosion.

"Okay, this is how we will do this," he whispered. "Follow my lead. We will conduct a sweep and clear of each room. We have to clear each room quickly. If we encounter hostile forces try to keep casualties to a minimum. There could be a mixture of Lumagom, Scarlet Moon and Earth forces scattered throughout the building so hold your fire until absolutely necessary."

Everyone nodded their acknowledgements.

"Kedge I need you to stay here and cover our escape," he added.

Kedge looked disappointed but nodded. Before we left I took one last look back. Kedge maintained a sour look but remained as ordered. He stood in the middle of the room, leaning against his staff.

We swept through each room swiftly as Embeth had instructed. The United Nations was unusually empty due to the state of emergency declared by the President. The lack of people was good news for us but we remained cautious as we moved between rooms.

At the end of the hallway, voices came from behind a set of wooden double doors. We readied our weapons and approached the doors carefully.

"Wait," Wraith whispered. "Stand back." He motioned for us to back away from the doors. Once we moved behind him he phased through the door. We never even had the chance to voice our protest.

"I hate when he does that," grumbled Embeth.

"Yeah, but you have to admit it comes in handy sometimes," Lianne replied.

"Handy indeed," Embeth spat. "He is going to get us killed."

"How does he do that?" I asked.

Embeth scowled at the door. "Umbrals have the ability to control their subatomic particles for a brief period of time, allowing them to 'phase' out of view. They can only do it for short periods of time which concerns—"

"*What the hell was that?*" A voice from the other side of the door interrupted him.

My first thought was the people on the other side heard Embeth. I clutched my neutralizer so tightly it almost went off. Lianne placed a finger against her lips and motioned for us to back up.

"*What was what?*" Another voice replied.

"*I felt something brush past me!*"

"*Afraid of ghosts, John?*"

More words passed on the other side but as we moved back they became harder to understand. Before we backed away completely another voice cried out, "*What did you say?*"

Calypso. My body went rigid. Just the sound of his voice angered me. It required all my willpower to stop me from breaking down the door.

"*Um, I asked him if he was afraid of ghosts.*" The voice responded, followed by a nervous chuckle. "*Why?*"

The room descended into silence. After several moments passed, I could no longer hold my tongue. "Should we keep waiting like this?"

As if in response, the door exploded outward. Fragments of shattered wood showered me and scraped across my cheeks before I hit the floor. I crashed against the floor hard and watched as my neutralizer slide across the floor.

Embeth and Lianne rolled to the side, weapons ready. Satou trained his neutralizer on the doorway, crouched against the wall. I scrambled to retrieve my weapon, but my sweaty palms made it difficult to grip the gun. With mounting frustration I dropped the weapon several times before finally managing to grab it with both hands. *Nathan Chambers—teenage warrior indeed.*

Security officers poured through the doorway, weapons blazing. The first four were the unlucky ones as a hail of neutralizer darts sprayed them. They crumpled to the floor in a heap. Several more exited and attempted to climb over them. They received an ample supply of neutralizer darts to their faces for the trouble.

"Fall back," a man in a black suit ordered.

The remaining officers retreated to safety. We moved in and I saw the pile of unconscious bodies move. Before I could ready my weapon, the pile shifted aside and Wraith climbed out.

"Are you guys alright?" he asked calmly.

"*We* are fine," Embeth growled. "But what the hell happened in there?"

"Well," Wraith brushed himself off before continuing. "Apparently one of them had been standing a little too close to the door." He smiled and for a moment I thought Embeth was going punch him.

Embeth's scowl was priceless. He bit his lip so hard that blood trickled from the corner of his mouth. He clenched his fists and I could see that he was resisting the temptation to strike him.

"*EMBETH!*" Lianne shouted.

Calypso appeared, flanked by several Lumagom soldiers. Behind them were the bodies of the Defense Fleet soldiers. My eyes fell on Klax, who stared accusingly at me through lifeless eyes.

Embeth saw what I did and roared with such fury that my blood turned to ice. "*NO!*" He screamed and leapt at Calypso. His sudden fury caught the Lumagom soldiers off guard, leaving them no time to react. He crashed into Calypso, sending them both tumbling into the room. Lianne fired her neutralizer at the two closest guards, dropping them. Satou, too close to fire his neutralizer, grabbed the closest guard's head and twisted. The crack sounded like a gunshot and I felt sick to my stomach.

Wraith and Lianne neutralized the remaining humans while Embeth and Calypso wrestled on the floor. Embeth threw Calypso into a nearby desk and smashed an elbow into his face. I heard a shot and Embeth's shoulder exploded in a spray of blood. Natronix appeared with a rifle in his hand.

My instincts kicked in and I fired the neutralizer, striking him in the shoulder. He didn't fall, but instead pulled the needle out and ducked through a side door. Calypso squirmed from Embeth's grasp and charged Lianne, who stood between him and the doorway. He picked up a broken chair and heaved it toward Wraith, knocking him out of the room. Satou lunged, but Calypso was able to reach a nearby rifle and crack Satou in the face with it.

Somehow I ended up in the path of Calypso. With a cry of rage I raised the neutralizer and fired. Several darts struck him in the chest. Before I could celebrate my victory, he looked at them and laughed. He brushed them aside and the darts fell uselessly to the floor.

"What the hell?" I blurted.

"Energy armor," he beamed.

I lowered the weapon. "So what now?"

Calypso edged toward the door. Before he walked through it, he fixed me with a look filled with sadness. "I wish it didn't have to be like this, Nathan. I know you don't believe me, but in time you will understand why."

"So why don't you explain it to me."

Calypso hesitated before going through the door. "I guess the short answer is I have no other choice."

I clenched my fists. "I know your planet isn't really dying!"

He chuckled dryly. "No, I suppose it's not."

"Where is the Universal Map?"

"Safe."

"That's not good enough," I replied. "I want it back. I can't let you travel back in time. We have too much at stake. One small change could screw up the entire time line."

In a gesture that surprised me, he brayed laughter.

"What the hell is so funny?"

A tear formed at the corner of his eye and he wiped at it with the back of his hand. "Oh Nathan, you are so naive."

"No more games," I demanded. "Where is the *map*?"

"I promise it is safe," he assured. "You can rest easy. I promise to leave the past alone."

Frustration took over. I grew tired of the cat and mouse games and desired straight answers, not more riddles. Picking up a nearby rifle, I moved toward him but he stuck a finger out and wagged it, mocking me. "I have the feeling we will meet again, Cartographer."

His taunts only served to enrage me further but he slipped through the door before I could pull the trigger. I ran to the door but stopped when Embeth started groaning behind me. Relief washed over me and I rushed to his side. Blood streamed from his left shoulder as he struggled to sit upright. "Are you alright?"

He nodded. "Check the others," he croaked.

There really was no need. Lianne and Wraith appeared okay as they helped Satou to his feet.

"I heard what Calypso said." Embeth propped himself against the wall and reached for his communicator. "Something isn't right about his story. We must stop him and get the map back."

"What's wrong?" Lianne strolled over, fastening her sword to her belt.

Embeth ignored the question. "Gard, get the shuttle ready for launch, we are heading back."

"*Sir, I detect a ship departing the area. I believe it is the Cirrus.*"

"Acknowledged." Embeth grimaced and balled a rag against the wound in an effort to slow the blood flowing from his shoulder. Satou approached and he turned to him. "I have a feeling the time hole doesn't travel to the past as we originally suspected."

Intrigued, Satou cocked his head. "What do you mean?"

Embeth ripped the shirt off a nearby soldier and tied it around his shoulder. "I think it comes from the future."

"You can't be serious," Satou gasped.

Embeth winced as he fumbled with the shirt. "I just hope I'm wrong."

SOLOMON CORVUS

"You have to stop toying with him, Calypso."

His back faced Calypso and he tried to hide the frustration in his words. A burgundy hood covered most of his head, shielding his face. Calypso had a knack for reading a person's expression, feeding off their emotion and anticipating responses. Corvus guarded himself well around him.

"Toying? I call it positioning," he replied.

Corvus sighed and turned. His lavender eyes reflected the overhead fluorescent lights, as he focused them on Calypso. "Positioning, you say?" he mocked.

Calypso shuffled uncomfortably under the stare. "I admit I have a soft spot for the boy." He paused before adding, "He reminds me of my son."

Corvus' eyes darkened. "More the reason to distance yourself and follow my instructions. Or have you forgotten what I told you?"

"No I haven't forgotten," Calypso muttered. "I found it hard to believe at first, but it's not hard to forget."

Corvus turned toward the window. A bright orb in the sky greeted him, backdropped by the dark wilderness of space. The Cirrus began its descent toward the moon. Time was short and they needed to move ahead with the next phase of their plan. He had no more time for Calypso's games.

"Your son is dead," Corvus stated calmly. He glanced at the former Council of Five member. "It's up to us to avenge his demise, not mourn it. If we fail then the universe..." The words died on his lips. When he turned to Calypso he had fire in his eyes and his hands were clenched at his sides.

"Don't you think I know?" he growled.

His features softened and he turned back to the window. He remembered the day he found Calypso. It was during his second trip through the Richat Structure portal. Calypso rarely traveled to Earth during routine maintenance missions but Corvus spent years studying seized Explorer's League archives and timed it perfectly to coincide with one such visit. After Corvus "persuaded" a private pilot to secure a flight to the United States, he landed in New Mexico the night before the scheduled mission. At first it was difficult to convince Calypso that he was more than some random hiker in the park. He knew secrets of the Consortium, however. Impossible things that no ordinary human could possibly know. Although reluctant to join Corvus at first, it took just under an hour to explain what had been planned for the future—including the fate of his son. After the tale was told Calypso practically begged to join.

"Meta sent him to war. Despite everything I had done for the Explorer's League, they sent him off without telling me," Calypso stated, as if reading Corvus' mind. He had an uncanny knack of doing it, which always made Corvus wary.

"They will send a lot of children to war, Calypso," he explained. "Unless we stop them."

"There will be no Explorer's League," Calypso's voice faded as he reminisced about the future. "No Science League... no Medical Society... nothing. There was no point in serving the lie anymore."

Corvus decided to let him ramble. He learned this after their first meeting. Over time the random musings helped him learn a lot of the Consortium's tactics not contained within the archives. The compilations will assist him in devising a plan to defeat the Consortium.

"Eternal war." Calypso continued staring blankly at the stars. "That's our future." He folded his arms across his chest and looked down. "With the entire technological might of the Consortium focused on warfare instead of exploration and science, nothing could stop them, not even you humans."

"Humans?" Corvus' eyes flared. "You know who I really am. We ceased being the sheep of the Consortium."

Calypso closed his eyes and placed the palms of his hands on the window ledge. "I'm sorry, not even the *Ascended* could stop them."

"Can we put the history lesson aside and get on with things?" A gruff voice asked behind them.

They turned to see Natronix standing in the doorway rubbing his eyes.

"About time you woke up," Calypso mused.

"Neutralizer darts are not a joke," he grumbled. "They are more potent than I remembered." His face became serious when an alert rang out from the communication station. He moved to a nearby communication panel and brought up an image on the main screen.

"Well hello, Shai," Corvus purred. "I was beginning to think you wouldn't show."

Shai curled his lip. "A mercenary makes sure to finish the job he is paid for."

Colonel Noz, the former warden of the prison planet Carcer-4, stepped into the picture. A bright red scar stretched from an eye patch down his cheek. "He will finish it thanks to me."

Corvus knew that Calypso had made arrangements to release the leader of the Scarlet Moon. He knew of Noz and judging by the scar the prison break did not go as smoothly as planned. When he saw him, however, it caught him off guard.

"You're human," Corvus said, mildly surprised.

The colonel's face soured. "Was," he growled.

"I'm afraid I don't understand," Corvus admitted.

"Colonel Noz had been found by the Erudites drifting near Neptune in a Russian space capsule," Calypso chimed in. "They mistook him for a member of the Lumagom and transported him to the prison planet. Eventually the administrators of Carcer-4 learned he was human and offered their apologies and compensation for the inconvenience."

"I chose to stay," Noz said. "They made me one of the administrators and over time I eventually became the warden."

"Noz is a strange name for a human," Corvus said with a hint of suspicion.

The colonel chuckled dryly. "Well my real name is Ivan Nozchevsky but in order to prevent the constant butchering of my name I just shortened it."

"Judging by your scenery, I assume you are at the rendezvous point?" Corvus smiled.

Rocky outcroppings split the stretched barren landscape that provided the backdrop to their conversation. Shai shrugged. "Yeah I guess you can say that," he groaned. "Quite a dump you have here."

Corvus ignored the barb. "Are your men in place?"

Shai looked annoyed. "Yeah, yeah. We got it covered over here."

His insolent tone grated his nerves. He clenched his teeth and bit back the rage. "Good we will be landing soon."

Corvus cut the connection and the screen went dark. Calypso shifted his feet restlessly and mumbled, "He is rough around the edges but will do what we need of him."

He is a loose cannon that must be dealt with when the mission is complete. He kept the thought to himself. Calypso considered him an ally and Corvus needed to measure how deep his loyalties rested with the mercenary.

"Do we have a shuttle ready?" Corvus asked.

"Um, yeah." The question surprised Calypso. "Can I ask why?"

"Because we are abandoning the Cirrus."

Natronix stepped forward, his cheeks flushed red with anger. "This is my ship! What the hell do you mean, you're abandoning it?"

Corvus ignored the question. "I suggest you prepare yourselves and join me on the shuttle."

It was Calypso's turn to flush. His face darkened and he placed a hand on Corvus' shoulder, stopping him at the door. "This ship can be a valuable asset in the upcoming battles against the Consortium."

"An exploration vessel against the mighty defense fleet," he scoffed. "What was I thinking, perhaps we should attack Caelum directly!"

Calypso backed down underneath his glare. "I just thought—,"

Corvus folded his arms impatiently. "That's your problem, Calypso. Perhaps I should do the thinking around here." He headed to the door but turned before walking through. "Oh before I forget, make sure to leave the Universal Map on the ship." He exited before Calypso could respond. The door slid shut and he chuckled. He caught the look of shock and confusion on both their faces and was pleased. He didn't want Calypso using any of his mind tricks to anticipate his moves. If he gained any type of advantage he will snatch it in an instant, tipping the scales in his favor. Corvus preferred setting up confusion among them. Confusion was good. It kept them in check.

Right where he wanted them.

Satou nodded and hoisted the President over his shoulder. "What about the rest?"

"We will have to come back for them," Embeth replied.

"What the hell is going on out there?" I hurried to the exit and held the door open for Satou.

"Gard, what the hell is going on out there?" Embeth repeated into his communicator.

"*Sir, the Defense Fleet is attacking. They have locked onto the Cirrus and are attempting to bring it down.*"

"Their aim is terrible. They are going to destroy the city," Lianne shouted. "And us in the process."

"We have to get out of here." Embeth agreed. On our way we were greeted by Kedge who had several unconscious security officers lying around him.

"Have some trouble?" Embeth grumbled. Still weak from his wound, he slipped and Wraith had to grab him to keep him steady.

"Nothing I couldn't handle," Kedge countered.

"Do you know what the situation is out there?" Embeth asked.

"It looks like your friends ran out of patience," Kedge said with a wry smile.

We hurried aboard the shuttle and strapped ourselves in. Satou shoved the President into a chair and buckled him in before jumping into the pilot's chair.

"*Sir, it appears the Cirrus has escaped. The Defense Fleet is in pursuit. I suggest we leave. It appears the United States government has dispatched fighter jets to intercept.*"

"Great, they probably think it's another 9/11." I frowned. "I guarantee the entire military is on its way to New York City."

"So much for discretion," Lianne growled. "What the hell was Meta thinking?"

"Set course for the Argus, Gard." Satou ordered before glancing at Embeth. "How are you holding up?"

Embeth grimaced. "I've been better."

Wraith retrieved a kit from a nearby cabinet and removed a clear jar filled with a green viscous substance. He took a handful and spread it across the wound which started to smoke. It sizzled like bacon on a hot frying pan. Watching the wound billow smoke made me nauseous. Embeth closed his eyes, grit his teeth and let out a grunt before settling in the chair.

The smoke died down and he opened his eyes. He looked over at me and offered a pained smile. "Don't look so pale, I refuse to die today," he assured. "If I die, who the hell is going to lead you sad excuse for soldiers?"

"Patch me through to Royal Command," Satou ordered.

Meta's face appeared on the screen. He did not seem pleased. I thought he looked disappointed, as if he didn't expect us to be alive. I dismissed the notion.

"Calypso escaped," he growled.

"You have to call off the Defense Fleet," I said. "We have the President of the United States on board."

Meta shrugged. "So?"

I clenched my fist and chewed back my anger. Embeth sensed my anger and answered for me. "He seems to be under the influence of some sort of drug. He could have been compromised by Calypso."

He narrowed his eyes. "What do you mean?"

"We are not sure, his eyes are different. Definitely not normal. He moved sluggishly, and his eyes are so red it looks like his blood vessels may have ruptured."

"Red you say?" Meta steepled his fingers beneath his chin. "I wonder..." he trailed off and paused.

"What is it?" Embeth asked.

"Bring him to me. Immediately."

The screen went blank and Satou turned to Gard. "Change course to the Astral Spirit."

"Astral Spirit?" I asked.

"It's Meta's flagship," Wraith explained. "The largest in the fleet. It's a cross between a battle cruiser and a pleasure barge."

Once we left Earth's atmosphere I understood what Wraith meant. The Consortium fleet lingered in the distance. Most of the ships were similar to others I had seen except for the lead vessel. It was enormous, even by galactic spaceship standards. The angular frame was longer than the Empire State Building, with two large wings at the center and several smaller wings attached to the rear. Hundreds of small, cylindrical objects were attached to the outer hull, but when we got closer I realized that they were actually smaller ships, like small escape pods. An enormous ring, attached to the rear of the vessel, looked like the largest Dyson fan ever created. My lips parted when we initiated docking procedures and my mouth hung open until we stopped.

Embeth chuckled at me. "Never seen anything like it, huh? You need to get off Earth more often." He bellowed laughter before becoming overwhelmed by a coughing fit.

Satou chimed in. "A ship the size of the Astral Spirit requires a large amount of power to rocket through space. That is where the technetium drive comes in."

"The what?" I asked.

"The large ring surrounding the rear of the vessel is a technetium drive. Technetium is the driving force behind the radioactive power feeding the propulsion engines," Satou explained.

"Oh sure, obviously," I retorted. It felt like he just explained quantum physics in Latin.

When we exited the shuttle, the High Prince was there to greet us with a frown. He pointed to the President, draped over Satou's shoulder. "Bring him to the Science Lab."

"Come on Embeth, we better get you to Medical," Lianne grunted and tried to lift him up. "Wraith, can you help me here?"

Wraith nodded and grabbed his waist. They stumbled out of the bay and down the hall.

"I shall remain behind with the shuttle and conduct routine diagnostics," Gard offered.

Kedge and I accompanied Satou to the Science Lab. They strapped the President to a gurney and bound him by the wrists and ankles, the same way they bound me all those months ago. I cringed when the disembodied tentacles slithered around his appendages. Just watching them crawl over his wrists made my skin break out in goose flesh.

Meta crouched over the prone form of the President. He switched on a miniature pen light and pulled back his eyelids, waving the light back and forth in front of each pupil. "How much longer until he awakens?"

"I would say at least an hour," Satou replied.

Meta stepped away from the gurney and glanced at us. "I hope it's enough time. He has indeed been infected." He removed a syringe from a nearby medical supply case and extracted a blood sample from the President.

"Infected by what?" I asked.

Meta held up his hand and moved toward an intercom mounted on the wall. "Hark-Kalech are you there?"

"Yes sir."

"It's true. The human has been infected. I need you to develop a cure. I am sending you a sample of his blood." He slid aside a compartment door next to the intercom and placed the vial inside. After he closed the door the vial was sucked skyward with a loud swoosh.

"Infections? What's going on?" I asked.

"The royal prince bloodline has the ability of precognition. It is how we are chosen to rule over Caelum and preside over the Consortium," he explained. "I can see pieces of the future, but they are nothing more than random images. Most of the time it takes considerable effort to translate the images into something understandable."

"What?" I gazed at him in disbelief. "If that's true then how could you not see this coming? How did you miss Calypso's defection? Are you telling me this could have been avoided?" My anger grew with each word.

"Calm yourself, Nathan," he cautioned. "As stated, I only see some images. Sometimes I can piece them together and understand the message. Other times they are nothing more than a random slideshow."

"You mentioned infection," I said, trying to control my anger at his latest revelation. "What is he infected with?"

He placed his hand on the President's forehead. "It is called the Dominion Curse." Meta spoke softly, as if he was in a trance. "It is synthetically manufactured but acts like a parasite, attaching itself to the victim's brainstem and making them susceptible to hypnotic suggestion. It's a cruel weapon, but effective. The victim loses their sense of self, becoming nothing more than a hollow slab of meat determined to follow any command they are given."

"Where the hell did it come from?" Satou asked, his eyes sparkled with interest but I saw the concern hidden deep within.

"From Earth," Meta replied.

"Earth?" I repeated incredulously. "There's nothing like that on Earth."

"That is because it hasn't been manufactured yet," he replied.

I threw my hands in the air. "What the hell does that mean?"

Meta removed his hand from the President's head. "It is from the future. Earth's future to be exact. The door is now open and we need to close it." He moved toward the exit but I blocked his escape.

"Wait a minute. What door? What are you talking about?"

"I don't have time to explain," he muttered. "We have to stop him. Get out of my way."

I didn't budge. "Explain it anyway. This is my planet we're talking about."

Anger flashed in Meta's eyes briefly and I wondered if I pushed him too far. He eventually relaxed and slumped his shoulders. "The time hole on Earth does not lead to the past as Ales originally believed. It leads to the future. We believed the portal was inaccessible due to its location deep under the ocean, but apparently he was wrong about its location as well."

"So, where is it?" I asked.

A strange smile spread across his face. "Oh but you already know where it is. Kell knew its location. That is why he made it part of the key to unlock the map."

I shook my head with confusion. "I have no idea what—" I stopped and suddenly remembered the quiz to unlock the map. "The Richat Structure," I concluded.

Meta nodded. "Only the Universal Map can reveal its exact coordinates."

"We have to find Calypso first. He has the map," I stated.

"There is another way." Meta glanced at Satou but he shook his head. "It's been done before."

"What is it?" I asked, my eyes darting between the two of them.

"Destroy the planet."

"What?" I blurted. "You can't be serious." I started toward Meta, but Satou held me back.

Meta leered over the prone form of the President. "Destroying the planet would neutralize the time hole."

"Calm down, Nathan, we will find another way." Satou's attempt at comfort fell on deaf ears.

Meta turned to me and frowned. "Unfortunately, there is no other way to close the time hole. The only experience we have to fall back on is the event on Mars. The destruction of the planet destroyed the time hole as well."

The world turned red through my veil of fury. "NO! There has to be another way! You are the Consortium, with access to technology I could only dream of. You need to find a way!"

Meta matched my anger. "There is no time!"

I attempted to wriggle from Satou's grasp but, despite my rage-fueled strength, he had a grip of steel. "We know Calypso has left Earth," Satou offered. "Our scanners do not detect the Cirrus. Since they are not on the planet that will give us time to capture him and recover the map."

I ceased struggling when I saw that Meta seemed to contemplate the suggestion. While he stroked the gray whiskers above his upper lip, deep in thought, an idea came to me.

"What about those transceiver things?"

"What?" Meta ceased his contemplation and looked at me.

"The transceiver like the one in the cave," I explained. "Those transceivers have the ability to harness the power of normal wormholes, maybe with some alterations to the technology we would be able to control and monitor the time hole. Maybe we could even close it."

Satou scratched his head. "Perhaps." He turned to Meta. "It might be possible. I can form a team and investigate this course of action."

Meta nodded slowly. "I will give you time to work on this solution."

An incoming message interrupted us. "*High Prince, are you available?*"

"Yes, what is it?"

"*Sir, we have received a communication from the DFS Proteus.*"

Meta sounded impatient. "Well? What do they want?"

The voice on the other end cleared their throat. "They have captured the Cirrus near Mars. They are starting boarding protocols."

"Advise them to put priority on locating the Universal Map!" He hesitated before adding, "Take the crew alive if possible, I will be right there."

Satou placed a hand on my shoulder and smiled. "Perhaps everything will work out after all."

"I hope you're right." I pulled away and followed Meta out the door.

Kedge Mal'Dineen

He removed his staff from its sling and laid it gingerly across the bed. The accommodations the Consortium afforded him were poor at best. A single bed, mounted against the wall opposite the front door, had a mattress but it was so thin it was about as comfortable as sleeping on the floor. A table and two chairs adorned the center of the room. He slid into one of them, wincing while he did. The chair was less comfortable than the bed. The Consortium held little love for him so he supposed he should consider himself lucky he wasn't sleeping in the engine room.

The time alone allowed him to reflect on the past. When Kedge rose to power and took over as head of the Lumagom they were dazed, scattered and leaderless. After years of exterminating life in the name of false religion, Ales Banda—their former leader—had been killed after a failed attack on Caelum. *He was a fool. A bloodthirsty, unreasonable fool.* Kedge vowed to become the opposite of what Ales represented. The fool had destroyed Mars, stole him away from his people and forced him to watch while he murdered countless innocents. After Kedge took over as their leader Calypso approached him and promised to help him return Mars to its former glory by traveling back in time to save it. He never revealed that the time hole on Earth led to the future, not the past. Calypso betrayed him and stole the Lumagom from him. Kedge's hatred festered like an open sore.

"If I ever see you again, Calypso, I will cut off your head and mount it over my bed," he muttered.

He sighed and picked at the titanium plate in his throat. It was one of the many cybernetic implants which has kept him alive through the centuries. As he caressed the device his thoughts drifted to the Ascended and Earth. He recalled one of his earliest voyages with Ales Banda. Their ship came upon an uncharted world in a galaxy which had long been forgotten. It bordered the edge of the universe. The planet flourished with life, which turned out to have been a mockery of everything Ales believed in, so he made the decision to exterminate everything on the planet. The first attacks scorched the planet's surface. Despite the attacks, some life remained. Ales had been furious and landed to deal with them personally. They came across a large cave which led to an underground village. The surprised villagers emerged from their hovels thinking the Lumagom raiding party were actually rescuers. Kedge recalled one villager in particular. A boy, similar in age to Nathan, had clutched his mother's hand and led her from their stony hut. At the time, Kedge had been surprised with their similarity to humans. Their amber skin and single ear were the only differing characteristics. The boy had been dressed in a leather jerkin with pants stitched from a material similar to denim and tucked into crude leather boots. The boy's eyes—*pale blue eyes that he will never forget*—looked past the Lumagom soldiers with their laser rifles, bandoliers full of grenades, bladed weapons and wrist rockets. He looked past them all until he locked on Kedge. His eyes were filled with hope. He seemed to hope Kedge would somehow rescue his people from the danger and lead them to safety. Kedge, weaponless and shackled, matched the child's hopeful eyes with sorrow. As soon as the mother realized who they were Ales shot her dead. In the child's face hope had been destroyed and replaced with horror. The horror only lasted for seconds before Ales shot him in the head.

A knock at the door yanked Kedge from his thoughts. Being the outcast he assumed no one would bother to call on him. The

There were no signs of shuttles launching from the Cirrus. Our conclusion is the ship launched from Earth without a crew."

"Is that possible?" I asked. I felt stupid asking the question but I was no starship engineer.

The captain turned to me. "It is."

"Any sign of the map?" Lianne asked.

He held his clawed hand up to the screen. A collective sigh of relief came from the room. He held the disk which contained the map.

Lianne smiled, clearly relieved. "Thank you, my friend."

I felt Embeth's hand on my shoulder. "We should reunite you two and locate that time hole."

"What about those on Earth?" I looked at him, filled with concern. His hand fell away when he understood the implication.

Everyone turned when Satou barged in, holding a silver beaker in his hands. "Meta, the President is conscious."

"What is that?" Meta asked indicating the object in Satou's hands.

"Hark-Kalech assisted me with synthesizing what I believe is an effective cure for the curse afflicting the President." He sounded confident but there was traces of doubt in his words.

"So what's wrong?" Meta asked, sensing the concern.

Satou frowned. "Well unfortunately I do not have a test subject and we are short on time. I fear we will have to administer it untested."

"We need to make it quick," I urged. "We have to return to Earth because Calypso is there with more of the infected."

"Yes," agreed Embeth. "I shall accompany you, Nathan. We must eliminate Calypso while we still have the opportunity."

Lianne disagreed. "You can't do anything in your condition, Embeth. You would be more of a hindrance than a help."

"Bah, what condition is that?" he bellowed. "I can take care of myself."

"I will take his place," a voice called from the door.

35

Kedge stood in the doorway. His fierce look of resolve dissuaded anyone from offering a counter proposal.

"I will go as well," offered Lianne.

"As will I," Satou added.

Meta shook his head. "No, Satou. I need you here to continue your efforts in working toward a cure. We will need more than that beaker."

Satou attempted to argue but Meta held up his hand.

"Don't worry yourself, I will send someone in your place." He turned to a nearby communication panel. "You will need someone who is an effective negotiator in case of human interference."

He pressed the button on the intercom. "Kale, I need you to report to the bridge."

"Oh no, not that dude. He hates me." I recalled our last unpleasant conversation aboard the Argus.

Meta turned to Satou. "Can you please show Nathan to the room I have prepared? It is on Deck Nine next to the visitor's lounge."

Satou nodded. "Come on, Nathan, you need some rest before your big homecoming."

*

I was back on Earth inside my own home in New Mexico. I don't remember when or how I got there. The house was still a mess and I frowned at the tower of dishes that came dangerously close to crashing to the floor.

"Mom? Dad?" Only silence responded to my calls.

I climbed the stairs toward their bedroom. At the top of the stairs a large cobweb tickled my face, forming a thin veil across my eyes. *What the hell?* I brushed it aside and spit out the remains. My hand fell on the doorknob to their bedroom.

"Mom?" I called out and placed my ear against the door. It was as silent on the inside as it was on the outside. "Dad?" *Nothing.* After several moments of continued silence I turned the knob.

The door swung open slowly. When it swung open completely it revealed the scene inside. I felt a sinking feeling in my gut and I had to hold onto the door for support. My parents hung upside down from the ceiling fan in the middle of the room. Thick hemp cords were wrapped around their ankles and their throats had been sliced open from ear to ear, creating macabre throat smiles. Blood collected on the floor forming gelatinous red pools on the carpet. In one darkened corner of the room the shadow of a man stirred. Moonlight from the nearby window barely illuminated him. When he stepped forward the moonlight caught his eyes, offering a faint glimpse of lavender. Those eyes were unlike any I had ever seen. The hair on the back of my neck stood tall. A burgundy hood covered his head, but his eyes pierced the darkness.

"Welcome, Cartographer," he purred in such a low voice that I could barely hear him. "It is unfortunate we have to meet like this."

"You killed my parents." It was a statement more than a question.

The stranger glided across the floor toward me. Despite the ill look in his eyes, his words had a soothing aspect to them. "It's not what I did, Cartographer, it's what you did." He stood before me, towering over me with his six-foot frame.

My mouth dried. It felt like someone had dumped a bag of sand down my throat. "Who are you?" I croaked.

He grinned. It was the grin of a demon wrapped in an angel's skin. His teeth were too white, his lips too perfect. "My name is Solomon Corvus." The smile widened, revealing more pearl-white perfection. His smile distracted me and I missed his hand sliding into his robe.

"What are you?" My question was barely a whisper.

He leaned in closer. "The future," he whispered in return. He produced a knife from his robe but I never felt the weapon in my stomach. He smiled even when he disemboweled me.

I heard my guts fall to the floor, but it didn't matter. His eyes had me in locked in their captivating embrace. "You are the past. I am the future, Cartographer. Your friends will abandon you. All will abandon you. Your cause is hopeless."

I fell to my knees in a pile of my own gore. My parents continued to swing from the ceiling fan above while the last of my lifeblood ebbed from me. Before I lost consciousness, I saw my dead father yelling at me.

"*Wake up, Nathan!*"

My head hit something hard. It felt like a long, smooth piece of wood. I opened my eyes to see Kedge standing over me, his face a mask of worry. He bopped me on the head with his staff again.

"Ouch!" I cried. "Stop doing that, I'm awake!"

"Sorry." Kedge frowned. "You were screaming in your sleep. I had to snap you out of it."

I rubbed my eyes. "I just had one hell of a dream."

Kedge straightened and put his staff away. "Dreams are portals into our subconscious. They can be a valuable resource."

"My parents were dead and I was murdered," I grumbled. "Remind me to thank my brain for its 'resources'."

His monocled eye adjusted, locked onto me and studied my face. "Death is easy," he responded.

"Excuse me?" I cocked an eyebrow.

"Death is easy, Nathan. It's life that's hard."

"Thanks, Buddha. What the hell does that mean?"

He slid into a chair. "Once death happens it is over and done with. Life is what's hard, Nathan. Life is filled with depression, pain and difficult decisions. Life is an eternal maze, with no exit."

"Aren't you just a big bag of sunshine this morning?" I quipped. "Life is also filled with wonders, love and happiness."

"I guess it depends on your perspective." He shrugged and studied my face. "It seems there might be more to this dream than you're telling me."

You got that right. I wasn't sure I wanted to reveal the details. Its violent brutality still haunted me. After several moments I closed my eyes and eventually relented. "Well...no."

Kedge leaned forward with his elbows propped on his knees. "Go ahead."

"Well, there was a person in the room with me. He seemed human except for his eyes. They were a color I had never before seen, sort of like lilacs. He told me his name was Solomon Corvus before he stabbed me in the stomach."

"Corvus?" Kedge mused and looked past me, as if the name alone held some hidden meaning.

"What do you think it means?" I asked.

He folded his hands underneath his chin, deep in thought. "I'm not sure. It could mean nothing or it could mean everything."

"Wow, are you always so full of answers?" I retorted.

He narrowed his good eye and shrugged. "There is a reason for my visit today, and it's not to provide answers to riddles. I'm here to warn you."

"Warn me?"

He lowered his voice to a whisper, as if the walls would hear what he had to say. "I do not trust Meta."

"Why is that?"

Before he could answer a knock came from the door. He looked at me with concern and I hurried over to the viewport.

Wraith stood outside with a box in his hands. He seemed to struggle with breath, as if he had just completed a marathon. I opened the door to see his normally pale cheeks flushed.

"Sorry for bothering you, but Satou insisted I bring this to you immediately," he said breathlessly before shoving the box in my hands. "I have to get back to the weapons locker before

Lianne and Embeth take everything not welded to the floor," he grumbled before leaving.

"Hey wait a minute," I started, but he was gone.

I sat on the bed and turned the box over in my hands. Kedge watched me with only mild interest when I opened it. Inside sat a four-inch wide, black metal bracelet with an octagon-shaped socket embedded on the top. Embedded in the socket lay a familiar object—the disk containing the Universal Map. I yanked it from the box, knocking loose a note which had been attached. My hand shook a little when I opened it, fearing the worst.

Nathan, sorry I couldn't give this to you personally. I designed a mobile computing device that will attach to your wrist and allow you to bring up the map anytime as a three dimensional holographic image. The metal is flexible and should slide over your hand and conform to your wrist. To activate the map, flip the switch along the side.

-Satou.

I tossed the note in the box and examined the bracelet. To the right of the socket I found a tiny green lever. After slipping the bracelet on, I flipped the switch. Suddenly the room was bathed in green light as the map sprang to life three inches above my wrist. It was no bigger than a laptop screen but I could still read the locations and designations clearly. I guided the screen past planets, stars and galaxies with the tip of my finger as if the holographic image was an actual computer screen.

"Well, that's interesting," Kedge mused. In my excitement I almost forgot he was in the room.

I flipped the switch again and the map vanished. "Yeah I suppose it is." I leaned back in the bed and fingered the bracelet. "Why don't you trust Meta?"

His look of curiosity vanished. "His decision to invoke Helios Protocol came a bit too quickly I suppose."

I sat up. "What do you mean?"

"Although the Consortium had been my enemy for centuries, I never underestimated their intelligence. Their wisdom seemed to always put them one step ahead of the Lumagom. I may be no Erudite, but I do realize a more reasonable solution could have been reached," he explained.

"I thought we were working on it?" I countered.

Kedge frowned. "He still resists the idea. His precognition leads me to believe he is holding something back. I have been around a long time, Nathan. Too much war and too much death have prevented me from trusting so easily," he lamented.

I narrowed my eyes. "So what are you getting at?"

"He has seen something. Something he does not want us to know."

"That is all well and good, but I am about to travel to Earth with a member of the Council to try to find Calypso and prevent a war. Why would he send us there if he is focused on destroying it?"

Kedge looked away. His monocled eye made a hushed buzzing sound as he focused it on the far wall. "I don't know."

"Maybe we should tell someone? Someone like Lianne or Satou," I offered.

Kedge shook his head. "I'm afraid my confidence in your friends isn't as high as yours. They are all part of the same organization, one that has already been torn by treachery. I don't trust them. They are ripe for more treachery."

"Why come to me then? I'm one of them now." His accusations didn't sit well with me.

He stared at me for a long time. His eyes peeled away my clothes, skin, and bones. It was as if he peeled everything away to stare into my soul.

"Not yet," he muttered ominously. "You are too new to have been infected with the corruption. It has been something that has been festering for some time."

"I don't believe it. I would trust some of them with my life. Satou, Lianne, Wraith...," my voice trailed off.

"You are still young, Nathan." He reached up and picked mindlessly at the metal plate in his throat. "I am not saying they are all victims of the same corruption that poisoned Calypso." He paused before adding, "Just be careful who you trust."

He started toward the door but I grabbed his arm. "What about you, Kedge?"

"Excuse me?"

"Can I trust you?" I narrowed my eyes with suspicion. I found it hard to believe a centuries old killer who once led the Lumagom did not have some sort of hidden agenda. *The irony would almost be comical if the situation hadn't been so dire.*

He stood up and made his way to the door. The question lingered in the air and he paused briefly as if to answer it before opening the door and walking out. The question fell to the ground unanswered. His statement, however, continued to linger.

Just be careful who you trust.

THE PRINCE AND THE
PAUPER

"The President is awake."

Lianne stood in the doorway with a grim look chiseled on her face. She was dressed in the familiar golden armor of the Defense Fleet. My heart sank when I realized she was prepared for battle.

"Just a security precaution." She noticed my concern and comforted me with a smile. "I don't want to take any chances."

With a nod I followed her to the Medical Lab. While we strolled the cavernous halls I chose to keep my thoughts to myself. Kedge's words haunted me. A guy I didn't fully trust telling me to be careful who to trust—the irony would have been comical had it not been for the seriousness of the situation. We stopped in front of the lab and Lianne turned to me. Judging by the look on her face she seemed to sense my angst.

"So, are you going to tell me or do I have to assume you have a bad case of gas?" She folded her arms with a frown.

Be careful who you trust. Her feline facial features crinkled and the fine whiskers above her lip hugged her cheeks and she studied me. I found it hard to distrust her. She was a starship captain who saved my life.

"I'm just worried about Calypso and our trip to Earth," I lied.

Her doubtful expression made me shift uncomfortably but she eventually relented and entered the medical lab. As one of the few people in the Explorer's League I could consider a friend it made me sick to lie to her.

I stepped into the lab to find the President sitting on the end of bed fumbling with a translator headset. Several armed Defense Fleet guards stood nearby, watching him intently. Meta stood next to him with his hands on his hips, looking irritated.

"So, run this by me again," the President said. "Everything Calypso told us was a lie?"

"I promise we have no plans to invade Earth," Meta assured before moving next to Satou who was too preoccupied with the screen in front of him to notice. Attached to the screen was a flexible strap which connected to the President's wrist.

"Well," Meta asked.

"It seems to be working," Satou replied. "I cannot locate any trace of the curse in his bloodstream."

"Mister President—," Meta started but the President held up a hand.

"Please, call me Tom."

"It appears you were infected by a synthesized parasite, Tom," Meta explained.

The color drained from the President's face. "A parasite? What did you people do to me?"

"We *people* did nothing," Meta replied with mild irritation. "It was your new friend Calypso and his allies who did this to you." He circled the bed. "Do not fret. We have engineered a cure."

The President breathed an audible sigh of relief, but concern remained etched on his face. "How was I infected? Is the country in danger?"

Satou circled the monitor. "It does not appear to be lethal. It may have been administered in a mist form, forcing the subject to inhale it. From that point it metastasized from the sinus cavity into the victim's brain stem. Eventually it makes one susceptible to hypnotic suggestion."

The President looked weary. "Can you repeat that in English?"

The way Satou cocked his head reminded me of the first time I met him—the look of a confused octopus. I had to resist the urge to laugh.

"I am sorry, is my translator not working?"

The President shook his head. "No, it's not that. Can you just explain it to me without all the medical jargon?"

"Basically, it is a drug which makes a person susceptible to suggestion," Meta grumbled. "Unfortunately we are short on time and need to continue if we hope to thwart Calypso."

The President hopped off the bed with a look of annoyance. "Fine, where the hell am I and what do you want with me?"

"Calypso mentioned one thing which was correct." Meta continued to pace around the bed while he explained. "Your planet *is* being invaded by a hostile force, but it is not we who are your enemies."

Exhaustion filled the President's face and his eyes sagged when he spoke. "One minute we're being invaded, then we aren't being invaded, then we're being invaded again. Can you people please make up my mind already?"

Meta seemed equally tired. "Perhaps *invaded* is not the proper term. Infiltrated would be more accurate."

"Infiltrated?"

Meta took a long look at me before continuing. "Earth has been infiltrated continuously through the centuries. It continues still to this day."

"What do you mean?" I asked, suddenly concerned. The President seemed to share my concern.

"Ever since the attack on Mars, the Consortium took a personal responsibility for the events which transpired. We felt our lack of a response led to the unfortunate events that followed."

"Attack on Mars? What are you talking about?" the President interrupted.

Meta held up his hand. "I'm sorry, but we don't have the time to explain that," he said, alluding to Martian history. "To explain the infiltration I can summarize. The humans who were displaced and relocated to Earth lost most of the technology they had acquired on Mars. As Nathan already knows, we installed a transceiver on Earth a long time ago which allowed us to monitor how the humans fared on Earth. We monitored your species' technological progress throughout the years. Unfortunately, your technological evolution took much longer than expected. Through discreet agents we helped you along by providing several advancements to assist with your growth. Electricity, cell technology, combustion engines, jet propulsion, computers and other such advancements had been provided."

The President interrupted. "Um, excuse me I hate to disagree but we were responsible for all of that."

Meta smiled with very little humor. "Who do you think our agents are, Mister President?"

"Are you telling me that Thomas Edison was an alien?" I scoffed.

Meta cocked an eyebrow curiously. "Who?"

"Earth records indicate that Thomas Edison discovered incandescent technology," Satou interrupted.

"Ah, yes. Incandescent technology," Meta recalled. "I remember reading about that in the archives." He fixed his gaze on me. "No, Nathan. Thomas Edison was very much human, but Harry Boynton wasn't."

"Who?" It was my turn to look confused.

"Harry was an agent of Caelum serving within the Universal College at the time," Meta explained. "He was picked due to his thorough knowledge of humans and his uncanny resemblance to the species. Based on his knowledge, he quickly became a favorite of Edison's."

I slumped into a nearby chair and rubbed my temples. Even though I had been with the Consortium for months, I still continued to discover new things about them. It was hard to believe all of Earth's advancements were funded in some part by an alien organization and I began to wonder how many people on Earth were actually secret agents of the Consortium. A memory of my third grade teacher popped in my head. She always seemed a bit odd. *Could Mrs. Wentworth have been an alien?*

"We must move on," Meta continued. "The infiltration continues but not only by us. Our agents returned when we observed Earth had begun developing better technology on its own. That didn't stop another, more sinister force, from continuing their observations, however."

"Who?" It was Lianne who spoke. In all the excitement I almost forgot she was in the room. She looked uneasy. I suddenly understood why. Meta was about to reveal information that members of the Consortium (even high ranking officers of the Defense Fleet) did not know.

"His name is Solomon Corvus." The name sent a shiver through me when I recalled the dream. "He is a human from the future and for years has been gathering allies," he hesitated before adding, "And strength."

"The future!" Lianne gasped. "How?"

Meta opened and closed his fists. It was subtle and he kept them close to his sides, but I noticed it and fear cradled my heart. The truth must really be disturbing to make the leader of the Consortium nervous.

"We can speak on the *how* later."

"What is he doing in the present?" I asked. I decided to keep the details of my dream a secret.

"The Council and I believe Corvus has come back to destroy the planet." His fist ceased clenching.

His face remained firm but it was hard to believe the explanation. Perhaps Kedge was right. He seemed to be holding something back, but I couldn't put my finger on it. His explanation did not make sense. *Why would a human from the future come back and destroy his own planet?* There had to be more to the story, but I decided to hold my questions for a later time. *Be careful who you trust.* The words returned to haunt me.

"The wheel has already begun to turn," he continued grimly. "It began with Calypso's betrayal and continues with his new alliances."

Calypso was once a member of the Council of Five—the closest confidants of the High Prince. If he could betray the Consortium, surely others could as well. Could another member be a traitor? Embeth had saved me from certain death and fought by my side—*could he be a traitor*? The entire Defense Fleet was under his command, a worthy army to turn against the High Prince. *What about Kale?* He was the diplomatic negotiator for the Consortium. He had not even tried to hide his disdain toward me from the first day I met him. His diplomatic ability to influence leaders, races and governments throughout the universe could prove to be troublesome. I had mistakenly believed him to be a traitor once before, however, that didn't mean I trusted him. Varooq and Hark-Kalech remain mysteries since I knew very little about the two. I promised myself to remain guarded when around all of them until the truth could be uncovered.

"I'm afraid we will have to send a force to the planet to engage Corvus," Meta finished.

"That is not necessary," interjected the President. "Just tell me where he is and I will send our military after him. I don't feel comfortable having an intergalactic conflict happening in my country or on my planet."

Meta looked at him incredulously. "With all due respect, your military is insufficient. Trust me, it is best that we handle this. I can guarantee we will be discreet and the matter will be dealt with swiftly."

The President started to protest, but when he looked around the room he stopped. Technology—well beyond what was available on Earth (including weapons)—was on display everywhere.

The President resigned himself to the obvious when he eyed the hand cannon strapped to Satou's belt.

"I guess you're right," he conceded. "But I want to be updated on the progress of your mission. This is not negotiable."

Meta bowed his head. "I promise it will be done. In return I ask for discretion from your government. Your species is not prepared to fully embrace us."

The President looked sad. "I'm sorry you feel that way. I truly think you are underestimating the human race." He ran his hand through his hair. "However, discretion will be tough since Calypso has conducted his little press conference for everyone to see."

Meta turned and strolled over to the communication panel. After punching several buttons, the large screen flickered to life and Kale appeared. He was sitting at a table with Varooq. Varooq sipped from a large mug which could only be described as a small keg. Judging by the smile on his face, he seemed to be enjoying its contents. Kale stood up and Varooq's smile faded when he looked our way.

"Kale, I'm sorry for interrupting your social hour," Meta droned. "We have a bit of a conundrum."

Varooq slammed his keg on the table and scowled at the screen. The sight of Bigfoot sitting at a table drinking beer made me chuckle, but I quickly bit it back. I didn't want to bring unwanted attention on myself.

"Conundrum?" Varooq bellowed.

"Yes, my furry friend. It's something I am confident we could resolve." Meta fixed his gaze on Kale. "It seems Calypso's little stunt on Earth may lead to some unwanted publicity for us and hinder our efforts to launch an effective counter attack on their location. Can you undo the damage?"

Kale folded his arms underneath the giant fishbowl that served as his head. I had never seen his face (I wasn't completely positive he had one). Only the tinted reflective glass globe on his shoulders ever greeted me. I meant to ask Satou why he never removed it, but recent events distracted me away from my curiosity. In the meantime I assumed it kept him alive like an astronaut helmet.

"His ridiculous blathering is nothing which cannot be undone," Kale responded. "We will just circulate a story that he was just some insane man under the influence of a new brand of synthesized narcotic."

"What about the people at the United Nations?" the President asked.

Meta turned and cast a curious glance his way. "I'm sorry?"

"Oh God, we forgot all about them," I blurted. "Most of them are under the same curse, whatcha call it?"

"The Dominion Curse is still active on Earth?" Kale asked. "Indeed that may pose a problem, High Prince. Those people are affected by whatever message Calypso inserted in their minds. We need to send a team in and cure them...or kill them."

The President stood up. "Absolutely not, I will not allow that!"

Meta placed a steady hand on the President's arm. "That is a last resort. I promise we will do what we can to help them."

The President relaxed slightly. "So, what do you propose?"

Meta looked at Satou who had just completed monitoring the President's vital signs. He began shutting down the machine but he sensed the High Prince staring at him. He stopped and looked up.

"Satou, with Kale tied up at the moment, would you please lead a small team back to the United Nations to administer the cure?"

Satou picked up a metal canister that sat on a nearby table. He shook it with a scowl before setting it down.

"I might have just enough for the people we came into contact inside the building," he muttered with uncertainty. He glanced at the President. "Did Calypso come into contact with any others?"

"I'm not completely sure, but I'm pretty sure he returned straight to his ship after his press conference."

Satou nodded. "If that is the case then we have enough, but we must be careful. Those who are infected will be aggressive and will not listen to attempts at negotiations."

"I want to go with you," I said.

Satou frowned but didn't protest. "I will need some people to return the President to Earth. We will also need a shield for us in case things get out of control at the United Nations."

"Take Lianne and Kedge with you," Meta replied. "I will have Wraith return the president. Use extreme caution."

Please, God, let this work, I prayed to myself.

CAPTAIN LIANNE

She tossed her cloak on the bed. The blur of exhaustion started to cloud her vision and she tried to rub them away. When she stepped into the bathroom her reflection stared back at her in the mirror above the sink. Lianne winced when she glimpsed her sandy hair hanging lifelessly around her shoulders. Even though she was only nineteen Earth-years in age, she felt decades older. She switched on the faucet and let the lukewarm water roll through her fingers. Aside from the Royal Command ships, none of the other Consortium vessels had cold water taps. She was so exhausted she would have sold her soul just to splash some icy water across her face. Time like these made her yearn for her home on Caelum where she could float among the cold waters of Steelglass Lake, chewing on some fleshfruit.

"You look like hell Lianne," she complained to the reflection.

She dried herself off and stepped into the bedroom. Taking her time, she laced each loop of her cloak carefully before slipping it on. She straightened her clothes as best she could. When she turned she noticed the picture on the chest at the end of the bed. The picture had been taken six years ago, when she graduated from the academy. At the time she was the youngest graduate ever, surpassing the record held by Embeth who graduated at the age of sixteen. Tears formed and rolled down her cheeks as she gazed at the photo. They clung to her whiskers briefly before finally falling to the floor in large droplets. It wasn't the memory of graduation that brought her reaction. It was the picture of the man with his arm around her. Her father, Captain Jasper of the

Explorer's League, rushed back from an exploration mission just so he wouldn't miss her graduation ceremony. He wasn't always so eager, however. When she announced at the age of nine that she was foregoing her studies at the Science Academy to enroll in the Defense Academy, she could taste his disappointment. He felt it was too dangerous and preferred for her to rise through the ranks of the Explorer's League as a science officer, or perhaps a geologist. He felt that would be the safer route. *No, wait. It was a xenoarchaeologist,* she recalled. Back then she laughed at him.

"But it wasn't safer, was it dad?" she mourned. *No, it wasn't,* would be his reply now if he could give it. He died as a member of the Explorer's League, yet she still lived as a member of the Defense Fleet. He died at the hands of Shai, the Scarlet Moon leader, when they invaded the Argus. "I would have been next," she whispered to the picture. If it hadn't been for her wrapping her bound hands around a guard's neck, snapping it like a twig, she would have died by his side.

Ever since becoming captain of her own ship last year she had seen very little combat. Most of her duties had been keeping the peace between the Caelumites and Aquanauts, transporting prisoners to Carcer-4 and providing security detail for foreign diplomats. There were other captains more suited for the upcoming mission. Captain Daranan battled the Lumagom during their failed invasion of Sirus Minor. Captain Muriel defeated the Yakizi on Remeese. Several captains had been involved in battles ranging from minor incursions to interplanetary war. Lianne never before felt as inadequate for a task as she did for this one. The feeling left a sour taste in her mouth.

"I hope I make you proud." She kissed the picture and returned it to the chest. After clasping the cloak around her throat, she turned to the picture one last time. "Saving this planet Earth better be worth the price we paid."

Nathan came to mind. The Cartographer had been an important position in the Explorer's League for centuries. Only special individuals with unique talents could read and understand the Universal Map. That alone made Nathan an important asset for them. Kell must have locked the map for a reason. It had remained that way for years before Nathan came along. There had to be a reason for that. It was her responsibility to keep him safe as a captain of the Defense Fleet. *What made him special, though?* The answer seemed to escape her for now. During her brief encounters with humans in the past they seemed barbaric to her. They endlessly war with each other, covet power, lust after money and seem rather disinterested in worlds beyond their own. Nathan seemed different but was he really? It was human blood that ran through his veins after all.

"*You* better be worth the trouble, Nathan." She clipped her sword to her belt. "If not I will kill you myself."

She slipped out the door.

THE UNITED NATIONS

Satou jumped in the pilot seat. For several minutes Kedge fumbled with his harness before finally locking it around himself with a grunt. I slid into the seat next to him.

"Here we go again," Kedge grumbled

I flipped the switch on my bracelet. The Universal Map sprang to life, bathing the interior of the shuttle in a pale green light.

"What are you doing?" Lianne asked. Her features cast an eerie green shadow which looked more demonic than feline.

"I have to see something." I squinted my eyes as galaxies flashed on the screen. I batted them aside with the tip of my finger. There was only one planet I was interested in. When I found the familiar blue-green marble (it glowed more like a green-turquoise marble within the color of the map). I zoomed in further. When I saw the flashing box over the western coast of Africa, I zoomed in further. Kell had left an annotation over the region. It was a section of Mauritania, more specifically an area between Mali and the Western Sahara. When I read it I almost fell from my seat.

"I knew it!" I exclaimed triumphantly, my lips splitting into a smile.

"What is it?" Lianne asked.

"Ales Banda was wrong about the time hole on Earth," I explained. "Kell knew it but didn't tell anyone. He did, however, mark it on the map. I think this may be why he locked it in the first place."

Satou unstrapped himself and lumbered over to me. Kedge and Lianne leaned in closer, tussling with each other to get a better vantage point.

"What are you rambling about, Nathan?" Satou asked.

I took a deep breath to slow my heart before it beat its way out of my chest. My thoughts raced through my head. "When Meta told us that Corvus came from the future, I wondered how it was even possible. I only knew about time travel through phone booths and Deloreans. I read about time holes in your archives but most of your records show that they only travelled into the past, never the future. Using Meta's explanations I began to question the universal time line. I had to ask myself, 'What if *we* are someone's past'?"

Satou stroked his chin tentacles, deep in thought. Kedge scratched his head and focused his monocled eye on me. Lianne slipped back in her chair with a confused look on her face. Frustrated, I clenched my fists. If anyone should understand what I was saying it should have been the people around me.

"Look," I directed them to the map, specifically at a caption hovering over the country of Mauritania.

This location houses a time hole unlike any I have ever encountered before. Preliminary tests concluded it does not lead to the past as originally thought. Science Officer Jharg passed through the hole completely with no adverse effects. The logical conclusion is that this is a receiver. We are standing in someone's past. This is a remarkable find. Someday, someone from the future may pass through this hole. How far in the future remains to be seen. Also, obviously this brings up concerns regarding any intentions this futuristic traveler may bring with them. Further studies must be conducted.–KELL

"That's an amazing find, Nathan," Kedge said. "Good job!"

"The Richat Structure," I muttered. "That's why Kell did what he did."

"What?" Lianne blinked at me.

Startled, I shook my head and realized my words had been uttered out loud. "Oh, sorry. I was remembering the riddle I had to solve to unlock the map. It involved the Richat Structure and now I know why."

"But what does all of it mean?" Lianne pressed.

I couldn't answer her question. Before I could admit as much, Kedge spoke up.

"It means Calypso lied to me when he recruited me," he said solemnly. "He only desired the power of the Lumagom, and my men." Kedge rubbed his chin. "I think I may know what Corvus is planning."

"Well, don't keep us all in suspense," I quipped.

"The only logical conclusion is he is using the time hole to bring technology from the future into the past. The Dominion Curse was only a sampling of that technology."

We were jarred in our seats as Satou guided the shuttle out of the bay. He activated the auto pilot and turned toward us. "Why do this?" he asked. "It doesn't sound very logical to destroy your own planet's past."

Kedge shrugged. "It must have something to do with the future. Unfortunately, without knowledge of the future, it may be difficult to determine their motives."

"Well whatever it is, it can't be good." I fumbled with my harness which took several tries to get hooked. "We have to complete our mission but we also need to go to the Richat Structure and stop Corvus."

"Well, since we can't be in two places at one time I will notify Embeth and see what he can do," Lianne offered. "Perhaps he can dispatch some of the Defense Fleet to that location."

Lianne hurried to the back of the shuttle and accessed the communication panel. Satou returned his attention to the shuttle's guidance system and guided the craft around an incoming asteroid.

"We should be landing in New York shortly," he stated. "In the meantime prepare yourselves."

As everyone double-checked their weapons, the shuttle's cloaking technology covered our landing in the East River. The scanners reported a lack of boats in the area and we unhooked ourselves and prepared. Satou retrieved a large metal canister from the cabinet and strapped it to his back. A one inch diameter hose was attached to it which he fastened to his wrist.

"What is that?" I asked.

Satou tightened the strap and met my gaze. "This is an air-borne version of the cure. All I need to do is spray this toward the victim and, if it works as intended, the antidote should enter through the sinuses and take effect."

"Are there any side effects?"

Satou shook his head. "No side effects, but the cure is only effective if the subject inhales it. It will still take about a minute for it to work."

"Which means we will need to disable them," Kedge acknowledged. He slid his staff into its sling and looked at me with a grim expression. "That means there is a chance some may need to be killed if the cure does not work in that timeframe."

Lianne burst into the cabin. "Embeth agreed to send a force to the Richat Structure. He still suffers from his wounds but Daranan will take the lead. He should be a reliable—," her voice trailed off and her smile faded when she saw our faces. "What's wrong?"

"Nothing," Kedge replied. "Just addressing a bit of unpleasantness."

Satou stood up and his face hardened. "Nathan, I have to ask you to stay here."

"What?" I asked incredulously. To say I was disappointed would have been an understatement.

Satou raised his hand to stop my protest. "Kedge is right, we may have to kill people in there."

A tense moment of silence passed between us. I attempted several times to respond but the words escaped me. *He is right.* I refused to admit it out loud, but my brain knew otherwise. I slumped into a nearby chair and dropped my face in my hands.

A hand fell on my shoulder. I looked up to see Kedge scrutinizing me with his bionic eye.

"If I was in your position I would feel the same way," he said. Sorrow crossed his face and I thought I spied a tear in his good eye but it could have been my imagination. "We will handle this and I'll do everything I can to make sure the casualties are minimal." He turned toward the exit but stopped with his head down. "Humans were my people too...at one time." Before I could say anything he exited the shuttle.

Satou grabbed a neutralizer and followed him out the door. Lianne tossed me a look of regret before she walked out as well. I watched the communication panel while the airlock disengaged outside. A feeling of uselessness filled me. *A lot of good I will do in here.* I moved to the pilot's chair and fingered some of the buttons and knobs that dominated the control panel. I removed my hand when I realized I might accidentally hit the wrong button and launch the shuttle into the side of the United Nations.

"Please God, let everything be alright."

Solomon Corvus

The time hole shimmered. To an untrained eye it was nothing more than heat rising from the sun-scorched desert. Occasionally, desert nomads would wander past the location seeing nothing more than strangers staring into empty space. They wisely chose to put a lot of distance between them. Solomon Corvus was no desert nomad nor was he some stranger who had wandered into the desert. He *felt* the power of the portal. He saw a portcullis, draped in bluish energy. As he watched, the color of the door became darker than usual and shapes formed in the background. Someone, or something, was ready to step through.

Calypso and Natronix exchanged nervous glances, expecting the worst. They hadn't travelled through the time hole and weren't sure what would come through. Not Calypso. He had been waiting patiently for visitors.

"What is it?" Calypso asked.

Corvus chuckled when two of the Lumagom guards raised their weapons and trained them on the portal. They put on a brave face, but couldn't hide the fear in their eyes.

Corvus smiled warmly. "Reinforcements."

Calypso visibly relaxed. "It's about time. The untapped potential of your technology will be useful against the Consortium."

Untapped potential. Calypso said the most amusing things sometimes, Corvus thought. He bit his tongue and continued to stare at the portal. The darkened swirls formed small blobs before splitting into one large blob soon followed by another, much smaller one. Eventually the mists came into focus and the blobs took shape. One male, one animal. They exited the portal and Corvus' smile widened when he recognized them.

"Sam Wells!" Corvus beamed. "You are a most welcome sight."

The male, a human in his fifties, was completely bald with thick rimmed glasses and a six inch brown goatee, mottled with gray. Thick, golden hoop earrings dangled from each ear and he clutched a large black case in one hand. The animal next to him was a wolf as white as snow. He fixed his pale blue eyes on them and growled.

Corvus cocked his head. "And you too I guess?"

"What the hell is this?" Natronix growled. "A man and his dog are our weapons against the Consortium?"

"If you are referring to Claw, then I must clarify that he is actually a wolf, not a dog." Sam frowned and reached down to stroke the animal's fur. The animal closed its eyes and let out a soft purr, almost like a cat. Natronix curled his lip.

"Dog...wolf, it makes no difference. We need an army, not animals," he grumbled.

Sam glanced at Corvus and ceased petting the wolf. "I would have thought you would have one by now. You seem to be slacking."

Corvus laughed and looked around. Ten Lumagom soldiers had escorted them to the Richat Structure. Most of them circled the portal with weapons raised, unsure of Sam and his pet. He rubbed his temple and knew that if so commanded, Sam's wolf would tear them to pieces before they could even fire a shot.

"This is just a contingent. The rest are up there." He raised a single finger toward the sky.

Sam looked up and scanned the skies. "The only thing I see there are clouds. What exactly do we have 'up there'?"

"Four Scarlet Moon warships, seven Lumagom battle cruisers and one science vessel Calypso managed to steal from the Consortium," Corvus replied.

"We would have also had one Explorer's League vessel if you hadn't abandoned it," Natronix grumbled.

Corvus ignored him. "We have a mix of roughly two hundred soldiers, science officers, and medical staff."

Sam scowled. "Not nearly enough to achieve our goal."

"That's why I need your assistance." Corvus nodded toward the case.

Sam shrugged and dropped the case. The soldiers took a defensive step backward. They focused their weapons on Sam with an air of uncertainty. He stepped away from the case and Corvus moved in to inspect his new gift.

"So this is the Richat Structure," Sam commented as he surveyed the desolate landscape around them. Countless desert hills and valleys surrounded them. They were a staple of the barren wasteland which comprised this particular section of Mauritania.

"Lovely, isn't it?" Corvus grunted.

Sam's eyes fell on the rifles that were pointed at him. "If you plan on using those, I suggest you get it over with."

Claw growled and the soldiers seemed unsure of the situation. They looked toward Calypso for guidance but before he could issue an order something growled behind them. They spun their weapons toward the sound. From behind a nearby acacia bush an African lion emerged. Its golden mane was caked with dried mud from recent rains. It swayed gently from the dry desert wind. When it turned its hungry eyes spotted their group. To him their group must have appeared like a buffet.

"Wait!" Sam's voice interrupted the soldiers before they could fire on the animal. He pushed his way past Calypso and Natronix.

Corvus looked up from the case and smiled. He knew Sam enjoyed "showing off" for an audience. It was one of his quirks for as long as they have known each other. The wolf trailed behind Sam with its head low to the ground and growled. It was his low, guttural growl that caused goose bumps to break out on Corvus' arms. He didn't know much about the animal but he *did* know Sam's skills. Their group was about to be treated to a show.

The lion's haunches tightened when Sam approached and he appeared poised to strike. Sam stopped and let his companion move past him. The lion showed no fear toward Sam, but paused when the wolf approached. The lion, although not afraid, sniffed the air in confusion at the site of the animal. Claw stopped about fifteen yards from the lion. He raised his muzzle toward the lion. His eyes, pale orbs of white totally devoid of fear, fixed on his quarry. Satisfied that the wolf was his enemy, the lion leapt.

It happened so fast that Corvus was still processing the event minutes after it ended. The lion stretched in mid-air, its paws— bigger than a grown man's hands—were extended and ready to strike. Then it happened. One moment the lion was there, the next moment it wasn't. There was fire, an explosion and the lion was simply gone. The only thing remaining was blood, a few clumps of fur and entrails which covered most of Claw's face and upper torso. Toward the rear of the wolf there was an open hatch and an empty metal enclosure. Smoke poured from the cavity and tiny flames licked the edges of the wolf's fur before burning out.

"What the hell just happened?" Natronix asked, his mouth agape.

The metal enclosure receded inside the animal and the hatch closed, covering the hole with fur. Sam approached the animal and crouched down and brushed away some of the burnt fur.

"Damn, I'm going to have to get that fixed now," he groaned. "He fired when the lion was too close."

Corvus bellowed laughter and clapped Sam on the back. "That is ingenious! Your experiments have improved since the last time we met."

Sam waved him off and continued to work on the wolf. Calypso approached the pair cautiously and gestured toward Claw. "What the hell is that thing?"

Sam looked away from his fur repair duties and smiled. "I guess I should have been more specific upon introduction. This is a Cybernetic Land Assault Weapon, Claw for short. This here is the Arctic Wolf model."

Claw looked up and chuffed. Calypso seemed entranced by the weapon. He crouched down and placed his hand on the wolf's head. The animal accepted it without resistance.

"My god," he gasped. "It's so realistic."

Sam's smile faded. "Of course it is, I designed it that way."

"Sam is our best weapons engineer," Corvus beamed. "He will help design weapons to use in the upcoming battle."

"I'm sorry," Natronix interrupted with a scowl "But how are animals going to help us defeat the Consortium?"

Before Corvus could answer his communicator chirped. He unclipped it from his belt and barked into it. "This better be important!"

"It is," Shai's voice growled from the other end. "There is a shuttle on the way toward New York."

Corvus narrowed his eyes and glanced at Calypso. "Oh really?"

"They must have found a cure for your little plague," Calypso offered. "I bet they are on their way to the U.N. to administer it."

"According to my sources, the Cartographer is aboard," Shai said.

Corvus dropped the communicator to his side and his lips tightened. "We now have our chance." He turned to Calypso.

Calypso nodded, grabbed Natronix and headed toward their shuttle.

"Wait, that's not all," Shai said. "Meta has dispatched a force heading your way. It seems they mean to intercept you, but since they only sent one ship it appears they want to maintain discretion."

"So, they have a Cartographer?" Sam asked.

Corvus nodded. He turned toward the departing figures of Calypso and Natronix. "Wait!" he called. They stopped and turned. "I need you to take Sam with you."

"Me?" Sam asked incredulously. "I still have work to do if you expect more prototypes."

"I need you to go with them Sam," Corvus whispered. "I need someone with them I can trust."

Sam wasn't pleased by the news. "You don't trust these guys? I thought they were our allies."

"They are, but they don't know what you and I know." Corvus grabbed his elbow and held him close, lowering his voice even more. "They cannot make the decisions that will be necessary soon."

"Because they don't know what we know," Sam repeated.

"Exactly."

"What about Claw?" Sam looked concerned.

"I will keep him here with me, along with a few soldiers to guard the Richat Structure."

Sam approached Calypso. "Guess I am tagging along for the ride."

He narrowed his eyes. "We don't need a chaperone, Corvus."

"I am not sending him as a chaperone," Corvus explained. "I'm sending him as insurance."

"Whatever," Calypso muttered before leading Sam to the shuttle.

Corvus watched the shuttle rise into the sky and disappear among the glare of the bright desert sun. He looked at Claw who seemed to study him with cold, calculating precision. "You will come in quite handy, Claw," he whispered to the wolf. Corvus was well aware of Sam's talents. His weapons would prove useful in the battles ahead.

Quite handy indeed.

KEDGE

"Can you hear me, Nathan?" Satou slapped the side of the headset. "Damn it!"

Kedge watched while he fumbled with the headset. Lianne had explained to him that the Explorer's League technology grew more antiquated every day despite the Consortium funding the League since its inception. Financing for new technology had been reduced drastically over the years. Calypso repeatedly complained about it, but his pleas fell on deaf ears. The refurbished equipment neared the end of its life cycle, but the crew had to make do with what they had.

"Bureaucratic shenanigans," Kedge grumbled. "You would think your High Prince would care more about the group that brings new worlds into their ranks."

Lianne took her headset off and frowned. "What do you know about caring? Have you ever cared about anything in all your years of leading the Lumagom against us, slaughtering millions of innocents?"

His jaw tightened. Her words stung with truth. It seemed no matter what he did he would never be able to wash his hands of the past. No matter what he intended to correct a lot of the wrongs of his predecessor.

"I have cared, *woman*, more than you know," he spat the word through clenched teeth.

"Stop it, both of you." Satou banged the headset against his thigh and reattached it to his head. "Nathan, are you there? Can you hear me?"

Lianne focused her attention on Satou, which turned out to be a good thing. Kedge felt a familiar pain radiating from his chest. It was like a dagger poking at his lungs. It radiated outward and gradually got worse. He had to resist the urge to reach for his chest. *Not now damn it.* With a grimace he bit back the pain.

"*Yes,*" replied Nathan. "*Sorry about that, but I had a hard time trying to figure out how to use the shuttle's communication system.*"

Kedge folded his arms across the chest, hiding the pain. Lianne turned and bored a hole into his soul with her eyes. Kedge feigned a smile. He knew she didn't like him but he didn't care. He didn't trust them. Any one of them could turn out to be a traitor, just like Calypso.

"We are about to enter the building, we will alert you if we see anything out of the ordinary." Satou cut the transmission and grabbed his scanner. After punching a few buttons, he stared grimly at the miniature screen.

"What's wrong?" Lianne asked.

"Nothing at the moment. It appears there are about fifteen people inside the building."

"That seems like a low number," Kedge admitted. "That's good."

Satou nodded and fastened the scanner to his belt. After double checking the canister, he made sure the wrist connection was snug. "Alright, we go in side-by-side. I want both of you flanking me but slightly behind me. I will take the lead and hopefully get the spray off before they have a chance to react."

Kedge nodded. He retrieved his staff and noticed Lianne's sword was already in her hand. He hoped for Nathan's sake that neither of them had to use their weapons.

Satou opened the door.

A Cure For Boredom

"This sucks," I muttered.

It had been twenty minutes since Satou contacted me. The walls of the shuttle seemed to close in around me and I felt the beginning stages of claustrophobia creep in. I tried to find a scanner on board that would have allowed me pinpoint their location inside the building. After accidentally starting the shuttle, activating some sort of horn, knocking a knob off a device that may have been important I finally gave up and slumped in my seat.

After several minutes of thumb twiddling I decided to activate the map and poke around the universe. I found myself bathed in familiar green light as the map lit up the room. The map remained centered on Mauritania, which seemed to be a built-in "save your work" functionality. I located the GX-750 galaxy and found the planet Xajax, the mysterious planet where we first encountered Kedge. It was categorized as a new planet (a new find for the Explorer's League) so the template next to the planet was blank. As the Cartographer it was my duty to make sure the Universal Map was updated. It served as the cosmic GPS unit for the Explorer's league. I filled out the template, adding the strange trees with their sap defense mechanism as well as the birds who could fly as well as burrow underground. Since it was also my responsibility to name new species I decided to call the birds Tunnel Owls due to their resemblance to Earth's barn owls and their ability to tunnel underground. The trees I decided to name Pitcher Trees. The name came to me when I thought about pitcher plants, which looked harmless enough until their prey comes close. Xajax's trees were certainly pretty to look at, until you got close. Images of the unfortunate bird that had been thrown against one of them by Satou came to mind. Visions of the bird as it struggled while the sap overtook it sent shudders through me.

We never got a chance to explore further on Xajax once we found out it was being used as a base for the Lumagom. Our priorities changed and I never got the chance to study any of the other wildlife on the planet. I left the rest of the template blank and marked it as incomplete. I hoped to fill in the blanks one day.

The airlock disengaged outside and I turned my attention toward the door. The familiar sound of the river filling the cabin soon followed.

"Well, that didn't take long." I breathed a sigh of relief. If they returned this quickly then that meant there had been hardly any resistance and that meant minimal casualties.

I went to the door and waited. The waters receded from the airlock and the inner door opened. "Thank God I hope everything went—," I froze in midsentence.

Calypso stepped through the doorway. Next to him stood Natronix, pointing a neutralizer at me. I didn't know whether to laugh or cry. I briefly wondered if I had fallen asleep and descended into some sort of nightmare.

Before I could pinch myself, Calypso spoke. "Don't make this harder than it has to be."

My mouth hung open. "How...Richat...gone?" When they both tilted their heads and peered at me strangely I knew my mouth was not conveying the correct message. I took a deep breath and tried again. "How is this possible? I thought you were at the Richat Structure?"

"We are everywhere, Nathan," Calypso replied mysteriously. "Your friends will be returning soon so I have to insist you come with us immediately."

"Why?" I crept closer to the control panel. Located inside a nearby compartment was a spare hand cannon. Satou showed it to me earlier when guiding me around the shuttle. Five feet separated me from the compartment.

"Unfortunately I don't have time to explain," he explained, not unkindly. "I promise once we get back to our shuttle I will explain everything."

A little over three feet away now. "Why should I believe you? Everything you told me was a lie."

Natronix stepped forward, gun at the ready. Calypso held up his hand to stop him. "What have I lied to you about?"

Two feet. "Your planet is not dying. Your reasons for betraying the Consortium is the biggest of the lies."

"A little white lie," he admitted. "My reasons for betraying the Consortium are truthful. They attempt to save insignificant worlds every day as major contributing planets are left to die. I did not lie about Charr, only about the timing."

I was about a foot away, close enough to reach out and grab the weapon. "What do you mean?"

"You will find out that it is not me who's lying, Nathan. The Consortium is one big lie. They will be revealed as the true betrayers."

I narrowed my eyes and fury rose from deep within my soul as I remembered all the people who had done nothing but help me. Lianne, Satou, Embeth, Wraith—they were no traitors. Then my thoughts drifted towards those that had been killed as a result of Calypso's treason—Madoc, Crag'Dughai as well as Lianne's father, Captain Jasper. Unable to contain my rage anymore I opened the compartment and reached for the gun.

Calypso's eyes went wide. "*NO!*"

I managed to get a shot off but had no idea who or what I hit. Natronix, however, was a former captain of the Explorer's League with military training. The first neutralizer dart hit me square in the chest. The second pierced the soft flesh at the bottom of my throat. I dropped my weapon and crashed to the floor. Drool fell in droplets from my mouth before it went completely dry.

"Urk you." The statement was unintelligible, but judging by the pained look on Calypso's face the meaning had been understood. I collapsed in a heap at his feet.

"Nathan, can you hear me?"

Satou voice beckoned me from the communication panel. He sounded frantic, but I wasn't sure if it was due to my lack of response or trouble inside the United Nations. It didn't really matter anymore, it was over. Calypso grabbed me and hoisted me over his shoulder before I passed out.

Game over.

SATOU

"Nathan, are you there?" He shoved the communicator into the belt clip. "Damn!"

He placed the antidote dispenser carefully in the pack and strapped it to his back. Scattered around them were the unconscious bodies of humans who were infected by the virus. Satou dispensed the cure with zero casualties. The news would please Nathan as well as satisfy Meta.

"Where the hell is he?" Lianne demanded.

Satou wondered the same thing. Lianne and Kedge were looking at him, wide-eyed. They sensed something was wrong back at the shuttle. He felt it as much as they did.

"Come on, we are going back," he barked.

It's happening all over again. Memories of Vaire came flooding back. Not the good ones either. Events led him back to his days before the Explorer's League. His son, Darus, had desired to be a member of the Vaire Royal Security Forces—a powerful militia who were held in the highest regard on the planet. He begged his son to reconsider. He had urged him to join the Order of Chemists instead like his grandfather. Darus had laughed at him. "*I am better with a weapon than a beaker,*" he said. The underwater empire required that all of their recruits travel to the surface to pass the Trial of the Sands. Traveling to the desert villages to slay a Shreen warrior had been considered a rite of passage. It proved the recruit's worth in battle. The Shreen were a violent race and their scorpion-like carapaces hard as steel. Every one of them had enormous claws three feet across which could snap a full-grown man in half. Each recruit had the opportunity to select a *Ka*, or protector, to guide them to the villages. The job of the Ka was primarily that of a guide and they could not interfere in the battle in any way or the recruit would be disqualified. The Ka were required to bring along video equipment to document the recruit's journey and discourage cheating. At the time of selection, Satou insisted Darus choose him, and he agreed reluctantly. His reluctant acceptance was the last words passed between father and son. They encountered a group of Shreen as soon as they surfaced from the ocean. They rarely ventured so close to the desert-ocean passageway. Normally they shunned the water. Battling one Shreen was a difficult encounter, a group of them were virtually impossible.

Satou looked at his communicator and remembered the claws of the Shreen warriors. The image haunted him. Darus' beheading had been quick, thank the gods. The sound had been louder than cannon fire and echoed across the desert. Its reverberations still resided in Satou's nightmares. He swore to protect Nathan just as he swore to protect Darus. *Have I failed again?*

They reached the shuttle and hurried aboard. After searching the cockpit, Satou slumped in the pilot's chair. He noticed the storage compartment door open and the gun lying on the floor.

Kedge saw it as well and picked up the gun. "He fought back."

Lianne ran into the cockpit. "There is no sign of him anywhere."

Satou's foot brushed up against an object. He scooped it up and pinched it between his fingers.

"A neutralizer dart," Lianne remarked.

"Which means his abductors took him alive," added Kedge hopefully.

"And I swear we will recover him that way," Satou growled. He closed his fist, snapping the dart in half.

Lianne jumped in the co-pilot's seat and punched in coordinates.

"I will not fail again," Satou whispered.

PERCEPTIONS

"How long will he be out?"

"The neutralizer has run its course, it should be any moment now."

"Satou?" The word fell from my lips as nothing more than a croak. My mouth failed me and my eyes felt like they had been welded shut. Neutralizer venom was potent and Satou mentioned that its victim could remain unconscious for hours.

"What was that? Do you think he is coming out of it?"

My eyes opened slightly which granted me the pleasure of Natronix's grim expression. The last of the welds faded from my eyes and they flew open. I leapt out of the bed but fell to the floor with a crash. My legs failed me and I panicked, thinking I was paralyzed.

"Relax, Nathan." Calypso revealed himself from a shadowy corner of the room. "You are suffering after-effects from the neutralizer venom so you need to give your legs time to regain their feeling."

He helped me into the bed gently. The room resembled the one aboard the Cirrus when I first came into contact with the Consortium. Several fluorescent lights lined the wall, however only two were on yet dimmed, giving the room an eerie torture chamber vibe. Besides the single bed, there was a monitor in the corner and a large unmarked cabinet beside it. Unlike my previous encounter I was not bound by writhing, disembodied tentacles which was a relief.

"What do you want with me?" Panic crept in when I remembered the Universal Map and I immediately looked at my wrist. The bracelet remained with the map nestled in the socket.

Calypso followed my eyes. "Do not fret, Cartographer. Your map is safe."

"Where am I?"

Before he could answer there was a knock at the door. Natronix opened the door and let in a familiar face. It was Zeek, the communications officer that used to serve on the Cirrus under the Explorer's League. Just another traitor to add to the list.

"Our guest was just wondering if the Cartographer was awake yet."

"Yes he is, but give me a few minutes with him," Calypso replied. Zeek left and closed the door. Calypso glanced at Natronix. "Alone, please?" With a grunt, Natronix followed him.

Anger started to bubble to the surface. "I won't join you so you might as well get this over with."

Calypso fixed me with a sorrowful stare. "Get *what* over with?"

I glanced at him suspiciously. "Aren't you going to kill me, like you killed Kell?"

His expression changed to shock. "What makes you think I killed Kell?"

"You sent him on that scouting mission. He was doomed from the start. You betrayed him as well as the Consortium by stealing the map. Everything you did up to this point is dripping with betrayal."

Calypso shook his head. "I did no such thing. Kell was killed in an accident. The scouting mission turned out bad. Everything I have done is for the future of the universe. I betrayed no one."

The sincerity in his eyes only served to enrage me further. His words, dipped in charisma and uttered with grace. I was well aware that his power resided within the spoken word. I refused to let his charms work on me.

"You murdered Captain Jasper. You killed Crag'Dughai and Madoc! Do you still want me to believe you're some sort of savior of the universe?"

"Shai murdered Captain Jasper. A most unfortunate incident, I'm afraid. The Lumagom killed Madoc and Crag'Dughai in their haste to loot your base camp. I had nothing to do with either of those incidents."

The feeling came back to my legs and I stood. "You have everything to do with those incidents. Those people are now your buddies...your friends....your amigos!" Tears of rage streamed down my cheeks but I no longer cared. "Am I reaching you yet? You are guilty by association!"

I could tell that my words cut because his smug expression shifted to sorrow. His genuine look of emotional pain caught me off-guard. My anger receded and I sat on the edge of the bed.

He turned away and paced to the door. His hand fell on the door handle and his head lowered. "You're wrong about me, Nathan."

"Wait a minute!" I tried to stop him but he was gone.

My thoughts raced while I studied the closed door. Was I his prisoner, cursed to stay here until I believed him? Before I could answer my own question the door opened and a man stepped through. His appearance shocked me.

"You're human!" I exclaimed.

When the stranger laid his eyes on me he froze with a look of shock. His lips parted slightly and a sliver of drool trickled onto his well-manicured goatee, merging with the gray strands that highlighted it. He fidgeted with one of the oversized hoop earrings that dangled from each ear and wiped his mouth with the back of his hand. "Oh my God, Nathan, you're alive."

I studied him suspiciously. "How do you know my name?"

The stranger let out a dry cough and rubbed his mouth with the back of his hand. "Sorry, I'm being stupid. I should have known you wouldn't recognize me. To you it's been just a few months, but to me it's been several years."

"What are you babbling about?"

The man took a deep breath and strolled across the room, toward the cabinet. From inside the cabinet he retrieved a large metal disk, about six inches thick and carried it over to me. I flinched, expecting something horrible to happen but instead he pushed a button alongside the disk and four metal legs unfolded from the bottom, making it nothing more than a stool. He placed it on the floor and sat next to me.

The man placed his elbows on his knees and wrung his hands nervously. I studied his face but his expression revealed no details of his motives or what he was thinking. Fear tickled the hair on the back of my neck.

"The media reported you dead when you disappeared. I tried to find you, but you were nowhere to be found."

I chewed on my fingernails nervously while I studied his face. His expression and tone seemed sincere but I wasn't sure if this was another one of Calypso's tricks. I needed to tread lightly and remember that they were the enemy.

"What are you trying to get at?" I asked defiantly.

"I ran into the cave but I was a fool and knocked myself out. I wanted to go back inside but the police wouldn't let me." Tears welled in his eyes. "I swear Corvus never told me your name when I returned."

"Who the hell are you," I croaked. My mouth was as dry as the area surrounding the Richat Structure.

"I'm Sam." he moaned. "I'm your best friend."

THE ASCENDED

"You can't be Sam. You're so *old*." The initial shock at his appearance was immediately replaced by skepticism.

He smiled and rubbed his gray-streaked goatee. "Yeah, I guess I am." His smile faded, however, when he viewed my skepticism. "I suppose it really is hard to believe." He stood up and stretched, arching his back to work out the kinks. "When the Ascended discovered the time hole on Earth it was hard for us to believe at first as well." A light, snapping sound came from his back and he let out a sigh. "But I'll tell ya this, even though it's hard for you to believe I'm this old, I certainly feel it sometimes."

"I'm sorry did you say the Ascended?" I continued to fix him with a look of suspicion. "Who the hell are they?"

Sam cracked his knuckles. The way he cracked them reminded me of my Sam. Whenever he got nervous he would ball his fist and massage his knuckles until they cracked. Perhaps this stranger really was Sam.

"The Ascended are the dominant species on Earth now," he explained. "They are the result of human genome experimenting gone awry."

"Human genome experimenting?" My confusion trumped my suspicion.

"In 2021 a company called Synthicon Labs developed a research project designed to cure autism. Their first attempt at singling out the gene and eradicating it failed miserably. The gene was different with each patient. The company experimented with identical twins who were autistic and it was discovered that the gene was different even in the case of patients who were related." Sam stopped and studied me.

"What's wrong?" I asked.

"Am I keeping you awake? You look bored."

I rolled my eyes and made a circling motion with my hand. *Get on with it.*

"You never had any patience, Nathan. Anyway, one of the scientists decided to create a test tube baby using DNA from autistic parents."

My eyes widened. "How would that help?"

Sam tugged on the other earring. "Well, since the DNA strand differed between patients perhaps they could somehow 'water down' the affliction, perhaps removing it altogether."

"I get the feeling that it didn't go according to plan," I muttered.

Sam shook his head. "In fact, quite the opposite happened. The DNA of the offspring carried an autistic gene. But the baby also carried something else."

"And that was?" I asked.

Sam looked nervously at the door before answering. "When the baby reached puberty he began to exhibit unusual signs." He took a deep breath before continuing. "At the age of ten he was confronted by three older boys in school. There had been a history of bullying between them." Sam paused as he recalled the event. "They attacked him."

Because of my intellectual ability I was often in advanced classes or sometimes found studying with older students. Before that day in the cave I actually qualified for college level engineering courses even though I was only sixteen. This drew the ire of other students who ridiculed me or in the case of Bradley Davis, physically beat me. I found myself empathizing with the subject of Sam's story.

Sam continued. "It was an unfortunate event."

"Was he hurt badly?" I interjected.

Sam let out a dry chuckle. "He came out unscathed." He paused. "The older boys, however, were not so lucky. Two of them were killed."

"Oh my God," I gasped.

Sam shook his head slowly and let out another dry chuckle which made me uncomfortable. I wasn't sure whether it was from the story itself or the way he reacted. "The boy never touched any of them. One minute the three older boys were taunting him, one even knocked the books from his hands, and the next minute two of them were dead and the third was against the far hallway wall unconscious." Sam looked down before adding. "The kid who knocked the books from his hands was actually the lucky one. He survived."

"How did it happen?" I devoured his words like they were slices of pizza.

"I wasn't there," Sam replied. "I was in college wrapping up my Bachelors in biology, but from what I read the boy attacked him with his mind."

I curled my lip in disbelief. "His mind?"

Sam nodded. "I never got the whole story because the scientists grabbed him and whisked him away to a private lab somewhere. Rumor has it though, that the boy eventually made his way up the ranks at Synthicon, eventually becoming President or CEO or some junk."

"What do they have to do with the Ascended?"

"I guess I should go into more detail." Sam closed his eyes briefly as he stroked his goatee. "Synthicon continued to experiment with autism. However their focus switched from curing it to replicating the case of the boy. By 2025 they gave birth to twenty five test subjects. Seventeen were male and eight were female and all of them exhibited similar qualities to the first boy. The company housed and schooled the subjects in secrecy in a remote location near Boulder, Colorado. In the year 2030 NASA encountered the Consortium during a flyover of the moon Europa. In 2035 the Consortium officially welcomed Earth into their ranks. The United Nations became the official diplomatic liaison between Caelum and Earth. Synthicon's funds started to dry up and they decided to clone current test subjects in order to save time. In 2040 they had two hundred test subjects and the company decided to end the project. The test subjects rebelled the following year and took over the company. With Synthicon under their control they spoke out against the Consortium and forged a business partnership with NASA, who was split off from the Federal Government years prior and became a private business."

"I have a feeling this story is not going to end well," I lamented.

Sam continued without responding. "With the cash flow of NASA, Synthicon continued cloning. Meanwhile NASA was contracted by the military to build space vessels embedded with heavy weaponry. When NASA asked why, the Government's reasoning was National Defense."

"Isn't it always?" I retorted.

"By 2049 NASA had built eighteen warships. Synthicon had cloned over 1000 test subjects."

I felt a sinking feeling in my stomach and a sandy taste in my mouth. I had a feeling I knew where this would lead.

Sam nodded when he saw my expression. "That's right. The original autistic test subject had been leading the company and declared war on the Consortium."

"Why?" I croaked.

"Well, apparently Synthicon discovered the worm hole located inside the Richat Structure. They claimed that they discovered time travel and that the Consortium had been using the worm hole in an effort to manipulate Earth's history. This, of course, soured relations between Caelum and Earth. There was a lot of teeth-gnashing and foot-stomping in the international community. Some governments chose to join Synthicon and others sided with the Consortium. Because of NASA's fruitful relationship with Synthicon, they continued manufacturing warships. Synthicon, on the other hand, was working the other side of the coin."

"What the hell does that mean?"

"The Ascended slowly took over the planet, converting the governments that sided with the Consortium over to their side. So you see, Nathan, the Ascended are superhuman. That was the name they gave themselves, because they were so disgusted with the human race's alliance with the Consortium. They believed that humans were mongrels and they were the evolved version of man."

"That's mighty cocky of them," I quipped. "So what happened?"

Sam once again looked at the door nervously, as if he was afraid one of them might step through at any moment.

"By 2053, the Ascended went to war. Most humans joined them, those that didn't were offered a chance to leave the planet. Those that didn't were arrested and quarantined. The Consortium was taken by surprise and their base on Mars was destroyed. Their Defense Fleet was forced to retreat to Jupiter. By 2055 we had defense outposts on the moon and Mars. Eventually, though, the Consortium Royal Command rallied the Defense Fleet as well as some other alien forces we were unaware of to their cause. Our bases were destroyed and we were beaten back to Earth. These defeats are what brings me here today."

I studied his face, no longer doubting that this was my friend from the past. Sorrow rimmed his eyes when he told his story and I realized he spoke the truth. So many unanswered questions remained that I barely knew where to start.

"How do you fit into all this?"

"At first I was thrilled of an alien encounter. The fact that we came to a point where we could have an intergalactic partnership with an advanced civilization excited me."

"So why are you here?" I prodded.

"I was hired by Synthicon as a biological engineer," he said at once. "I helped design the cloning process." He stood up and paced the room like a cat. "When I learned that the Consortium was possibly manipulating our timeline I immediately thought back to that day in the cave. The police never found you but you never came out of the cave, Nathan." The pitch in his voice became higher, another trait that future Sam and past Sam shared. It happened when he became overly emotional. That was when I saw the tear linger at the corner of his eye. "I began to suspect alien abduction, as crazy as it sounded. I found myself wondering if the Consortium abducted you." He flicked the tear aside and locked eyes with me. "I guess it wasn't crazy after all."

A few tense moments of silence passed between us. I was the one who finally broke it. "It was Solomon Corvus, wasn't it?"

Sam tugged at his earring. "I'm sorry?"

"The boy who killed those kids, the one who eventually took over Synthicon, it was Solomon Corvus, wasn't it?"

Sam lowered his head but remained silent. I took his silence as an affirmation.

"Why would you align yourself with him?"

"We were both smart kids, ahead of our class in school. However, I always knew you were smarter than me." He turned toward the door and let his hand rest on the handle. "Not about this, though. You're on the wrong side."

"Oh really?" Anger took over when I remembered Calypso's crimes. "Do you want to know a something about your new friends?" I balled my fists in fury.

Sam shook his head and opened the door. "You are my friend, Nathan. They are not my friends, only tools needed to complete the mission. The Consortium is not what you think they are."

I clenched my teeth, barely controlling my anger. "Oh? What are they, Sam?"

"The bad guys."

I frowned. "I refuse to believe that."

His disappointment was apparent. "It's nice to see you again, Nathan." He turned and left.

Corvus

Claw uttered a low, throaty growl and turned toward the time hole. Corvus followed his gaze and noticed that someone, or something, was coming through. With nervous anticipation his Lumagom guards raised their weapons. Whatever was about to step through wasn't very big, only about a foot high.

Corvus turned to the closest guard. Their ship stood just up the ridge to the east, about a quarter mile away. "Take someone with you and get back to the ship. Focus the scanners on the time hole. We will deal with whatever comes through."

The guard nodded and motioned for the closest soldier to follow. That left Corvus with two armed guards and Claw. More than enough to take out whatever happened to come through the portal. As if in agreement, Claw let out another growl.

The form in the portal materialized and out sauntered a large cat, a Maine Coon to be exact. It was dull yellow in color and extremely furry—fluffy would have been an accurate description. Claw let out another growl which caused the cat to pause and sit on its haunches. It turned its head, and with folded ears surveyed the area, ignoring Claw's growls of protest.

"Well what do we have here?" Corvus asked. The guards lowered their weapons and approached the animal.

Corvus moved towards the cat and it let out a purr. That was when he noticed the animal's left eye. It was not an eye at all, but rather a solid piece of tinted glass. Startled, Corvus took a step back and the cat opened its mouth. Instead of a meow, purr or any other such feline sound a voice came from the beast. A human voice.

"*Please identify yourself.*"

Corvus chuckled. *The animal must be another of Sam's toys.* "My name is Solomon Corvus of the Ascended." He took a step forward. "Who am I speaking with?"

The voice on the other end chuckled. "*Wow, this is actually our lucky day! They said you would be miles away by now and this mission would be a waste.*"

The guards were busy examining the cat, apparently more interested in its technology than its message. In a sense of irony Claw refused to approach the cat, but it was the wolf's demeanor that unsettled him. Claw remained close to the ground with his nose twitching, as if he were trying to catch the scent of the cat. He thought the appearance of the cat was a godsend—another weapon to use in the fight against the Consortium. The voice coming from the cat, however, had raised his suspicions.

"And what mission is that?" Corvus asked.

"*Assassination,*" the voice replied. Suddenly the cat's mouth widened and its eyes changed colors. They became red like blood.

Corvus dove head first away from the cat. The guards, unfortunately didn't have time to react. The cat exploded in an eruption of white light. Corvus planted his face to the ground, tasting dry, desert soil as he attempted to shield his eyes. After a moment passed he stood up and brushed himself off. Claw was untouched; fortunately he sensed the danger surrounding the cat and stayed far enough away to avoid damage. The same thing couldn't be said for his guards. There was nothing left of them but smoldering shoes. As for the cat, there was no sign of it at all. The only thing left behind was a charred circle with bits of smoldering fur.

"Very interesting," he muttered flatly. Despite its attempt to kill him, Corvus admired the technology. It made a useful assassination tool and he made a mental note to ask Sam about it when he returned.

The sound of his communicator snapped him from his trance. With a frown, he reached down and unclipped it from his belt. When he grabbed it, he noticed his tunic was singed around the edges, still smoldering. He batted at the flames mindlessly and lifted the communicator to his lips.

"What is it?" he barked.

"*Is everything okay?*" It was Sam. "*We were on our way to base and Calypso detected strange readings from the Richat Structure. Did something happen at the portal?*"

"Something came through," Corvus replied.

"*Reinforcements?*" Sam asked.

"Not really." Corvus let out a dry cough and dirt fell from his lips. He swatted at the last of the flames with a grimace. "It was a cat."

"*A cat?*" Confusion marked Sam's voice. "*What the hell does that mean?*"

Corvus ignored the question. "Two of the Lumagom are dead. I'm afraid the enemy will be coming through the portal soon. Do you have the Cartographer?"

"*Yes.*"

"What about the Consortium?"

"*A Defense Fleet contingent is heading your way,*" Sam replied. "*The rest of the fleet is outside Earth's orbit, apparently waiting for word from the group in New York.*"

"Good," Corvus sneered. "Let them wait. We will rendezvous on Xajax. Stop for nothing or no one, is that understood?"

"*Acknowledged.*"

Corvus severed the connection and clipped the communicator to his belt. Claw chuffed behind him.

"Don't worry, boy. You will get your chance to spill Consortium blood soon enough."

A rifle lay near the charred ground where the cat once stood. Corvus reached down and picked it up. The weapon was intact with not so much as a scratch on its surface. Pointing the weapon toward the sky, he fired. The weapon functioned normally. With a smile, he admired the ingenuity of their weapon. The cat had to have been engineered by Sam's people. Whoever sent it must have stolen it or worse, commandeered Sam's lab. Corvus wondered if it was the Consortium or someone else who tried to assassinate him. He had many enemies in the future.

"Some people are just jealous of my intelligence and ambition," he muttered to Claw and strapped the rifle to his back.

The wolf growled in response and padded off toward the ship.

REDEMPTION

Days passed since Sam's visit but I had eventually lost track of time. The only person to enter my room had been a five foot tall turtle-looking creature who served me stale bread and warm water twice a day without a word. The first time he brought my tray I couldn't tear my eyes from his hands. Four fingers, thicker than plump sausages and scaly like a fish, adorned each hand. When he dropped the tray in front of me, I grimaced at the sight of him. For days, I thought of him as nothing more than a servant until one day he came in with a rifle strapped to his back. That day he licked his leathery lips and locked on me with his soulless black eyes. I recalled almost soiling myself in fear, assuming it was my time to die. My fear proved unfounded. He merely dropped another tray of bread and water at my feet and left.

I stared at the crusty bread and found myself longing for even a scrap of recycled Sustanant pizza. My eyes drifted from the bread toward the lone window in the room. It was circular, about three feet in diameter and allowed me to watch the planets and stars as they passed by slowly, like the days. Sometimes the ship would pass close enough to a planet for me to make out distinguishing features. Occasionally it would be a dead planet like Mars, others had land, clouds, water and even mountains that reached the sky. We passed planets that were red, green, blue and even purple. As time passed, I rarely glanced out the window and only with passing interest as my thoughts turned to my friends. Were they still alive? What had happened on Earth? Too many questions churned through my mind.

I choked down the bread between sips of tepid water. Once I swallowed all I could muster, I crawled into bed and fingered the bracelet fastened around my wrist. *How did you get yourself into this mess, Nathan?* I should have been playing Call of Duty or World of Warcraft like the other kids in my school. Maybe if I was a less of a nerd and more of an average teenager, I would have never been in that cave. I wouldn't be aboard this ship, prisoner to a misguided psychopath.

There was a knock at the door but it sounded a million miles away. Calypso walked in and I rolled my eyes. I had just about enough of his delusions, his plans and his company. My hands fell to my sides in frustration and that was when I felt something in my pocket. When my hand located the object my fingers wrapped around it. My heart leapt into my throat when I realized what it was—one of the stun grenades Wraith handed me back on Earth. I completely forgot about them. As I sat up in bed I locked eyes with him and gripped the weapon tightly.

"Have you had time to think about what I said?" he asked, but his eyes revealed it to be a rhetorical question. It seemed he knew my response before I even uttered it.

"I think you are a deluded lunatic," I spat, my hand tightening around the grenade, gaining inner strength with each passing moment. From what Wraith told me all I had to do was toss the grenade toward my intended target and stand back. My only concern was whether the door was locked, but when I looked past him it was slightly ajar. There would never be a better opportunity. I had no real plan of escape, I just hoped the grenades bought me enough time to form one.

Calypso ran the back of his hand across his forehead. "I'm sorry you feel that way, Nathan. I was hoping—,"

He never had a chance to finish the sentence. I threw the grenade. Wraith warned me to look away when tossing grenades such as these. He said the bright light which explodes from the weapon causes a majority of the stun effect. Even though I heeded his advice, the intensity of the explosive light surprised me and I fell backward, crashing my head on the corner of the bed. I expected the explosion would bring the attention of my guard outside, but the bomb was strangely quiet. It detonated with a hiss rather than a bang. I listened intently for what seemed like an eternity for stomps of approaching guards, but no one came. Calypso's unconscious body lay crumpled across the doorway. I stepped carefully around him and grabbed another grenade. *This one is payback for the moldy bread and sewer water,* I thought as I looked for the guard.

I pulled the door open slowly because I couldn't take the chance that a squeaky hinge would alert someone. My fears proved unfounded when the door opened, revealing an empty hallway. I was momentarily stunned at my unusual timing of good luck. I slid along the wall like a shadow clutching the grenade, ready to toss it at a moment's notice. A sign ahead marked the way toward the docking bay. I hustled around the corner when I bumped into Sam. His look of surprise was brief before he grabbed his sidearm and pointed it at my face. My fingers held the grenade in an iron grip as we stared at each other like some sort of Wild West standoff.

"What the hell are you doing, Nathan?" Sam's face was flushed and a thin veil of sweat formed above his brow.

"I'm getting the hell out of here, Sam," I muttered. "Come with me."

Sam lowered the weapon. "I can't do that."

"These are bad people, Sam," I pleaded. "You need to help me get back to my friends."

Sam frowned. "Your new *friends* are not who you think they are, Nathan. You need to return to your room."

His words weighed heavily on my heart. At that point I knew Sam could not be swayed. He was always bullheaded but this was an unnatural stubbornness that unnerved me. I had no choice, if I wanted to escape, it would have to be through my old friend.

"I can't do that." I drew my hand back, prepared to toss the grenade. Before I could throw it I felt something slam into the back of my head. My face smashed into the floor and the coppery taste of blood filled my mouth. The grenade rolled uselessly toward Sam's feet. Someone grabbed my arm roughly and I blacked out.

I dreamt of a great stone building towering over me. I couldn't make it out completely because the sun rose behind it, blinding me in its glare. The shadow of the building engulfed me in its dark embrace. I shivered, despite the shroud of sweat on my face. A great forest surrounded me but seemed to close in, forcing me toward the building. The sun's glare fell behind the building as I made my way closer. Several stone steps ascended toward a large oak door. Two twenty-foot granite columns flanked the entrance. Above the door a single word was etched into the stone—*Archivist*. As I climbed the steps I was jolted by an earthquake. I grabbed the stair above me to steady myself and prevent a tumble off the stairs. I surveyed the area and noted that everything was calm. Not even the leaves stirred. I shook it off and climbed the remaining stairs. The tips of my fingers brushed the bronze door handle but before I could pull the door open another explosion rocked the world around me. *Wait a minute, earthquakes didn't explode.*

I was yanked from the dream by another explosion which rocked the ship, sending me crashing to the floor. The lights in the room flickered momentarily before going out. Several smaller lights switched on and I found myself bathed in the sapphire light of the emergency lights. Alarms began blaring.

Reeeeee! Reeeeee! The alarm sounded like a robotic cicada.

I hoisted myself up on one knee before a warm wetness trickled down my forehead. Alarmed, I rubbed my palm across my

face and held it in front of my face. *Sweat, not blood, thank God.*
I certainly didn't need to be injured and locked in a room on a
hostile ship while it blew up around me. I forced myself to stand
up. The door was also bathed in the eerie blue light.

Reeeeee! Reeeeee! I thought my eardrums were ready to burst.
The alarm weaved its way through the base of my skull and I
had a feeling if I didn't escape the room I would soon descend
into madness. I pressed my face to the window, hoping to catch
a glimpse of whatever caused the explosion. A planet stood in
the distance and I recognized it almost immediately—Xajax. We
were close to reaching the Lumagom base. The source of the dis-
turbance was not visible through the window, and I was afraid
if I pressed my face against the glass any harder I would have
went right through.

Several shouts followed by gunfire brought my attention from
the window to the door. I looked around frantically, hoping
to secure some sort of item that would serve as an adequate
weapon. Outside of the metal tray with the yellowing piece of
bread, there was nothing in sight. Loud thumps came from outside the door followed by another gunshot. I swept the crusty
bread off the tray and wielded it like a samurai sword. Looking
back I'm sure I looked quite absurd as I stood close to the door,
ready to slam the tray down on the first person to walk through
the door. *Death by platter.*

A muffled thump outside the door was the final sound before
the ship slipped into complete silence. I stepped toward the door,
readying the tray for a fatal blow. The blood rushing through my
ears was the only sound. My heart pounded like a drum and I
took another step closer to the door. Craning my neck toward
the door I listened to the faint breathing coming from the other
side. The hairs on my arms stood at attention and I gripped the
tray tighter. Who was on the other side other side of the door?
Was it even a "who"? Who knew what unspeakable creatures lay
within the blackness of space, ready to pounce on unsuspecting

vessels? My mind flew astray and I began to envision a cosmic kraken enveloping our ship with space tentacles.

A voice called out from the other side. It certainly didn't sound like a hideous creature from the bowels of the universe. It was a male voice, deep and commanding. "I can hear you breathing."

I stepped back. "Oh yeah? I can hear you breathing too!" As soon as the words left my mouth I realized how pointless they were.

"Identify yourself," he commanded.

I loosened my grip on the tray. "I am the commander of the Consortium Defense Fleet! Also, I am heavily armed so I wouldn't come in here!" I had no idea why I tried to bluff the person outside. The stupidity just flew from my mouth.

After a brief hesitation, the voice cleared his throat. "Well, that is strange," he snickered. "You certainly don't sound like Embeth."

Not knowing whether the voice on the other side was a friend or foe was unsettling but I felt helpless at that particular moment. Trapped inside a room armed with nothing more than a serving tray didn't make me comfortable with my odds. I decided to cease the pointless bluffing.

"My name is Nathan Chambers." I drew in a deep breath and exhaled slowly. "I am the Cartographer."

"Ah, the Cartographer," the voice bellowed. "That's much better. For a second I was concerned that I had invaded the wrong ship."

The door swung open and the owner of the voice stepped through. Once I saw him, I dropped the tray. The uselessness of the thin metal pan was never more apparent than at that moment. The man had to duck to enter the room which put him at a shade under seven feet tall. I cowered under his gaze, despite his lack of eyes. The lower half of his face seemed almost human with two fleshy lips parted slightly to reveal a set of sparkling white teeth. That was where his humanity ended. Above the lips, starting where the nose should have been, was an elaborate, violet helmet embedded with several lenses resembling that of a camera. I counted five, but they appeared to form a ring around his helmet. They were of several shapes and sizes with the largest approximately four inches in diameter and the smallest no more than an inch. He wore a suit of violet armor comprised of similar material as the helmet. Angular shoulder pads were concealed underneath an ebony cloak which contoured the muscular stature of his body. He clutched two obscenely oversized hand guns—one in each hand. When his gaze fell upon me two of the larger camera lenses rotated counterclockwise and were replaced by two of the smaller ones. I could see them zooming in on me as he studied me.

"You are much younger than expected," he muttered and holstered his weapons. He inspected each corner of the room as if an assassin hid within every shadow before returning to the doorway.

When I looked past him into the hall I saw my bread and water servant sprawled in a pool of his own blood. As his lifeless eyes studied me a pang of sorrow filled my heart. Not for him, of course. I would never miss his sour look nor his crappy bread, but for Sam who was most likely among the casualties aboard the ship.

"Who are you?" I asked, not taking my eyes off the corpse.

The stranger was busy rummaging through the corner cabinet, which I found out during my earlier exploration of the room contained nothing more than a blanket and dust. He turned when I asked the question and studied me through his helmet of eyes. "I am sorry I seemed to have forgotten my manners in all the commotion. I am Vayne." He bowed low in mock greeting. "Now that we have dispatched with the pleasantries I can tell you I have been dispatched to rescue you."

"Dispatched?" I asked. "By who?"

He slammed the cabinet door and waved his hand. "Unfortunately we are short on time so I will have to explain later. Several people aboard this vessel escaped before we completed the boarding process so it will not be long before reinforcements arrive."

"There is nothing in those cabinets," I stated as he sorted through another one on the far side of the room. I secretly hoped Sam was one of the escapees although I decided to keep those feelings to myself since I wasn't completely convinced Vayne was one of the good guys. He grunted, slammed the cabinet door and looked at me as if he read my mind.

"Don't worry, you will be safe with me." He waved me through the door. "We better go."

I stepped around Turtle's corpse with a grimace. Vayne was behind me in an instant and pressed his hand gently into my shoulder, guiding me along the hall. He moved swiftly and silently, blending in the shadows like a ninja. As we stumbled through the hallway navigating our way around the Lumagom corpses I caught glimpses of the battle through the blue haze provided by the emergency lights. Blackened holes dotted the walls accentuated by occasional smears of gore. I had to duck underneath a light fixture that had been blown away from the wall and hung halfway across the entrance to the main corridor. A neon sign, flickering with a threat to go out at any moment sat mounted on the wall. *Evacuation Shuttles*, it read. I turned to make my way down the hall but Vayne stopped me.

"Not that way," he said, turning me toward the bridge instead.

"But aren't we trying to get out of here?" I asked.

"All of the shuttles are gone," he grumbled. "So unless you have wings and plan to fly out of here you will find that path a dead end."

I looked down the corridor I noticed that most of the emergency lights had died. It seemed a large chunk of the fighting had taken place in that area and a few wayward shots struck them instead of their intended target. Apprehension took over and I found myself wondering if Vayne was leading me into a trap. When I glanced at him he stared straight ahead through those emotionless lenses. As if in response, they rotated and two smaller lenses revolved from the rear of his helmet to the front. They were tinted with a green color and I had a feeling they were some sort of night vision devices.

"Follow me, Nathan. I will lead us through the dark." He pointed his weapons forward and made his way along the hall. I hung onto the back of his cloak like a child being led by his mother.

We made our way around the corner and darkness gave way to a faint light radiating from the control room. A shadow exited the room and crept toward us. Vayne trained his weapons on the object while the faded green light of his lens reflected off them. A brief moment of tense silence passed between us while he studied the unknown person or thing that approached us. Vayne surprised me by letting out a hearty sigh of relief when the shadow spoke.

"*The control room is clear, sir. We have taken control of the ship.*"

The mechanical voice was familiar but my mind had a hard time processing the owner. He couldn't possibly be aboard because he was light years away aboard the Astral Spirit. When I stepped in front of Vayne a beam of light escaped from the shadow and illuminated the hall, revealing his identity.

"Gard!" I cried in disbelief.

He cocked his head and studied me. "*It is good to see you again, Nathan. I hope to have time to celebrate our reunion at a later time. We must depart quickly.*"

Before I could offer any sort of protest, Vayne led me to the bridge. A hooded figure hunched frantically over the controls, twisting knobs and pulling levers in an effort to gain control of the vessel. I looked down at a battered corpse on the floor beside him. The body was positioned on its stomach but the head was twisted completely around in order for the victim to stare lifelessly at the ceiling. It was Natronix, the former Explorer's League captain turned traitor. I felt no remorse for his death, it was no more than he deserved. Vayne slipped past the corpse and positioned himself beside the shrouded figure. My interests turned to the view screen which showed an image of a vessel attached to the side of ours. Immediately I understood how the rescuers managed to gain control of the ship. I couldn't help but admire the design of their ship. It's long, gray hull was similar to a submarine but came equipped with triple tail fins like a jet plane. Two oversized thruster engines flanked the body while the front of the craft formed a "T" shape which gave the vessel an overall appearance similar to a hammerhead shark. *Predators in space*, I chuckled silently.

"What is our status?" Vayne barked.

The hooded figure slammed his hands on the control panel in frustration. "Our status is exactly what you see. Your blatant disregard for our surroundings during your berserker fueled rage pretty much killed this ship."

Vayne frowned. "My mission was to rescue him." He flicked his thumb toward me. "Not the ship."

An audible sigh of frustration escaped the mysterious stranger and he pulled back his hood to reveal a pale, hairless head. When he turned around his displeasure was noticeable, but when I saw his face I found it hard not to crack a smile.

"Wraith!"

His frustration ebbed and a smile played at the corner of his lips. "I am glad to see you safe, Nathan. We have much to discuss."

Before I could ask him to clarify he motioned me to follow him. Vayne led us back through the darkened halls toward the breach made by his ship. Where there was once a wall near the engine room, there was nothing more than a cavernous hole sealed by some sort of flexible connector wall, not unlike a jet bridge. We hustled through the walkway until we came upon the bridge of Vayne's ship.

Vayne took off toward the bridge. "Hang on, we are getting out of here."

"Wait, where are you going?" I asked.

"We have a long trip ahead of us. I'm sure Wraith can catch you up to speed."

When I looked at Wraith a sorrowful look came over him. My worst fears bubbled to the surface. My friends were dead. Something bad had happened on Earth and Corvus was responsible for it. We were all that were left of the Consortium. All of those negative feelings soared through my brain and I was helpless to control them.

"Let's head to the Observation Lounge and I will explain," Wraith offered solemnly.

Gard studied me with his emotionless eyes before rolling himself to the corner of the bridge. It seemed apparent he did not want to be a part of our discussion. I glanced at him one last time before following Wraith.

The inside of Vayne's ship was nicer than any other vessel I had been aboard. It was obscenely luxurious. The halls were covered in a dark colored wood, similar to cherry, and adorned with shelves filled with trophies and pictures of Vayne posing with several different people. Wraith moved swiftly toward our destination so I only managed to catch a glimpse of some of the images. The one that caused me to pause was one of Vayne shaking hands with Bree N'Dadi, the leader of the Erudites. All of the photos were concealed behind glass cases so I couldn't touch them but I pressed my face against the glass in order to get as close as possible. Both Bree and Vayne were smiling while surrounded by several representatives from different planets. They were all clapping and cheering.

"Hey, come on," Wraith barked.

I turned back to the picture and it was Vayne with his arm around someone else. "What the hell?" I muttered.

A hand fell on my shoulder and I flinched. "Those are Memory Frames." Wraith looked at me and smiled. "They are rare and very expensive. The item absorbs a person's memories, periodically cycles through them and puts them on display. In my opinion only narcissists, braggarts and bandits put them on display."

Wraith moved on and I followed. "And under what category does Vayne fall under?"

Wraith ignored my question and instead led me through a set of double glass doors that opened into a room similar to a boardroom. A hardwood desk was surrounded by nine black leatherbound chairs. The entire room was surrounded by outer space. Only a clear window separated the occupants of the room from the great beyond.

Wraith walked to the window and stared at X-1, the closest moon to Xajax. It was barren and devoid of life, similar to Earth's moon. He lowered his head and without turning around said, "You may want to sit down."

I slumped into the nearest seat and waited for him to tell me the bad news—*they were all dead.* That had to be the news, what else could it possibly be? When he turned to face his cheeks were moist. Whether it was from sweat or tears I could not tell. He cleared his throat and wiped at his mouth with the back of his hand. He started and stopped several times. Words seemed to escape him. The news seemed to be worse than I could imagine.

"I'm sorry, Nathan, but there is no way for me to say this, so I'm just going to come out and say it." He slumped his shoulders and leaned against the pane of glass. "The Consortium initiated Helios Protocol on Earth."

I was wrong, it wasn't the worse news I could imagine. I could never imagine this. I sat motionless, frozen in disbelief.

"The planet is lost."

THE FIRST BLOW

My hands were perfectly flat on the table but body did not feel them. After Wraith's revelation my entire body went numb. I think I licked my lips but it felt like another person placed a finger in my mouth. Wraith sat down after breaking the news and watched my reaction. I attempted at least three times to say something, but the words wouldn't come. They finally came on the fourth attempt.

"Are they dead?"

He scratched his head, confused with my question. That was when I realized he didn't understand if I meant Satou's group or all of mankind. I quickly clarified the question.

"They managed to escape before the attacks started," said Wraith, his face nothing more than a grim mask as he told the tale. "Satou led them to safety. Once news of the impending attack reached us, Embeth, Gard and I escaped and gathered on Vaire to recover our forces and plan our next move. Our first order of action was to rescue you."

Relief washed over me when I realized they were safe. My concern switched to other matters. "This couldn't have happened quickly. How long was I captured?"

"Six Earth days," he replied.

I rubbed my temples and felt the beginning stages of a headache tugging at the recesses of my skull. *Six days.* A lot could happen in that time and judging by the expression on Wraith's face, a lot had. Suddenly my lips felt dry and I ran my tongue over them but there was not a drop of moisture to be had in my mouth.

"I need you to tell me everything," I croaked and cleared my throat in an attempt to regain my lost voice. "How could Corvus do this?"

Wraith sat down and folded his hands in his lap. "I better start from the beginning," He wiped a thin sheen of sweat off his brow. "Satou's mission was successful with zero casualties. They managed to cure the few people left at the United Nations building who had been affected by the curse. When they returned to the shuttle they realized you were gone. They thought you had left to follow them into the building and they were about to go in after you but that was when Satou realized you had been kidnapped."

"How did he know?" I asked.

They found the hand cannon on the floor and the compartment door open. There was also a neutralizer dart on the floor." He winced when he stood up and rubbed his chest. It appeared the wound he suffered during our first visit to Xajax still affected him. He placed his hands on his hips and stared off into space. "They ran scans in an effort to locate you but ran out of time when Meta ordered them off the planet."

"Ordered them off the planet?" I repeated.

"The Astral Spirit was attacked by the Scarlet Moon. The Defense Fleet forces we sent to Mauritania met resistance from the Lumagom. It was a two pronged attack and we were unprepared and overmatched. Meta panicked, despite reassurances from Embeth that he had the situation under control."

"What do you mean, 'panicked'?"

"That was when he initiated Helios Protocol," Wraith said somberly. As he recited the events, each word seemed to cause him physical pain. "It was the beginning of the end for the humans." He turned away from the window with a sympathetic look. "Embeth refused to lead the Defense Fleet against Earth. He was removed from the Council and court martialed."

"Why?" I shouted and my cheeks flushed with anger. "This doesn't make any sense!"

Wraith lowered his head. "Embeth thought as you did, as did most of the Council. But in the end Embeth stood alone. Men abandoned their posts and chaos took hold among the Consortium commander ranks. In his rage, Meta ordered the absconders to be put to death for treason."

My breath caught in my throat. "*Death*? Has he gone insane?"

"Embeth escaped with defense fleet forces who were still loyal to him. A battle ensued aboard the Astral Spirit between loyalists and absconders. The battle raged between former colleagues and former friends. Eventually the loyalists gained control of the ship at the expense of their former crewmembers. Meta proceeded to lead the attack against Earth."

I stared past Wraith, toward Xajax and the space beyond. I tried to imagine the planet was Earth but the vision escaped me. In my grief it was like my mind guarded against the memory. "Why did he have to attack? Humans weren't a threat to the Consortium."

Wraith shook his head. "As soon as humans from the future came through the time hole, they became a threat. Corvus' forces defeated the Defense Fleet on Earth but fled shortly after. It was rumored that they were bringing technology from the future through the time hole and that sent Meta into a frenzy. Blinded by rage, he made the decision to attack."

Mortified, I had the sudden urge to vomit. Wraith viewed my discomfort and softened his gaze. He leaned against the wall. I had never seen him look so exhausted.

"Your people fought valiantly," he said, his voice barely above a whisper. "I'm not sure what comfort that news would bring."

I chuckled derisively as I stared at my feet. "I'm sure their spirits are dancing in the streets." When Wraith didn't respond I looked up into his eyes. They were nothing more than two orbs filled with sorrow. "Are there even streets anymore?"

Wraith shook his head. "This is a path you do not want to travel down right now, Nathan. There will be time to explain what happened Earth in detail, until then we have important work ahead of us."

Vayne stepped into the room but remained silent when he glanced at the furious look on my face. My rage had built to its boiling point, however upon the sight of my rescuer I felt it ebb a bit. Before it completely vanished, I wanted release my final thought on the matter.

"I want to go back there."

Wraith and Vayne exchanged puzzled looks. It was Wraith who finally responded. "Go back where?"

I slammed my fist on the table. "Earth! I want to see what those sons of bitches did to my planet! I have friends and family there."

Wraith looked uneasily at Vayne, who remained stoic. It was hard to read the emotions of a man with a helmet of goggles covering half his face. "We do not have time for that," he barked. "My orders are to deliver you to the Insurgents on Xajax."

Confusion replaced my rage. "The Insurgents?"

Wraith rubbed his hands impatiently. "A lot has happened since you were taken. In due time you will understand the consequences of our actions." He looked uneasily at Vayne.

Vayne's mouth formed an unreadable white line. The inability to read his expressions frustrated me. I had a feeling the mysterious stranger was much more than a cosmic pirate flying a fancy ship around the universe saving teenagers from the clutches of bad guys.

"What my ashen companion over there is trying to say is *you* are the Insurgents," Vayne grumbled as he pointed to each of us. "The Consortium branded you as such."

"You are as well, Vayne," Wraith corrected.

Vayne brayed like a donkey. His laughter was dry and humorless and sent chills up my spine. "Oh, I needed a good laugh. It amazes me how little you know about us. We held no part in your rebellion."

His usage of the word "us" intrigued me. I saw very little of Vayne's crew since I came aboard, I assumed he flew solo. Judging by Wraith's clenched fists, I knew there had to be more to story regarding this uneasy alliance.

"Our goals are the same, Vayne. Don't mock me like I am some rock grinder that just emerged from the Charr obsidian mines. Never forget I was a member of the Explorer's League."

Vayne bowed low in mock admiration. "Excuse me your eminence. Pardon my intrusion in a room aboard my own ship, but I wanted to advise your highness that we will be making our descent to Xajax shortly. According to ground forces, we are clear to land."

Wraith seethed. His pale face was outlined in red. He was not used to this brand of insolence. Instead of verbally retaliating he offered Vayne the pleasure of a curt nod. With one last glance he was gone.

"Who is he?" I asked.

Wraith turned to the window as we broke through the planet's atmosphere. We passed a large, snow-covered mountain range which opened up into a grove of familiar pink trees. It wasn't until the hastily constructed landing strip became visible that Wraith responded.

"A pain in my ass."

XAJAX

It wasn't until we landed that I started to see signs of Vayne's crew. They scurried from various rooms performing different tasks. Some monitored control panels, others were busy polishing his numerous trophies. Each of them looked exactly like Vayne. Well, not exactly. Some were different shapes and sizes— a few were short, almost dwarfish, others were a bit taller and stocky but in the end they were all miniature replicas of Vayne. From their goggle helmets to their ebony cloaks, they were spitting images of him. Wraith explained they were clones and I laughed at first, assuming he was playing some kind of joke on me. Vayne confirmed it, however, when we were descending the landing ramp. Vayne had seventeen crew members and they had been cloned from Vayne. They may have been as narcissistic as their host, but they were equally dangerous. Seventeen cloned fighting machines in total. As we passed one of his clones near the exit ramp, I shuddered, despite the warm air of Xajax drifting in.

Wraith followed me down the ramp with Gard taking up the rear. Vayne remained on board to conduct "diagnostics". I pictured him looking at himself in the mirror and patting himself on the back for a job well done. I rubbed my eyes when we reached the bottom. In my haste I forgot how bright the dual suns of Xajax could be. Before my vision cleared, I felt strong arms wrap themselves around me, sucking the breath from my lungs.

"Nathan, you're alive! Thank the gods!"

The sun spots faded from my eyes and I gazed upon the smiling face of Lianne. Tears of joy tickled the corners of her eyes and her fine whiskers tickled my cheeks. Behind her stood Embeth, Satou and Kedge. Their expressions were bleak. Behind them, a makeshift camp comprised of tents, mobile labs and campfires provided the backdrop. Several crew members scurried around moving things such as scanners, weapons, food, medicine and other supplies to several large pavilions in the center of camp.

"Headquarters," Embeth grumbled and eyeballed the pavilions. "This is what we have been reduced to."

Lianne let go and her smile faded. The mood around the camp was grim. The past events weighed heavily on their hearts. One could read it in their tired faces.

Kedge stood next to Embeth and leaned against his staff. "I know what it's like to have your home stolen from you."

Satou wandered over with a grave look. "I am sorry, Nathan. I never knew what the High Prince had planned. He promised me Helios Protocol would be the last resort." He twisted uncomfortably as if the memory made him ill.

"Tell me everything." I growled. I felt a drop of water trickle down my cheek. At first I thought it was a tear but when I wiped it away another fell on my hand. I looked up to see the clouds darkening. A storm was coming.

Satou nodded and directed us to the closest pavilion. Inside, a metal table sat in the center of the makeshift room with a glass partition. Surrounding the table were several folding stools similar to the one Sam had back on the ship. A three dimensional map had been called up on the glass and I realized it was a view screen. A Defense Fleet soldier slid his hands back and forth on the partition as he navigated through galaxies. Standing next to the soldier was a man of average height, with flowing curly blond hair. A brown vest covered a plain black shirt. The vest intrigued me, because it was made from some sort of animal pelt. The hollowed head of the animal extended from the back and lay on top of the stranger's head. In the dim light of the tent I couldn't make out what sort of animal it was but it looked like a saber-toothed tiger. The rest of him was ordinary. His plain brown denim pants were battered with dirt and grime. He was unarmed and adorned only with a silver bracelet chiseled in the likeness of a falcon head. His eyes, blue like the sea, sparkled like diamonds. Underneath each eye was a tattoo of a triangle with the point facing down. The stranger tore his eyes from the monitor and fixed me with a steely gaze.

"This is not the place for children," he grumbled.

"This is no child," Embeth admonished. "This is the Cartographer."

The stranger seemed unimpressed. "That means nothing to me," he said, each word dripping acid. "The title may have held meaning before the Consortium decided to turn their back on the universe."

Satou stepped between us. If the stranger's statement bothered him, he did not show it. "Nathan, this is Vigil." He gestured toward the man.

"Vigil the Surveyor," he stated gruffly.

"The Surveyor?"

Vigil grunted but it was Satou who clarified. "He is Vayne's ally, and they are here to assess the situation."

Vigil held up a hand. "Let's not get carried away. I am not Vayne's ally. How many times must I explain this simple fact to you people?"

Satou folded his arms across his massive chest and shrugged. "Maybe you should explain it to us again," he grumbled.

Rain battered the outside of the pavilion as the two squared off. Several tense moments passed in silence before the flap of the tent blew open violently, startling everyone. A storm was brewing inside as well as outside. I looked uneasily at Lianne and she returned the look. I decided to interrupt their staring contest before the tension boiled over.

"How about explaining it to me since I just got here."

Vigil turned his head with such force that I thought it would roll off his shoulders. His narrowed eyes fell upon me.

"Ah yes, the human child who unlocked the Universal Map, destined to restore balance to the universe," he mocked. "Instead, your people brought the universe to the brink of destruction."

"My people?" I shouted, fury bubbling to the surface. I barely felt Lianne's hand on my shoulder.

"Stay calm, Nathan," she whispered. "He is only looking to provoke you."

"Provoke me?" I roared, shrinking from her touch. "Well, he's doing a pretty good job." I fixed my gaze on Vigil, who smiled wryly, which only served to stoke the flames of my rage. "What's preventing me from leaping over this table and strangling the life out of you?"

Kedge laughed and Lianne elbowed him. Vigil, however, kept his smile and shrugged. "Nothing I suppose." Despite his unexpected passiveness, he fingered his falcon head bracelet with a cocked eyebrow. His expression stole some of my rage and I backed up a step, half-expecting the falcon to spring to life and leap for my throat. "But I would hold off on that act of aggression. You see, as the Surveyor, my job is to monitor the situation and report back to The Progenitor. Your act of aggression might be construed as an act of war. That would be a most unfortunate turn of events."

As I looked around the tent at the concerned faces I understood the implication. No matter how arrogant Vigil could be, his assistance was more important than my bruised ego. "So tell me what's going on," I snapped.

Vigil took no solace in his moral victory and he ignored my curtness. Instead he clenched his jaw and switched his attention to the map. "Six days ago Solomon Corvus slaughtered a Defense Fleet squadron just outside the Richat Structure on Earth. His defiance enraged Meta and he lost all sense of reason. In his zeal to destroy the time hole and prevent any more of Corvus' forces from arriving he declared Earth an enemy and attacked under the guise of Helios Protocol. The Astral Spirit led an attack on Earth. Unleashing plasma weapons and chemical agents ended up ripping holes in the atmosphere. The Explorer's League distanced themselves from Royal Command and attempted to rescue some of the population. Meta declared them traitors and attacked them as well. War raged on the planet's surface between human forces and the Defense Fleet but their technology was no match for the destructive power of the Consortium. They were routed."

My blood boiled and I clenched my fists. "What about the Ascended?"

Vigil shook his head. "We don't know what happened to them. Last scans led to a point beyond the Milky Way." He pointed to a coordinate on the map. "We believe they retreated to Carcer-4 and are setting up a base there."

A lit waypoint lay where Vigil pressed his finger, highlighting the prison planet of Carcer-4. I guess it's a former prison planet now, God only knew what Corvus did with the prisoners who inhabited the planet. *Most likely integrating them into his army*, I thought gravely.

"Where is Meta now?" I demanded.

"On his way back to Caelum, I assume."

I turned to Embeth. "I need you to take me to Earth."

Silence blanketed the pavilion. Everyone looked at me sympathetically but no one acknowledged my request. After several moments I repeated my request. Satou finally responded.

"I do not think that's wise, Nathan."

Kedge interrupted. "The boy is right."

Satou looked incredulous. "You cannot be serious. Going back to see the destruction of his home serves no purpose."

Kedge picked at the metal plate covering his throat—a consequence of the technology that kept him alive for centuries. The lens of his bionic eye dilated when he fixed it on Satou. "It serves a great purpose." He turned to me. "You need to see it, Nathan. You need to see what these people have unleashed. Use all of your anger to water the seed of rage until it blooms into a flower of hatred unlike any you have ever seen. Use it to strike back at them."

"That's morbid!" Lianne exclaimed. "He is only a child."

"He is no older then I was when my home was taken from me," he stated plainly.

"There is enough hatred in the universe to last a billion lifetimes," Vigil grumbled. "My take on the subject would be advising against revisiting the planet, but it may actually do the boy some good to see the destruction that can be wrought during times of war."

"Who are you?" I asked.

"Ageless," he responded as if the word explained everything. The rain continued to pound the large tent and the wind dislodged the main flap of the door. He strolled over and secured it before continuing. "I am one of the Twelve Timeless and the Surveyor. My job is to make sure that order and chaos maintain balance in the universe. For millennia sentient beings have used worm holes for many reasons. No matter their reasoning, whether it be good or bad, people have always respected the power they held. The wanton destruction of these portals are frowned upon by the Progenitor, and we are forced to act."

"Who is this Progenitor?" I asked.

A smile formed on his lips. "In time, you will see. Only then will your eyes truly be open."

The storm calmed and the rain ceased its endless pelting of the pavilion. "What the heck does that mean?"

Before he could answer a loud commotion sounded outside. One of Embeth's soldiers popped his head into the tent. The golden helmet of the Defense Fleet covered most of his face, but judging by his heaving chest he just finished running back to camp.

"What's wrong, soldier?" Embeth asked, suddenly concerned.

"Sir, I think we have a problem," he gasped. "You better come outside."

Concerned looks were passed around the pavilion. Embeth hurried out the door with the rest of us in tow. The camp appeared normal but it wasn't until I looked in the sky, toward the mountains, that I understood the soldier's concern. In the distance were several winged creatures closing in around us. I immediately recalled our earlier encounter on the planet and assumed they were the burrowing owls we faced. As they approached I immediately knew that was not the case. Soldiers scrambled around us and formed a defensive perimeter. Kedge had his staff in hand and Lianne reached for her sword. Embeth and Satou reached for their sidearms. Vayne stood on the ramp of his ship with Wraith not too far behind. Vayne rested his hand on his weapon, but did not draw it from its holster.

"What are they?" Satou asked a nearby soldier holding a scanner. The soldier wore no helmet and the lone antenna centered on his head glowed brightly. He hailed from Exorg-7 and memories of Madoc came flooding back.

"I have no idea," he responded with a confused look. "According to this, they are not organic in nature."

"Fascinating," uttered Vigil. "I would bet that Scribe would love to be here right now."

I didn't know who "Scribe" was nor did it matter at that moment. The winged beasts were closing in fast. Vayne removed his weapons and were holding them stiffly by his side. I felt Kedge brush up against me and noticed his knuckles were white dots against the staff. If he clutched it any tighter it would snap in half.

The beasts were about two hundred yards and closing fast. They weren't birds at all but humanoid beings with oversized wings sprouting from their backs. From this distance I could see they were mostly gray in color with a dark brown stripe covering the top of their wings, as if someone poured a gallon of melted dark chocolate over them. They had long horns protruding from the sides of their heads which gave them a gazelle-like appearance. Their eyes were a deep red, like blood, and their fingers ended in sharp claws. *Demons.* All rage seeped from me, quickly replaced with a combination of fear and morbid curiosity. I still held a small place in my heart for exploration and discovery, despite recent events. Soldiers surrounded us as they formed a defensive perimeter around the camp with rifles pointed toward the sky.

The first one landed in a clearing about a hundred yards from camp. The creature studied us intently but made no move toward us. He was unarmed, which was very little relief when I spotted his razor sharp claws. As more of them landed behind the newcomer I noticed they were much smaller in size, no larger than five feet tall, and clutched crude weapons such as hammers and spears. Thirty in all landed and despite their archaic weapons they were no less fearsome.

"Hold the line," Embeth shouted. Soldiers stood shoulder to shoulder in a semi-circle between us and the beasts.

The largest of the group—the one who landed first—approached us. Despite his stunted legs, he moved quite gracefully, almost gliding across the landscape. When he got closer, I noticed the brown stripe across his wings reflected light and was actually bronze in color, and metallic. Everyone raised their weapons until Vigil cried out.

"No!" he pointed at the claws. "He comes to us unarmed, wait and listen to what he has to say."

"You call that unarmed?" Lianne responded skeptically, gesturing toward its claws.

My first instinct was to believe they were demons sent from the bowels of hell to wipe us sinners off the planet. When I looked at the other creatures I observed a nervousness about them. They continued to stare at our ships like they were creatures themselves. One of them sniffed the air near Vayne's ship and hopped back defensively, unsure if it would attack. It seemed they were as afraid of us as we were of them. Out technology frightened them.

Their "leader" stood approximately ten yards away but would come no closer. He held up a clawed hand and uttered several guttural sounds. The sound reminded me of rolling gravel. Everyone exchanged confused glances before Satou hurried over to a large metal case sitting on a table under a canopy. Opening it hastily, he yanked out a translator headset, however when he offered it to the newcomer he flinched and hopped backwards. He let out a scream that turned my blood to ice. Rows of pointed teeth, the color of obsidian, filled his mouth. Soldiers returned to their defensive position and aimed their weapons at the creature.

"Wait, lower your weapons," Satou said. "They are as distrustful of us as we are of them. We need to find another way to communicate."

It appeared the newcomer understood and thrust his hand to the ground. He drew something. Curiosity took over and everyone moved in closer to see. I slipped between Kedge and Lianne and craned my neck forward. On the ground was a large circle. The creature pointed to the circle, uttered several guttural syllables and pointed to the sky. His finger was directed toward the sun.

"It seems our new friend thinks we came from the sun," Kedge said with mild surprise.

"*No, not quite.*"

All of us turned as Gard rolled down the ramp past a startled Vayne. "Are you saying you understand him?"

"*A little,*" Gard replied as he rolled onto the open field between us and our new friend. "*The dialect is crude but reminds me of a language I picked up from tribal leaders during a trip to Arkon-2. He believes we were sent by the sun. It appears these creatures worship the sun.*"

Gard uttered several guttural syllables in reply. Their leader turned and responded in kind. He gestured toward our vessels and growled a few more syllables while flapping his arms animatedly. Vigil folded his arms across his chest and observed the dialogue with interest. Satou let out a dry chuckle.

"*His name is Urlan and he is the leader of the Quark. Those that are with him are his personal guard. From what I can translate, it seems they are mistrustful of our technology. More specifically, our starships.*"

"They do appear to be primitive," Satou agreed.

"*I concur. I have run preliminary diagnostic scans and it appears they are inorganic.*" Gard rolled up to Urlan who stepped back tentatively. Gard stuck out his clawed hand and touched his arm. Once Urlan realized the robot meant no harm, he relaxed. "*It seems his epidermis is comprised of a mineral mixture of sandstone and quartz. I detect organs underneath and blood flow which means he is not entirely made of stone.*"

"Well, I guess that's a relief. We have enough stone-heads around here," quipped Vayne.

Gard ignored him. "*Their 'skin' prevents long range life scans. That is why we did not detect life upon initial scans. It also makes for a formidable protective layer.*"

Urlan stared at Gard like he was some sort of god who descended a heavenly escalator from the sun to smite them all. I chalked it up to his distrust of technology.

"They would make fine warriors," Vigil commented.

Everyone understood the implication of his statement. Our list of allies was small. We would need many in order to fight a two-sided war with the Consortium and the Ascended. I had no idea how many allies we had but we had no more than forty soldiers on Xajax. The Quark would prove useful.

"Gard, ask them what they want from us," I said.

"*I'll try.*" He turned to them and uttered several raspy sounds, followed by something between a growl and a choking noise. This went on for several minutes before Gard stopped and turned toward us. "*He says curiosity brought them from the mountains which is their home.*" Gard pointed skyward, beyond the grove of trees, to the mountain towering on the horizon. "*They have not had visitors for several centuries until strangers came riding great silver chariots adorned with metal flags. I am not sure if this is a translation error, but that is the best I could gather from his statement. He insisted that these chariots brought a great flood of other flying vessels, of which many looked different.*"

"Great silver chariots adorned with flags?" Kedge repeated and scratched his chin. "I came here with the Lumagom a while ago to set up a base camp, but our ships looked nothing like what he describes."

"I wonder if he means the Scarlet Moon," I offered, remembering our encounter in space. Their ships reminded me of pirate ships except their sails were silver and comprised of some unearthly metal which made them appear like they were sailing in space.

Embeth nodded. "That could very well be. Which would mean our enemies are here."

"More reason to endear ourselves to the natives," Vigil grunted. "Our forces are a bit thin at the moment."

No one argued his point. When I surveyed our camp I knew our handful of soldiers could not repel a full assault from our enemies. Embeth and Lianne were veteran soldiers, skilled at the art of defense and warfare and were more than capable of holding the camp against smaller groups, but if either the Consortium or Corvus' forces attacked, we wouldn't have the manpower to repel them.

Embeth turned to Gard. "Do you think you can explain to them who we are and why we are here?"

He nodded. "*Urlan, we mean you no harm. We must set up camp here because we are in trouble. We are former members of an organization called the Consortium, but we turned against them when they did something unspeakable. We need your help.*"

Urlan cocked his head and sniffed the air, as if our stench would answer all his questions. Showers have been at a premium lately so he would have to make do with stale sweat and grime. His eyes fell upon the object in Satou's hand—the translator headset. He pointed and growled.

Gard rolled over to Satou and took the headset from him. After grunting out a few words, he placed the headset on his head. Urlan nodded and approached. Gard handed the headset to him and he placed it gingerly on his head. Because of the horns sprouting from each side of his head, it hung at an awkward angle.

"A strange device," Urlan growled before gesturing his contingent to move closer. Soon the Quark surrounded us. Dark orbs studied us from behind their gargoyle-like faces. "We are simple people who live peacefully in the mountain. We have no desire to enter your conflict but we will allow you to stay as long you do not bring the pain of warfare here. Rest your weary and tend to your wounded, we shall leave you at peace."

With that, Urlan's forces took to the sky. When they were nothing more than dots in the sky, Vayne turned to Vigil. "Well that went well," he remarked sarcastically.

Vigil groaned and fixed him with an angry look. "Shouldn't you be counting gold coins or admiring your paintings or something?"

Vayne smiled. "Perhaps," he replied nonchalantly. "I give you my leave so you can continue playing in the grass."

Vayne strolled up the ramp and disappeared within his ship. Vigil clenched his fists and fumed. It didn't take a genius to see there had been no love lost between the two. "Let us discuss our next move," he stated gruffly before disappearing inside the pavilion.

I watched the Urlan and his posse disappear into the mountain. Long after they were gone I continued to study at the mountaintops, watching as the sun glistened off its snowy peaks. I have not received the full story of what happened since my kidnapping, but if we were attempting to recruit strange beasts from alien worlds to our cause, than the situation must be dire. I felt a knot in the pit of my stomach and I started chewing on my bottom lip.

"Nathan, are you feeling okay?" Kedge's hand fell upon my shoulder.

"I need to go back to Earth," I replied without turning from the skyline. "I need to know what happened."

He let out a long sigh. "I'm not sure I like that idea." I turned to protest but he stopped me with a raised hand. "But there is a lot you should know, and a trip to Earth will give me the time to explain."

Hope filled my heart. "Do you have a ship?"

Kedge looked away and I followed his gaze. He was looking at Vayne's ship and that was when I spied the name upon its hull—*Talon*. "Are you suggesting—," I began.

"I'm suggesting we hitchhike a ride with the only person in this camp that has been itching to get out of here." He turned to face me. "You saw the dislike between Vigil and Vayne. Perhaps we can use that to our advantage."

"So what do we do?"

Kedge laughed. "You grab Gard and hop aboard. I will grab some people who I think will help us."

"Shouldn't Vayne and his crew be enough?" I asked.

Kedge's smile faded and he shook his head. "I have a feeling Vayne will take us there." He dropped a hand on my shoulder.

"Let me form an exploration party," he hesitated before adding, "One last time for the Explorer's League."

CALYPSO

"Already the time lines have split," Calypso muttered. He was mad at Corvus for being reckless and enraged at Meta for attacking Earth but when he observed Vayne carving a path of destruction aboard his ship another emotion took over. Fear. This was something he hadn't felt in a long time. Their actions have awoken forces that were better off asleep.

"I'm sorry?" Sam asked who had been busy plotting a course into the navigational computer.

"The universe is a living entity, Sam. Meta's attack scarred it, but it will heal." Calypso hunched over the shuttle's steering controls and acknowledge the waypoint that Sam entered. When finished, he turned and faced his copilot, who studied him intently. "We are nothing more than a virus that needs to be expunged from its system."

Sam cocked an eyebrow. "Is that who attacked us? Some sort of universal immune system?" he scoffed. "That was no entity, it was simply a man with guile who caught us by surprise."

"Fool!" Calypso growled before continuing. "It is his impatience that has cost us. I told Corvus to gather his forces quietly and give me more time to sow seeds of doubt within the Consortium. We had the Universal Map, we had the transceivers and we had the planets. He could have continued bringing his forces through the Richat Structure while I gathered more allies."

Sam acknowledged his point with a slow nod. "I agree. He may have been too quick to show his hand."

Calypso slumped in the seat and stared off into space. "No one could have foreseen Meta's attack on Earth," he conceded. "I'm afraid I erred in snatching Nathan. Perhaps he could have prevented the attack in some way."

Sam did not respond, instead choosing to pour over the control panel and enter additional coordinates. Calypso glanced at him and noticed the fluorescent lights of the shuttle reflecting off the corners of his eyes. Could they be tears or just a trick of the light? He could have been imagining things but he was aware of their friendship.

"I know this must be hard." He spoke so softly that Sam cocked his head in order to hear. "But Nathan is so damn stubborn. He needs to be on our side and I know how much that means to you."

Sam stopped fussing over the control panel, closed his eyes and rubbed his forehead. "Yeah," he muttered before reaching into his shirt pocket. He lifted a box of Marlboro cigarettes out of his pocket and shoved one in his mouth. He produced a lighter from his pants pocket and lit it. Calypso had been amused the first time he laid eyes upon it. The lighter was a miniature human skull forged from bronze. The mouth of the skull spat the flame that lit his cigarette. He inhaled deeply and shoved both skull and pack into his pocket.

Corvus. Just thinking of him made Calypso boil with anger. Too many mistakes have been made. Calypso's counsel fell upon deaf ears, and sometimes it seemed Corvus would go out of his way to do the opposite of what he suggested. It all came down to Calypso's son, Draeger, who became a general in the Defense Fleet. A General who some suggested would replace Embeth on the Council. Draeger, the man who questioned the Consortium when he found out how deeply the High Prince's corruption ran. The son who never got his chance because he was sent to die on some hostile planet during a meaningless exploration mission before the High Prince could be questioned.

Of course all of that happened during Corvus' time period. In the present, Draeger was four years old, safely bundled in his mother's arms probably watching the sun set over Charr. His thoughts drifted to his wife, Simone. They met during an Explorer's League meeting on Charr long before he had been named to the Council. He was just a captain sailing around space. She was an event coordinator and the head of the tourism department for the Charr Civics Council. He remembered the first day they met. Her hair had been so red it had looked like it was kissed by fire and her skin was pale and smooth like fresh milk. They were introduced by his father who was head of the Charr Mining Company—sponsors of the event. When their lips met for the first time it was like the heavens opened and fireworks fell from the sky. When Draeger was born, he felt like their life had been complete. He came into the world with one red eye and one blue eye, a sign from each of them.

"What did you mean by 'the time lines have split'?" Sam asked.

The image of Draeger and Simone faded and Calypso rubbed his eyes. "The universe is a living entity. Traveling through time is risky, both to the traveler and to the universe. One small change in the past could disrupt the future. The Explorer's League was very careful when it came to documenting time holes and even more so when traveling through them." The control panel beeped to advise them of an oncoming asteroid. Calypso made the necessary course correction and continued. "When Meta attacked Earth, he altered the future. Many were killed. You were there...well your young alter ego was there, yet here you are. That can mean only one of two things. You either survived or were killed. If you were killed then the universe healed the rip in its fabric by its only means available."

Sam's eyes widened when the realization struck. "By splitting the time line."

"You cannot simply vanish as if you never existed," Calypso continued. "That would be against the natural order of the universe, yet you can't die in the past but be alive in the future."

"It's possible I survived," Sam argued. "Why do you seem sold on the timeline split?"

Calypso recalled the ease with which the many-eyed stranger cut through his crew. He practically unscrewed Natronix's head with his bare hands. Fortunately for him all the years spent in the Explorer's League taught him the art of stealth, which allowed him to barely escape the man's rampage. Sam had the good fortune to be working on the escape shuttle at the time otherwise he would be making this journey solo. A man who could tear through an entire crew with such ease was no man at all.

"Calypso?" Sam's eyes were fixed on him, filled with concern. It was only then that Calypso realized he had been so deep in thought that he bit his lip bloody.

"I'm not completely sure about the timeline split," he admitted. "I worry more about the person who attacked our ship. He wasn't a part of the Consortium."

"You mean 'people', don't you?"

Calypso bit his lip and withheld the truth from Sam. The information received from his sources was unreliable so he had decided he would wait until it could be verified. He had too much to worry about now. *Sam was Corvus' soldier and trusted confidant*, Calypso reminded himself. It was for the best to keep some things unsaid until the right moment.

"Yeah, right," Calypso replied, turning his head to hide his face. Some people had the ability to observe a lie before it even left the lips. "I meant people, of course."

Because if Calypso's hunch was correct, the alternative would turn out to be much worse.

META

He sat, cross-legged, at the end of the jetty. The sun settled upon the horizon of the Obsidian Sea like a top hat. During the summer solstice, the Caelum sun shone for two days before ceding to darkness. It was only now beginning to rise. A crisp breeze tickled his cheeks while the roar of the surf provided the background music. He always came to this spot to meditate, and reflect on the hard decisions which had to be made. His fingers formed a steeple underneath his chin while he contemplated the consequences of the hardest decision he ever had to make. The decision to attack Earth was not made lightly nor was it easy. His precognitive abilities allowed him glimpses into who Corvus was and what his plans were for the Consortium. Once those plans were revealed, he felt better about his decision. Breathing deeply of the salt air he closed his eyes and became one with his ancestral spirit. By the time the footsteps approached he had been so deeply entranced that he didn't even hear them.

"Sir," the voice called out uneasily. "I bring news."

Meta opened his eyes. "I hope it is good news finally."

Varooq sighed. "We have stabilized the unrest, however we have lost more of the Defense Fleet than originally estimated."

Good news seemed to travel with the bad lately. Meta stood and pulled his hood back, revealing fine strands of gray hair intermixed with auburn which clung to his shoulders. He folded his arms across his barrel-like chest. "Damn Embeth for having soldiers so loyal," he muttered. "Have any captains remained loyal, or are they all traitors?"

Meta glanced somberly at Varooq. Even though Meta was large by Caelumite standards, Varooq towered over him. He stood over seven and a half feet tall and twice as wide as Meta. He was naked with the exception of orange hair that covered every inch of his body, making him the Consortium's version of Sasquatch. He stood upon legs like tree trunks with arms to match. The native of Sirus Minor had the strength to rip Meta in half without barely breaking a sweat. It was a relief to learn that Varooq had remained loyal to the Consortium.

"Captain Daranan remains aboard the Swallowtail with a crew of seventy five, loyal to us," he growled. "Captain Markus has a crew of fifty aboard the Lunar Breeze. Hark-Kalech is aboard the Astral Spirit taking inventory of our remaining strength."

Meta turned back to the sea. A great fin broke the surface of the murky depths briefly before returning to the gloom below. *A giant daggerfish most likely*, thought Meta. Most of the creatures who called the Obsidian Sea home were beautiful yet deadly. As deadly as the waters themselves.

"Did you know my father died upon these waters," Meta said without removing his eyes from the horizon.

Varooq let out a dry cough. "Yes, I believe I heard the tale. He was traveling to Black Isle, was he not?"

The Black Isle, a small island no bigger than a half mile across, mysterious and unreachable by air. The only mode of transportation viable enough to travel to the island was by boat, and across the treacherous expanse of the Obsidian Sea. His father was more adventurous than Meta and lived his life on the edge. Meta preferred study and quests for knowledge, choosing the halls of the Archivist Library over the jungle of the Black Isle. Even to this day, Meta approached problems with caution, preferring to weigh the risks first. *Except for the attack on Earth.* He pushed the argument away as fast as it came.

"He was," Meta acknowledged. "He loved risk and drank in adventure like it was a fine wine."

"He was a great man," Varooq offered weakly.

Meta chuckled humorlessly. "He was a wise leader, but risk led him to death. When I donned the mantle of High Prince I vowed that I would never make decisions without weighing all the risk."

"That is a wise course, sir."

"Don't pander, Varooq. It is very unbecoming." Meta glanced over and caught him shuffling his feet uneasily. "I have a point I am trying to make. I have been High Prince for almost a century now and have never made a decision without calculating the consequences." Meta picked up a stone and tossed it into the sea. It skipped several times before vanishing into the gloom. "Until Earth, that is. I acted rashly based on a precognitive fear."

Varooq looked puzzled. "I'm afraid I don't understand. You did what you had to do to preserve the Consortium. You said so yourself."

"I know what I said," he replied with minor irritation. "Our bloodline had been blessed with the gift of precognition for generations, ever since the first High Prince emerged from the depths of the Emerald Quarry to lead the Caelumites to glory. But I fear the ability has grown weak over the centuries. These visions are harder to come by and provide less information for me to dissect. My vision of Corvus and the dissolution of the Consortium may have been misinterpreted."

Varooq remained silent and Meta was thankful. He needed to air his concerns and remove the block of guilt that slowly crushed his conscience. "I'm afraid there are dark times ahead, Varooq. We need to remain vigilant and stand united." He knew worlds formerly loyal to the Consortium had changed sides, vowing support for the Insurgents. He had even heard rumblings of some pledging assistance to the Ascended. "I need you to be my envoy."

"I would be honored," he responded. "What do you need me to do?"

He had to stop the bleeding of his forces. For every world that joins their strength with either the rebels or the Ascended, the Consortium becomes weaker. He vowed the Consortium would not fall while he drew breath. The oldest cosmic organization in the universe would not fall due to some insignificant planet located in a remote galaxy. It was time to end this war before it truly began.

Meta reached into the pocket hidden within the folds of his robe. He shoved the paper into Varooq's hand. "I need you to rendezvous with Daranan and travel to the planets on this list. Affirm our strength and verify their loyalty to our cause. I will need their strength in the upcoming skirmish."

Varooq raised his head and cocked an eye. "Skirmish?"

"I had another vision," Meta replied. "Despite my reservations regarding the others, I must believe what I have seen and take the necessary precautions."

"What did you see?"

"I would rather not discuss it at this time. Please do as I request and all will be explained in time." Meta sat upon the rocks once again and returned his attention to the sea.

"It will be done," Varooq grunted. The resignation was obvious in his voice."

Meta watched the water crash upon the rocks and contemplated recent events. A large bird flew above and circled the water, waiting for prey to surface. It eventually locked on a target and it dipped low, hoping to catch it by surprise. The bird touched the water surface briefly before an oversized mouth breached the surface, filled with rows of razor sharp teeth. It swallowed the bird whole. The fish vanished beneath the surface as quickly as it appeared.

How easily a predator becomes the prey. Meta closed his eyes and returned to his meditation.

THE VOYAGE HOME

Vayne stood with his hands on his hips and licked his lips. He stared at us through the smallest goggles on his helmet. Kedge glanced at me and I wasn't sure whether we should have been insulted. "You can't be serious," he clucked.

"*I have completed the calculations and the danger level is low,*" Gard responded. "*Hostile forces have moved from that galaxy.*"

"I have to go back," I pleaded.

"Why?" he asked.

One word, uttered so effortlessly. It was just a simple question, but I found it difficult to answer. Everyone told me Earth was lost. *Why should I go back?* A part of me just had to see the destruction for myself but that was the only reason. *My family.* My parents weren't always there for me, but they were still my family. If I gave him that answer he most likely wouldn't budge. He doesn't care about them any more than he would care about a gnat buzzing around his face. If I were going to win him to my side, I had to appeal to his more *practical* side.

"My reasons are my own," I replied. "But wouldn't you be interested in the treasures?"

He cocked his head inquisitively. "What treasures?"

I had him. "The Earth is a dying planet, surely there are some items you can collect from the planet's surface that would prove priceless. Items from an extinct race perhaps?"

He looked at me for a long time before bursting in laughter. "Oh you are a clever one, Nathan Chambers. You hope to woo me with promises of priceless treasure." He tightened his gun belt and acted indifferent, but his words betrayed him. "If truth be told, I am somewhat attracted to the concept."

"So take us there!" I demanded.

His smile faded. "Alas, I am needed here, take your folly elsewhere." He turned to leave.

"He's right, Nathan," Kedge interjected. I fixed him with an icy stare but he held up his hand. "Vigil warned us he would be of no use. We should heed his advice. Maybe Vigil will be willing to help us."

Vayne stopped. His back faced us but I could hear his rapid breathing. "Vigil warned you," he growled without turning around. "Perhaps you should listen to him." Slowly, he turned toward us. His face darkened before adding, "Or maybe we should depart as soon as possible."

"Well, if I didn't know better, I would say you people were plotting something devious," a voice called from the doorway. We turned to find Wraith in the doorway, looking smug.

"It's about time you showed up," Kedge grumbled.

Wraith held up his hands in feigned innocence. "Hey when you told me what you were planning, I thought you were lying... or at the very least crazy. Sheer morbid curiosity led me here."

Kedge shrugged. "It doesn't matter what brought you here, so long as you are here."

I turned to Vayne. "How long until we reach Earth?"

Vayne stroked his chin. "So you intend to go through with this?"

I nodded.

"About five days," he sighed. "In the meantime, I suggest you get some rest." He glanced at an extravagant watch strapped to his wrist. The golden band shined bright but it was nothing compared to the luminescent gems that encrusted the face. "We will take off shortly, in the meantime I will direct you to your quarters."

"I suppose I will head to the lab and rummage through the collection of junk you have stashed there. Hopefully there will be something of use," Wraith griped.

"I'm not tired," Kedge grumbled. "Perhaps I will head to the weapons locker and see what toys you have."

Vayne waved them off. "Come, Nathan. Let's stuff you in an uncomfortable corner of the ship." A smile played at the corner of his lips but I wasn't sure if he was serious.

I followed him along the cavernous halls, passing various pictures and trophies. Some were familiar from our last voyage, but as we turned down different halls I noticed new treasures. Platinum goblets sat behind thick glass cases and exotic paintings adorned the walls. At the end of the hall a door slid aside revealing a lavishly decorated room. A u-shaped couch, lined with fur sat in the center of the room along. An oversized cherry wood desk stood in the corner with a computer connected to two monitors. The room was as lavishly decorated as the halls with a panoramic window which offered a view of the outside. An empty trophy case sat in the corner of the room, however the walls were decorated with paintings similar to those in the halls.

"I hope you find your accommodations comfortable," Vayne said. "In the next room you will find a bed, hopefully to your liking, as well as a washroom. Feel free to roam the ship if you get bored, just don't bother me." He turned to leave.

"Thanks a lot."

He waved me off and left the room. I strolled over to the window and looked outside. The window offered me a view of the main pavilion. Several Defense Fleet soldiers stood guard outside, their golden armor reflecting the bright Xajax sun. A few science officers entered the adjacent tent, followed shortly by Satou. He appeared to be in the process of setting up a mobile science lab. *His home away from home*, I mused. Turning from the window I glanced at the couch. Its comfort called to me and I obliged. I stretched out and laid my head on the armrest. It was even more comfortable than it looked. I started to nod off when there was a knock at the door.

"Of course," I griped. I sat up and shambled over to the door. "Who is it?"

"Me," Kedge responded flatly.

I opened the door and studied him with mild irritation. "Come to give me another inspirational speech?"

He wandered into the room and sat on the couch. With his head down, he laid his elbows across his knees and let his hands dangle between his legs. Suddenly I grew concerned. He looked like a man defeated.

"Sit down, Nathan."

Kedge motioned to the seat next to him. His sour expression didn't exactly fill me with confidence. I sat and prepared for grim news.

"Since we have some time before we land on Earth, I figured I would explain some things." He lifted his head slowly, his monocled eye focusing on me. "I am sure you have some questions to ask."

"You could say that," I chuckled but there was no humor in it. Lately it had been difficult to locate my funny bone.

"I guess I will start with our new allies. You know Vayne and Vigil, but there are twelve altogether."

"Wow, a whole twelve. I'm sure our odds are a lot better now." My sarcasm bone was much easier to locate.

Kedge narrowed his good eye. "These are no normal twelve. They are called the Twelve Timeless. They are older than the universe itself."

I rested my elbows on my knees and rubbed my temples. Exhaustion had begun to settle in and I was becoming quite irritable. "Kedge, I'm tired and really don't want to play this game."

"Game?" He looked genuinely confused.

"Yeah, I know you are messing with me." I threw up my hands and rolled my eyes. "It was hard to believe that you were centuries old until I learned about the cybernetic devices, but those two don't look a day over forty. With the exception of Vayne's ridiculous goggle monstrosity I don't see anything that would make me believe your story."

Kedge sighed. The cybernetic implant in his throat turned it into a growl. When his eye locked on me I recognized an iciness that sent shivers up my spine. "I guess I will start from the beginning." *He's not joking.* "Meta attacked while we were still on the planet. New York wasn't the initial point of attack, thank the gods." Kedge moved to the window and looked out. Folding his hands behind him, he continued. "Satou was furious, hell we all were. After we docked we confronted Meta. The pompous bastard had the audacity to throw it back in our faces. 'I did what was necessary to protect the rest of the universe'." Kedge looked over his shoulder and chuckled dryly before returning his gaze outside. "Boasted! The guy actually boasted about it. Well to make a long story a little less long we managed to commandeer two shuttles before he had the chance to react."

"Where does Vayne fit in?" I asked, my curiosity increasing.

"He doesn't," Kedge replied. "At least not yet." He turned with a smirk. "Are you going to let me finish or interrupt me every minute?"

I frowned and motioned for him to continue.

"We were passing Mars when Embeth radioed from the other shuttle. Wraith picked up a life form reading coming from the planet." I opened my mouth to protest and he stopped me with a raised finger. "I know what you are about to say, so save it. We questioned the findings as well. According to Embeth something was not right. The scanners registered the life form as a sentient being but the energy readings received were insane."

"Insane?"

"The energy readings had been solar in nature and equal to the power output of a sun. Our curiosity overwhelmed us. We decided to investigate, and when we landed," he hesitated to clear his throat, "Let's just say we were a bit surprised by the discovery."

"What was it?" I leaned forward, straining to absorb every word. I practically fell off the couch in anticipation.

"*It* was Vigil. We found him staring at the sky through one of the largest set of binoculars I had ever seen. Although we needed respirators and suits in order to navigate the planet's surface, he stood there just as he is now. He breathed in the toxic Martian atmosphere like it was nothing. When we found him we scanned him three times just to make sure he wasn't a mirage."

"What happened?" I asked.

"Well, he introduced himself. '*I am Vigil the Surveyor,*' he said. Except his voice was in our minds since words did not travel well through the air there. When he mentioned he was one of the Twelve Timeless I remembered a story my mother used to tell me when I was young. Some people called the Timeless gods, others called them the founders of the Universe. A small minority called them crackpots."

Is he kidding? Although I had to admit that Vigil was a bit strange, he seemed far from a god. *Does he expect me to believe that gods walked among us now*? Vigil seemed strange and Vayne had an overabundance of treasures, but that didn't qualify either of them as gods. For a moment I wondered if Kedge had been toying with me until I saw his expression. He was as serious as I had ever seen him. His look melted away any doubt.

"So are they gods or crackpots?"

He folded his hands across his laps and turned to me. "The universe is an enigma, Nathan. We could travel across it for a million years and discover only a small percentage of its secrets. Our new allies are one of those secrets."

The intercom interrupted us. "*We are preparing to launch for Earth. Before we lift off, I would like to bring your attention to the window on your left,*" Vayne's voice came across like he was in the middle of conducting a guided tour of a zoo. "*If you are care-*

ful you will catch a glimpse of a very special animal." Kedge and I exchanged confused glances and made our way to the window as Vayne droned on. *"Outside, my friends, is the rare Red-Faced Baboon."*

Outside Vigil looked up at our ship and screamed with such fury that his face turned blood-red. Embeth, along with the assistance of one of his soldiers, restrained him and attempted to calm him down.

"As you can see, folks, the beast can become agitated quite easily," Vayne continued. *"His handlers are having a hell of a time restraining him."* Outside, Vigil tossed the soldier aside and Embeth tripped trying to maintain a hold on him. *"Whoa!"* Vayne snickered. *"It looks like he is really ornery!"* The intercom clicked off.

We were soon out of visual range of the scene below. I ran my hand through my hair and shook my head. "What the heck was that all about?"

"It appears there is very little love between them. It seems Vigil did not approve of our little side trip." Kedge moved toward the door.

"Wait a minute, I have another question."

He turned with a smile. "You have almost a week to ask." My frown explained my lack of satisfaction with his answer. He groaned and shrugged. "Very well, go ahead and ask it."

"Are they really our allies?"

Kedge licked his lips as he considered the question. His hesitation caused a pit in my stomach. If these people weren't truly our allies and the Consortium had forsaken us, who *were* our allies? *Calypso? Sam? The Ascended?*

After a moment passed, Kedge answered. "They are."

I thought of Vayne and the way he brutally carved a path of destruction through Calypso's ship. Images of Natronix came to mind, his head practically torn from his shoulders. He had been no friend of mine, but I still couldn't deny the viciousness of it all. Kedge must have recognized my doubt because he moved from the door to stand face-to-face with me.

"They are our allies because they have to be."

"What does that mean?" I asked.

"We are on the brink of a war," he replied glumly. "One that threatens to tear at the very fabric of the universe. The Consortium had been protectors of the peace for centuries. They are broken. Your friends back on Xajax are all that's left of the old guard who wish to undo everything Meta has wrought." He turned to leave.

"What about Calypso and the Ascended?" I grabbed his elbow, turning him toward me. He stared at me with a mixture of surprise and annoyance but I didn't care. "Where do they fit in?"

"Nathan, I may be part machine, but in the end I am really only a man." His annoyed look faded and switched to resignation. "I don't have all the answers you seek. To be honest, I have no idea where they fit in. All I know is I have a score to settle with Calypso and I mean to settle it. If it means forging an alliance with these people then so be it."

The door slid open and he walked past a startled Gard. "*I hope I am not interrupting.*"

Kedge grunted and continued down the hall. I motioned Gard in before the door slid shut. "Well, it's nice to see you," I grumbled sarcastically. "Were you off frolicking among Vayne's treasures?"

Gard cocked his head. "*I do not frolic.*"

"Never mind." I rubbed my temples. I felt another migraine coming on. "What are you doing here?"

"*Talon suffered minor damage to the landing gear. I had just finished repairing it before Vayne took off. Once the work had been completed, Vayne had no more use for me. So I came here. After all, you are still the Cartographer and I am still your humble servant.*" His eyes flashed in quick succession and I recognized it as laughter.

"I'm glad to see you didn't lose your sense of humor," I groaned.

"*Vayne mentioned that we are on our way to Earth.*" The flashing stopped. His pale azure eyes were studying me instead.

I strolled to the window and watched Xajax fade into the distance. "Yep." We passed the planet's closest moon which was nothing more than an ashen rock devoid of life according to earlier scans. I turned to Gard. "So what are we going to find once we get there?"

Gard joined me at the window. Being only four feet high he couldn't quite reach the window. Instead he rolled to a stop next to me and locked on me with his luminous blue orbs. His right hand—the normal one—rested on my forearm.

"*Death.*"

AFTER EARTH

I opened my eyes to see Vayne standing over me. He welcomed me back to consciousness with a smile. "We're here."

I fell out of bed in my haste to get moving. "Where are the others?"

His smile faded. "Thanks for flying me back to my home planet, Vayne," he replied sourly. "My job is such a thankless endeavor."

I rolled my eyes. "Thanks for bringing me home." I threw on my shirt and washed my face with cold water. "Now, can you tell me where the others are?" I asked impatiently.

Vayne chuckled. "You're a funny guy. The others are outside waiting for you." He shoved something into my hand.

I looked down and saw it was a gun, similar to one he had in his holster. "What's this?"

"A precaution."

I followed him to the exit ramp. He remained silent until I grabbed him at the exit. He turned and gave my hand a look like he was about to bite it off.

"Is it bad?" I asked. In my zeal to come home I never imagined I would need a weapon as a precaution.

He moved past me and stood on the ramp, surveying the landscape. "I suppose it depends on what your definition of 'bad' is."

I stepped onto the ramp and looked around. Kedge, Gard and Wraith waited for me at the bottom. When I saw where we were my heart skipped a beat.

"I know where we are!" I ran to the bottom of the ramp and looked around. Vayne landed his ship in the middle of Highway 180 overlooking Carlsbad Caverns National Park. Not only were we in New Mexico but we weren't far from where I first ran into Satou. I was truly home.

"Gard had records of your first encounter with the Consortium," Vayne explained. "I figured it was only appropriate that we land here."

The sun was beginning to rise but the highway was empty. Normally this wasn't unusual in such a remote area of New Mexico but when I saw the charred body of a Cessna embedded in what was once Big Tony's Country Store reality had begun to settle in. Corpses littered the parking lot. Crows pecked away at their burned husks and I felt my gorge rising.

"I can't believe it," I moaned. I looked up and my heart skipped a beat. Although there were only a few clouds in the sky and the sun was shining, portions of the sky looked darker. Blacker.

Wraith followed my gaze and removed a scanner from his belt. He held it up to the sky and scowled. "I hate to be the buzzkill here but we must hurry. The atmosphere is beginning to deteriorate."

"What does that mean?" I glanced at him nervously.

"It means that the ozone layer is depleting," Kedge responded. "I have seen it before… on Mars."

"Which means I will be getting out of here soon, so do whatever it is you came here to do," Vayne said calmly.

My rage boiled. Meta's indifference to mankind doomed them. I clenched my fist and vowed to pay him back tenfold. Humans may have been an imperfect species but they were *MY* species.

"*Something is coming,*" Gard said.

My heart skipped a beat. *Survivors!* I looked to where Gard pointed and saw someone running toward us along the highway. They were about a half mile away. I stepped forward and waved my hands furiously.

"HEY!" I shouted. "OVER HERE!"

"Wait a minute, Nathan." Kedge's hand fell on my shoulder. He gripped it so hard a felt fingers of pain radiate through my neck.

"Ouch," I cried. "What the hell?"

"That's no human," Wraith said. His weapon was in his hand. "Look at him. He is about a quarter of a mile away yet he is huge. He must be eight or nine feet tall."

I squinted against the glare of the sun and agreed. If the person coming toward us was human, he was larger than any human I had ever seen. Fear took over and my hand fell on the butt of my weapon. I looked over at Vayne. His thumbs were buried in his belt and he made no move toward his weapons. The lens of his helmet moved clockwise before settling on a pair of over-sized tubes. He remained silent and studied the figure, who continued moving at a high rate of speed with no sign of slowing.

"Vayne," I said, trying to hide my nervousness. "Who is it?"

He remained silent, choosing to instead stare off in the distance. The stranger was less than three hundred yards from us and gaining. My fingers closed around the butt of my weapon and I looked at Vayne for a sign. He gave none. The figure closed to within two hundred yards. When he closed to a hundred I froze.

"What the hell is that?" Wraith gasped.

The figure was at least ten feet tall, but that was only because it wasn't a single person at all. It was actually two people, one riding the other. The figure on the bottom was large, at least six and a half feet tall and covered from head to foot in gray hair. He was pumping his arms (which were as big as tree trunks by the way) running as fast he could. Every muscle in his body flexed as he carried the smaller man along the highway. The smaller man was slightly under four feet tall and straddled the larger man's shoulders with his hands buried up to the wrists in its shaggy mane. The shorter of the two wore a metal hat that resembled a garbage can lid wrapped in fur lining with a white overcoat to match. It was like I was watching some kind of macabre piggy back ride in the circus.

"I can't believe it," Vayne grumbled.

The unlikely duo slowed before coming to a complete stop in front of him. "Vigil is not happy with you," the shorter man said, pointing at Vayne. His tanned cheeks were flushed and a thin veil of sweat glistened on his forehead. The larger of the two, however, looked as if he had just crawled out of bed. He wasn't even breathing heavily.

"When is he ever happy with me?" Vayne responded cheerfully. "If you ever notice that he is happy with me I am probably dead."

The beast growled and the man on top slapped him on the head. "Calm down, Liath. Our friend was only joking."

"I think I just stepped into the Twilight Zone," I said, wide-eyed.

The shorter man looked at me and a wide smile crossed his face. He turned his index finger toward me. "I know you."

I took a step back and my hand fell from my weapon. "That's nice. That makes one of us."

His smile faded. "It seems Vayne only talks about himself and his treasures when he should be talking about more important things. Menjaro the Messenger, fastest among the Timeless, at your service." He slapped Liath upside the head. "Bow, you fool!"

Liath let out a squawk and attempted to bow but the gesture was so awkward it looked more like he would vomit instead. Menjaro clutched his fur tightly to prevent himself from sliding off. I placed my hand over my mouth to stifle the laugh rising from my throat.

"You cannot do anything right," Menjaro sighed and rubbed his face in frustration. "I apologize for my hairy friend here but

I will forgive him this one time and blame it on exhaustion from our trip."

"How long have you been here?" Vayne asked.

"Long enough to know I want to be gone as soon as possible," he replied sourly. "I followed you here only because I owed Vigil a favor. Of course as soon as I knew you were coming back to Earth I raced to beat you here. I waited on the other side of a ruined warehouse about two miles back and hid my ship. I didn't want survivors or something more...undesirable...stumbling across it."

"Are there survivors?" I asked hopefully.

Menjaro looked at Vayne. "He doesn't know, does he?" When he spied the confusion on Vayne's face he slapped his forehead. "Oh, that's right, you decided to skip the meeting. That reminds me, Ibune is also not happy with you by the way."

Vayne waved his hand dismissively. "You and your damn meetings."

"Wait a second," I interrupted. "What am I supposed to know?"

Liath growled and licked his lips. Menjaro reached down and patted the side of his neck. "Settle down Liath, we will be leaving this place soon enough." He reached into his jacket and pulled out a rolled up piece of paper. He flattened it against the back of Liath's head and scanned it with his index finger. He looked up apologetically. "Sorry, I had to recall the minutes of the meeting. According to Scribe the battle took its toll. Meta attacked everyone in his determination to destroy the time hole. He took out half the planet along with the Ascended forces unfortunate enough to remain behind."

"It seems I was right about the High Prince," Kedge grunted.

Kedge was indeed right. As much as I trusted the Consortium to do the right thing, this was the worst thing Meta could have done. He was no better than the Lumagom who destroyed Mars.

I was about to ask him the status of survivors when Menjaro interrupted with a scowl.

"I know you as well." His cherub-like demeanor vanished and his face darkened. Liath seemed to sense his master's emotional change and let out a menacing growl. They took one step closer to Kedge. "Oh yes, Kedge Mal'Dineen, I remember you as well."

Kedge folded his arms across his chest, unperturbed. "It seems a lot of people know me. Rumor has it I've been around awhile."

"Indeed," Menjaro muttered. "Are you happy with your former friends' actions? Does Lumagom blood still flow through your veins?"

"I guess you two know each other?" Wraith asked.

Kedge narrowed his eyes and matched his scowl but remained silent.

"Those aren't his friends anymore." I stood next to him in a show of support.

"We shall see." Menjaro eyeballed him before turning his attention to me. "I apologize for bringing such grim news, but there is nothing more you can do here. If you notice the sky, the atmosphere is starting to degrade and soon the air will become toxic. If there are survivors here, they won't live for long." He turned Liath around and looked over his shoulder, focusing his attention on Vayne. "Vigil does not normally rage for long, but Vayne has a habit of rubbing him the wrong way. If I were you I would return to Xajax before his anger causes his head to explode like a volcano."

"That would be a sight to see," Vayne replied. "I would sell my ship to see that."

"Always pushing boundaries." Menjaro shook his head and turned to leave.

"Wait," I cried. "What about my parents?"

He stopped. "If I am correct, they do not live far from here." He reached into his pocket and pulled out a small circular object. Its gold surface glittered in the sunlight. His mouth tightened while he studied its surface. "According to my calculations you should have enough time to find out for yourself." He returned the object to his pocket and stared at the sky. "Atmospheric tearing....hmm. If I were you I wouldn't linger for long." He turned and sped down the road, becoming nothing more than a mirage on the horizon.

"I will stay here and run some scans to check for survivors," offered Vayne.

"*According to my calculations your home is approximately two-point-four miles from here*," Gard said.

"Hold on a minute." Wraith popped the clip from his weapon and checked the ammunition. "Full load." He slammed the clip closed with a grunt. "Now I'm ready to go."

My hand brushed against the butt of my weapon. I checked it earlier so I knew it contained a full clip.

"Let's go." I turned down the road.

Solomon Corvus

The goblet flew through the air and crashed against the wall. Calypso stood, wide-eyed, with fists clenched closely by his sides. Corvus missed his head by inches. He also missed the window which was fortunate for everyone. The outline of Earth floated in the background as the shuttle orbited the planet.

"How the hell could this happen?" He roared.

Calypso composed himself and lowered his head. "I underestimated Meta. I never imagined he would attack Earth."

Corvus ran his hands through his snowy hair and paced the room. Rage flowed through his veins but he had to shove it aside so he could think clearly. He agreed with Calypso. He never thought the High Prince would attack Earth. Perhaps Meta's attack on the planet was a blessing. The Consortium was now fractured and weakened. He breathed in deeply and let the rage ebb before looking at Calypso. *Were their forces strong enough to attack Meta directly?*

Calypso flinched under his gaze. "What?"

By his calculations, the Scarlet Moon provided him with six ships and over five hundred soldiers. The remaining Lumagom forces came with ten ships and seven hundred soldiers. Without the use of the time hole on Earth, he could not hope to gain allies without manipulating events in the present. "What do you think of the Consortium's manpower at this moment?"

Calypso closed his eyes and flexed his fingers as he mentally calculated. "Meta's personal fleet is made up of ten ISS class warships, twenty-five IPS class scout vessels and ten royal barges which are nothing more than entertainment and transport ships. I am not sure how many of the Defense Fleet forces Embeth took with him. I assume Meta still holds at least half of the Defense Fleet which means he has an additional thirty ISS warships at his disposal."

"What about the Explorer's League?" Corvus asked.

Calypso shrugged. "They are nothing but science and research ships, limited to self-defense weapons."

"It is the quantity I am interested in," he countered.

Calypso held up his hands. "I think it's safe to assume they followed Satou. They were loyal to him." Calypso chuckled.

"What's so funny?"

Calypso stopped and shook his head. "Oh nothing, I was just thinking what some had been calling them."

"Insurgents," Corvus finished. He had heard the term himself, mostly from intelligence gathered by Shai. "It appears they may not be made up of only disgruntled Consortium folks though." He had heard the rumors.

Calypso nodded. "The Timeless."

"Again with this term," Corvus grumbled. "How is it I never heard of these people before?"

Calypso dropped his head and stared at the floor, but not before Corvus spotted his incredulous eye roll. He hated him for that. *Calypso the great universal explorer.* He continued to treat him as if he were a moron. As if for some ungodly reason, a human—even one from the future—could not possibly know more than the great Calypso. His insolence created a red waterfall of rage to wash over him.

Calypso let out a choked gasp as hands closed around his throat. He dropped to his knees, flailing at appendages that weren't there. Corvus stood across the table with his eyes closed as his fury consumed him. He also stood next to Calypso with his hands wrapped around his throat, choking the life out of him, but no one could see his projection.

"Urk," Calypso gasped. His hands reached for his throat, but came away with empty air. He tried to stand but the pressure from the phantasm kept him on his knees.

"Your disrespect is really starting to grate on my nerves," Corvus said calmly. "Next time I will not let go." He opened his eyes and the phantasm disappeared.

Calypso collapsed on the floor, gasping for air. As he struggled to breathe, Corvus circled the table and stood over him.

"You think of us as nothing more than sheep," he sneered. "You may be right about humans. The Ascended, however, are not."

Calypso raised his head with the fires of rage burning in his eyes. Tears streamed down his cheeks as he coughed and rubbed his throat. "Ascended or not," he rasped. "You do not know everything." He stood up on one knee and slowly massaged his injured neck. "The Timeless are real. We were attacked by them. If you decide to disregard them, they will destroy you."

You. No more "we". It could have just been a mistake on Calypso's part. Or perhaps he was already distancing himself. Either way, Corvus made a mental note to keep a closer eye on his colleague. He was correct in one regard. If the insurgents had new allies, it would be prudent for him to gather more as well.

"You're right."

Calypso seemed taken by surprise from his quick agreement. He narrowed his eyes with suspicion. "I guess you came to your senses." He stood up and backed away, as if distance would keep him safe from Corvus' wrath. "What do you plan to do?"

Corvus smiled. "I plan on finding us some new friends."

"And how do you plan on doing that?" Calypso asked.

"Leave that to me."

INVITED GUESTS

Our trip along Carlsbad Cavern Highway was rather uneventful until we reached the intersection of National Parks Highway. That was when things took a turn toward bizarre.

"What is that, Nathan?" Wraith pointed ahead.

He pointed toward a small brick building with six garage doors. All of them were open but empty. A big white sign hung along the front of the building. *Joel Volunteer Fire Department.* A ladder truck was parked outside. It was nothing more than a scorched shell of metal on four smoldering tires. The only reason I knew what it had been was half of the ladder remained. It was a charred skeletal reminder of the attacks. Before our discovery, it felt like nothing more than a peaceful Sunday where the streets were empty because everyone had gone off to church.

"It's the remains of a fire truck," I replied. Before I could turn away and continue down the road I spotted the charred corpse next to it.

"There is no sense lingering here." Kedge grabbed my arm but I brushed it away.

"No," I growled. *I have to see this.* I embraced the rage I felt at that moment.

The remains of a patch, half-blackened from whatever had killed the poor guy, stood out on his shirt. *Joel Volunteer*, it read. The rest of the patch was burned beyond recognition. I saw others burned inside the fire truck. Their charred remains were unrecognizable. With a grimace I headed toward the building.

"Hey, be careful," Wraith called out. "We don't know who or what we may run into down here."

"*I am picking up no life signs in the area. There seems to be no immediate danger,*" Gard offered.

All I had to do was look up to the dark tears in the sky to know what "immediate danger" we would be facing soon. "How did they do it?"

Kedge poked the charred corpse with his staff. "Do what?"

He followed my gaze toward the sky. His mouth tightened and his monocled eye focused furiously in the glare of the sun. "I'm not sure it was intentional."

I turned toward him incredulously. "Not intentional?"

It was Gard who responded. "*Chlorofluorocarbons did this, Nathan. The emissions from so many battleships combined with weapon discharge contributed to the degradation of the ozone layer.*"

"I suppose it doesn't matter," I replied, my words laced with venom. "They are responsible, whether it's intentional or not." I moved next to Wraith who had been busy scanning the corpse. I pointed at it. "They did *this*!"

No one argued my point. Wraith completed his scan and shoved the scanner into his belt clip. "This person is dead," he said flatly. He looked into my rage-filled face and frowned. "There is no point dwelling on this. It will be worse in more populated areas of the planet."

I looked from the corpse to Wraith. "You think?" I asked, my voice dripping with sarcasm.

He pursed his lips with a confused look. "No I don't *think*. I can confirm it with facts."

I rolled my eyes and moved toward the bays. Wraith remained behind, apparently confused by my outburst. He could be so thickheaded at times.

"What goes inside there?" Kedge walked behind me and motioned toward the building.

"Fire trucks," I responded.

He rubbed his chin. "Fire trucks? Are they always on fire?"

I looked at him to see if he was serious. His frown and hard stare answered my question. "Um, they aren't on fire. We use them to help put out fires."

His frown changed into a wry smile. "Oh, I see. We had something like that on Mars. We called them water transports." He grabbed a fireman's helmet off a shelf and turned it over in his hands. "Warriors piloted these *fire trucks*?"

"No." A smile played at the corner of my lips as I watched him study the helmet. "Normally it was volunteers from the community." Kedge held the helmet up to his monocled eye and examined it.

"Interesting," he mused. "These helmets are hard. They would be useful in battle."

We stepped out of the bay and joined Wraith, who was preoccupied with examining the charred husk of the fire truck. He scraped off a burnt piece of metal and pinched it between his fingers. He brought it up to his nose. "Smells like plasma."

"So?" I asked.

Wraith frowned. "I just wanted to verify the cause."

"The cause?" My anger started to rise. "What else do you think caused this? Do you think this fireman was out here just washing the truck when suddenly it spontaneously burst into flames?"

Wraith opened his fingers and let the debris fall to the ground. "We should go," he chuffed.

I felt bad for snapping at him. I had to remind myself that he helped bring me back home. He may be snobbish at times but he had been instrumental in rescuing me from Calypso and bringing me here. "I'm sorry," I apologized.

He brushed me off and started down the road. "It's this way, right?"

I nodded and followed him. Gard fell in behind us. As we passed Kedge he grabbed my arm. "It is alright to be angry. Anger keeps us focused on the task at hand."

I turned to him. "And what is the task at hand?"

He stopped walking. "Why it's to defeat the—," Gard's communicator interrupted him.

"*I don't know where you guys are but you better wrap it up quickly. Two ships have entered the sector and are headed in your direction*," Vayne's voice barked.

"Consortium ships?" Wraith asked.

"*Are they Consortium ships?*" Gard repeated.

"*They don't appear to be*," Vayne responded. "*That doesn't mean you shouldn't be careful. If I were you, I'd start making travel arrangements out of there.*"

I squinted and looked to the hills on the horizon. Two black circles appeared just above the Shell gas station sign in the distance. They looked like thick dishes with antennas attached on the top. *Remote controlled Frisbees.* I laughed out loud.

"What's so funny?" Wraith grumbled.

I gestured toward the incoming objects. "You've got to be kidding me...real flying saucers!"

"*Those appear to be Kamilian vessels*," offered Gard.

I recalled the Kamilian I observed onboard the Argus during my first voyage with the Consortium. I remembered how their similarity to Bugs Bunny made me giggle. The question was: *whose side were they on now?* It didn't seem so funny now.

"Friends?" I asked.

No one offered a response. Kedge grabbed my elbow. "We should go."

"It's too late," Wraith said.

He was right. The ships were no more than a quarter mile away. As they passed over a nearby Rodeway Inn, the lobby doors burst open and a young couple ran out. When they turned and saw us the man pointed and ran in our direction. The ships veered to the left and followed. As they approached I appreciated the size of the ships. They were enormous and had to be the size of a football field.

"We better get inside," Kedge said, motioning toward the fire station.

"I agree," I replied.

We hurried through the nearest bay door. Inside was another door leading to an interior office where I led the group. There was a lone window in the office which faced the highway. Blinds partially concealed us, but we could still be seen from the outside. I reached up to close the blinds and spotted the couple outside. The ships were directly over them, blocking out the sun and covering them in their shadow. The woman let out a scream as the man pulled her along.

"Those people are leading them right to us," Wraith grumbled.

I pulled the string controlling the blinds, but it became twisted around the gear. After muttering several curses under my breath I managed to unhook the string. Before I could close the blinds a beam of light exited the bottom of the ship and engulfed the couple and they vanished. One minute they were running toward the fire house, the next minute they were gone.

"*Fascinating.*"

I turned toward Gard wide-eyed. His tone of voice was detached, as if he had just watched a gymnast do a triple somersault rather than observe two humans get vaporized.

"Fascinating?" I croaked.

He ignored me and continued to stare out the window. The ship that fired continued to hover while the other ship departed the area.

"It appears that they are looking to land," Wraith whispered.

He wasn't wrong. The ship hovered above the firehouse for a moment before darting across the main intersection toward the Rodeway Inn. It descended, kicking up large dust clouds and scattering debris everywhere. Two parallel bars extended from the bottom, allowing the disk-shaped craft to land safely in the parking lot. Due to its size, the corner of the ship crushed a portion of the iron fence surrounding the outdoor pool.

"Sorry folks, the pool will be closed for the remainder of the season," I uttered before laughing hysterically.

Kedge smacked me on the back of the head. "This is no time to lose your head, Nathan. Stay focused."

"Stay focused he says," I mumbled. "Two people were just disintegrated—,"

Before I could finish, a ramp descended from the ship. Two of the Kamilians cautiously moved down the ramp and surveyed the area. One of them was armed with a rifle which he kept straddled close to his chest. He was naked from the waist up except for thin, gray hair that covered him from his neck to his waist. He wore baggy cargo pants and high combat boots, which reminded me of a furry Rambo. He broke off from the other and examined the damage to the pool fence. The other was naked from the waist up as well, with the exception of darker hair and a bright red sash straddled across his shoulder. He wore similar attire but carried no visible weapon. His long ears stood erect at the top of his head, but when he turned I saw one of them had a big hole in the center.

"Are they Meta's people?" I asked.

Wraith craned his head forward and peered out the window. "I don't recognize them."

"Yeah, well, he is looking right at us." Kedge unhooked his staff and backed away from the window.

Mr. Red Sash exited the parking lot and started walking up the street toward the fire house. His friend ceased his inspection of the mangled fence and shouted something. Red Sash turned and yelled something in return. His armed companion joined him in the street, holding his weapon defensively and surveying the area.

"Damn, let's hope there's only two of them in that ship," Wraith muttered doubtfully before removing his weapon from its holster.

"I don't care," I growled. "I will kill them all." My gun was in my hand before I even realized I pulled it out.

The Kamilians were no more than one hundred yards away from the fire house and closing. The armed escort continued to sweep his rifle to the right and left while Red Sash stared in our direction, moving slowly. He couldn't possibly see us with the blinds and distance masking our presence, but I couldn't shake the feeling that he "sensed" our presence. He would stop periodically and sniff the air, like he was trying to smell us.

"Kamilians have an enhanced sense of smell," Wraith said, as if he read my thoughts. "He is trying to locate us.' He moved toward the door leading to the bay and placed his hand on the doorknob. "Gard keep watch and see what they are doing. As soon as they cross the street, let me know."

"*Acknowledged.*"

"I got your back," I said.

Kedge moved toward the door and kept his back against the wall. "I'm ready."

"*They stopped,*" Gard said. "*The Kamilian with the red belt has stopped smelling the air and has engaged in conversation with his companion.*" Gard's eyes flickered. "*Wait, they stopped talking. They are crossing the street.*" Several tense seconds passed before he continued. "*They are examining the corpse.*"

"At the count of three we will rush outside," Wraith said. "Gard you stay here."

When we nodded our agreement he began to countdown. "One," Wraith whispered. "Two." I felt Kedge place his hand on my shoulder before I moved closer to Wraith. "THREE!"

We burst from the door and into the bay, practically tripping over one another. Startled, Red Sash looked up from the corpse. His companion swung the rifle in our direction. That was when everything turned to chaos. Kedge's staff came to life. One minute it was nothing more than a piece of wood with a snake head engraved along the top and the next minute it was a living serpent. The eyes lit up with an emerald fire and it let out an ungodly sound. The hiss which escaped sounded like steam escaping from a broken valve. The living weapon left Kedge's hands and lunged for the Kamilian holding the rifle. It wrapped itself around the weapon and let out another hiss. The Kamilian dropped it and screamed.

"NO, WAIT!" Red Sash shouted.

That was when the action slowed to a crawl. I watched everything unfold in slow motion. The rifle shattered as the staff serpent squeezed its body around it. Red Sash held up his hands and his lips curled slowly. Wraith shouted something but I didn't hear it. I was no longer paying attention. My gaze looked past the screaming, weaponless Kamilian. My gaze switched to their ship. Two people were coming down the ramp. It was the couple, whole and intact. They stopped and stared at the scene with confusion.

"NO, WAIT!" I echoed.

The serpent slithered back into Kedge's hands where it became a staff again. Wraith fired his weapon well wide of his target. My shout, thankfully, threw off his aim. Red Sash put his hands down and his companion stopped screaming, looking at the shattered ruin of his weapon with disbelief.

"Wait!" Red Sash repeated.

I looked from the stunned couple to him. "What? How?" I stuttered. "How did they survive?"

Red Sash turned to me and held up his hands. "Bree N'Dadi sent us."

I recognized the name. He was the leader of the Erudites, a group of cosmic messengers, whom I met aboard the Argus long ago. From what I understood they held no affiliation and were simply messengers zooming across the cosmos delivering messages. "Bree from the Erudites?" I asked. "Aren't they just some sort of galactic FedEx?"

"Why would Bree do that?" Wraith asked incredulously.

"My name is Ehoro," he replied. He pointed to the couple. "We are here to rescue the people of this planet."

HOPE?

"My name is Jimmy, and this is Amber."

The man was really just an older kid. He looked pale and ready to vomit but remained strong. I thought it was more of an act to impress the girl more than anything. The girl, on the other hand, had a look on her face like she bit had into an onion. Her hair hung in her eyes and she brushed it aside several times trying to study us. Her hair had been dyed red to clash with her name.

"What were you two doing inside the hotel?" I asked.

"Well, mister cheapskate here insisted on staying at Rodeway instead of the Holiday Inn like I wanted," Amber pouted. "All he had to do was wait until we got to 285 like the GPS said."

Jimmy's mouth tightened. "Amber, shut up about the damn Holiday Inn already. You heard the reports on the radio." He walked over and pointed at Ehoro who cocked an eyebrow. "Look at this guy." Ehoro started to voice a protest but was interrupted by Jimmy turning dramatically toward their ship. "Look at their ship. They are aliens, Amber. We were attacked by aliens. Do you think they really give a damn what hotel we stayed at?"

Ehoro's companion, who ran back to the ship earlier to replace his shattered rifle, approached.

"What is it, Merren?" Ehoro asked.

"A report from Rok," he responded. "Ships have been sighted over Australia, heading northwest."

"Not ours, I suppose?" Ehoro asked sourly.

Merren shook his head. Jimmy and Amber exchanged nervous glances.

Ehoro frowned. "How many survivors have been recovered so far?"

Merren looked down at a large square object, no bigger than an iPod. He touched the interface and muttered something unkind under his breath. "It appears we have rescued thirty-five thousand." He slid his finger across the screen. "Rok reports we are nearing capacity and will need to finish soon. We would have been able to rescue more but Bulwark 7 blew a plasma converter core and had to be escorted back to Kamil-Isa by Bulwark 1."

Ehoro turned to us. "Come with us. We need to leave."

"Wait. I need to see if my parents survived." I placed my hand on his arm and he pulled away from it like it was on fire.

"There is no time," he countered. "We are a search and rescue team." He pointed down the road toward his ship. "These vessels are not machines of war. The reports of unidentified ships entering Earth's atmosphere is a cause for concern. We have over seven hundred humans on board. We need to get them to safety."

"Where are you taking them?" Kedge asked.

Ehoro narrowed his eyes and studied Kedge. "Somewhere safe," he replied dryly. He looked at Wraith and Gard. "You are not humans. Who are you?"

Kedge and I exchanged nervous looks. In the end I determined Ehoro could be trusted with our information. "I am Nathan Chambers," I replied. "I am...was...the Cartographer."

"We are nothing but rebels now," Wraith added.

"No." Ehoro frowned. "Not rebels. *Insurgents.*"

I took a step back and sensed Kedge stiffening beside me. Wraith's hand slid slowly to his sidearm where it came to rest on the grip. I lowered my hand to my belt, closer to my weapon.

A broad smile split Ehoro's face. "Such a terrible name. Insurgent implies rebellion against established authority. The title alone lends power to the Consortium as if they were some sort of galactic governing body." He bellowed laughter and Merren followed. I exhaled and felt the tension leave my body. He clapped a hand on my shoulder before leaning over to whisper in my ear. "Bree believes in you, lad. If he believes in you then I believe in you. The Consortium is decaying, and you are all that's left of what it stood for."

"I'm not sure about all that," I argued. "All I want to do right now is find my parents."

His smile faded. "Then what?"

Before I could answer, Merren fell in behind Ehoro. "Sir, we have to go. The ships are passing over the southern tip of Africa and closing."

Ehoro nodded and Merren ushered Amber and Jimmy back to the ship. "Bree said that you were smart. If that is true than I trust you will do the right thing." He placed a finger against his temple. "Think about what's happening right now. Really *think* about it. Despite the despair, despite the bloodshed and despite the heartache, there is a real *chance* to do good." He turned and walked away.

"Opportunity for what?" I called out after him.

He stopped and turned. "You will know when you discover it." He continued down the road.

"Gee thanks Aristotle," I grumbled.

He turned one final time. "We will be back, Nathan. I promise. I made a vow to Bree to rescue as many people as I could. If you do decide to stay here, look to the sky for the Ark."

"The Ark? I asked.

"It was dispatched from Kamil-Isa but is much slower than the Bulwarks. It will come for most of your indigenous wildlife, but it is capable of holding up to one hundred thousand people. The last I heard it entered your solar system with only a skeleton crew in order to house more survivors. It should arrive soon."

"What about those other ships? Won't the Ark be in danger?" I asked.

"I hope not," he replied before continuing down the street. "But if the ships are hostile, the Ark is better equipped at defending itself than we are."

"We are running out of time, Nathan," Kedge urged. "Let's go."

I watched Jimmy and Amber board the ship. *Should we have followed them?* Even if my parents survived, there is a chance they had been picked up by one of the Kamilian ships. Was it really worth risking our lives only to come away empty?

"Let's go," I said. I led our group down Carlsbad Cavern Highway. As we passed the Rodeway Inn, the humming from Ehoro's ship grew louder, eventually becoming a giant hornet's nest inside my skull as the ship lifted off. The ship ascended slowly into the sky and hovered over us. Several blue globes of light rotated counter clockwise around the hull of the ship one time before it shot out of view like a ball from a sling. *Textbook flying saucer,* I mused.

We got a half mile past the Rodeway Inn before we saw our first real signs of battle. A trailer park entrance was located just off the main highway. The property was surrounded by a chain link fence which allowed us to see inside. Most of the trailers had been obliterated. They were now nothing more than smoldering metal carcasses. I wandered past a red Ford pickup truck with a smashed windshield that had crashed into the ditch. There was a bumper sticker on the back window that read "I'll give you my gun when you pry it from my cold, dead hands." A hulking man in brown camouflage hung out the driver side door with a charred hole in his chest. Clutched in his hand was a tactical shotgun. Kedge approached the scene cautiously before reaching down and prying the gun from his hand.

He took one look at the bumper sticker and glanced at me. "Irony, huh?" There was no humor in his voice.

Several Eddy county Sheriff vehicles were parked across the street with doors and trunks open. Shotguns and AR-15 assault rifles were scattered around the vehicles along with the bodies of several deputies. The Eddy County Sheriff is the first line of defense for the residents outside the city limits but against the Consortium, they were no defense at all. Wraith rushed to the nearest corpse—a burly cop clutching an AR-15. He waved his hand scanner over the corpse.

"This person was shot at close range," he observed. "The wounds appear to be consistent with a hand cannon."

"So what?" I asked.

"It means Meta put soldiers on the ground," answered Kedge. "It means that he wanted to wipe the humans out. This wasn't some insane quest to destroy the time hole. There was a hidden agenda here. These people were assassinated."

I looked into the lifeless eyes of the deputy. They stared accusingly toward the sky, as if blaming heaven for unleashing hell. "There is nothing we can do for them now."

"Retribution," Wraith said.

"Huh?" I turned and watched as his mouth tightened.

"That is what we can do for them. Retribution for all that had died as a result of Meta's misguided actions."

Wraith was right. This was just a small sample of what happened on Earth. This was just a small rural area with a relatively small population. I could only guess at what kind of carnage waited at the larger cities. *Thirty-five thousand.* That's how many the Kamilians rescued on a planet inhabited by billions. They said an Ark was coming, but how many people were left to rescue? Scowling, I reached down and pried the assault rifle from the dead deputy's hands. His hands were stiff with death and he clutched the weapon as if he planned on taking it with him to the afterlife. I pulled with such force that his index finger broke, which added to the sick feeling already present in my stomach. I popped the clip and examined it, relieved to see it was still full of ammo. I slammed it back into place with a resounding thud. I noticed Kedge looking at me with a curious expression.

"What? I have seen this done a million times in Call of Duty," I joked.

Kedge narrowed his good eye and studied me with the monocled one. "Call of Duty?"

Before I could respond, a transmission from Vayne came over Wraith's communicator. "*Hey folks, I'm not sure what island you people are vacationing on, but I suggest you hurry. I have several ships heading our way. I know I am good and all that, but several is a few too many for me to handle solo. At this time I'm not sure if they are hostile, but why take a chance?*"

Gard stared off into the sky, northeast of the sun's position. The blue orbs of his eyes flashed like a disco light. "*Do you have the Kamilian ships on your radar, Vayne?*"

I heard Vayne fidgeting with something in the background. He muttered something under his breath before coming back to the radio. "It looks like the Kamilians took off like an Umbral Ice Hound on fire."

I wasn't sure what an Umbral Ice Hound was, but I supposed they didn't enjoy being on fire. Either way, we were running out of time. "Where are the ships now?"

"*About two thousand miles southeast of our position,*" Vayne responded.

"Let's get out of here," I said.

"Are you sure?" Kedge asked.

I swung the AR-15 over my shoulder. "We need to get out of here. Those ships may be looking for us. If my parents are still alive, I won't do them any good leading a fleet of ships to their doorstep." I walked over to the closest police vehicle and rummaged through the trunk. I found a clip full of ammo for the AR-15, a bulletproof vest, two tactical knives, a portable defibrillator and road flares. I grabbed the clip and one of the knives. I shoved the clip in my pocket and stuck the knife in my belt. "Now I'm ready."

We doubled back past the scorched trailer park. As we moved past the Rodeway Inn with its mangled pool fence I noticed a crushed Cadillac on the far side of the parking lot. It seemed Ehoro's parking job wasn't as smooth as first suspected but I figured the owner had more important things to worry about now. When we got to the abandoned fire house, Wraith grabbed his communicator.

"Vayne we are about a half mile from your location. What's your status?"

Dead air responded. "Vayne?" Wraith repeated.

An antenna extended from the back of Gard's head. "*Perhaps he had to relocate due to imminent danger. Let me try using long range communications.*" Gard rolled up a nearby hill to gain a better vantage point. "*Vayne, this is Gard. Are you there?*"

More silence followed until Vayne's frantic voice broke through. "*Gard...had to...under attack.*" There was too much static to understand what he said afterward. Gard looked toward us.

Even though he was an emotionless robot, for a brief second I imagined an expression of hopelessness nestled within his eye orbs. Kedge and Wraith stood along the edge of the highway and they seemed to sense the same thing.

Suddenly the radio sprung to life. "*GARD... THE SHIPS... HUNDREDS... RUN!*"

No one questioned the panic in the voice. Vayne was one of the Twelve Timeless. I had witnessed his combat abilities aboard Calypso's ship and I did not doubt his courage. If he was telling us to run, we must run.

"GO!" Wraith commanded.

"Where?" I cried. "We are in the middle of nowhere."

"Back to the fire house," Kedge suggested.

I turned and ran as fast as I can. We were about a quarter mile from the building when suddenly a humming sound came from the sky behind us. It sounded like the world's largest dial tone which got louder over time. *They were here.*

"Don't look back, Nathan," Kedge shouted. "Just run as fast as you can."

I put my head down and pumped my arms as fast as I could. It became awkward eventually as I struggled to maintain control of the AR-15 strapped over my shoulder. It bounced painfully against my arm. Gard whizzed past me and I realized for a small robot with tank treads he was quick. He must have been going at least forty miles per hour.

"Hey, wait," I shouted breathlessly. "Give me a ride at least!"

We were no more than thirty yards from the fire house when the humming became too much to bear. I tripped, fell hard on my side and lost my grip on the rifle. It went skidding into the gravel alongside the highway. Gard reached the fire house and stopped in front of the first bay. He turned and waved his arm frantically.

"Get up!" Kedge grabbed me roughly and hauled me to my feet.

I hurried over to the rifle and swung it over my shoulder. As soon as I did, a large shadow fell over us and I glanced back. During my lifetime I had wished for a lot of things: money, fame, good looks, but never have I wished for anything more than I wished to have never looked back.

Vayne was correct. There were hundreds of ships. There were so many that they blocked out the sun.

"My god," Kedge gasped.

The ships were all different shapes and sizes, making it difficult to tell their allegiance. I spotted the familiar crescent moon flags of the Scarlet Moon. But they were only a few of the many ships in the sky. I saw the blimp-like vessels of the Lumagom. There were triangle-shaped ships, round ships, square ships, ships shaped like an X. My jaw dropped at the sheer volume of spacecraft.

"This isn't the Consortium," Wraith stopped. "This may actually be a good thing."

"What?" I replied incredulously.

"Hear me out. The Consortium wants us dead. They want mankind dead. But Corvus is human. His first goal would be to save the survivors of his home planet, wouldn't you think?"

When I looked back to the sky the ships' actions seemed to confirm Wraith's statement. They flew past us. The ring tone in my head went from deafening roar to dull hum. Several of the Scarlet Moon ships lagged behind the main pack. The largest among them broke from the smaller group and headed toward us.

"Uh oh," Kedge lamented.

It approached for landing in a nearby dirt field off the main highway. Several small wheels emerged from the hull extending along the base toward the rear of the vessel. The metal sails adjusted to form a parachute-like canopy above the deck. Bright red halogen lights blinked rapidly along the "masts" of the ship, signaling its approach. It landed and rolled to a stop about twenty yards from the fire house. Despite the similarity to a pirate ship it was almost as big as a full-sized aircraft carrier. A door opened and a ramp lowered to the ground.

The first person to exit was an Exorg. They resembled angler fish with their toothed maw and glowing appendage sticking from their forehead. Despite their ugliness, I was reminded of an ally from long ago who had been taken from us before his time—Madoc. Behind him exited a human with an eye patch. He looked familiar and I struggled to recall who he was. It wasn't until he descended the ramp that I remembered a conversation long ago with the prison planet, Carcer-4. Colonel Noz appears to have picked a side in this conflict. The Exorg grasped a rifle tightly to his chest and moved off to the side of the ramp once he reached the bottom. Colonel Noz had a sidearm strapped to his waist. He moved aside as well once he reached the bottom of the ramp. The last person to exit caused my blood to boil.

"Shai," I growled.

I barely noticed Wraith sliding his hand to his sidearm. My focus was solely on the man who had killed Captain Jasper who was murdered in cold blood before our eyes. Whether he was our enemy or not I couldn't stomach an allegiance with him. I clenched my fists in anger. Kedge gripped his staff tightly. The move made the Exorg uncomfortable and he shifted the rifle in his hands. Shai reached the bottom of the ramp and smiled broadly when he saw our group. He was armed with nothing more than a slender, curved sword strapped to his waist. *I could take him out with one shot from the rifle,* I thought. One shot and Lianne would have her justice.

"Look what we have here," Shai beamed. He pointed and turned to Colonel Noz. "Do you know who this is?"

Noz squinted his eye and shook his head. "Can't say I do."

"This is the Cartographer," he chuckled. "Map reader extraordinaire and prized possession of the Consortium." Noz only responded with a grunt of disinterest.

I stepped forward, clutching the rifle tightly. The Exorg lifted his rifle and pointed it at me.

"Maybe you haven't heard, but we aren't part of the Consortium anymore," I said through clenched teeth.

Shai's smile faded. His gaze fell upon Kedge. "Well then," he sneered. "That seems to lower your value significantly. What should we do with you?"

"Can you cook, boy?" Noz asked. "Some of the crap the Scarlet Moon serves I wouldn't serve to a dog."

"Maybe they consider you less than a dog," I retorted.

Noz stared coldly at me before eventually breaking into a smile. "Ha! The boy has balls, I'll give him that."

Shai didn't take his eyes off me. "Perhaps. But unfortunately for him we can't afford to have a cook with 'balls'. Normally I would kill you based on your recent value reduction but today is your lucky day."

"Oh really," I mocked. "Why is that?"

"It seems Corvus needs you for something. He can be such a diva sometimes," Shai grumbled. "He always *needs* something but for now it's you he requires." He turned to the Exorg. "Kill the others, but take the boy alive."

The Exorg approached while Noz retrieved his sidearm.

"NO!" Kedge shouted.

Before the Exorg could lift his rifle the staff was in the air, once again transforming from pale wooden stick to a living snake. It wrapped its body around the rifle and the Exorg dropped it in a panic before being shot in the chest by Wraith. Dark blue blood washed over the snake, turning it into a macabre blue-and-white candy cane. The creature shattered the rifle in its embrace and turned its head toward Shai, who backed up a step and removed his sword.

Wraith got off another shot but missed Noz wide to the right. Noz fell to the ground and somersaulted to his left. He leapt up and fired a shot, clipping Wraith in the shoulder. Wraith fell back a step and dropped his weapon.

"NO!" I echoed Kedge's battle cry. The AR-15 was in my hands and flame burst from the barrel as I pulled the trigger. I sprayed the area in front of me. In Call of Duty I had been an expert marksman. The reality of it was that I was a terrible shot. Bullets flew everywhere. I hit the side of their ship, the ramp, a stop sign, the ground—everything but my intended targets.

My terrible aim did very little damage, but it bought Kedge and Wraith valuable time. Noz was busy ducking my cover fire. Shai had his sword in his hand and was busy between parrying the snake on the ground and dodging an occasional stray bullet. Kedge produced a bolo from the folds of his cloak and threw it at Shai. It caught the Drith-Nar in the ankles and he fell backward against the bottom of the ramp. Wraith recovered his senses and fired another shot which grazed Noz in the arm. He ducked behind the ramp.

The AR-15 was empty. I killed nothing but the stop sign. In all the confusion none of us saw the rifle barrel poke out from ramp entrance. The sniper fired. The bullet travelled past me and I turned in time to see the top of Wraith's head explode. The bullet took him above the left eye. He buckled to his knees before falling to the ground face first. A pool of blood spread underneath him.

"*NOOOOOO!*" I cried. I fell to my knees and watched his life pour out of him before the sniper turned his rifle toward me. I lifted my gun and pulled the trigger only to hear the sound of dry clicks. I saw a flash of light and was knocked back from the impact of the shot.

I fell to the ground but felt no pain. I looked over and saw Kedge parry Shai's sword thrusts. The snake was once again a staff in his hands. Metal clashed against wood, yet the staff remained unmarred. Blood poured from my left shoulder and I wondered if I would ever get the chance to inquire about the mysterious staff. Shai parried a staff thrust and plunged his sword into Kedge's midsection. He dropped the staff and fell to the ground. Shai removed his sword and held it out, letting the blood drip to the ground.

I closed my eyes and heard boots approaching.

Dead is Dead

My shoulder was on fire. The wound oozed blood and it felt as if someone had their finger inside trying to pull a bone out. The warmth of the sun splashed on my face and I knew I was still outside. I cracked my eyes open but the glare made it difficult to open them completely. Dust covered my face and rolled into my eyes when I turned my head. My face was flushed and I wondered if I had an early onset of sunburn while baking on the highway. I reached up and brushed the sand from my eyes. I heard the crunch of gravel as someone walked toward me.

"Nathan." Lianne's voice.

I turned toward the sound. The sound of it was music to my ears. She crouched over me and never looked more beautiful. I smiled in spite of the pain.

"Lianne," I croaked.

She placed her hand on my cheek, a welcome cool touch in the desert heat. "Don't die on me," she said.

"Wraith's dead," I grunted and tried to sit up. She placed her hand on my good shoulder and gently pushed me back.

"Don't get up." She started to fade. I thought it was the heat of the sun playing tricks on me.

"Wait," I said. "Don't leave me. Where is Kedge? Did he survive? Where is Gard?"

"Stay alive, Nathan," she said. She seemed to phase out of existence and I could see the horizon through her body. "You will be faced with difficult decisions soon. We will come for you as soon as we can. Stay alive!" She urged before vanishing completely.

"No, wait!" I coughed while trying to get up. "Don't go."

"Oh, don't worry. I'm not going anywhere." Shai looked down and laughed. "Not without you."

Fury bubbled to the surface when I saw him. I wanted to reach up and tear his smug face off and shove it down his throat. Unfortunately the wound in my shoulder prevented me from even the minor act of sitting up. "I hate *you*."

"Now, that's not very nice." He feigned a wounded look. "I thought we were becoming good friends."

Noz walked up to them favoring his right arm. "I can't find the damn robot anywhere."

The Kamilians were gone and Vayne went missing so I wasn't sure where he could go. He was a resilient fellow, though, and probably in a better predicament than me.

"Doesn't matter," Shai replied. "The other one scampered off too. It seems our enemies are nothing more than cowards."

Kedge escaped? I breathed a sigh of relief. I thought for sure he had been killed. "They will come back for you. They will kill you," I muttered.

Shai crouched over me. "Oh they will, will they?" He stuck his finger inside my shoulder wound and I screamed. "But I should have plenty of time to make you miserable."

I didn't doubt him. Tears from the pain formed in the corner of my eyes but I blinked them away. I refused to show him any sign of weakness. The sour taste of sweat filled my mouth as I tried to move. He removed his finger and I bit my lip until the pain subsided. "I will kill you," I uttered through clenched teeth.

He grabbed me under the shoulders and hauled me to my feet, bringing a fresh wave of pain. Dizziness overwhelmed me and if it wasn't for him holding me I would have fallen to the ground. He leaned in and put his face next to my cheek. "No, you won't," he whispered. "If it wasn't for Corvus, I would snap your neck right here and be done with it. Perhaps by the time we reach the end of our journey, you will beg me to do just that." He looked at Noz. "Take him inside."

Noz wasn't gentle as he dragged me up the ramp. By the time we reached the top the pain was so unbearable I almost begged for death. I faded in and out of consciousness as he dragged me through the halls of the cavernous ship. We came to a room guarded by a squat, lizard-looking fellow with a massive rifle held firmly against his chest. His cold black eyes looked disdainfully at me.

"The room is ready," the lizard man muttered. "I removed most of the blood stains. Our last *guest* was such a bleeder."

"I don't think our friend here will mind," Noz replied. He looked down at me. "Do you mind?"

I coughed out something unintelligible. The entire room spun out of control. The door opened and I fell face first into the room. It smelled of mold and urine.

"Get a medic down here," Noz grunted. "We don't want him dying before Shai gets a chance to question him."

That was the last thing I heard before mercifully blacking out. When I regained consciousness I found myself lying on a gurney in the center of a cold and dreary room. The room had dull gray metal walls, dull gray metal ceiling and pretty much dull gray metal everything. It was as if I was inside the world's largest lunchbox. There were no decorations anywhere except for a single table next to the gurney. On the table lay a small blue box with a red laser light coming from the center that had been angled to point at my forehead. I looked away from the box and noticed that my wounds had been dressed. Despite a dull throbbing coming from the site of the wound, there was no actual pain. I tried to sit up but found I could not. There were no restraints holding me back and for a brief moment I feared that I had been paralyzed by the gun shot. *Can shoulder wounds lead to paralyzation*? Panic crept to the surface. Luckily before my head burst from the anxiety, the door opened.

Being completely paralyzed I couldn't even move my head to see the person until they stood over me. It was a woman with flowing auburn hair, a warm face a slightly bent nose and full, pouting lips that were red like blood. She wore a tattered, gray uniform with no visible markings. Despite her lovely face there was one feature that really interested me.

"You're human," I croaked.

She tossed me a dry smile. "Yes, I am."

My head was pounding. It was as if a cement truck was being dismantled by a jackhammer inside my skull. Although the room had been dimly lit, I still had to squint. The fluorescent tubes bordering the ceiling had been dimmed significantly but it felt like tiny daggers of light poked my eyeballs.

"Were you one of the survivors?" I asked.

Her face twisted with confusion. "Survivors?" She looked behind her toward the door. "Oh no, the Scarlet Moon found me during a scouting mission about a month ago."

"You are one of them?" I asked incredulously.

She placed her finger to her lips. "No," she whispered with a frown. "Don't get yourself all worked up." She leaned over and placed her hand on my good shoulder. Despite my inability to move I felt it. She was warm to the touch. "I was taken," she explained. "I was on my way to a friend's house after work when I came up to a road that was closed due to construction. I took the detour but the road was unfamiliar. It was dark and my GPS wasn't working. For some reason it was unable to locate any satellites. Anyway, there was this car on the side of the road that looked like it was in an accident. The front end was smashed and someone was underneath the car with a flashlight. So being a nurse I figured I'd stop and see if anyone needed help. My father always warned me of strangers and…well…I wish that was the one time I had listened.

"It was *them*, wasn't it?" I asked.

She emitted a dry chuckle. "Yep. Apparently I stumbled upon them dismantling the car for parts." She looked nervously toward the door and lowered her voice. "Ironic, isn't it?"

"What?"

She sighed. "We always view aliens as being technologically superior to us. But they needed parts from us in order to repair their ship. I guess we aren't as backwards in the universe as originally thought, eh?

"You're Canadian, aren't you?" It was the "eh" that got me.

"I'm from Hamilton," she replied.

I wanted to tell her there was no Hamilton anymore. I decided not to because she appeared depressed enough already. Instead I switched the conversation toward my current predicament. "Why am I paralyzed? I never heard of anyone becoming paralyzed by a shoulder wound."

She nodded toward the box on the table. "They call it a cerebral inhibitor. The beam is programmed to prohibit movement."

"Why?"

She shrugged. "Captain's orders."

I closed my eyes and tried to move. Despite my best efforts nothing moved, not even my pinky. I grunted with frustration. "Why are you with them?"

Sorrow lined her voice. "I helped one of them with some injuries. Once they realized I had medical training they decided to keep me around. I guess I was more useful to them alive."

She flinched. The fluorescent light reflected the pain in her eyes. As bad as it was I needed to exploit her pain if I planned on making it out of there alive. "What's your name?"

A smile cracked the corners of her lips. "Deena Trask."

"How old are you?" I asked.

"Twenty-four." She relaxed and tapped a button on the side of the box. "What about you?"

"Well, I kind of lost track of time, but I was sixteen at one time."

She giggled. "Yeah, I suppose time sort of loses its meaning in space."

"Are you going to be my nurse?" I asked with a smile. It was good to feel my facial muscles working.

"Yes," she said with a smile.

"Can you turn that machine off?" I smiled mischievously.

Her smile faded and she looked at the box uneasily. "Sorry, I can't do that."

Frustrated, I blurted, "They killed my friends." When she narrowed her eyes suspiciously I softened my tone. "What do they want with me?"

She looked down at the machine and refused to look at me. "I don't know," she said in a hushed tone. "I'm only here to make sure the wound is healing and make you comfortable."

Before I could press her further, the door opened. Because of the paralysis I couldn't see who walked in, but judging by Deena's face it was bad news. The voice confirmed my suspicions.

"How is our patient faring?" Shai asked.

"Stable and restrained," she replied.

"You can go," he growled. "Nathan and I have some catching up to do. I'm sure he has questions."

She turned and walked out. After the door closed he leered over me. "Why am I here?" I demanded. "What do you want with me?"

He looked me up and down before smiling. "Bah, you are no threat," he spat. He turned toward the box and switched it off. The beam vanished and I felt a slow numbness creeping along my extremities. "Corvus needs you," he responded as if the statement was the answer to everything. "Don't bother asking me why because I have no idea. I am just a simple mercenary for hire who does what his boss tells him to do."

I turned my head away and stared at the far wall. A mirror hung over an oversized basin sink. It was big enough to bathe a baby. I wanted nothing more than to fill it up and shove Shai's head in it until he drowned. "You're nothing more than an over-rated pirate," I muttered.

His fist smashed against my jaw. Lucky for me my head was already turned which made it more of a glancing blow. Despite the angle, my vision still filled with stars and I felt a dull pain as the numbness from the inhibitor began to wear off.

"You better watch your mouth," he warned. "Corvus asked me to deliver you but he didn't say anything about it being in one piece."

I turned my head and narrowed my eyes. "Go to hell."

I readied myself for a blow that never came. Instead he simply smiled. "I'll give you that one. You have balls, kid. I understand your anger at that bit of ugliness on Earth." There was one chair on each side of the gurney. He eased into the one closest to the machine. "It was business, mind you. I was paid to recover you, but your friends wanted to make a big deal out of it."

The memory of the events in New Mexico brought forth a fresh bout of anger. I reached for Shai but crashed to the floor, bringing a fresh stab of pain to my shoulder. My limbs failed me. The numbness lingering in my extremities prevented me from controlling them effectively. Shai's heckling filled the room.

"Whoa, don't go getting yourself in a tizzy, soldier," he mocked. He scooped me up like a rag doll and tossed me back on the gurney. "I wouldn't want you to hurt yourself."

"What do you want from me?" I roared. "Congratulations, you caught me. Take me to Corvus. If I have to hear your voice any-more I'm going to rip off my ears and shove a blade into my brain."

"There's a bit more to it," he replied. "Corvus wants informa-tion regarding his enemies." Shai pushed a rolling cart toward me. On top of the cart were several tools. A scalpel and needle was just two of many. "You're special in that you have been a part of the Consortium as well as the Insurgents."

"I won't tell you anything," I sneered.

He picked up the needle and worked the plunger. The needle spit out a tiny amount of golden liquid. He turned and waved it back and forth with a smile.

"See, that's where you're wrong."

LIANNE

When she stepped off the ramp, her thick synthetic fiber boots crunched the gravel underneath. It sounded like the crunching of bones and she shivered, despite the warm, New Mexico air. She placed a hand over her eyes and surveyed the surroundings. The sun settled upon the horizon. In the distance along the highway she spied a small building. Further up the highway was a corpse. Due to the distance it looked like nothing more than the carcass of a large animal, perhaps killed by one of the fast moving metal conveyances the humans used to move about.

"Are you sure they were here?" She turned to Embeth.

"Captain Muriel assured me that Gard's emergency beacon leads to this region," Embeth replied grimly.

"It still pings here." Muriel confirmed as he emerged from the ship and wiped at his beaked maw with the back of his hand. "By the gods, is it this hot everywhere on Earth? I feel like my brains are broiling inside my skull."

As they approached the building, Lianne's heart sank when she noticed the smoldering wreckage in front of the building. It sank further when she saw the corpse. It wasn't an animal carcass after all.

"Oh no!" Lianne exclaimed and ran to the body. She slipped her hand behind his head, but it was hard to lift due to the congealing blood causing it to stick to the ground. She tried to locate a vital sign, but she knew Wraith was dead.

"Damn!" Embeth exclaimed bitterly. Captain Muriel ran up to them with a Defense Fleet soldier in tow.

Lianne removed her hand and looked past the corpse. She spied a trail of blood leading off into the distance. "Look," she pointed at the fire house. "That trail of blood leads to the building over there."

"So does Gard's beacon," Muriel added.

"Weapons out," Embeth growled. "Be on alert."

They approached the building cautiously, keeping their weapons locked on the fire house. They passed the burnt corpse of the fireman. Lianne acknowledged it with a grimace.

"The beacon is getting stronger," Muriel acknowledged.

Embeth gestured toward the side of the building. The Defense Fleet soldier acknowledged with a nod and moved to the location. Muriel crouched low and approached the lone window. Embeth covered him. Lianne leaned against the burnt shell of the fire truck with her weapon pointed toward the open bay.

"It's coming from inside," Muriel whispered.

Muriel crouched in front of the window. Embeth waved her in. With a nod she rushed in. The bay was dark. She flipped a switch located at the top of the rifle and a beam of light penetrated the gloom. Embeth stepped in beside her.

"Nothing," she said. "But look." She pointed at the trail of blood leading into the office.

Something hard and heavy fell in the other room. They turned their weapons toward the door to the office. They approached it carefully. Inside they heard a crackling sound, like bacon frying.

"Are you gonna sit out there all day or come in here and join us," a gruff voice called out.

They entered the office and the scene was grim. Kedge sat on the floor propped up against the wall. Gard was hunched over his midsection and a small blue flame burned at the end of his clawed hand as he welded something in Kedge's gut. Kedge himself was surrounded in a pool of blood.

"Don't worry, it's only a flesh wound," Kedge laughed dryly.

"What the hell happened?" Embeth demanded.

"Where's Nathan?" Lianne asked.

Kedge flinched. "Ow! Gard watch it! That was flesh."

"*Sorry the light is limited in here,*" Gard replied. "*Now quit moving.*"

Kedge sighed. "Robots! They are so damn temperamental. Anyway, there is a lot you need to hear so take a seat."

"Muriel. Barlow. Get in here," Embeth ordered. They appeared in the doorway. "Barlow return to the ship and keep an eye on things. Muriel keep a watch outside."

They nodded their acknowledgement and vanished. Lianne kept an eye on Kedge who clenched his teeth as Gard worked on him. His abdomen was sliced open from hip to sternum. Tiny red lights could be seen inside where his stomach should have been. Kedge caught her staring.

"Yeah, it's not pretty but it keeps me alive," he grunted. He looked over at Gard. "Can we hurry this up?"

"Will he live?" Embeth asked.

"*The sword strike pierced his abdomen but fortunately most of the damage was to mechanical parts,*" Gard responded.

"What happened?" asked Lianne.

Kedge grimaced as Gard welded some piece of him back together. His staff lay on the floor next to him and it looked like it had been through a battle. Large chunks of wood were hacked out of it. Between the blood and the dust, the formerly white staff took on a charcoal gray appearance.

"It's dead," Kedge lamented.

"What's dead?" she asked.

"The staff." Kedge groaned as Gard stopped welding and started sewing. "I found him during an excursion through the Forests of Nisus. The Forest Monks taught me the commands to bring the wood to life."

"Are you trying to tell me that thing is alive?" Embeth crouched over it. He poked at it with his index finger.

"Was," Kedge moaned. "He had fought by my side for decades. Always tireless, forever faithful. To think a lowborn, bandit scum like Shai killed him is only adding salt to the wound."

"Shai is here?" Lianne asked.

"They were. Him and his merry band of idiots," Kedge sneered. "A sniper got Wraith." He hesitated and drew in a deep breath. "The sniper got Nathan too."

The news was like a shot to the gut. *The sniper got Nathan too.* The words haunted her. She hoped he was alive since his body wasn't nearby. "Where is Vayne?"

Kedge winced as Gard stitched him up. "I don't know. We thought he was coming to get us but then the ships came." He bit his lip as Gard welded something else together. "There's something else you should know."

"What's that?" Lianne asked.

"There is a new player in the game," he muttered. "It seems the Erudites have teamed up with the Kamilians to rescue human survivors."

Embeth fixed him with a confused look. "The Erudites are watchers and scholars. They never interfere." He folded his arms across his chest and his lips tightened. "Why would they do that?"

Kedge shrugged and struggled to stand. Lianne hurried over and caught him under the arm before he fell over.

"*You should sit and rest for a bit,*" Gard stated.

"We don't have 'a bit'," Kedge grumbled and leaned against the wall. "I have no idea why Bree would get involved. But the Kamilians mentioned something about an Ark coming to Earth."

"An Ark?" Lianne repeated. "Do you mean *THE* Ark?"

"Wait a minute." Embeth ran his fingers through his beard. "During a Council meeting I heard rumors of the Kamilians developing a ship large enough to contain independent ecosystems. This ship was also large enough to hold over a half a million people. The High Prince was toying with the notion of including it during Helios Protocol missions. They called it the Ark. Are you telling me that this is what is coming here?"

Kedge shrugged.

"If so," Lianne said. "The ship is large enough to rescue a lot of human survivors," Lianne added. "Perhaps they have a chance after all."

"Are you okay to move?" Embeth studied Kedge.

He looked pale and leaned a bit too much on the wall for Lianne's comfort, but for a guy who just took a sword through the gut he seemed to be holding his own. She wondered how many battles he had seen and how many grievous wounds he had suffered. She also found herself wondering how many grievous wounds it would take to kill him.

"Yeah, I can move," he grunted. "Let's try not to go on a cross country hike though."

They made their way out of the fire house. At first Kedge needed to lean against Gard for support but once they emerged from the bay he started to move under his own power. Captain Muriel led them back to the ship. They climbed the ramp and the Defense Fleet soldier met them at the entrance.

"Sir, several ships are approaching."

"It's them," Kedge warned.

"Get inside!" Embeth commanded.

Lianne looked to the horizon. It was too late. There were at least four ships hurtling toward them at top speed. She knew they would never get off the ground in time. "Gard get Kedge inside," she ordered. She sprinted toward the gun deck which was nothing more than a dome at the top of the ship equipped with two pulse-arc plasma cannons.

"Lianne, what the hell are you doing?" Embeth shouted after her.

"Saving our asses," she yelled back. Throwing open the hatch she hopped into the tilted chair and put on the targeting headset.

Two more Defense Fleet soldiers appeared. Embeth barked some orders before glaring up the ladder toward her. She slammed the hatch door shut. There was no time for argument. There was no time for escape. Their only option was to stand and fight.

"*Targeting system online*," the computer said through the headset.

The closest ship fired at them. Their shots were well wide of their intended target. Lianne returned fire. Plasma exploded from the cannons in short bursts, but they just missed her target. The green targeting lens over her right eye flashed a red box over a black X. She had a lock on the target. Squeezing the trigger, she let another series of bursts fly. This time the shots found their mark. The front of the enemy ship exploded in a torrent of flame and crashed in the desert. Before she could savor her victory another ship appeared and fired. This one hit its mark. The explosion rocked her turret and threw her from the chair. The headset went flying and smashed against the side of the dome. Her chin cracked hard against the console and she tasted blood.

Screams came from below and she could only assume that someone got it worse than her. It wasn't until she propped herself up that she felt the heat coming from the hatch door. She smelled smoke. She tried to open the hatch door but the latch was melted by the enemy ship's blasts. She looked outside the dome and saw the ship double back for a second attack. Its cannons glowed like a pair of demonic eyes as it approached. She placed the palm of her hand on the glass. They couldn't have been more than three hundred yards away and closing. *A can't miss shot.* Smoke started to fill the turret and her eyes began to water. Through the blurriness she saw the ship approach. She closed her eyes and braced for impact. The explosion came but not from her ship. Confused she opened her eyes to see the remains of the enemy ship which was nothing more than a fiery corpse on the side of the road.

She kicked the glass surrounding the turret. It spiderwebbed but did not break. A second strong kick did the job. As she wiggled her way outside her arms and legs were cut by slivers of glass. She collapsed on the ship's wing where she laid smoking and coughing. She looked skyward to see one of the remaining ships being pursued by a newcomer to the battle. It was Talon.

"Vayne," Lianne wheezed. The remaining ships were much smaller than Talon, no bigger than scout ships. They had no discernible markings which meant they could have been anyone. She moaned and rolled herself to the edge of the wing where she dropped the ten feet to the ground and landed on her feet with feline grace. Her Defense Fleet training allowed her to remain agile in spite of her injuries. She came face-to-face with Captain Muriel's sour face. He held a radio in his hand.

"*I can't do all the work for you,*" Vayne's voice boasted through the radio. "*You've sat around long enough.*"

"Cocky, isn't he?" Lianne said.

Muriel nodded. "While Vayne is taking out the trash here, Embeth is busy assessing the damage to the ship. From what we could tell so far the gun turret, positional guidance and one landing gear is lost."

Lianne looked to the sky. The rips in the atmosphere were growing, forming darkened veins within the otherwise blue sky. Time was running short on Earth. If the Ark was indeed coming, it better hurry.

Embeth extinguished the last of the fire and climbed down the ramp, muttering curses under his breath. "We lost most of the crew. Shep and Brocke are the only crew left and they will be tied up making repairs for days. Barlow is a good soldier but he doesn't know a flux wrench from a plasma cutter."

Talon landed nearby. Vayne exited the ship, looking quite flustered. "Ran into a bit of trouble?" Despite the quip the cocky swagger usually accompanying him was gone. "They got Nathan. I tried to catch up to them but some of their ships hung back long enough to keep me distracted which allowed their flagship to escape." He examined the ship he shot down. "These aren't Scarlet Moon vessels."

"They look like scout ships," Lianne admitted. "They are too small to fly long distances."

"Which means the mothership is around," Embeth added. "It seems the Ascended have made new friends."

"Which does not bode well for us," she added dryly.

A dry smile flickered across Embeth's face. "We should get out of here before more come."

Vayne stood with his hands on his hips, inspecting the ship. "You aren't going anywhere in that thing."

Lianne followed his gaze. "We need every ship we have." She ran her fingers through her golden braids. "We need to repair it."

Vayne nodded and barked some orders into his communicator. Three of his crewmembers—the mini-Vaynes, as Nathan had so affectionately called them—exited Talon and approached.

"See what you can do about returning the ship to functionality," Vayne ordered. They nodded and entered the ship. It wasn't long after that the clanging of hammers and turning of wrenches echoed throughout the halls. "She'll be flyable at least," he offered.

Lianne winced when she heard something large and metallic crash to the floor. One of the mini-Vaynes cursed loudly. She exchanged uneasy glances with Embeth.

"Hopefully," Vayne sighed.

THE GAME

Deena returned to the room pushing a cart. On it sat a small machine filled with dials next to a digital interface. Beside the interface was a small screen with one single unmoving horizontal line across. She parked the contraption next to me.

As if sensing my unease her face softened. "Don't worry this is just a heart and blood pressure monitor."

Shai injected me with the needle long before she entered the room. When I asked what I had been injected with, he simply laughed. Now he was watching me with a cold, empty look. *It was the face of the devil.*

I flinched when she slipped the cuff around my arm. "Sorry, hun," she apologized. "I didn't mean to startle you. This will monitor your blood pressure." She placed a plastic clip around my right index finger. The machine started beeping. She studied it and her mouth tightened. "His heart rate is currently 84 BPM which is a little high." When Shai didn't respond, she turned and eyed him impatiently.

He waved his hand dismissively. "It's nothing to be concerned with."

She turned and I recognized the concern on her face but was too calm to care. Whatever Shai injected me with created a euphoric state of mind. At that moment I had no worries. I smiled when she placed her hand on my forearm.

"Leave us," Shai ordered. He stood and Deena shuffled out of the room. He looked down through his pale gray eyes. In the dimly lit room they contrasted with his ebony skin. I wasn't sure if it was the drugs but it looked as if they were two ghostly globes flittering over me.

"What do you want?" I slurred. The drugs were making it difficult to control my mouth. The words came out "Wut d'ooo 'ant?"

Shai frowned. "It's a long ride back to Gorganna. Frankly, between you and me Noz is poor company. I decided to start a game to entertain me for the duration."

"Game?" I croaked. My throat was as dry as a desert riverbed. It was as if I swallowed a bucketful of sandpaper. *A side effect of the drug.*

He grabbed a scalpel off the tray. He placed the tip of the blade near my eye. In my relaxed state I didn't flinch. "The drug I injected you with is a muscle relaxer mixed with a pain inhibitor." He slid the tip of the scalpel down. The cold steel felt like a metal tear running along my cheek. "The game is this: I will ask you several questions regarding the Consortium as well as your Insurgent pals and you answer them truthfully. If you manage to answer them all correctly you win."

"And if I don't," I rasped, trying to summon any amount of saliva I could find within the desert of my mouth.

"Well." He paused and slid the scalpel up my cheek only stopping once it reached the corner of my eye. He leaned over, his face inches from my own. "Then I win," he whispered.

"I don't think Corvus would like that very much." It was a weak argument but the only one I had at the moment.

He chuckled and glanced at the blood pressure machine. "Wow, your heart rate is high." He turned to me and laughed. "Deena was right. You need to calm down, buddy." He stood up and placed the scalpel down on the tray. "As for Corvus, he didn't say anything about delivering you in one piece."

Under normal circumstances his implied threat would have caused concern. Under the effect of the mind numbing drugs, however, I started to giggle. Shai's confused expression only served to make me laugh harder.

"What the hell's so funny?"

Biting back the laughter I responded, "I'm going to kill you," before the laughter overwhelmed me again.

His confused expression faded and his smile returned. "Good luck with that," he mocked. "In the meantime while you are busy planning your brave assault, I will ask my first question."

"What do I win if I answer all the questions correctly," I asked.

Shai hesitated, as if it were an unexpected question. He rubbed his chin with the scalpel. Eventually he pointed the tool at me. "If you win then I will release you, how's that sound?"

"I'm sure that will go over well with Corvus." My statement dripped with sarcasm.

"If you provide all of the correct information, then Corvus won't need you," he admitted, recognizing my suspicion. "At that point you will just be in the way."

His answer could have been the truth. Then again, it could have been a lie. Or it could have just been the drugs messing with my mind. "What happens if you win?"

His lips twisted into a cruel smile. While he leered at me I no longer had the urge to know the answer.

"If I win, I get the chance to inflict pain upon you," he purred. Before I could ask him why, he turned on the cerebral inhibitor. I collapsed on the gurney and once again found myself paralyzed. My legs hung uselessly over the sides. Shai gently straightened me out.

"Why?" I whimpered.

He shrugged. "I suppose the simple answer is 'because I hate you'." He brushed his silvery hair from his eyes and tugged on one of his quarter-sized hoop earrings. "But I feel it's much more complicated than that. The Consortium destroyed everything I loved. I had a wife, a daughter and a thriving business. The Scarlet Moon Trade Organization was a thriving trade cartel which dominated our galaxy: We owned patents, created medical breakthroughs and marketed the most advanced weapons systems." Shai looked past me and his pale eyes sparkled with remembrance. "I ran it all and made the people of Drith rich. Until the Consortium came, that is." He curled his lip in anger and held his balled fists tightly to his sides. "They opened new trade routes and introduced even better technology. Gliese, Vexall and Gorganna, our biggest trade partners, engorged themselves with their new technology. They became addicted to it like an addict towards a new drug. As fast as I built our empire, the Consortium tore it down." He turned his hate-filled eyes toward me. "Eventually they reduced the Scarlet Moon to nothing more than vultures, scavenging whatever we could locate to survive. A lot of the Drith-Nar joined the Consortium, but those who didn't remained with us as outcasts."

"What does that have to do with me? I wasn't even there," I croaked. My throat was once again descending into desert-like status, an apparent side effect of having my brain inhibited.

"You're one of them," he growled.

I tried to shake my head but the effort was futile. I had to resort to shutting my eyes in frustration. "Not anymore. You realize I am being hunted by them, right?"

He chuckled. "Calypso was right. You are naïve." He shook his head and retrieved a small drill from the tray. "The Insurgents had been born from a reaction to an action the High Prince took. They still believe in the same basic principles of the Consortium. Their goal is to remove Meta at all costs, but what happen if they succeed?"

The question lingered, unanswered. I considered his question and realized he had a valid point. Our goal was to defeat Meta, but the ideals of the Consortium still hold true in our hearts. I never had a chance to speak with Satou or Embeth but I was sure once Meta was defeated that a new Consortium would rise.

"I don't understand what your point is," I responded. "Once Meta is defeated new leadership will take over and return the Consortium to what they were."

"Exactly!" Shai thrust his index finger at me. "That is the problem. The Consortium will be reborn. I want them destroyed."

"What about the insurgents?" I rasped. The inhibitor made it harder to talk. It felt like I had a mouth full of marbles. "What happens to them?"

Shai casually used the scalpel to dig out a piece of dirt from underneath his fingernails. "Casualties of war my friend."

Between the drugs and fatigue I had little strength left to ask questions. "Let's get on with your stupid game," I sighed.

He smiled and stood with the scalpel gripped tightly. "I will take it easy on you. I only have three questions." He circled the bed but because of the inhibitor I could barely keep my eyes on him. "First question: Why did the Consortium attack Earth?"

I closed my eyes and drew a deep breath before letting it out slowly. "I wish I knew," I sighed.

Shai placed the palm of his hand across my forehead. His calculating eyes locked on mine. Without blinking he studied me for what seemed like an eternity. He brought the scalpel up so I could see it. "I may be crazy but I believe you," he snickered. "On to the next question. How does the Universal Map work?"

Only then did I remember that I still had the map attached to the bracelet on my wrist. I would be the first to admit that I hadn't spent nearly enough time learning how to navigate with the map nor how to use it properly, but I found the timing of his question odd. *Does Corvus plan on using the map to get back at the Consortium?*

"I'm not sure," I admitted. "I never got the chance to spend enough time with it."

Shai's mood darkened. "Now that I *don't* believe." He slid the scalpel down my right arm, toward my wrist. "I find it hard to believe you know nothing about the map or how it works." I felt the scalpel come to rest on the back of my hand. He glanced at it for a long time before changing the subject. "Did you know that Deena was a human nurse on Earth?"

"Yes." My voice was barely a whisper. The inhibitor continued sapping what little strength I had left.

Shai frowned and nodded. "It was good news for us because we were lacking medical personnel within our ranks at the time." He switched his gaze from the scalpel to my face. "Unfortunately she wasn't too adept with advanced medical tools. We had to salvage some human devices so she could help us when needed."

"Why are you telling me this?" Exhaustion begun to take hold and I just wanted this entire ordeal over.

"With a laser-imbued blade one can cut through flesh quicker and with less pain." He removed the scalpel from my hand and held it up for me to see. "With these archaic devices, the pain is much greater." In a flash he brought the blade of the scalpel down.

Even in my weakened state I managed to scream. It was high pitched and intense in the beginning, eventually tapering off to a raspy wail. The only thing I could see from my position was the top of the scalpel jutting from my right hand. The inhibitor prevented me from moving but it did not prevent me from feeling the burning sensation radiating from the center of my hand. It also did not prevent tears of agony from streaming down my cheeks toward my ears. The monitor started squawking loudly but Shai ignored it.

"I'm winning, Nathan," he sneered. "You better answer the next question correctly or you are gonna lose."

I blinked back a fresh wave of tears. "Why the hell did you do that? I answered your question."

He shook his head. "You know more about that map than you are willing to share." He shrugged and retrieved what appeared to be a drill from the tray. When he held it up in front of me

I observed a fine, steel saw blade attached where there should have instead been a drill bit. The blade was about six inches long and no thicker than a pencil tip. "You used your freebie, Nathan. You only have one more chance to win."

If I wasn't already paralyzed by the cerebral inhibitor I would have been from fear. Shai was a nutcase with a saw. Only God knew what he planned to do with it. He waved it back and forth in front of my face like he was conducting an orchestra.

"Last question, Nathan. This one is for all the cash and prizes." He smiled. *A snake's smile.* "Where are the Insurgents hiding?"

Oh, God no. This answer I *did* know but my response would doom them. Between the Scarlet Moon and the Lumagom, Corvus' forces outnumbered Embeth's. Even with the help of Vigil and Vayne they would be no match. I witnessed their might on Earth. Their ships nearly blocked out the sun. If I answered him correctly I would be passing along their death sentence. On the other hand, if I didn't then I was most likely passing along mine. I shut my eyes and prayed. God, Allah, Odin, Zeus; I prayed to whoever would answer.

"Well?" Shai pressed. His smile was wide. He knew I would never answer the question and he reveled in it.

"I don't know," I whispered as another tear fell from the side of my face.

His smile remained. It didn't even waver. "I see." He pulled the trigger on the drill and the blade began to oscillate. It barely made a sound. "I'm sorry to say, Nathan, but you lost." He let go of the trigger which cut off the power to the tool. He mysteriously returned it to the tray. It was only then that I realized I held my breath. I let it out slowly. He grabbed the handle of the scalpel and turned to me. "I suppose you won't be needing this so I will take this off your hands. No pun intended." He yanked the scalpel out of my hand and tossed it on the tray. He studied the hand pouted. "I'm afraid that your wound is going to be difficult to repair."

The drill was in his hand again. "No," I grunted weakly.

"Don't worry, this won't take long," he replied. He pressed the blade of the saw to my wrist and pressed the trigger. At first I felt a burn but I was too weak to cry out. Eventually the pain subsided followed by wisps of smoke. "Almost done," Shai purred.

The blade of the saw squealed when it met resistance. Smoke rose in larger plumes and the scent of blood reached my nostrils. The room spun, eventually fading into grayness. It wasn't long before one of the gods answered my prayers.

I fell into darkness.

STARTING OVER

"Come on, Nathan. Hurry up!"

I finished tying the rope around my waist and looked up. Sam eyeballed me impatiently. "What's your hurry?" I asked.

He stuck out his bottom lip in a pout. "My mother needs me to run to the grocery store."

I sighed and rolled my eyes. Shoving the rock hammer in my waistband I checked the integrity of the knot one final time before stepping into the cave.

"*Final time*".

I stopped. Sam clutched the rope in both hands, watching me through eager eyes. "What did you say?" I asked.

His face crinkled with confusion. "Huh?"

I cocked my head and studied him, trying to figure out if he was messing me. His expression didn't change. "Um, nothing I guess. I thought I heard you say something."

He waved his hand at me impatiently. "Come on, let's get this over with. I gotta go soon!"

I switched on the flashlight and made my way to the collapsed wall. It was in the same condition as the last time we left it with the exception of the small gap I found. I took out my rock hammer but before I could work the hole I froze.

"Wait a minute, this isn't right," I muttered. "The hole was bigger." Looking down at the rock hammer in my right hand a distant memory came flooding back. "I lost this hammer on Xajax." I looked at the flashlight in my left. "I lost this here." Suddenly a sharp pain shot through my right hand and I dropped the hammer. I broke out in a cold sweat and backed up against the wall. "What the hell is happening to me?"

"*Nathan.*"

I whipped my head around and looked back toward the entrance. I thought Sam made his way down but the cave was empty.

"*Nathan.*"

Sweat stung my eyes and the pain in my wrist worsened. I fell to one knee and realized the sound came from the hole in the wall. I stumbled and fell against it. I raised my head so I could look through the hole. On the other side stood the shadowy outline of a woman. When she approached the hole the light hit her and I recognized her.

"Deena," I muttered.

She put her hand up to the wall and leaned in close. "Nathan, stay with me."

Before I could respond, her face vanished and was replaced by a bright light. Everything around us fell into darkness. A steady beeping echoed off the walls. A warm touch fell on my forehead before the stone walls of the cave gave way to the metal walls of prison. The darkness faded and I found myself surrounded by familiar fluorescent lights. Deena hunched over me with her hand pressed against my forehead. Her panicked expression broke through the remaining fragments of the dream.

"Stay with me, Nathan." The beeping, frantic at first, slowed eventually. She continued monitoring my vitals as the pain in my wrist subsided, giving way to a dull throbbing.

"I'm not dead?" I croaked.

She tossed me a weak smile. "Not yet." She returned her attention to the monitor.

I was glad to see that the cerebral inhibitor was no longer in the room. Another item had replaced it. The mysterious box was no bigger than a toaster. Concerned about Shai's sadistic nature, I asked, "What's that?"

Even though I was too weak to point at it, she knew immediately what I was alluding to. Her smile faded and she turned slowly and removed her hand from my forehead. She pushed the table away quickly. "It's nothing," she replied before returning her attention to the monitor.

Although she tried to hide it, her mouth tightened when I asked again about the box. She knew what was inside but withheld its contents. I found myself wondering if Shai was playing another one of his games. I changed the subject. "Where is he?" I asked instead.

Her eyes were full of sympathy. "He returned to his quarters. You're safe now."

"Am I?" I replied, perhaps a bit harsher than intended. "I'm aboard his ship flying toward a meeting with my enemies. How safe am I really?"

She turned to the monitor, watching my vital signs with brooding silence. I felt a tightness on my right bicep and looked to find a quarter-sized rubber patch fastened there. Attached to the patch was a lead and a wire leading back to the machine.

"What's this?" I asked, nodding my head toward it.

"A blood pressure monitor," she replied quietly. "I attached it after your meeting with Shai." She turned from the monitor and her face hardened. "Despite what you believe, I'm here to make sure you make it out of here alive."

My gaze drifted to the far wall. Someone had moved the gurney since my meeting with Shai. During our meeting walls were on both sides. Now the door was on one side. I watched it fearing Shai's return.

"He won't be back," Deena said, watching my gaze. "He is done with you."

"Is that what he told you?" I asked sharply.

The beeping of the monitor slowed. Instead of answering the question she rubbed my shoulder. Her touch was not unkind.

"Your blood pressure is coming back up. I was worried, for a while it was critically low."

She continued to rub my shoulder and I found myself strangely aroused by her touch. Looking at her it would be difficult for any man to not be aroused by her appearance. She was one of the hottest girls I had ever seen. My teenaged hormones must have been in overdrive because of the drugs I had been given. I never had such a reaction to a woman before.

"What's wrong?"

She caught me gawking at her. I shut my eyes violently and tried to shake the feelings of lust which suddenly gripped me. It didn't work. As soon as I opened them I found my eyes drifting over every curve in her body.

"Um, I...uh," I stuttered and looked away. "Boobs." I felt a flush creeping into my cheeks.

Embarrassed, I reluctantly looked at her. I expected her to be horrified, irritated or perhaps even angry. Instead she smiled. "It's the side effect of the drug I gave you. It helps coagulate the blood." She stifled a giggle. "It also increases testosterone."

"So are you trying to tell me that this drug you gave me makes me horny?"

She laughed and nodded. "Yeah, I suppose it does."

I smiled weakly. "Well, I guess that's better than other drugs on Earth where the side effects could be diarrhea, cramps, bloating or even death." She laughed harder and for a moment I joined her. It felt good to laugh again. Eventually the pain in my right wrist became too much and overcame the laughter.

"What's wrong?" she asked, suddenly concerned.

"It's my wrist," I grunted. "The pain's starting to come back. Why the hell does it hurt so much?"

"I'm sorry, Nathan," she said, glancing uneasily at the box. She tried to hide the look, but I caught it.

"What's in the box?" I asked.

"You didn't tell him?" A voice from the door spoke. Colonel Noz leaned against the wall, smoking a pipe made of glass. A dark substance sat in the bowl of the pipe while white smoke wafted from the top. In our brief moment of hilarity neither of us heard him enter. Whatever he was smoking was completely odorless, which helped mask his entrance.

"No I didn't," Deena replied coldly. "What are you doing here anyway? Shai assured me he had no further use for Nathan and promised he wouldn't come for him until we reached Gorganna."

Noz held out his hands innocently. "Hey I'm just checking on our patient and making sure he is going to make it. Can't a guy show a little concern around here?"

I turned toward Deena. "What's in the box?" I repeated.

Deena shook her head and drew a deep breath. "They never told me they would do this," she exhaled slowly. "I would have never agreed to help them if I knew." She turned slowly toward the box and picked it up. She laid it gently beside me.

Grimacing with pain I tried to roll over but I was too weak. She removed the lid and tilted the box. I blinked while my eyes adjusted to the gloom inside. Once the overhead lights penetrated the shadows I noticed the map bracelet that Satou had designed for me. Next to it was a hand.

"What the hell?" I muttered. In one violent motion I knocked the box to the floor and struggled to sit up. "What the hell did you do to me?" Noz chuckled but I ignored him. Deena tried to stop me from sitting up and I almost fell out of the bed fighting her. Finally she conceded and helped me into a sitting position. I looked down at my right hand. My wrist throbbed so bad it felt like someone was playing drums on it. When I looked down I froze. My right arm ended with bloody bandages. My hand was missing. For the first time since emerging from the bowels of unconsciousness I found inner strength.

I used it to scream.

BROKEN

"Is he gonna be okay?" Noz hovered over me, exhibiting a surprising amount of concern.

"Yes. His heart rate is steady. His blood pressure has been stabilized," Deena responded with her eyes glued to the monitor.

Noz looked relieved, although it wasn't out of concern for my well-being. He needed to cover his rear. Bringing damaged goods to Corvus was okay, but bringing dead goods to Corvus would be crossing the line.

"Good. We are approaching Gorganna and should touch down within the hour." He turned and left.

When the door closed I turned toward Deena. She fiddled with a knob on the side of the monitor. The pleasant exchange we had only a short time ago was now a distant memory. The joy I felt when we laughed was gone. I now viewed the universe through a red curtain of rage. A hole formed in my heart that would never be filled with anything except hatred. My anger had no outlet at the moment. I was angry at Shai for what he did. I was angry at Deena for letting him. I was angry at Kedge for abandoning me. I was angry at Meta for starting this war. Hell I was even angry at Embeth for allowing us to leave Xajax. My anger didn't have any reasoning behind it. My anger had no path and stumbled through my soul like a headless chicken.

"You have to help me get out of here." I reached over and grabbed her arm with my left hand.

She looked at my hand as if it was a ghost until she saw it was my left. "There is nowhere to go." Her face suddenly hardened and she pressed her lips together tightly. "Don't you think I've been thinking of a thousand ways to get you out of here? We have reached our destination, there is nowhere to go but down."

"There has to be a way to get to a radio or something," I pressed. "If I can get to a communicator I can call for help."

She shook her head sadly. "All communications are conducted from the bridge. There are at least twenty crew members in there right now."

I wasn't a warrior like Embeth or an infiltrator like Vayne. I wasn't a charmer like Calypso or a tactician like Wraith. There would be no way for me to get around the issue of the crew. I was no one but Nathan Chambers, one-handed failure who spent more time captured than asleep. I was nothing but an intergalactic stray dog. Her tone reinforced the impossibility of the situation.

"Why are we going to this planet?" I chose to change the topic since the conversation was leading me toward a pit of despair.

"I don't know." She shrugged. "All I know is the Scarlet Moon chose to set up camp down there for the time being." She turned to the door. Without looking at me she added, "He never tells me anything. I'm just a slave." Her hands balled into fists. "They never let me off this goddamn ship. For all I know the planets we visit could be empty or they could have cities paved in gold."

"I'm sorry." It was a weak response but all I could think of to say.

She turned to me with a look of surprise. "Listen to me. Here you are with your hand recently cut off and I'm bitching that I don't get enough fresh air." She wiped at the side of her face and it was only then that I realized she had been crying. "Let me replace your bandage and cauterize the wound so it won't reopen when they come get you." When she noticed my unease had returned she offered me a smile. "Don't worry, I will be here with you this time."

Her statement didn't offer much comfort. She had no chance against Shai if she interfered with another violent outburst toward me. I didn't tell her that, I was just glad she would be by my side. For the first time in a long time the feeling of loneliness had subsided.

She reached into a drawer underneath the monitor and retrieved a small canister that resembled a can of cooking spray. "Okay, I am going to remove the bandages and spray this on the wound. You will feel a sting at first but it shouldn't last for long. It will be followed by a cold numbness."

I looked at the can apprehensively but nodded. I must have had anxiety written all over my face because she leaned over and kissed my forehead. Her lips were soft and unexpected. A flush crept along my neck, eventually filling my cheeks. "What was that for?"

She leaned back and smiled. "To let you know it will be alright." She unwrapped the bandages around my wrist carefully. Despite the extreme care she took in removing them I still winced every time she brushed against a nerve. She removed the cap of the can and sprayed the bloody stump. I looked away and clenched my teeth. The sting felt more like someone slowly ripping the skin away from my wrist. Just when I thought the agony would overwhelm me, it stopped. The merciful numbness took over. It was as if the lower half of my arm fell asleep.

"Are you alright?" She asked, and shoved aside a sweaty strand of hair that had fallen across my eyes. When I nodded she proceeded to place a new bandage over the wound. "Okay, finished."

I looked down and noticed some swelling along the wrist but the wound looked much cleaner than the bloody roast beef it looked like before. The bandage she placed over it was black and similar to a wool cap rather than a conventional bandage. It was like I had the world's biggest sock puppet for a hand.

"What kind of bandage is that?" I asked.

She shrugged. "It's an Umbral medical device according to Shai. It keeps the wound area clear and dry as well as filter any bacteria from the air. It's usually used for limb loss or in cases of severe trauma." She shook her head and frowned. "Listen to me I sound like a spokesman for the company that makes them. Anyway, I spoke with one of the engineers on board to try to get you some sort of prosthetic replacement for your hand." She smiled and placed her hand on my head. "I told you I'm gonna take care of you."

"I appreciate it." I didn't return her smile. I tried to focus on the task of escaping the clutches of the Scarlet Moon before they or Corvus decided to cut off other parts of my anatomy. I sat up and swung my legs over the side of the gurney. Before I could hop off I was stopped by another kiss. This one was on my lips. Surprised, I didn't know what to do so I just sat frozen on the bed and accepted it. It was long, warm and pleasant. Eventually her lips parted and I accepted a much deeper kiss. No longer frozen, her kiss awoke desires I never knew I had. Being my first kiss I didn't know what to expect. I just passed the "cooties" stage and entered the exploratory stage. Before I could enjoy it any further she stepped back.

"What's wrong?" I huffed, working to catch the breath she sucked from me.

She looked past me, toward the door. I turned to see Shai standing in the doorway.

"Well lookie here," he sneered. An evil smile played at the corner of his lips. "This just tugs at the heart, doesn't it?"

Her hand fell to my knee and gave it a reassuring squeeze. "What do you want?" she asked.

His smile faded. "You know what I want. I hate to part you from your new *boyfriend*, but we have people to meet." Two guards appeared behind him with weapons drawn. They were Drith-Nar like Shai, except more lean as opposed to muscular. They had the same ebony skin as Shai but had blue hair instead of white. They were so similar in appearance I assumed they were twins.

"I'm going with him." She grabbed my shoulder.

He folded his arms across his chest. "This isn't a vacation," he growled. "We aren't going on a tour. This party is by invite only."

"I don't care," she barked and placed her hands on her hips with defiance. "He is injured and will need someone to tend to those injuries."

Shai and Deena stood and stared at each other for what seemed like hours. Finally he picked up a communicator and barked into it. "Varl, patch me through to the surface."

"*Direct link engaged,*" Varl replied.

"This is Captain Shai of the Scarlet Moon vessel *Victory*. I have a medical situation on board. Do you have medical personnel on the planet?"

After a brief pause, a mechanical voice responded, "*We have medical droids who are well versed in the anatomy of over three million species.*"

Shai smiled again before terminating the connection. "See sweetie, your boyfriend will be safe with us."

"No, I have—" she started but Shai cut her off.

"You will stay here!" he barked. "Besides, I have a project and I need your help."

Deena and I exchanged nervous glances. I really wanted her by my side when I walked into the hornet's nest of enemies I was sure waited for me on the planet.

"Let's go!" Shai ordered. The guards moved toward me.

One grabbed my arm but before he could haul me off Deena leaned over and kissed me on the cheek. "One for good luck."

The guard pulled me to the door and I followed him reluctantly. Before we left the room, however, I turned back to Deena who smiled in return. As we went toward the door I passed Shai. He was smiling as well. He looked at Deena and the smile never wavered, but hers did. The door closed behind us, leaving the two of them alone together. A sinking feeling formed in the pit of my stomach. I couldn't shake the bad feeling no matter how hard I tried.

I couldn't shake the feeling that I would never see her again.

GORGANNA

The guards led me to the open doorway. I stepped onto the boarding ramp and observed a night sky filled with three crescent moons and a million stars. Mixed among the stars was a constellation that resembled a DNA helix. It was the most beautiful sky I had ever seen.

"*Nathan Chambers, you have been directed to accompany us to the temple.*"

At first I thought two monks had approached, but upon closer inspection I noticed that they were robots. Cyborgs, to be exact. Their smooth, black bodies were dotted with tiny blue lights. Their eyes were glowing red orbs that were identical to the red orbs which served as their belt buckles. Originally it appeared like they were wearing long dresses but when they got closer I noticed the "outfit" was actually designed from metal as well. They were unarmed with the exception of their silver hands. Their fingertips ended with small barrels—gun barrels.

A road led from the ramp. Approximately thirty yards away, in the middle of said road, was parked a taxi that seemed to have been pulled out of 1950s New York. The only difference was that it had no tires. It floated two feet above the ground. Standing next to the taxi was another robot holding the rear door open. My two escorts led me to the waiting vehicle and stepped aside when I reached the waiting robot.

"*Greetings, Nathan Chambers of Earth,*" the robot buzzed. "*This conveyance will take you straight to the Temple. Once there you will be escorted to your awaiting party.*"

I slid into the vehicle and rubbed my eyes in disbelief. "Well, I am ready to go in my 1950s New York *conveyance*." I laughed in spite of the absurdity of it all. The robot closed the door left. I looked at the front seat and noticed that there was no driver. With the exception of a large metal plate embedded in the driver seat, the cab was empty.

"Um, who the hell is driving this thing?" I turned to the window but the robot was gone.

"Manny, driver number four-oh-four, at your service," a voice boomed from the front of the cab.

Where there was once an empty plate there was now a holographic projection of a driver. "Manny" was a human hologram with shoulder-length white hair and wild eyes. His appearance reminded me of Doc from *Back to The Future*. His attire consisted of a yellow cap with a black brim, a yellow tuxedo and black bowtie. He started the car and looked at me through the rear view mirror.

"We are now departing for the Temple."

The ride to the Temple was smooth which I supposed should be expected from a car that floated above ground. He guided the car through the wooded area with relative ease. As for me, it was so dark I couldn't see anything except what the headlights illuminated ahead.

"So what brings you to Gorganna today sir," Manny asked pleasantly.

I had been so wrapped up with the concept of a floating car that thoughts of escape never crossed my mind. After the question, however, I found myself wondering what my chances were. Instead of bursting out of the car like a kidnap victim, I decided to let fate play its hand. "Well, Manny, I was kidnapped and forcefully brought to Gorganna."

He kept his eyes fixed on the road ahead. "That is indeed unfortunate," he said stoically. "Perhaps Janero can assist you with your predicament."

"Janero?" I repeated.

"Yes sir. Janero lives at the Temple. He is the creator and author of our history."

With a frown I stared out the window. Trees reflected by the vehicle's lights whizzed by. Once or twice I thought I saw something pop their head out of the brush but it could have been a trick of the lights or simply exhaustion messing with my mind. "So Janero is God?" I asked.

"God?" Manny asked with confusion. "I don't think so. Janero is Janero. I don't know anyone named God, sir."

"Never mind." I continued to stare out the window.

Manny slowed the vehicle as we came to an obstacle in the road. "This was supposed to be a short cut. I apologize for this inconvenience."

When I looked out the front window I had to blink to make sure my eyes were working correctly. A boat lay across the roadway. It was one of the last things I would have expected in the middle of a forest. It had a flat design like a pontoon boat but it was cracked in half over a fallen tree so it formed an inverted V. The rear half of the boat was the part that was blocking our path.

"Hold tight, sir," Manny stated. "I believe I can navigate over the obstacle. I have conducted a six foot vertical push before with this vehicle but I don't like doing it." He offered me a friendly smile.

I felt like I was inside an elevator as the car ascended. Eventually we cleared the boat's height and Manny steered the vehicle over the obstruction and onto the clear road ahead. Manny smiled in the rear view mirror once we were over it.

"See, that was a piece of pie."

"Um, I think you mean 'piece of cake'," I corrected.

Manny scrunched his face in confusion. "Cake?" He scratched his head. "No that can't be right, I'm sure it's pie."

I rolled my eyes and looked out the window. The trees gave way to a clearing and I swore I saw charred remains of an aircraft but couldn't be certain in the surrounding gloom.

"You know, you never forget your first fare," Manny said. "You may forget their name, what they looked like or what they were wearing, but you never forget that they were your first."

"What?" I asked.

Manny laughed. "Sorry I was just passing the time sir.

"Oh," I responded. I was amazed at how realistic he was and wondered if this Janero character was his creator.

"You know, the guy before you had a hard time figuring out the seatbelt mechanism," Manny said.

I cocked an eyebrow. "Is that so?"

"Yeah," he responded. "But then it clicked."

Manny stared at me through the rear view window with a deadpan expression. I scratched my head. *Did a hologram just make a joke?*

Manny remained silent for the remainder of the trip, which lasted about twenty minutes. He brought the vehicle to a stop in front of large white building that resembled a church. Spotlights surrounded the building and highlighted the front of the structure. Large steeples stabbed the night sky. Small angular windows surrounded the building while golden light filtered out to illuminate what wasn't covered by the spotlights.

"We have reached our destination," Manny announced. "Please make sure to keep all arms and legs inside the vehicle until we come to a complete stop." He exploded with laughter.

"Where are we?" I pressed my face against the glass and studied the Temple as his laughter died down. It had to have been the biggest church I had ever seen. The spotlights couldn't even cover every corner of the massive structure. After several moments passed and Manny didn't answer I turned toward the front seat. He was gone.

I moved to open the door, but a face stared at me through the window. "Whoa!" I exclaimed and fell back against the seat.

It was another robot, similar to the first. He held his hands up apologetically. "*I am sorry sir for startling you.*" He opened the door and I tumbled out onto the pavement. "*I am Model 35. Please identify yourself.*"

"My name is Nathan Chambers," I replied.

His eyes changed. They went from a dark red to pale green before returning to red again. It happened quickly but I caught it. "*Welcome to the Temple, Nathan Chambers. Please follow me.*"

A pad was on the wall beside the Temple door. It was one large square which contained four smaller, colored squares—purple, orange, green and blue. The robot stood in front of the pad and hesitated.

After several seconds I asked, "Are you okay?"

The robot turned to me and his eyes changed colors again. "*Remain calm, sir. I was just trying to remember the passcode.*"

He pushed the smaller squares and they lit up in sequence with their particular color. The first time he did it an alarm sounded.

Braaaaaaaaaaa!

I thought I heard the robot growl in frustration but wasn't sure if it was my imagination. He balled his fist in irritation. "*Damn it.*" He furiously punched the buttons again. This time, instead of an error alarm, a voice boomed from the speaker. "Welcome to the Temple."

The door swung inward and the bottom of the door scraped against the floor, creating sparks. The door looked wooden but when I ran my hand across it felt more like metal.

We stepped into an immense hall illuminated by flame. Blazing torches adorned the walls and flames filled a large hearth at the center of the room. Instead of pews, several leather-bound chairs had been placed around it. Even though the hearth raged with flame the room was unusually cool. At first glance I thought the room was empty but then I spied the top of some-one's head poking from behind one of the chairs.

"*You guest has arrived,*" the robot stated.

The man in the chair stood and turned. The flames filled the room with ominous shadows that seemed to swirl around him, but even in the gloom I still recognized him.

"Corvus," I spat.

He gestured to the chair next to him. "Please sit down, Nathan," he said, matching my anger with pleasantness. "We have a lot to discuss."

Despite my anger I was torn I really wanted to hear what he had to say but I also wanted to throttle him for sending Shai after me. Eventually I slumped into the nearest chair. While shifting in the seat to get comfortable I observed Corvus looking at my handless arm.

"How did that happen?" He curled his lip with a mix of sur-prise and revulsion.

"Don't you know?" I responded harshly. "Your pal did this. Shai tortured me and blamed me for what the Consortium did to his people."

"Did he?" He responded with bewilderment. "If that's true than I offer my deepest apologies. I realize it has been a long trip and surely you are exhausted. Our host had a room prepared for your arrival."

"My last host 'prepared' a room for me too." I complained.

The flames in the hearth crackled and danced, casting eerie shadows across Corvus' face. "I'm sorry for what happened to you, Nathan. I truly am." He ran his hand through his snowy hair. "I assure you the room is comfortable and we are confident you shall find it to your liking."

"What do you want with me?" I briefly wondered what my chances of escape were. I grimly realized that my chances weren't very high

He folded his hands, smiled and leaned back in the seat. "Right to the point. I like that." He crossed his legs and drew a deep breath before continuing. "I suppose the simple answer would be that I would like the Insurgents to join us."

I laughed dryly. "Join you?" I sat up and stabbed a finger at him. "*You* are the reason for this entire conflict in the first place."

Corvus held up a hand. "Wait a minute. It was the Consortium who started it. Their constant meddling in our affairs is the reason I am here. I am trying to preserve our race!"

"Preserve our race?" I mocked. "Those events are from another time period. Your fight doesn't belong here."

It was Corvus' turn to laugh. "I am human, am I not?" He pounded his chest for emphasis. "Earth needs defending, I agree. The Consortium had established themselves as the defenders of the universe. But who would have defended Earth against its 'defenders'?"

"Did it need defending?" I asked incredulously. "It seemed fine to me before you came."

His face darkened. "Don't fool yourself. Things are not *fine!*" He stood up angrily.

"Settle down, Corvus," a voice from the shadow purred.

From behind a pillar stepped a man. He was pale, almost a light green. I wasn't sure if that was his actual skin color or the flames playing tricks on my mind. He stood about three inches taller than me and wore a faded black t-shirt, cargo pants and combat boots. The entire left side of his face bore burn scars which had healed to an angry red. He was missing most of his hair on that side of his head. What was left was black lined with streaks of gray. The burn scars ran to the top of his head, covering most of the spots which must have contained hair at one time. Despite the room being dimly lit, he wore aviator goggles with dark lenses. He was unarmed but when he moved closer two robots accompanied him.

"Janero." Corvus relaxed when the man emerged from the shadow. "I was just attempting to correct some misconceptions by our young friend here."

Janero took a seat and both robots moved into a flanking position behind him. I didn't need to look at them to feel their scarlet eyes boring into me. "Misconceptions?" Janero sounded surprised. "The entire universe is made up of misconceptions so why waste his time? Our friend here has traveled far and must be exhausted." When he saw that my right hand was gone he cocked his head curiously. "Old war wound?" he asked.

"Not old," I replied and tossed a sour look toward Corvus.

Janero caught the glance. "Unfortunate." He turned to one of his guards. "Tell Thirty-Five that I require him to accompany our guest to his chamber." The guard nodded curtly and left. Turning back to me he said, "Get some rest. I had your room stocked with food and water. I apologize if it seems meager, but harvest was weak this season."

My stomach grumbled at the mention of food and I realized it had been quite some time since my last meal. Thirty-Five entered the room. He was my red eye-green eye companion from earlier. I stood and yawned as exhaustion settled in.

"Thirty-Five, please show our guest to his room," Janero commanded.

With a nod the robot motioned toward the door. "*Follow me please.*"

I followed him down a narrow, stone hallway. Square light fixtures were fastened to the tops of the walls in rows of three which kept the hallway well lit, despite the lack of electricity in the main room. The walls had been constructed from some type of bare cobblestone that reminded me of the inside of a castle.

"Do you know what they plan to do with me?" I asked.

He turned to look at me. "*They do not plan to do anything—*" He stopped and his eyes changed from red to green once again. He stopped walking and grabbed my elbow. His voice changed.

It morphed from a mechanical dryness to a melodic sense of urgency. "*Nothing good I'm afraid. Stay vigilant. We will come.*"

Before I had a chance to ask him to clarify his statement, his eyes returned to their original color. A confused expression crossed his face and he shook his head. "*I'm sorry about that. I must have experienced a slight malfunction in my neural processor. Initial diagnosis detects no long term damage.*" He let go of my arm and continued walking. "*What were you saying?*"

"Um, never mind." I followed him along the hallway until we came upon a thick wooden door painted white. Thirty-Five turned the doorknob, opened the door and motioned me inside.

"*Welcome to your quarters.*" He flipped a switch on the wall and the room lit up.

Once inside I saw that Janero took great pains in setting up the room. A chest of drawers sat in a corner beneath a large stained glass window. A large round chair with a cushion about 12 inches thick stood in the center of the room. A king-size bed was tucked in another corner of the room. Next to the round chair was a stone table that looked as if it had been carved by hand. On top of the table were three plastic tubs and two large gallon jugs of a clear liquid which I assumed was water.

I strolled over to the table and looked inside the tubs. Inside the first one was a stack of paper plates and cantaloupe-sized fruit that resembled oranges. Inside the second tub were bags of maroon, shelled objects that resembled some sort of oversized nut.

"*The first box contains moon fruit. The second box contains unshelled cave nuts,*" Thirty-Five explained.

I removed a moon fruit from the box. It was as heavy as a coconut but had a rind like an orange. "So how do I eat it?"

"*You just dig your fingernail into the skin of the fruit and peel it back. The fruit inside is edible, but save the rind please.*"

Having only one hand I found it difficult at first to open the fruit. It was easier to hold it tightly against my torso and use the fingers on my good hand to peel the skin back. Inside the fruit wasn't orange at all but an angry purple. "Why do I need to save the rind?"

"*We use it to make fuel for the taxi,*" he replied.

"Interesting," I dug a piece of fruit out that was about the size of a golf ball and stared at it. What if the fruit on Gorganna was great for the natives but poisonous to humans? My grumbling stomach overrode my concerns and I shoved the fruit in my mouth. It was sweet and tasted like a strawberry. I tore a larger chunk out of the fruit and shoved it in my mouth so fast I nearly choked on it.

"*I will take my leave now. Two guards will be posted outside the door to make sure you remain undisturbed.*"

I popped a cave nut in my mouth and crushed it open between my teeth. The nut was chewy but tasted like an almond. After spitting the shell into the tub I picked up a second. Thirty-Five began making a strange grinding sound. I turned toward him and noticed his eyes were green again. I dropped the nut and it fell to the floor with a thump.

"*We will come,*" he said.

GRUNTS

After gorging myself on moon fruit and cave nuts, I hopped on the bed and stretched out. The bed was comfortable but my right wrist throbbed with pain, as if crying out for its missing appendage. Despite being completely exhausted, sleep eluded me. My mind raced after my odd exchange with Thirty-Five. *Could robots be bi-polar?* Although he blamed it on a malfunction I thought there was a more sinister reason behind his outbursts. To whom was he referring when he said "we will come"? Whoever it was I hoped wasn't an enemy. Lately, I had enough enemies to fill a stadium. My thoughts drifted to my mysterious host, Janero. On the outside he seemed friendly but so did Corvus and Calypso. He was their ally and I didn't trust him more than I could throw him. Eventually all my worries subsided as exhaustion overwhelmed me. Despite my brain's best effort to keep me awake my body finally succumbed to sleep.

I awoke to light filtering through the stained glass window and washing over my face. Stretching, I rubbed the cobwebs of sleep from my eyes. For the first time in a long time I felt refreshed. I stood up, shambled to the table and devoured another moon fruit. I glanced toward the far side of the room and saw what appeared to be a small trough attached by a pipe in the wall. My curiosity drew me to the object and I recognized it as an archaic plumbing system. I did my business and stood back, looking for the flush handle but there was none. Afraid I had just urinated in the water supply, I frantically looked around the object until a sucking sound erupted from it. My bodily fluids were sucked through the pipe and into the wall like a vacuum.

"A waterless plumbing system, that's pretty cool," I admired.

A knock at the door interrupted my admiration of the toilet. I opened it to see one of my robot guards standing in the doorway. "*Janero would like to see you.*"

I nodded and followed the guard to the main room. A roaring fire still burned in the hearth. The torches continued their endless flickering along the walls. One of the chairs was occupied by Janero. He stood when we approached.

"Good morning, Nathan. I hope you slept well." The aviator goggles were perched on top of his head which allowed me to see his eyes for the first time. They were as black as his glasses. His eyes reflected neither the fire from the hearth nor the flame from the nearby torches. It was like staring into two tar pits.

"I slept well," I admitted. "Your robot said you wanted to see me."

He smiled and slid the glasses over his eyes. "Yes. If you feel up to it, I would like to show you around. You probably didn't get to see much last night."

I narrowed my eyes suspiciously. "What about Corvus?"

His smile remained. "Corvus is going to sit this one out. He has other things to attend to."

"Why are you doing this?"

His smile faded. "Doing what?"

"Why are you being nice to me?" My wrist started to throb as my blood pressure rose with my anger. I held up the stump to show him. "Your allies have treated me like an enemy! Look what they did!"

Janero ran his fingers through what was left of his hair. When he moved the hair away from his scars I couldn't help but think they looked more like scales rather than burns. "I'm not your enemy," he replied coolly. "I didn't do that to your hand and I certainly would not have authorized such an act." He opened the door and motioned outside. I hesitated before stepping through the door.

Despite his friendly tone, I still couldn't shake the feeling that he held more sinister goals in mind. There was more to this than a tour. I certainly didn't feel any better when one of the robot guards accompanied us out the door. When I stepped outside the sunlight stung my eyes. As they adjusted to the brightness, dark shapes began to come into focus. Manny's taxi was parked out front, although Manny seemed to be hiding in his seat-plate. I placed my hand over my eyes to block some of the sun's rays and looked past the taxi. What I saw left me stunned.

"What the hell?" I muttered.

Beyond the taxi lay a paved road that extended for about a half mile before curving to the right. Brick buildings stood in rows on either side of the road. The buildings were in such disrepair that they seemed ready to collapse at any moment. One such building had a plane sticking out from the top. The remaining buildings were blanketed in vines, ivy and moss. Skeletons of several vehicles were lined along the roadway. Most had been charred beyond recognition. Large chunks of fallen concrete littered the road, making a majority of it impassable. Our robot guard strolled over and picked up one of the larger pieces of debris and tossed it aside like it was cardboard. I admired and feared his strength.

"I see by your reaction that you are amazed. I feel as you do sometimes, even after all these years," Janero sighed. "Although I see it every day but it is still a bitter pill to swallow."

"What happened?" I inquired.

"Come with me, I will explain on the way."

He started down the road but I hesitated for a moment. Although I was eager to learn what had happened, my distrust made me leery. In the end my curiosity buried my reservations.

We travelled along the road, passing several rotting buildings that seemed to house spectres of the past. Janero glanced at each building as we passed and I thought I spied a bit of sorrow in his eyes. "Earth isn't much different than Gorganna from what Corvus has told me," he said as we walked past a building I thought would collapse if a bird landed on it. When I looked up I thought I spotted a pair of eyes looking out from a window, but when I blinked they vanished. *Must have been the sun.* "We were a simple but prosperous people," he continued. "Farming, textiles and metalworking were our biggest industries but one day a company called Gentix Biosystems popped up seemingly out of nowhere. Their products were primarily genetically enhanced produce, medicine and biological agents which had been used as weapons for the military." We stumbled across the charred remains of a vehicle in the roadway. Janero's robot grabbed the frame and dragged it off to the side. Without skipping a beat, Janero continued. "Gentix absorbed most of the farmers, metal workers and tradesmen into their conglomerate. Whoever didn't join got forced out of business. The poverty level rose as more and more people became unemployed. The poor were eventually labelled 'Grunts' by the rich. Occasionally one of them would hire a Grunt to do menial tasks such as dig ditches, clean houses or, if they were lucky, cook meals for them."

"That doesn't sound fair," I replied. "Why don't they work together? Maybe if all these Grunts pooled their resources together they could create a market of their own and help rebuild some of these areas." I gestured toward the rundown buildings.

Janero smiled but the sadness in his eyes remained. "You are wise but the Grunts are long gone, Nathan. So are the Elites. Look around and bask in their legacy." His hand swept sadly across the rotting landscape.

My eyes widened. "Gone? You mean—"

"Yes," he interrupted. "I am all that remains of the Gorganos."

"But how?" I glanced at the scars on his face and wondered what horrors were unleashed on this world.

Janero halted while our robot escort moved aside more debris from the road. "The poor outnumbered the rich by a five to one ratio. They rose up against those they viewed as oppressors. They stocked up on weapons and overwhelmed local police forces in a bloody revolt. The Elites owned the military, including the chemical and nuclear weapons that had already been developed. They went unchecked by the government and spiraled out of control in their quest for power. They eventually owned and controlled everything. They murdered Grunts by the thousands. Grunt section housing complexes had been burned to the ground. The villages which managed to survive were later nuked into oblivion. A Grunt leader by the name of Kozbe Mayfair led a contingent into a secure military facility and stole several nukes. The Grunts retaliated by using those nukes. Gentix headquarters was leveled. Caillumet City was destroyed." After the road ahead was cleared by his guard he turned to me. "You seem upset, Nathan. Does this story ring a bell of familiarity?"

"These actions do hit close to home," I admitted. I studied his face. "Those scars are radiation burns, aren't they?"

"Yes," he replied dryly.

As I surveyed the surrounding landscape I began to question the timeline of his story. "I don't get it, the air here is breathable. If what you're telling me is true than the air should be poisonous. These buildings wouldn't have any vegetation on them. The landscape would be a whole lot more barren."

"You are very perceptive." Our robot escort stopped. Janero stopped and followed its gaze.

"What's wrong—" I started but Janero held up his hand to silence me.

"We are being watched," he whispered.

I followed their gaze and scanned the buildings. I saw nothing but empty windows, damaged walls and rotten rooftops. At first I thought he was stalling in order to avoid answering my question but then I saw something. Out of the highest window of the closest building, a pair of eyes, shining with the reflection of the sun, was watching us.

"I thought you said you were the last remaining survivor?" I whispered.

Our robot companion took a step closer to the building. His fingers made tapping noises against each other as they twitched in anticipation. Janero simply stared at the building in silence, either ignoring the question or simply sizing up the situation. My wrist throbbed as it cried out for its missing appendage and I longed to have a weapon by my side. I felt vulnerable standing out in the open.

Janero looked over at the robot and nodded. The robot returned the nod and advanced on the building silently. Janero turned to me and whispered. "I am the last of the *Gorganos*. I never said I was the last living being on the planet. I may have survived the poisons my kind unleashed upon the world, but so have others." He gave me a hawkish look. "There are things worse than me that walk this land now."

Before I could respond something leapt out of the top window. As it fell several stories to the ground the sun revealed it in its nightmarish entirety. With its pale skin my first thought was it was a phantasm, perhaps some long lost victim of the war coming to claim its revenge on those that have poisoned the land. It landed on the robot and knocked it to the ground. The creature was something hellish that my mind couldn't fully comprehend. Its torso resembled a hairless dog about the size of a Doberman with an extra set of legs along the front of its torso that were much shorter and clawed, similar to a Tyrannosaurus. Its head was that of a giant lizard. When it opened its mouth to gnaw the robot I witnessed two rows of razor-sharp teeth. The pale body of the creature nearly enveloped the black, armored carapace of the robot.

I was about to turn and run when Janero dropped a hand on my left forearm. "Don't run," he commanded. "You won't out-run it."

"What the hell do we do?" I asked, consumed by panic.

"We wait."

Shocked, I turned toward the carnage in the street. The crea-ture clamped down on the robot's right wrist and mine seemed to throb in response. Its teeth tore and pulled at the armored arm but the beast seemed to grow more furious at the lack of meat and bones on its prey. It hopped off the robot and turned its amber eyes toward us. I could almost taste the hatred in those eyes. It sprang at us before I even had time to react.

A blast rocked the creature's flank but it turned, unfazed. It whirled in the direction of its attacker. The robot stood behind it with an arm raised. Its fingers pointed at our attacker. Smoke billowed from his mini-barrel fingertips. Red eyes met amber in an old west standoff. An angry scorch mark marred the crea-ture's rear flank as a stark contrast to with its pallid flesh. The creature's haunches flexed as it poised to strike. It sprang again through the air with a feline grace but an explosion took out the entire left side of its head in midair. It fell dead at the robot's feet.

When the smoke cleared I shook my head at what had just taken place. "What in the world was *that*?"

The robot wandered over to us and spoke in a dry, emotion-less tone. "*Threat has been eliminated, sir.*"

"We simply refer to them as mutants," Janero replied. "They are mutated versions of what used to graze the plains beyond the city."

Now I realized the reasoning behind Janero bringing the guard with us. It wasn't to deter an escape attempt by me, but rather to protect us from *them*. My heart sank with the realiza-tion that I would never escape this place. If the guards didn't get me, the mutants would.

"Come, let's move on." Janero continued and I followed. After about a quarter mile I started to see the signs of a tunnel in the distance. "We will go as far as that tunnel but no further."

"Why's that?" I asked.

He chuckled dryly. "Because one guard won't be enough to protect us against what lies beyond."

I swallowed hard. "So I wanted to talk about this war of yours." I followed Janero's guard so close I practically rode piggyback. I had no desire to get jumped by another one of the mutants. "It must have happened a long time ago because the air is no longer poisonous."

"Ah yes, you did ask that question earlier didn't you. I apologize but in all the confusion I had forgotten." The buildings eventually receded in the distance and we came across some of the plains that Janero mentioned. It was nothing more than open flatland with sparse patches of spiny weeds and tufts of grass. Ahead the road led toward what looked to be the remains of a train station and beyond that was the tunnel. "You are correct, the war happened long ago. It has been over a hundred years but to be honest I lost track of time in that span."

"Are you trying to tell me you are over a hundred years old?" I asked dubiously.

He touched the side of his face, tracing the lines of his scars with his fingertip. "I think so, although I have to admit I have lost track of time. Some days I feel like a spry teenager, other days I feel like an elder." We stopped in front of the train station. "I outlived the survivors. Sometimes I believe that's a curse more than a blessing. I cheated death, Nathan. I don't know how and I don't know why but I do know this; surviving death has a way of changing a man." His jaw hardened and he bit his lower lip. "I was an Elite. I never had to worry about money, entertainment, or where my meal would come from. I had the highest quality clothes and enjoyed the best out of life. My father was an engineer for Gentix. He helped develop some of the very bioweapons that destroyed us. He died during the initial Grunt revolt. They shot him in the face as he pleaded for his life."

"I'm sorry," I offered. I had no idea what to say. I figured it would be better if he just got it off his chest.

He held up his hand. "There is no need for that. Whether we were Elite or Grunt it made no difference. In the end we were nothing more than stupid savages who preyed on each other. When I crawled from the shelter three weeks after the war I looked at the destruction we wrought and cried. I was nothing more than a thirteen-year-old kid alone in the world. For a week I did nothing but cry, forage and sleep. After a week I decided to do something else."

"What did you do?" I asked. The explorer in me took an interest in his story.

"I came across my first mutant and barely escaped with my life, that's what happened," he responded bitterly. "I couldn't survive on my own. I made my way to my father's lab in an attempt to find anything that would help; weapon, food, shelter, anything. The only thing I found were journals detailing his research, a super computer and a still functioning robot. Before the end Gentix had been researching ways to create an android army to bolster the military's ranks and help in the war against the Grunts."

We stepped into the train terminal. Our guard pressed ahead and swept the area to make sure no hidden threats laid within the tangled overgrowth inside. Thick vines wrapped around overhead computer screens and ticket counters, encircling them like an anaconda around its prey. Despite the heavy vegetation, the similarities to train stations I had seen on Earth was eerie. Janero kicked at ceiling chunks which had fallen long ago.

"My first order of business was to get the robot running. As I look back I think it was more of my desire for companionship more than any strategic maneuver. I'm glad I did though, because once the robot was functional he proved invaluable. He could forage for food, cook, clean, hunt and build. The first thing I used him to build was another robot using metal scavenged from nearby vehicles and machines and wiring from broken computer systems, inoperable vehicles and wherever else we could locate some. I was successful in getting communication systems up and running and learned my planet was officially dead. When I got the camera systems online, all I saw was nothing but death and destruction."

"Nuclear winter," I muttered.

Janero cocked his head. "Excuse me?"

"Oh sorry I was just remembering some things we learned in school about post-apocalyptic war scenarios. Creating survival scenarios was a big thing during the Cold War period. The books described the time following a nuclear war as nuclear winter. It was also big theme for a lot of video games. As a matter of fact—"

"Video games?" he interrupted.

"Yeah, it's these things we used play on a television," I explained. "We had several different systems that we could play them on and stuff."

"Oh," he said as his interest in the subject waned. "Anyway, I eventually built ten robots using scavenged material. Using some of my father's journals I integrated defense weaponry into their specifications so I could travel outside and defend myself against mutant attacks. After I completed robot number ten I named them 'the Reborn'."

"The Reborn?" I repeated.

"I desired to reshape the history of Gorganna," he stated. "I wanted the Reborn to be an example of how a perfect society should live."

I thought that a bit strange but assumed that everyone reacts differently when they discover their world had been destroyed. I had first-hand knowledge on the subject. "So how many of these Reborn do you have?"

Janero fingered a patch of moss covering the keyboard of a computer terminal. "I lost count at forty but I'm pretty sure the number is closer to fifty."

"That sure is a lot of robots to defend against mutants," I responded suspiciously.

Janero stopped playing with the moss and turned to me with a smile playing at the corner of his lips. "You are smarter than you look, Nathan." He proceeded to a staircase which led down to the tunnel. Next to the staircase were the remains of a vending machine. He stuck his hand inside and moved it around, as if he was looking for something. "I built twenty after Corvus approached me." He removed his hand, covered in grease and dirt. He looked at it with disdain and rubbed it on his pants. "I am still scavenging for material, but with his help I was able to build more."

"Why?" I asked. I wondered why he needed so many robots.

Janero smiled and wagged his finger back and forth. "Oh no, you won't get me to reveal our strategy no matter how crafty you are."

I had an overwhelming desire to pry for more information. "Okay, so be it. What about your alliance with Corvus? Why do you ally yourself with a bunch of murderers and kidnappers?"

Janero scratched his chin and glanced at our companion. "Seventeen, can you please go downstairs and make sure it's clear?" He watched the robot descend into the gloom of the tunnel before turning to me. "Corvus' allies are his own to choose. I realize he does what he does in order to achieve his goals. I have no control over what his allies do. Corvus himself has not murdered or kidnapped anyone."

"What about me?" I asked incredulously.

Janero offered me a wry smile. "Corvus had you brought here in order to convince you to join us. Despite what you may think, we share a common goal."

"Oh, and what's that?"

"To stop the Consortium," he swept the room dramatically with his hand, "To make sure that this doesn't happen again."

"The Consortium had nothing to do with this," I argued.

"True," he replied coldly. "But did they do anything to stop it? They are supposedly self-proclaimed galactic defenders. We had no contact at all from them. They had the power to stop this and they sat back and did nothing. How many more planets will end up like this as a result of their inaction?"

Before I answered, I contemplated the question. It wasn't inaction on their part that ruined Earth. The irony of the situation is inaction on their part may have saved Earth but his point was made. The Consortium had been responsible for too much destruction either through their actions or their inactions. Janero's words may have been poisoned honey, but they had a ring of truth.

"Join us," Janero urged. "Together we can make sure what happened to our planets will never happen again."

I had to admit the offer was tempting. The chance to adventure with Sam once again appealed to me, but then I thought of Lianne. I wondered if she would ever forgive me if I joined Corvus. Would Satou understand? Would Embeth? But then I thought of Shai and my wrist began throbbing with remembrance. My hatred for him trumped any other feeling I had. I hated him more than Calypso, more than Corvus even more than Meta. It was impossible for me to align myself with such a person.

"I'm sorry, Janero. I can't," I replied. "I need to return to my friends."

His look of disappointment shone through the gloom of the train station. "I'm sorry you feel that way."

At that moment Seventeen came up the stairs. "*The area is secure, sir.*"

"Thank you," Janero replied. "I suppose there isn't much more to talk about since you have made your decision." He made his way to the exit with Seventeen in tow.

"Hey, wait," I called out. "Does this mean I am free to go?"

"We shall see," he replied.

HOMECOMING

I stared out the stained glass window, deep in thought. Although Janero seemed pleasant enough I still questioned his motives. What did he need from me? I kept returning to that same question. I wasn't a soldier, I wasn't a strategist nor did I command vast armies. He wanted to bring the Insurgents over to his side but there would be no guarantee I would be able to convince them to do the same.

A knock from the door dragged me from my thoughts. I opened the door to reveal a grim face. "Well, lookie here," I mused. "It's a ghost from my past."

Sam smiled wryly. "Hello, Nathan."

My gaze drifted past him and I almost slammed the door shut in a panic. The largest wolf I had ever seen padded in a circle behind Sam. My robot guards were busy watching it, unsure if it was friend or foe.

"What the hell is that?" I gasped, backing into the room.

"That's my friend, Claw." Sam narrowed his eyes toward the guards and addressed the wolf. "Claw, stay here and guard those two." The wolf growled and sat next to the closest guard.

Sam entered the room and closed the door behind him. He took a seat on the couch and lit a cigarette. "Hey, this room is much better than mine," he joked.

"Smoking is a bad habit," I quipped. I took a seat on the bed and studied him. He looked older than the last time I saw him. His goatee seemed grayer and lines of age road mapped their way around his face. It was hard for me to believe that this version of Sam was my old friend. His age made him nothing more than a stranger to me.

Sam inhaled deeply and nodded. "Yeah, you're right," he coughed and looked at the cigarette like it was the first time he had ever seen one.

"What do you want, Sam?" I asked distrustfully.

An expression of pain flashed across his face. "I see you still don't trust me."

I shifted uncomfortably. "I don't know you Sam. You're not the Sam I remember."

He nodded slowly and took another drag. "I came to you for help, Nathan. I hope you could at least hear me out."

"You need help from me?" I asked cynically. "I definitely need to hear this." A low growl came from outside. Apparently one of the robots moved a little too close to Sam's pet. I smiled as I imagined the scene outside the door.

"I'm concerned with Corvus' allies, Nathan." Sam tugged on his hoop earring anxiously. "He is growing impatient and is beginning to recruit anyone who stumbles through the door. I am beginning to think his desire to destroy the Consortium is overriding his common sense."

My smile faded. Shai immediately came to mind. "I could have told you that," I replied sourly. "It started with Calypso and hasn't stopped. It won't stop, Sam, until he destroys his enemies."

"You're probably right. That is why I need your help." Sam replied somberly. "Don't get me wrong, I respect Corvus and his decisions until recently. We have been through a lot together."

"We were through a lot together," I muttered bitterly.

Sam sulked. "I know, Nathan."

"Why come to me?" I asked. "I can't control the decisions he makes."

"True," he agreed. "But you have influence with the Insurgents. I need your help bringing them to our side."

I shook my head. "I have already had this discussion with Janero. There is no way they would join forces with a murdering scumbag like Shai."

Sam dropped his face into the palms of his hands. "I know, Nathan." For a long time he remained in that position, breathing heavily through his fingers. Finally after several moments passed he looked up. "When we were kids I loved you like a brother."

I looked down and kicked at a dust ball the size of a cotton ball. "I know, Sam."

His face hardened and he sucked on the cigarette. "Now I am coming to you as a brother. The Consortium has been rotting from the inside for a long time. You know that," he pleaded. "Corvus needs everyone he can get to accomplish that. As it currently stands he can't win."

"So what?" I looked up. His face changed to a mask of shock and confusion. "Who cares if he loses? The Insurgents are determined to defeat the Consortium. We will do it without the assistance of murderers and thieves. If you really want to help then get me out of here."

Sam stood. The look of disappointment on his face cut me like a knife, but I remained resolute. "I'm sorry you feel that way. I'm sorry to be the bearer of bad news, but the Insurgents will not win either. The only way the Consortium can be defeated is by combining our forces." He turned and tossed the cigarette into the vacu-toilet before heading to the door.

"Sam," I called.

His hand rested on the door handle. Without turning he responded. "Yes?"

I stood but when I did my wrist started to throb, reminding me that my hand was still missed. "Join us, Sam. Forget Corvus. Take me back to the Insurgents, we will defeat the Consortium together."

He did not respond and instead opened the door. The two guards stood across from the wolf in a twisted parody of a Mexican standoff as they eyeballed each other. Sam stepped into the hall and turned around with sadness in his eyes. "I can't do that, Nathan." He closed the door without another word.

Two days passed before anyone else came to visit. Fortunately I had enough food and water left over from Janero's initial offering. I passed the time by counting the stones in the ceiling and thinking about the welfare of my friends. Occasionally I heard people pass my door on their way to other areas of the church, but their muffled voices were unidentifiable. As the time passed I began to refer to the church as a prison. It wasn't until my third day of confinement that Janero finally returned.

"I'm saddened by your decision," he mourned.

I held up my stump. "If you knew what I have been through, you wouldn't be so sad."

He looked at the disfigurement and nodded slowly. "You are probably right. Corvus and I agree that it would be unwise to release you." He lowered himself on the couch and studied me.

"Why is that?" I asked.

"We feel you might be inclined to reveal to your friends what you have seen," he explained. "Sam told me everything. He had explained our current strategic position and strength to you. I can't release you with that information."

Sam betrayed me. I was speechless.

"I'm judging by your silence that you are reevaluating your position?" Janero inquired.

"No," I replied softly.

He stood up, clearly disappointed. "I'm sorry to hear that. I'm afraid we will have to reevaluate your situation." He surveyed the room. "Normally these accommodations are reserved for people who are essential personnel."

"So I am no longer convenient for you?" I growled. "What are you going to do, throw me to the mutants?"

Janero's demeanor grew *colder*. "We are not quite the savages you make us out to be." He turned and opened the door. "I choose to deal with... *problems*... swiftly." He stepped into the hall and the door slammed shut.

BREAK OUT

When I first heard the commotion outside my door, I thought it was part of the dream I was having. I dreamt I was back on Earth before everything went to hell. I was in my house, enjoying a nice bowl of Hamburger Helper (don't knock it until you try it) and watching an episode of Family Guy when the commotion began. I originally thought it came from my parent's bedroom upstairs but then I was jarred from the dream. The noise was actually coming from outside my door. It sounded like the two guards outside were involved in a scuffle.

"What the hell?" I muttered. Soft thuds were quickly replaced by loud crashes. As soon the sounds started, they ceased. A long silence followed and I sat up briskly, straining to hear. The only noise coming from the room was the droning buzz of the overhead lights.

The door handle turned and I froze. With everything I had been through during the past 24 hours my mind pictured a ten foot tall mutant stepping through the door, coming to munch on my bones. Someone stepped through the doorway but it wasn't a mutant gorilla or flying monkey-shark-dragon thing. It was Thirty-Five. His eyes found me cowering on my bed. I noticed that they were green. In his hand he clutched the head of one of my robot guards.

He dropped it and uttered a single word. Although it had been only one word I heard the difference. It was less mechanical but sounded forced, as if it was coming from another source. It was one word which jolted me into action.

"*Run.*"

I didn't bother to ask questions. I sprang from the bed, rushed past him and into the hallway. In my haste I nearly tripped over the decimated remains of the two guards. They had been pummeled into piles of unrecognizable slag. I hesitated and wondered how one of their own could take out two armed guards with such ferocity. I didn't get the chance to ponder the question for too long when the booming voice of Thirty-Five resonated from inside the room. "*GO!*"

I did as commanded. I ran out the door, through the hallway, past the main chamber and out the front door. Outside the starless sky blanketed everything in darkness with the exception of Manny's taxi which remained outside with its lights on. When I hopped into the back seat I heard the shouts coming from inside the building as Janero's guards searched for me. I ducked down in the back seat and heard Manny's voice.

"Where to, kid?"

I peered over the seat. "Anywhere but here," I shouted.

Manny turned around. "Sorry pal I need a point of reference. Anywhere but here means everywhere with the exception of here."

I frantically surveyed my surroundings, expecting robot guards to come pouring out of the building at any moment. I needed to think fast. "Take me to the landing zone."

Manny scrunched his face in confusion. "The landing zone?"

"Yes!" My voice became more frenzied by the minute. "Wherever the hell you picked me up from."

A smile crossed Manny's face. "Ah, you mean the airport!"

I smacked my forehead on the seat cushion as Manny threw the vehicle in drive. In the dust cloud we left behind I saw four of Janero's guards burst out the door. They pointed their fingers at the cab but before they could fire, Janero ran out behind them with a robe wrapped around him. Even in the dark I could his face reflected in the church light. His face was a mix of anger and disappointment. He shouted something and they put their hands down. I turned around and slumped in the seat. I contemplated my next move and realized I had no next move. Where the hell would I go on a barren planet filled with nightmarish monsters?

About halfway down the road the vehicle came to a stop. When the holographic image of Manny vanished I realized that the vehicle died. Everything in the vehicle went out, leaving me surrounded by darkness.

"What the hell?" Frantic, I turned and looked out the back window. There was no sign of Janero or his robots. I drew a deep breath and tried to figure out my next move. The taxi stopped about 30 yards from the train station and I remembered Janero's warning. *Terrible things live beyond the tunnel.* I was unarmed, short one hand and alone. My current predicament did not exactly fill me with hope. I jumped in the front seat but the console was devoid of any type controls. Although there was a steering wheel there was no accelerator, brake, or light switch. The entire car had been controlled by Manny.

"Damn it!" I banged my left fist on the steering wheel but it was my right wrist that throbbed in response. *Where the hell am I supposed to go*? A little more information from Thirty-Five would have been useful but he was gone. I started to think the entire situation was some sort of trap. After all, it was one of Janero's personal robots who freed me. Was Shai behind this? I was aware of the "games" he liked to play.

I heard the clank of metal against pavement and saw Janero's robots in the distance, approaching fast. They were about a hundred yards away. I did the only thing I thought of at that moment. I left the cab and ran for the train station. Once I was inside the station I realized the folly of my actions. The darkness was only kept at bay by a single emergency floodlight outside. As I continued further into the station, the gloom eventually took over and I ran around like a headless chicken. I heard Janero's robots as they closed in. I changed direction and ran toward the tunnel. I took the stairs two at a time. By the time I reached the bottom it was so dark I practically fell down the final stair. I was blanketed in murky blackness. Even though there was oxygen down there I found it difficult to breathe. The air tasted old and stale, as if I just strolled into an old basement. I heard my pursuers muffled footsteps upstairs. I fumbled in the darkness for a light switch but felt nothing but cold steel walls. I fell back against the wall in resignation.

"Maybe this wasn't such a good idea," I muttered to myself.

I heard the robots scurrying around at the top of the stairs. Flashlight beams rolled over the floor at the bottom of the stairs only twenty feet away. "*Do you have him?*" Janero asked. The beams grew larger as the robots descended the stairs.

"*No sir, he escaped from the vehicle,*" one of them replied. "*We are currently pursuing into the tunnels.*"

"*No damn it!*" Janero's agitated voice boomed over the communicator. "*Get him before he reaches the end of the tunnel. He's dead if we don't stop him.*"

The end of the tunnel? I asked myself. I can't even find my hand in front of my face down here. I definitely had no urge to find out what lurked beyond the tunnel but the robots were coming. I slid along the wall, deeper into the tunnel. I froze when I heard a noise up ahead. It sounded like someone dropped a roll of quarters on the ground. I held my breath and listened. After a moment of silence I continued, but thought my lungs would explode. Only then did I realize I was holding my breath anxiously. I took one step forward and another sound from inside the tunnel caused me to freeze. This time it sounded like someone kicked an aluminum can against the wall. I strained my eyes in the hopes that I would see any sign of the source, but my eyes couldn't grow accustomed to such enveloping darkness. There would be no way I could continue through the tunnel without some source of light. I was trapped between the known threat of Janero and the unknown threat lurking in the gloom.

I stopped and tried to measure my options when two globes of blue suddenly pierced the dark. They began as no bigger than a pen tip but increased in size as they approached. The unknown threat was coming toward me! I turned and looked behind me and saw that the robots had reached the bottom stair. The first robot turned and held out his hand, palm open, as a white beam of light pierced the darkness.

The known or the unknown? I struggled with the path I should take. The blue light was almost upon me. It was larger than a quarter now and bright enough to illuminate the area around it. Behind the light I saw another larger blue light as big as a softball. Suddenly I was covered in white light as Janero's robots trained their lights on me.

"*We found him!*" one of them shouted.

Their lights shone past me, illuminating the blue orbs in front of me. They revealed a person donned in silver and black armor with a helmet to match. The softball size blue orb was actually a light in the center of its helmet. The quarter size light encircled the barrel of the pistol currently pointed at my face.

"Get down!" the newcomer growled.

Without hesitation I fell to the floor. Sparks fell on me as the weapon roared to life. I placed my arms over my head and buried my face in the ground. I stayed that way until silence filled the tunnel.

"Oh, get up off the ground," a mousy voice squeaked. "Do you humans always lie down on the job?"

I looked up into the face of a dwarf. He had so much hair on his face that I wondered if he even had one. His blond beard flowed down to his chest like a waterfall of hair. He had wild eyes which bulged from their sockets. As I stood and brushed myself off I was immediately covered in light when more of the armored strangers approached. The lead soldier removed his helmet. His features were similar to those of a human with the exception of a thick bony ridge which extended from the center of his forehead down to his upper lip. Two small dots above his upper lip flared and I assumed they were his nostrils. I looked toward the stairs to find the shattered, smoking remains of Janero's robots. They were riddled with holes and nearly unrecognizable. The scarlet brightness of their eyes faded until their sockets descended into shadow.

"Hey, I may be small but I'm not invisible," the dwarf barked. His eyes bulged as he studied me. For a minute I was worried they would drop out of their sockets. A buzzing sound came from behind him and a metal arm slowly emerged from his shoulder blades clutching a small circular object. The disk stopped in front of his left eye and he peered at me through it. "According to my calculations you are at least four hundred yards off course." He muttered something under his breath before continuing. "Of course I didn't anticipate Janero to cut power to the taxi." He wore a yellow overcoat which resembled a rain coat with many pockets. He reached into one of the pockets and pulled out a small book. He opened it and a 3-D holographic image popped up. The image looked like a car engine. After twirling the image 180 degrees with his index finger he frowned. His other hand opened and closed rapidly. "I really need to re-examine the Android Neural Inhibitor. I expected the android override to be more effective. My instructions to Thirty-Five were not relayed properly at all. *Not at all!*" He closed the book and shoved it into his pocket.

"Who are you?" I asked.

"Clean that up, please." He turned to the helmet-less soldier and motioned toward the pile of mangled robot carcasses. He nodded and put on the helmet. Turning to me he said, "My name is Grillick. Some people call me The Artificer. Others call me the Tinkerer. Vanth calls me a pain in the ass. But whatever you do, don't call me late for dinner." He glanced at my handless arm with disdain. "Oh deary-dear. This will not do. Not do at all."

I held it up. "What's wrong?"

He squinted at me. "Well, for one thing your hand is missing."

I scowled. "Thanks, Captain Obvious."

Unperturbed, Grillick continued. "Unfortunately for you, where we are going will require the use of two hands." He reached into a different pocket and removed a pad. He reached inside the jacket and retrieved a pen. "I am writing you a prescription for a new hand. Please hand this to the desk clerk upon arrival." He tore the paper from the pad and handed it to me.

I took the piece of paper. **Prescription: Cybernetic Hand Implant, Version 3.1. Please make sure to use the latest revision.**

"Are you serious?" I asked incredulously.

He waved his hand dismissively. "There is no time to explain. Janero will come once he finds out he lost his toys." Grillick cocked his head strangely and stared at the pile of robotic corpses. "Robots he calls them! They are nothing more than mobile rust magnets," he snorted. He turned around and barked orders to three soldiers standing at attention nearby. "We are going back through the tunnel. Let's go!"

"Wait a minute, do you think that's a good idea?" I argued. "Janero mentioned that there were bad things living beyond the tunnel."

"To hell with Janero and his bad things," Grillick sneered. "There are bad things living everywhere. Hell, I have worse things living in the storage compartment of my ship. Did you know I can make the Kessel Run in under five parsecs?"

"What?"

He brayed with laughter. "Oh, you humans and your movies! Star Wars provided me many hours of comedy that I will cherish until the end of time." He shuffled deeper into the tunnel, choking laughter, as I hesitantly followed.

As we made our way through the tunnel I wondered what these people wanted with me. Grillick was an odd duck but as he guided me safely through the tunnel he didn't seem to have malevolent intentions. My gut told me he was one of the good guys and my gut was the only thing I could trust anymore.

As we progressed through the tunnel, the soldier's lights fell upon the rusted carcass of a train. It had rounded edges like a monorail but was now nothing more than a reminder of what used to be. Even deep within the tunnel, the train wasn't immune to the ivy and vines which surrounded the buildings. The ivy circled the front of the train in a death grip and was about as thick as my leg. Grillick prodded me along before I could admire the scene any further.

We exited and stumbled over the moss-covered tracks the tunnel spit out. On the opposite side was the body of a mutant dog, similar to the one which attacked us earlier except this one had a gaping hole in its torso. We passed it and continued towards the barren wasteland that made up the plains. The ground was cracked with very little vegetation. As we traveled there had been some areas that vomited up a weed or two but mostly cracked earth greeted us. We continued for several hundred yards before a blood-curdling roar in the distance broke the silence. It was guttural and seemed very unhappy.

"What the hell was that?" I asked.

"Bad things," Grillick muttered sarcastically. I had to resist the urge to slap him in his furry mouth. We walked another hundred yards before coming to a stop.

"Okay, we're here," Grillick stated.

I looked around. The surrounding landscape was lit up by the soldiers light beams. We were surrounded by nothing but barren plains. My frustration boiled over. "Here? We are in the middle of nowhere!" I shouted irritably

Grillick sighed. "You humans," he grumbled and shook his head, "always thinking in terms of absolutes."

Aggravated, I continued walking and smacked my face on something hard. "What the...?" I extended my left hand and it flattened in front of me, as if hitting an invisible wall. Ahead was nothing but the barren environment yet something stopped me from going forward.

"The middle of nowhere, you said?" Grillick asked smugly. He reached into another pocket and retrieved a cylindrical object with a large, glowing red button on top. I found myself wondering how many things Grillick kept in his pockets. He pushed the button and the wall slid upward revealing a large ship.

"Well, that was certainly an interesting bit of camouflage," I mused.

The top of the ship was round, similar to the Kamilian saucers I witnessed back on Earth. Above the hull were several structures which resembled radio towers. Three long legs extended from the body toward the ground like an oversized tripod. Because of the darkness I had no idea what the overall height of the vessel was but by my estimates it had to have been at least three hundred feet high. A ramp led from the ground to the belly of the ship.

"All aboard," Grillick squeaked.

The roar we heard earlier got louder. The creature attached to it was getting closer. The soldiers tensed and swept the landscape with their weapons. Grillick hopped on the ramp and called out over his shoulder.

"And might I suggest we hurry."

THE ESCAPE

"Set course for Exorg 1," Grillick barked.

"Yes sir," the closest soldier responded before running off.

"Exorg 1?" I asked.

"Yes. That is where Vanth calls his home." Grillick led me down the hall to an archway with a large sign painted in bright blue letters. "Grog's Bar, Grill and Sundries" was written on the sign. Sitting at a desk underneath the sign was an ornery looking toad. His pale green skin, thick torso and puffy cheeks made him look like Kermit the Frog on steroids. His narrow yellow eyes locked on us as we approached the desk.

"What do you want?" he grumbled.

"His customer service may be lacking, but when it comes to his goods there is no equal in the universe," Grillick stated. "This is Grog. He is grumpier than a gutter snake, but since I don't see Preek around I could only assume he has pulled desk duty today."

"You're damn right," Grog grumped. "He says he doesn't *feel well* today. Maybe he shouldn't have been up all night drinking my stash of Orgellian Ale."

Grillick let out a long sigh. "Anyway, Nathan, please show him the piece of paper I gave you earlier."

I reached into my pocket, retrieved the "prescription" and handed it to Grog. He glanced at it with a look of indifference. He eyes went from the paper to me. "Broken, are we?"

"Occasionally," I muttered.

His hawkish eyes widened and he brayed laughter. It sounded like a cat getting run over by a car. "Grillick, you bagged a funny one, you did."

He turned to a nearby cabinet. That was when I realized he wasn't sitting to begin with. His torso was that of a toad but his bottom half reminded me of a horse. He had four thick limbs ending in hooves. They sounded like coconut halves slapping against metal. He reached inside the cabinet, retrieved a small, silver box and slapped it down on the desk. "It's the latest, greatest version of cybernetic implants. I designed it myself."

Grillick cleared his throat.

Grog sighed. "A little fairy helped too."

Since Grillick was too short to reach the top of the desk, I took the box and handed it to him. He opened it, examined the contents and seemed satisfied with what lay inside.

"Thank you, Grog. Always a pleasure," Grillick said with a touch of sarcasm.

"While you're here, would you care for a devilfish sandwich or perhaps a grilled sunbird pot pie?" Grog asked.

Grillick placed his hand over his abdomen. "No thanks, my stomach is still trying to process the fried jackalope you made last night."

Grog grunted and waved us away. "Take a hike then. I need to work on restocking the shelves. Preek decided to neglect those duties as well." He turned and clomped toward the back room.

Grillick opened the box and inhaled deeply. "Ahhh, I love the smell of invention in the morning." He closed the lid and handed it to me.

The top of the box was labeled "Cybernetic Hand, Human Model, Rev 3". I opened it and sure enough there was a hand inside, coated in some kind of dark-colored metallic substance. "What am I supposed to do with this?" I blurted.

"Vanth won't even consider you if you are short a hand," Grillick explained. "This cybernetic replacement can be attached to your wrist and will function like a real hand."

I looked at the object with skepticism. "How?"

We stopped in front of a sliding glass door marked "Lab". "I will attach the hand to your organic tissue via a synthetic neural interface that will allow you to control and use it as if it were the real thing. I will cover the joint with some synthskin and you should be good to go."

The inside of the lab looked more like a research center. There were several wash basins, stainless steel stools and tables, a bench which connected to an oversized machine which reminded me of a CT scanner, as well as several trays of beakers and vials filled with liquids of various colors. I followed Grillick to a workbench where circuit boards had been tossed in a pile. He pointed to a chair with armrests big enough to fit small tree trunks.

"Sit there."

I was hesitant at first. I was unsure of Grillick's plans for me. He never told me why he rescued me and I had no idea who this Vanth character was. I sat reluctantly, ready to bolt for the door at the first sign of trouble.

"Put your right arm there," he motioned to the right armrest and I did as requested. He placed the cybernetic hand about two inches from my wrist and retrieved a syringe from a nearby table. He held it to my neck. "Now this will sting for only a second."

I watched the needle warily. "What's that for?"

Grillick cleared his throat and uttered a dry chuckle. "The process of attaching a cybernetic appendage to existing flesh is rather... *unpleasant*. This will render you unconscious and allow me to conduct the procedure without you squirming like a stuck fish."

Being unconscious was really not what I had been planning, but my options were limited. "Okay," I muttered.

He placed the needle against my neck and depressed the plunger. At first it felt like the normal pinch of a needle but it suddenly became a burning sensation which enveloped the entire right side of my neck. It was as if someone placed a bag of hot coals there. It became nearly unbearable but before I could voice my protest everything went black.

When I woke I felt a tingling sensation radiating from the right side of my body. Grillick was standing on a stool hunched over one of the wash basins. The right side of my mouth felt ten times too heavy and when I spoke it was mostly from the left side. "What happened?"

Grillick jumped. "Holy Griselda and the Seven Isles!" he exclaimed. "Don't scare me like that."

"What did you do to me?" I cried. "I can hardly feel the right side of my body." I looked at my right arm and saw the cybernetic hand attached but no matter how hard I tried I couldn't move it or any of the fingers. "The hand doesn't work!"

He hopped off the stool and waddled over. "Of course it doesn't work, silly. I had to wait until you were awake to calibrate. Is your kind always this impatient?"

He grabbed something that resembled a neon flathead screwdriver from a nearby toolkit. He pressed down on my wrist, like he was feeling for a pulse. Once he reached the bottom of the palm I could no longer feel his touch. I heard a snapping sound and a small panel opened to the left of my thumb. Grillick shoved the screwdriver inside and sparks flew. Every finger closed in on itself, forming a fist.

"Oops, wrong wire," he muttered. "Let's try that again."

"Wrong wire, he says," I grumbled but he ignored my barb.

The second time he did it I felt an itching-burning sensation, as if ants were building a colony underneath my skin. "This itching is driving me crazy," I complained. "Can you do something about it?"

Without looking up, Grillick muttered, "Son, never rush an engineer during a calibration. If I make one mistake, I might have to take your entire arm off in order to fix it."

My eyes widened but I shut up and let him work. With one hand I was nearly useless. With only one arm I was an appendage away from being a floor mat. He stabbed at my wrist again and my fingers twitched. Grillick stuck his tongue between his lips in a comical parody of a person deep in thought. "I almost got it." He poked again and my hand formed a fist.

"Hey I felt that!" I cried triumphantly.

"That is the desired result we were looking for," he acknowledged. He closed the panel and tapped my forearm. "Okay, we are almost done. Can you flex your hand?"

I squeezed and the fingers moved, forming a fist. I could hardly believe my eyes. The movement felt so natural. It was like Grillick magically returned my hand. "It's a miracle," I gasped.

Grillick waves his hand in front of his face like he was trying to swat a fly. "No, no, no. I simply applied a formula for success. Calculations and skills are not miracles." He tossed the screwdriver aside and slapped his hands together. "Do you want to know what a miracle is? Trying to get Grog to part with his Hydrophanic laser swords, now *that's* a miracle. Now that we're done here, I suppose you want to know why you're here and where we're going."

I squeezed my new hand a few more times. "I guess that would be nice," I replied with a hint of sarcasm. "Why don't you start from the beginning and make it easier on both of us?"

Grillick let out a dry hacking cough that proceeded to get worse. Patches of skin shone crimson through his furry face. He continued to hack and I realized he was choking. I put my hand on his shoulder but he waved it off.

"Hey, are you alright?" I asked with concern.

He started making a god-awful retching sound and coughed up a ball of fuzzy slime at my feet. After taking a few deep

246

breaths he admired it as a cat would an unconscious mouse. "Whoa," he wheezed. "That was a big one."

"What is it?" I curled my lip in revulsion, trying to get as far away from it as possible.

Grillick wiped his mouth with the back of his hand. "Hair ball. They come on every once in a while, usually when I get excited."

"Hair ball?" I watched the thing on the floor as if it were about to come alive. "What are you?"

"*What* am I?" He looked insulted. "I am not a what, I am a who. Grillick the Artificer is my name. Science, invention, alchemy and chemistry is my game." He bowed.

"What do you want with me?"

He cocked his head. "Well, for starters a thank you for giving you a new hand would be nice. But to be honest it isn't I who needs you."

I scratched my head in confusion. "Who does?"

"I have my orders," he replied calmly, "to deliver you to Vanth."

"I don't want to go to Vanth. If you really want to help you will take me to my friends," I explained. "They are on Xajax and could use the information I have."

Grillick folded his arms and rubbed his chin, giving him a very philosopher-like appearance. "Where to start... where to start?" He held up his right index finger and began to count off. "Dilemma one: I suppose I will start with the Insurgents, if these are the friends you speak of. They are no longer on Xajax. Dilemma 2: Word has reached Vigil that human survivors are being transported to Vexall by the Kamilians so he has agreed to assist in the safe transition of the survivors. They are relocating their base to Vexall. Dilemma 3: um... oh, wait. Where was I?"

"Wait a minute," I interrupted. "You know Vigil?"

Grillick sighed. "Such a silly boy, of course I know Vigil. He is one of us."

"Do you mean to tell me you're one of the Twelve Timeless?" I looked at him with disbelief.

He narrowed his eyes. "I'm not sure I appreciate your tone, but yes I am." He strolled over to a workbench and picked up a vial containing a bright green liquid. "I am the inventor of the group. I'm charged with coming up with new gadgets, trinkets and designs to keep the universe going."

"Wow, the whole universe," I replied sarcastically.

Grillick began to cackle. "Ha-ha-ha, I see he doesn't believe the almighty Grillick!"

He waved his arm dramatically before hurling the vial at my feet. It exploded in a plume of green fog. As soon as it cleared a black bear the size of a bus appeared before me.

"Holy hell!" I cried and leapt from the chair, tripping over a stool and smashing the side of my head against a cabinet. A crown of stars fell before my eyes.

The bear stood on its rear haunches and let out a blood-curdling roar. Just as it was about to pounce, it vanished. Grillick brayed like a donkey. "Oh-ho-ho-ho!" he shouted as tears streamed from his eyes. "HA-HA-HA! Not so brave, are we, against the might of Grillick the Great!"

"What the hell was that?" I asked and rubbed the side of my face as I checked for blood.

"I haven't given it a name yet because it still doesn't last as long as I would like," he admitted. "As of right now, I file it under Liquid Holography." He waddled over, picked up the stool and set it straight. "Oh well, as I was saying, the Insurgents are not strong enough to fight a war on two fronts. They are going to build their forces, assist with Earth's relocation and let the Consortium and Ascended fight it out. Corvus and Calypso have gained strength. With the assistance of Janero and the bolstered ranks of the Scarlet Moon added to his pieced together Lumagom army they make a formidable foe. Meta and his cronies are flying around the universe making sure that planets aligned with the Consortium are truly loyal. Right now they hold the edge over Corvus' forces, but the margin is growing thinner by the hour."

"Who is Vanth?"

Grillick chuckled. "Vanth the Adjudicator. In short, he judges. If you ask me his true purpose is King Grump. But if you ask the others, his true purpose is training. He is proficient in all forms of weapons combat, hand-to-hand combat as well as the art of transcendence."

"Transcendence?" I asked.

"It's an ancient art form that originated on his home planet. I'm not entirely sure how it works but supposedly it's some form of meditation." Grillick shrugged matter-of-factly. "If it doesn't involve science than I have no time for it, to be honest."

"Why are you taking me to him?"

Grillick turned and fiddled with a pile of circuit boards on a nearby desk. "I am never going to get this thing functional," he muttered. "If I have to make another prototype I will simply blow my top. If only I could find my magnetic tube wrench the repairs would be much easier."

"Can you please answer me?" I demanded.

Grillick sighed. "We fear that there is sinister work afoot. Corvus' appearance is not a coincidence. Destroying a time hole may have dire consequences. The stability of the entire universe is at stake."

"What does that have to do with me?" I asked.

"I suppose there is time," he mumbled as he glanced at a wall clock above the work bench.

The clock read 31:43:11. So much for me figuring out time while aboard Grillick's ship. "Time for what?"

He looked at me and smiled. "Time to start from the beginning."

The Beginning

Grillick led me to a room down the hall from the lab. It came equipped with a bed, desk, two chairs, a bathroom and a couch. All the comforts of home; a home aboard a flying research center in outer space that is.

"Have a seat and I'll explain everything."

I plopped down on the couch and admired its softness. It was like sitting on a cloud. I kicked back, stretched and laid my head back. On the ceiling hung a large ring, about the size of a chandelier. A cool breeze wafted from it. I recognized it as some kind of air recycling system.

"Do make yourself comfortable," Grillick said, slightly annoyed. "Anyway, in the beginning this universe was created after an enormous explosion on a cosmic scale."

"Yeah, yeah," I interrupted and waved my hand in the air. "I paid attention in school. I know this already."

Grillick stopped and fixed me with a hard stare. "I'm sorry was I interrupting you? Do you have somewhere to be? You know nothing, Nathan Chambers, so I suggest you sit back and shut your face hole."

I felt the blood rush to my cheeks and looked away. Sometimes I let my immaturity get the best of me and Grillick's scolding was an embarrassing reminder.

"As I was saying," he continued. "That is how *this* universe was created. I won't rehash the birth of this universe because frankly it is common knowledge and the subject bores me. But what few people realize is the explosion destroyed the *previous* universe."

"Previous universe?" I sat up. He now held my interest.

"The Timeless were the only survivors of the Big Bang." Grillick paused for a moment before breaking out in a high-pitched giggle. It sounded like a squeaking mouse. "*Big Bang.* What a silly name. Since sound does not travel through space it should have been called the *Big Light Show.* Anyway, I digress. Where were we? Oh yes, the beginning."

Watching Grillick babble was like watching a crazy person in a straitjacket sitting in a padded cell discussing chess tactics with a toilet. I remained silent, however, and listened to what he had to say.

"Vigil's home planet of Kron was the first to be destroyed. Mine was the last. Ibune gathered us like a shepherd but we fell into a state of suspended animation from the cosmic radiation. Time passed while we drifted aimlessly aboard her ship."

I blinked. "This story is ridiculous. Are you telling me that you not only survived the Big Bang, but you lived *before* it even happened? That would make you billions of years old."

"That about sums it up, but I suppose the suspended animation helped along the way," he responded coolly. "So I guess maybe we are only millions of years old. Who knows?" He shrugged. "You tend to forget a lot during such a large amount of time but I will never forget the beginning." He paused. "None of us will."

I closed my eyes and rubbed my face. "I'm sorry, I don't believe that at all. You don't look like you're older than forty-five," I muttered sarcastically.

Grillick tapped his foot impatiently. "I will ignore your japes for now. I may be ancient, wise and good-looking, but I don't have all the answers. The universe is mysterious and no one will ever unlock all of them. I have done billions of calculations and conducted twice as many experiments but it all revolves around the cosmic radiation. I assume I will achieve enlighten-ment on the subject someday. This brings me to the part about why you are here." He cleared his throat for a long time and I was worried that he would cough up another hairball. After a few moments of dry hacking he continued. "The universe is beginning to destabilize again. Not because of any natural oc-curring phenomena, but because of the actions of High Prince Meta and this Solomon Corvus fella."

When he saw that I was completely confused, he shook his head and continued. "Traveling through a time hole for research is one thing, but traveling through a time hole and starting a war is another thing altogether. When Corvus stepped through the time hole, his actions disrupted the flow of time. We must repair the damage before the universe become one big fire-works show again." He ran his hand through his thick beard and scratched his chin. "Meta on the other hand attacked an inhab-ited planet, destroyed its atmosphere thereby starting a chain reaction which will ultimately lead to the demise of the time hole on Earth. Destroying time holes also disturb the balance. He needs to be stopped."

"I'm sorry, but what does this have to do with me?"

"Ibune hopes you will bring balance by restoring the Consor-tium to what it once was. They have lost their way. They have forgotten their primary mission."

"Who is Ibune and how does he propose I do that?"

"Ibune is a she," Grillick clarified. "I'm not exactly sure what she has in store for you but I'm sure she has a plan."

"Oh. Well, that makes me feel much better now." I rolled my eyes.

"There is a reason I am explaining this to you so be quiet and listen. Over the centuries we have seen much. Species had been born and species had died. Wars have been fought. We lived through the destruction of planets, galaxies and a universe."

"So, are you guys some sort of gods then?"

He shook his head. "We are immortal only in the fact that we do not age. We can still be killed." He stopped suddenly and rubbed his hands together, as if he were recalling a distant memory. I thought I saw pain in his eyes.

"There were more of you." I meant it as a question but it came out a statement. His fidgeting at the mention of death gave it away.

He nodded slowly. "Sixteen of us, originally," he lamented. "I will not bother delving into their history at this time. But it serves a valid point. We can die."

When I didn't press the issue further, he continued. "Wars have come and gone in this universe. There was the War of Galaxies, the Vaire-Charr trade embargo, the Lumagom-Consortium war, the Exorg conflict and many others. Throughout the centuries there was one constant. That constant was us. We remained vigilant but stayed out of the conflicts. We chose to stand aside in order to let the natural order of things progress. We agreed to be the watchers, only interfering if the integrity of the universe was at stake."

"Which is now, I assume?" I asked.

"When Corvus came through years ago, we took notice but stayed our hand. We were alerted every time someone traveled through a wormhole. Heck that was the only job Lapiz the Protector had. His job was to monitor wormholes. He was alerted every time someone stepped through. We realized that people have been traveling through wormholes for centuries."

"Aren't you concerned that what they do in the past could affect the future?" I found it difficult to believe that these sentient beings did not interfere with people who jumped through time.

Grillick shook his head. "What they did in one time period would have not affect the one they came from."

"Why not?"

He scratched his head vigorously before replying. He scratched so hard I was afraid he would remove his hand with large tufts of his hair. "Time is like a river. If you place a rock in the water, the waters will simply flow around it. If you try to block it with a dam, the force of the river will tear it asunder. Time cannot be stopped. It can only be *redirected*."

"What does that mean exactly?" I pressed.

"It means you cannot simply travel back in time within your own time period. What has passed has already passed. It can never be recovered."

"But how do you explain Corvus?"

"Easy!" Grillick smiled. "Corvus is from another *timeline*. His past has already been written. Even though this time *period* is technically from his past, he is in the wrong timeline. Nothing he does here will affect where he came from."

"I'm so lost right now," I admitted.

Grillick chuckled. "I admit it is enough to blow one's mind. It was many moons ago when I discovered the truth behind time-lines. Sometimes I wonder if I blew a cerebral gasket back then trying to piece it all together." He dug a finger into his ear and pulled out a large glob of greenish wax. "Sorry mister glob of wax but we are no longer accepting passengers for this flight." He flicked it aside with a scowl before looking at his watch. "Uh oh, we are late. I better get you to Vanth," he gasped.

Watching the interaction between him and his earwax I found myself agreeing with his assessment. Perhaps he did blow a cerebral gasket years ago.

FEAR

Grillick led me to a set of dark, oversized doors with a large, red bird engulfed in flame etched on the surface. It didn't look very inviting. I paused, fearing what might wait on the other side.

He noticed my apprehension. "Vanth can be...*quirky*...but effective. You will go in a mouse and come out a lion."

"I'm not here to become a lion," I mumbled.

I looked down at him and he looked up at me, matching my gaze. Suddenly he began scratching at his beard as if something was irritating him. He stopped and pulled out a metal bolt and tossed it aside with a look of disdain. "Strange," he muttered. "That must have been left over from the Mitochondria Capacitance Meter. Useless thing blew up in the lab." He conducted one final sweep of his beard. "That appears to be it." He tossed me a smile. "I'm sorry what were you saying?"

"Never mind." I moved to open the door but he grabbed my arm.

"NO, WAIT!" Grillick shouted. He shoved me aside violently.

"What the—" I blurted with surprise.

"No, no, no, NO!" Grillick stomped his foot in irritation. "Vanth enjoys his privacy and prefers seclusion," he replied, drawing a deep breath. "The door is warded."

"Warded?" I repeated.

"Yes, yes, YES!" he replied impatiently. "Anyone who touches it wakes the Phoenix." Grillick pointed at the bird on the door. Carefully, he moved to the side and opened a panel in the wall. Underneath was a smooth, glass interface which was currently blank. Grillick pressed his face into it and a bluish light engulfed his face.

"*Welcome, Grillick the Artificer,*" a pleasant female voice chirped from the interface. The door swung inward slowly. The creak that followed sounded like ancient hinges screaming for oil.

"Now, let's go before you blow us all into the next universe." He muttered several curses under his breath before leading me through the door.

The room inside was dimly lit by a single lamp attached to a desk in the corner of the room. Bookshelves lined the walls. Books were stuffed into them like sausage into a casing. When I passed one I thought the breeze of my passing would cause it to burst and rain books all over the place. A hooded figure sat in an oversized chair that looked to be carved from bone. Its bleached whiteness shined with an internal luster which kept the shadows at bay. In the dimly lit room it was impossible to see his face. The hood covered his face and the shadows made it seem like I was looking down a deep well. The armrests of the chair had been carved into serpent heads and his hands were gripping them tightly. With dread I looked for Grillick but he was no longer by my side. He remained next to the door.

"Don't look at me." He squeaked. "I'm not going in there."

"What the—" I stopped myself before I said something I would later regret. Cautiously I turned toward the hooded figure. He remained seated, completely motionless—dark and silent like the shadows. The door slammed shut behind me and I knew Grillick had left.

"Son of a bitch," I griped.

"There is no need for that language here," the hooded figure boomed. Inside the confines of the room, his voice was that of God. He rose from the chair and pulled back the hood. His face was pale, rivaling only the whiteness of his chair. His skin, like the chair, glowed with its own luminescence. The shadows feared him and remained in their respective corners. I wasn't sure if it was the effect of being inside such a dimly lit room, but it seemed that the being standing before me radiated power. He was barrel-chested and stood over six feet, but despite his size he was as graceful as a cat. He glided toward me, almost floating above the cobblestone floor. His eyes were milky white like someone affected with cataracts. His eyes were more oblong than a human's, forming boomerangs along the side of his face. His eyebrows seemed to be missing—either that or they blended in with his paleness.

"I'm s-s-sorry," I stuttered, shrinking against the door. My back slammed against it as Vanth towered over me. He leaned in to the point where I tasted the smell of musty tomes and mildew radiating off him. His nostrils, the size of quarters, flared as he sniffed the air around me.

"I smell your fear, human." As he continued to study me his movements suggested that he was blind. He smelled the air around me and traced my face with cold fingers.

My fear subsided and became disappointment. "You have to be kidding me."

He leaned back with an expression of confusion. "Excuse me?"

I peeled my back from the door and folded my arms in irritation. "You're blind, aren't you?"

He paused. "Blind is a relative term," he replied with a frown. "I see more than you realize."

"Great. Grillick said you would help train me to fight. You were supposed to make me some sort of lean, mean fighting machine," I replied with dismay.

Vanth bellowed laughter but there was no humor in it. "Who do you think I am? Do you think I am some simple potter and you are this block of clay to be molded into whatever your little heart desires?" He stepped aside and touched the wall with his index finger. Light bathed the room, drowning out the shadows cast from the desk lamp. "I am here to teach you the things you need, not the things you want. Today is the day to let go of the things that no longer serve you."

"What does that mean?"

"It means everything," he replied gruffly. "Your training hinges on your ability to let go. Let go of your weaknesses. Let go of the past. Embrace your strengths. Prepare for the future."

"Thanks a lot Sun Tzu," I replied, dripping with sarcasm. "What do you suppose I let go of first?"

"Your attitude, for one thing," he replied, unsmiling. "Aside from that, what do you think is your biggest weakness?"

The question caught me by surprise. I pondered it for a long time before answering. *What would be considered a weakness to him?* I was skinny, not very strong, not that attractive, my hair sucked, I couldn't run very fast, I wasn't athletic. The "weaknesses" poured into my brain like water from a faucet until I looked down at the hand Grillick designed. The loss of my hand culminated from my inability to do what needed to be done to save the ones I loved. In the end my weakness caused me to get captured twice, get several people killed, created failures of epic proportions. I took a deep breath and said the word slowly. "*Fear.*" When I muttered the word his scowl faded.

"Fear?" He seemed amused.

I nodded. "I can't stop being a scared kid. I realize I am no longer some naïve teenager from Earth. I need to put my big boy pants on and become a man."

Vanth folded his arms across his barrel chest. "Fear is a tool. Use it. Wield it like a weapon and strike your enemies down with it. Learn that and nothing can stop you."

His words reminded me of something and I chuckled.

"What's so funny?" he demanded.

My smile faded quickly. "Sorry, I was thinking of something someone said long ago. A former President of the United States once said; 'the only thing you have to fear is fear itself'."

For several moments he stood and stared at me. Finally he shook his head in dismay. "That is a statement for the weak. Never fear an emotion, control it."

"Well, anyway," I muttered. "It's probably my biggest weakness. That and these skinny arms," I added. He glanced at them with a disinterested look. When I looked at them, however, I grimaced. I hadn't exactly been eating well these past few months and it showed in my arms. They looked as if they could scare off a few crows.

"So be it." He retrieved a six-foot-long staff from the corner of the room. The shaft was an angry gray, like a stormy sky. At the top of the staff was a carving which resembled a lantern and at the bottom was a baseball-sized knob shaped like a skull. Two black gems, similar to onyx, were embedded in the eye sockets. "If you are prepared to forget the past, improve the present and lay the path for the future, follow me and begin your voyage."

Without taking my eyes off the staff I nodded and followed him out the door.

TRAINING

Day 1

Sunlight fell on my face, waking me. I stretched and felt a renewed sense of purpose after my conversation with Vanth. Outside my window, the barren wasteland of Exorg 1 greeted me. Even though I was anxious regarding my upcoming training, I looked forward to conquering my fears. Clasping my hands over my head I stretched one last time before strolling over to the mobile Sustanant. Grillick had been kind enough to bring one in yesterday.

"Time for me to start my voyage to the unknown," I said with a yawn. "Let's start it with a coffee."

I punched in "COFFEE" and the door slid open, revealing a steaming cup of the black stuff. With a smile I grabbed the cup and lifted it to my lips. It only took one sip for the smile to fade.

"My God, this tastes like used motor oil," I spat. I put the cup down and punched in an order for water. As soon as the door opened I guzzled the water down in the hope it would drown out the taste of engine. I also ordered some toast with butter which tasted bland, but I was able to choke it down.

A knock at the door interrupted my breakfast. "Come in," I shouted through mouthfuls of toast.

Grillick entered along with one of his armored soldiers. I swallowed hard. *What does he need a soldier for?* He quickly put my suspicions to rest. "Good morning, Nathan. I trust you slept well? This here is Sergeant Cantrell, he will show you around the complex before you meet with Vanth today."

When the soldier removed his helmet I recognized him as the person in the train tunnel on Gorganna. "I'm no babysitter so let's make this quick," he grumbled.

"Sergeant Cantrell's pleasance has no equal," Grillick countered sarcastically. "Fortunately for him the tour will have to be quick because Vanth is expecting you in one hour."

"Bah," the sergeant barked. "Follow me and try to keep up."

I followed him out the door and tried to keep up as best I could. For every step he took I had to take two. He was a big man and his legs were long. In the beginning of the tour I could tell he wanted to get it over quickly but eventually he slowed and explained areas more thoroughly, especially when it came to the barracks area and mess hall. The entire complex was designed as a perfect circle. The walls of the halls were constructed of some sort of gray synthetic material that lit up as we walked past. Vanth's complex had been designed with four guest rooms, a medical facility, a mess hall, a barracks, a weapons storage room and his office. Every room surrounded what Cantrell referred to as "The Octagon"—a room designed with eight angled walls that served as a training room. "Oh, you are gonna have fun in here," Cantrell scoffed when we passed by the room.

The tour ended in front of Vanth's office. Unlike my first visit, this time the door was open. "This is where our little tour comes to an end," Cantrell said gruffly. "Hopefully he doesn't break you like he did with the last one." He hitched his belt and stomped off towards the barracks.

"Gee, thanks," I muttered before stepping into Vanth's office. I found him hunched over a tome as big as a dictionary with a single candle burning nearby. A feeling of déjà vu came over me as I recalled our first meeting.

"Good morning, Nathan," he said without looking up from the tome. "Are you ready to become the person the universe needs you to be."

I shifted uncomfortably under his gaze. "Wow, the entire universe," I mumbled. "No pressure, I guess."

Vanth stared at me, and despite his blindness I felt his cloudy eyes studying me. He lifted his hood over his head, enveloping his face in shadow. "There will be pressure. You will deal with it or you will die." He grabbed his staff and led me from the room.

I chewed a fingernail off on the way to the training room. To say I was nervous would be like saying a tornado was just a mild breeze. *Set panic mode to DEFCON 1 please.* When we entered the training room I was convinced I would piss myself.

Cantrell rushed me through the room during the tour so I didn't get a chance to take in everything around me. Now that we were about to start training I examined the room with a bit more scrutiny. Paintings of people (some slightly human, others with faces so unearthly they seemed to be yanked directly from the nightmares of hell) lined almost every inch of the walls.

"Who are they?" I motioned to the images, but then I remembered he was blind and mentally facepalmed myself before adding, "The people on the walls."

Vanth placed his hand upon the closest wall, covering one of the images. He closed his eyes and spoke slowly and methodically. "They came to me seeking the way. Some days I can feel their souls crying out. They beg me for a second chance; one that I cannot give."

"A straight answer would be nice sometimes," I grumbled.

Vanth let out a long, deep sigh. "This is your first day so I will forgive your impatience. Just remember that I will not always be so forgiving." He clutched his staff tightly and the skull scraped ominously against the stone-tiled floor. "They failed their training and paid for that failure with their lives."

I swallowed hard and studied their faces. There had to have been hundreds of pictures hanging on the walls. Some looked like warriors, others could have been no older than kids. *Just like me.*

Vanth led me to the center of the room which was separated by four foot metal poles scattered around the area, forming a smaller octagon. The "mini-octagon" was roughly thirty feet from corner to corner. The floor felt soft underneath my boots, sort of like the wrestling mats we had at our school gym. "This is where most of your combat training will take place."

"Is this where they failed?" I asked, indicating the people on the wall.

"That question is the first in what will surely be a long list of failures on your part. Let us pray that you do not fail when it counts." Vanth scowled and gripped his staff tightly. "Do not focus on the where or how, focus on the *why*. Your question should have been: 'Why did they fail'?" He leaned against a nearby pole and rested his chin against his staff before closing his eyes. "They all failed for various reasons. Several did not *believe* my words. A few did not *listen* to my words. Others did not *hear* my words."

I had no clue what the difference was between the three but decided to remain silent. It didn't seem to be the proper time to be asking such questions. Vanth left the inner octagon and I followed but he held up his hand.

"Wait here," he commanded. "Your training will begin shortly. This part is just an assessment and will not be used toward the final judgment."

I stiffened. "What am I supposed to do?"

"You fight." Vanth turned and slammed his staff into a notch in the ground. Electricity passed between the poles, forming an electric fence. The center of the floor began to glow bright orange and an image formed above it. At first it was nothing more than a dark-colored shadow. As the seconds passed it swirled, molded and morphed like a large black chunk of modeling clay. Eventually it stopped and took on the form of a man. When the transformation was complete, Shai stood at the center of the room, tossing me the same smug smile I left him with. I looked to Vanth for guidance. He held out his hand, palm facing me as if he were expecting me to high-five him. "Go."

I turned my attention to my adversary who looked at me like a predator and I was the prey. I clenched my right hand and looked at it, recalling what he did to me which only filled me with rage. He took a step forward and my mind went blank. Everything was covered in a red blanket of rage. I rushed him with the intent of caving in his smug face and pummeling it until it was nothing more than a slush pile.

He apparently had other ideas. He easily side-stepped my advance and punched me in the side, knocking the wind out of me and bringing me to my knees.

"No," I gasped and got back up on one knee.

Shai knocked me to the floor with a blow to the back of my head. It felt like he dropped an anvil on it. I laid face down on the ground, gasping for air as the world dimmed around me. I turned to see his boots. I felt like I had just been run over by a bus. I struggled to move and braced for a blow which never came.

"There is more work to be done than I had originally estimated," Vanth said. The fence disappeared and he entered the ring. Shai was gone.

"What the hell was that?" I asked, struggling to catch my breath.

"That was your first test to measure your ability in battle. I have concluded that you have none." He brought the staff down and clubbed me over the head.

"Ow, what the—," I cried.

"That was for being absolutely terrible in a simple skirmish. What would have happened had there been two adversaries?

What would have happened if there were ten?" He tapped the staff on the ground impatiently.

"I probably would have gotten my butt kicked," I mumbled. I rubbed my head and would not have been surprised had I felt a lantern-shaped indentation in my skull.

"You would be dead," he clarified.

"So does that mean I fail?" He was right. If I couldn't beat a holographic image of Shai, how was I supposed to beat the real version? I have never felt more disappointed.

"No." He clutched the staff in both hands and leaned on it. "I was disappointed by your performance but not surprised. You were never expected to beat him. You can savor one small victory. You got up and continued to fight. That is a start."

"But I lost," I argued.

"Combat rule number one." He held up his index finger. "Some people fight for riches, others fight for glory. A few fight for honor. It is only important that you fight."

"What do you want me to gain from all this?" I felt the back of my head where Shai struck me. A lump was beginning to form. Vanth's training partners were more real than holograms.

"This training is like life. It's a journey where you will encounter many obstacles. You will also come to crossroads. A person may guide you but in the end only you can walk the path." He motioned toward the door.

"That's it for today?" I asked incredulously.

Vanth nodded. "I will send Grillick for you at first light. Your grace period is over."

"Great," I muttered and headed to my room.

Day 2

Vanth was right. I ended up in the training room at first light. Unfortunately for me, Exorg 1 only experienced twelve hour days. Grillick collected me and half-dragged my groggy body down the hall.

Grillick stopped at the entrance. He turned to me and frowned. "Why so grumpy today?"

"Are you serious with that question? I couldn't have slept for more than an hour," I groaned.

"Actually, you slept five and a half hours." When he saw my frown deepen, he smiled. "I know what will cheer you up! A joke!"

I glared at him. This did not stop him. "Why do they call curium and barium the medical elements?" He hopped up and down and clapped his hands together. He was exploding with eagerness to reveal the answer.

"Go away," I groaned.

My request did not faze him. With a broad smile he responded, "Because if you can't curium than you will have to barium!" He braced himself against the wall and roared laughter.

He continued roaring with laughter after I entered the octagon. The door slammed shut but didn't drown out his incessant tittering. I shook my head and pressed my lips together tightly. Vanth stood in the center of the room, staff in hand, unperturbed by the mousy laughter booming from the other side of the door. The laughter only died down when Grillick began coughing violently. After a few seconds of retching, the halls went silent and I knew he had coughed up another hair ball.

"So, what's on the agenda today?" I asked sourly. I felt my gorge rising at the thought of stumbling into a slimy hairball in the hallway.

"Your initial physical assessment has been completed," Vanth responded, unperturbed by the events outside his door. "It is time for the mental assessment." He touched the wall and the lights dimmed. His dark purple robe blended into the shadows cast throughout the room. He pulled the hood over his face, blanketing his face in darkness. "Our exercise today will test your mental prowess in the face of adversity." The lights dimmed further, creating a fog of gloom. Vanth vanished into shadow. "This is just an initial mental assessment which will not be counted toward your final score but do not let that fool you. Do the best you can."

Suddenly the room lit up around me. I was no longer in the octagon nor was I alone. Kedge stood next to me and Wraith stood behind us. I was in New Mexico again. Shai and his ship stood before us.

"Oh, please God no," I pleaded. "I can't go through this again."

"You must," Vanth's voice boomed from an overhead speaker like the disembodied voice of God. "You will."

Noz, Shai and the soldier were on the ramp, just like last time except I was not present—well at least my physical body wasn't. The New Mexico version of myself stood next to Wraith. I was still in Vanth's training room acting as a spectator. That was when I noticed everything moved in slow motion. New Mexico Nathan lifted the AR-15 for what seemed like an eternity. When Wraith started firing, the bullets sailed by me so slow I reached up to grab one but my hand slipped through it like an illusion.

The barrel of the sniper rifle gleamed in the sun just before the side of Wraith's head exploded like a watermelon under a sledgehammer. New Mexico Nathan was out of ammunition and cried out in rage. Kedge parried Shai's blow. As quickly as it had started, it stopped, frozen in time. I noticed brown spots in Shai's teeth when he clenched them together to put his weight behind the blow. Flame encircled the barrel of the sniper's rifle and the bullet was frozen just outside of it. Wraith was frozen in death, bent backwards, halfway to the ground.

"WHAT DO YOU WANT ME TO DO?" I screamed. I looked around but the only thing surrounding me was the New Mexico landscape. "I can't stop this from happening."

"Of course not," Vanth boomed from overhead. "I want you to remember this day and what you were feeling. Think, recall and remember."

I clenched and unclenched my fake hand as I recalled my feelings. "I remember being afraid at first," I admitted. "But after they killed Wraith I became angry."

"What were your mistakes?" Vanth asked.

I answered quickly. "I missed my shots."

A long, drawn-out sigh came from the loudspeaker. "No," he responded curtly. "Your first mistake was fear. Fear led to indecision. When your enemy first appeared you should have struck. Instead, you hesitated."

"Wait a minute. I didn't—"

"QUIET!" he roared. Never speak during assessment. "Your second mistake was uncontrolled anger. The anger blinded you. Fear started what anger finished, therefore leading to complete failure."

New Mexico vanished and the lights came on. Vanth strolled to the middle of the octagon and rubbed the top of his staff thoughtfully. "Your emotions are the reason you failed."

I shook my head in disbelief. "Do you think that perhaps my poor aim had something to do with it?"

"Perhaps," he sighed "Or perhaps an army of giants could have flown from the heavens on the backs of unicorns and killed your enemies for you."

I got the hint. "So what do you expect me to do, forget my emotions? Should I never fear or be angry again? I'm sorry, but I am not a robot," I argued.

"No, you must never forget your emotions. You need to learn to use them, to control them and to make them work for you."

"How do I do that?" I asked.

"This will be the basic building block of your training. You will learn to turn a negative emotion into a positive one." He stepped out of the octagon and I found myself once again at the

beginning of the encounter in New Mexico with one exception—
I wasn't there. Kedge and Wraith were accompanied by Vanth.
Instead of an AR-15, Vanth carried his staff.

"What the heck?" I cried out in surprise.

"Watch and learn," he said. "The key to controlling a negative
emotion is to convert it into a positive. Turn anger into gratitude. Turn fear into hope. Hate becomes love and sorrow becomes joy." The scene behind Vanth was frozen in time as he
lectured me. "You had two primary emotions during this encounter; fear and anger. The first emotion I will change will be
fear into hope."

"Hope?" I repeated.

"Yes," he replied calmly. "Hope that my enemies provide me
with the opening I need and that my actions result in their destruction. The second emotion I will change is anger. I will turn
anger into gratitude. My gratitude will be toward my enemies.
I will thank them for providing me the strength and motivation
to fight."

"Um, okay," I muttered skeptically.

The action continued as soon as Vanth turned around. He
approached the ramp where the three members of the Scarlet
Moon descended. Without a word, Vanth slipped past Kedge and
stood at the bottom of the ramp. Shai looked at him. Although it
was Vanth playing out the scene, Shai still addressed him as me.

"Look what we have here," Shai beamed. He pointed and
turned to Colonel Noz. "Do you know who this is?"

Before Noz could answer, Vanth's staff danced through the air.
Crack. The lantern end smashed Shai in the face and knocked
him off the ramp. Before Noz could react Vanth was airborne.
His boot caught him firmly in the center his chest. The momen-
tum of his body knocked the Exorg through the entranceway.
Vanth somersaulted backwards just as the sniper stuck the rifle
barrel out the door. He fired and once again Wraith lay dying
on the ground. Both Kedge and Vanth descended on the sniper

and dispatched him with ease. Vanth's facial expression did not change during the entire encounter. He had a calm, almost Zen-like demeanor while he tore through his enemies. He stepped off the ramp and the landscape disappeared leaving me once again in the octagon.

Vanth entered and tapped the bottom of his staff on the floor. "For a blind man you sure fight well," I quipped.

He ignored my jape. "Did you see how I used my emotions against my enemies?"

I shrugged. "It's easy to fight when you already know how the battle will go. Even knowing that you still managed to get Wraith killed."

"Nothing could have changed that," he replied. "These results were not due to any foreknowledge on my part. I simply did what was necessary to dispatch my enemies."

"I suppose so," I replied skeptically.

Seeing the disbelief written on my face, he slammed his staff on the ground. "Enough with the past. I am here to carve your path as one would carve a statue from stone. It is now your turn. Since you think events of the past skew the test results I will allow you the same luxury." The lights dimmed and he faded into shadow.

I was once again in New Mexico. However, this time I was in the hallway of my high school. The ringing of the school bell jarred me into focus.

"Hey, come on. We are gonna be late." A hand fell on my shoulder. I turned to see Sam standing next to me.

"Late?" I asked.

Before he could answer his face froze as he looked past me. I turned and followed his gaze to see two of the biggest seniors in our school, Brett Raines and Tommy Stewart coming toward us. They were locked on us as they approached.

"Oh no," I muttered. I was about to relive the biggest school beating in my academic career. The prior week I had caught them trying to cheat off me during our chemistry exam. I purposefully wrote down the incorrect answers and waited for them to turn in their papers. When they did I went back and replaced all the wrong answers with the correct ones before I turned in mine. When we got our graded papers back they knew they had been conned when their F's were compared to my A. That day I received a broken jaw and black eye for my trouble while they both received suspensions. They got a vacation from school while I couldn't talk right for weeks.

Turn fear into hope, Vanth's voice commanded me from the back of my mind. "Oh yeah?" I asked his voice. "Well, I *hope* they miss," I muttered.

Tommy was the first to approach me. He was as big as a barn and star lineman for our football team. He shoved me against a locker. "You're dead, Chambers!" Each word was accentuated with a generous helping of spittle.

"You changed the answers, didn't you, you little shit!" Brett shouted from the peanut gallery.

Whenever I got nervous I became extremely sarcastic. This was a trait that did not serve me well at all. "The cheaters got cheated? Oh the humanity!" I responded. Tommy pushed me into the locker again, this time much harder than the first. *It is you who control your emotions, not the other way around,* Vanth bellowed from above. Tommy's hand dug into my shoulder and he cocked his fist back for a strike.

"You think you're funny? You're gonna pay for what you did."

I did the first thing that came to mind. I fell to the floor so hard I thought I heard my coccyx crack. Tommy's fist flew harmlessly over my head and slammed into the locker. His cry of pain brought a smile to my face before I slammed my fist into his crotch. *Wow the bigger they are the harder they DO fall,* I admired when he fell like a sack of rocks.

"Son of a bitch," he cried through clenched teeth as he covered little Tommy.

I stood up and smiled but never had time to truly admire my handiwork. Brett grabbed my hair and smashed my face into the locker. "How do you like that, you little jackwagon?" he sneered.

I fell to the floor and the coppery taste of blood filled my mouth. Before I could get up he slammed me in the back of the head with his fist. Unfortunately for me my face wasn't too far from the floor and I slammed into it. I heard the sickening crunch of bone as my nose shattered. Before I blacked out the lights of the octagon fell over me.

Vanth stood over me. "Grillick will take you to the infirmary to get that taken care of. This will conclude our lesson for today."

I spit out a thick, red ball of snot and hoisted myself to one knee. "So how did I do?"

"You knew what was about to happen just like I did in New Mexico. Why did you not win?" He stood over me with his staff resting across his shoulder.

I pondered the question. He was right. If my theory was correct then I should have won the fight easily. "I did take Tommy out of the fight which was better than the last go around," I argued.

Vanth nodded. "True. But you still failed. Do you know why?"

I shook my head.

"Because you were overcome with pride. You were too busy admiring one fallen enemy that you forgot about the other. There is no room for pride on the battlefield."

I rubbed my face and my hand came back sticky with blood. Vanth looked at it with disdain. Get that taken care of. We will continue tomorrow.

Day 10

The next several days consisted of lessons similar to the first two. I received beatings and dished out a few. As the days wore on I learned to gain control over my emotions. I also gained about five pounds of muscle. As a result of the generous menu programmed into the Sustanant I was eating much better and each battle provided a great cardiovascular and strength training workout. Vanth watched my progression with growing interest. He still would not confirm whether he was truly blind or simply messing with me. Grillick insisted he was blind but he also insisted gremlins sabotaged some of his inventions.

As the days passed I grew fond of Grillick despite his pass-fail invention ratio. For every invention that worked at least ten failed or, as he called it, achieved undesirable results. After the fifth day he insisted he had created a pocket-sized flamethrower. He showed me an object that was no bigger than a wallet. He pulled a pin out of it and tossed it on the ground. The wallet opened up into a long gun barrel on a tripod. He pressed a button on his wristwatch and the turret melted into a smoldering pile of sludge.

"Hmm, perhaps I used the wrong fuel," he pondered that day. "I seemed to have exceeded turret output capacity."

It was on day ten that Menjaro arrived. Grillick explained to me he was bringing news of the war. I asked about my friends but he only shrugged. "They didn't invite me to the meeting," he explained.

Day ten was also the day that I completed my hand-to-hand combat training. During the previous ten days all of my combat had been weaponless. When I needed to fend off armed attackers I asked Vanth where my weapon was. He responded, "Weapons are tools for the weak." I countered by explaining that he carried a weapon after pointing to his staff. He looked at me with a deadpan expression and responded, "I have no idea what you are talking about. This is simply a walking stick."

We started weapons training the next day.

Day 30

I learned a lot over the past twenty days. As before, I participated in skirmishes ranging from one to five opponents. This
time however I practiced with weapons ranging from daggers to
rifles. During this period I gained another ten pounds of muscle and started to change from scarecrow to an actual man. My
birthday passed during this time according to the Earth calen-
dar Grillick hung in my room. It had officially been a year and a
half since my first encounter with the Consortium. I was now 18.
"Hey, I can now buy cigarettes legally," I joked to Grillick. He responded with the curium/barium joke and I wanted to slug him.

Vanth acknowledged I was better at controlling my emotions.
He put that to the test on day 27 when he put me in the octagon
against two of Vaire's Shreen. I had to admit I almost crapped
myself that day. That day I had been training with a lightning
rod—a staff with a large electrified bulb at each end. I managed
to catch the first Shreen by surprise before the second even had
time to react. I was amazed at my reaction times in battle. I won
but I believed it was more of slow reaction time by the holograms as well as their smaller size. Vanth noted that they were
not full-grown warriors because in his words he didn't want to
"kill me yet". He did acknowledge that I was one of the fastest
learners he had ever trained. I felt better than ever before.

Day 90

The past sixty days went as expected. I participated in more
battles and became proficient in most hand weapons as well as
all trigger-based weapons. My battles went as Vanth expected.
I won some and lost some but the most important factor had
been that I never gave up. I controlled my emotions and used
them when needed. We replayed the fight in the halls of the high
school and I won with ease. During the fight in New Mexico

I still had some issues controlling my anger. On day 88 Vanth thought he had lost me. We replayed the New Mexico battle for the third time and I managed to dodge the sniper's bullet, but it ended when Shai stabbed me in the chest. It took Grillick two hours to stitch me up and get my blood pressure under control.

"If the sword were two inches more to the left we would be jettisoning your corpse into space," Grillick grumbled in the infirmary.

On day 90 I stood within the dark recess of my doorway when Menjaro arrived again. He did not seem pleased. This time Vanth summoned Grillick to the meeting, but when I asked him what was going on he brushed me aside and muttered something about his "geometric tribulometer being on the fritz". I had no idea what he was talking about but the look on his face told me something bad had happened. I found myself wondering what messages Menjaro was bringing them.

Day 173

On Day 102 I graduated from skirmishing. Despite a broken nose, near fatal stab wound and an accidental gunshot to the thigh, I came out of training relatively unscathed. Vanth praised me as being one of his "best students he had seen in a long time". Grillick brought me aboard his ship and bought me a drink. Grog was his usually grumpy self that day until Grillick dropped a silver coin on the desk and his expression changed.

"How can I help you fine gentlemen?" he beamed.

"I need a glass of your finest Kamilian wine for my friend here," Grillick said.

Grog studied me and rubbed his scaly chin. "Um, are you sure about that?"

Grillick insisted. Grog reluctantly slid a goblet of golden liquid across the counter. I should have heeded his warning because after that I blacked out until morning. I woke up the next day with the worst headache of my life. My lungs felt like I had swallowed ten pounds of ash. Grillick entered my room and simply stated, "It'll pass" before dragging me to Vanth's office. When I arrived Vanth looked at me and shook his head disapprovingly.

"This isn't the best day to be suffering from the ill effects of alcoholic beverages," he grunted.

I tried to run the alcohol-induced fog from my eyes. "How did you know?"

"I know everything," he stated matter-of-factly.

For the next 72 days I learned the art of "transcendence"—the ability to leave one's body and become one with the universe. For the first week all I did was sit cross-legged in the middle of the octagon with my eyes closed and my mind clear of all "impure" thoughts. The first three days of that week all I could think about was how much my legs were cramping. On the fourth day my stomach cramped along with my legs. By the end of the week I had been convinced I learned nothing but how to sit cross-legged in the middle of an octagon trying not to fart.

The next week we did the same thing with one exception. Vanth decided to pump sounds of battle over the loud speaker. I tried to clear my thoughts but it was awfully hard with the sounds of people being shot, bludgeoned or stabbed to death coming from all around me in stadium surround sound. By the end of the week I wondered if I would go insane.

During the third week Vanth pumped images of the universe around me, giving me the sensation of floating in space. That week he wanted me to clear my mind with my eyes open. He told me to start by focusing on the single brightest star and hold my gaze until the universe started to vanish around it. Once that had been accomplished he asked me what I saw. At first all I could see was the one star. The next day he asked me the same question but that time the star had been twinkling. I responded, "A twinkling star." He narrowed his eyes and dismissed me for the day. The following day he asked me the same question. As I stared at the twinkling star it started to expand and a hole formed in the middle, turning it into some kind of cosmic donut.

"A cosmic donut," I responded.

By the end of the week the star was no longer a star. It wasn't even a cosmic donut. It was a portal. A dark frame encircled what appeared to be a smaller universe swirling inside. It was the most beautiful thing I had ever seen.

"Close your eyes," Vanth commanded.

I did as he asked. At first I saw nothing but complete blackness. After several seconds passed, the portal appeared in my vision. Shocked, I closed my eyes tighter but the vision remained.

"What do you see?" Vanth asked.

"A door," I responded. "A portal leading to another universe."

The lights came on and I opened my eyes. Vanth entered the room and for the first time since I met him he smiled. "Amazing!" he exclaimed. "It has been a long time since I have met another like you." He placed both hands on his staff and leaned his chin against the lantern. "Another human, what are the chances?" he breathed.

"I'm sorry, did you say 'another human?'" I asked with confusion.

Sergeant Cantrell burst through the door, breathless. "Sir, we have a situation!"

Vanth turned, his smile fading into a deep scowl. "What have I told you about interrupting during training?"

Cantrell cringed and looked torn. "I know sir, I'm sorry... but... but... your presence is required in your office."

Vanth let out a long sigh before turning to me. "I'm sorry, Nathan, but it seems we must conclude our training for today. We will begin again in the morning." He followed Cantrell into his office and slammed the door shut but it didn't catch and hung ajar.

I was excited and confused by Vanth's announcement. I was glad I passed but I wanted to learn more about the mysterious human he mentioned. Excitement gave way to curiosity as I stared at the partially open door. Muffled voices came from inside and they seemed agitated. I crept to the door. I felt guilty about eavesdropping but as the voices became more agitated I strained to make out what they were saying. Several voices started shouting at each other in unison and I no longer needed to strain to hear what they were saying.

"This is terrible news. Terrible indeed," Grillick's mousy voice cracked over the others.

The voices died away when Vanth spoke. "Menjaro, can this be confirmed?"

"Vigil has first-hand knowledge of the situation," Menjaro responded. "He relayed everything to me and requested I share this information with you." He paused and took a breath. "Do you think I would have brought him with me if this wasn't important?"

"Is the boy ready for this?" Cantrell asked.

"I'm worried what will happen if we tell him," Grillick added.

"The Ascended have struck a blow that will cripple the Consortium," Vanth noted. "Not only that, but they decimated the Insurgents while doing it. This is dire news indeed."

My heart dropped as fast as my jaw. *Decimated the Insurgents.* Immediately my concern turned toward my friends. "No!" I cried and threw open the door.

Inside everyone grew silent. All heads turned to me. "NO!" I repeated, as if for some reason they didn't hear me the first time. I studied their faces. Grillick looked stunned. Cantrell looked irate. Menjaro fixed me with eyes of sadness. Vanth simply stared with those murky eyes of his. However, there had been a newcomer in the group. It was the *him* whom Menjaro referred to earlier. When I saw him a familiar anger rushed forward. Even using all of Vanth's training it was hard to restrain. To see him again after all that happened was too much to bear. I growled between clenched teeth. "What the hell is he doing here?" When I took a step forward, he took a step back, unsure of my intent.

It was *Kale*—Council member of the Consortium.

DECEPTION

Cantrell grabbed my arm to restrain me. I was so close I could see myself in the mirrored finish of Kale's helmet. My head looked like a football and my contorted look of rage made me appear as something straight out of a nightmarish funhouse.

"Back off son!" Cantrell shouted.

"No!" I exclaimed. "You don't understand what he is. He is one of them!" I cried, pulling against Cantrell's grip. "Earth is gone because of him."

"It's not his fault," Vanth responded. "Contain your rage, Nathan. Remember your teachings!"

I ceased struggling and Cantrell loosened his grip. I closed my eyes and drew in deep breaths, as I had been taught. I felt the rage roll back like the tide. When I opened my eyes Kale was unbuckling the restraints around his helmet and removed it. His hair was nothing more than a blue stripe running down the middle of his head. On each side of the stripe the skin was dark and cracked like a desert floor. The lower half of his face was covered by a tan bandanna like some bandit from the Old West. He looked over his angular nose and studied me. His golden eyes scrutinized me. "I am not who you think I am."

"Who are you, then?"

He looked at Vanth who nodded softly. "I am Scribe the Chronicler."

"The Chronicler?" I repeated. "Does that mean you are—?"

"Yes," he confirmed and held up one of his gloved hands. "I am one of the Timeless."

"Where is the real Kale?" I asked dubiously.

"Dead," he responded coldly. "When the opportunity presented itself, Moro assassinated him."

"Moro?" I asked.

"There is no time to explain," Vanth interrupted. "We used the opportunity presented us to infiltrate the Consortium. Meta had already planned to attack Earth before we could get to Kale. The important part is the news he brings."

"What happened to the Insurgents?" I demanded.

Scribe shook his head. Without looking at me he told his story. "Satou and Vigil agreed that it would be best if they moved their base from Xajax to Vaire. Despite the planet's loyalty to the Consortium in the past, their allegiance was tenuous at best. The leadership on Vaire had not been pleased to learn of the events on Earth. Unfortunately before they could gather their full strength the Ascended attacked. Most of Vaire's defense forces were far away on Consortium missions. The Ascended swarmed the planet. The Insurgents made a valiant defense against the Scarlet Moon's air attack but the combined ground forces of Janero's men of metal and the Lumagom overwhelmed them. Vanth and Lianne doubled back with their ships to rescue as many people as they could but it was too late."

"What about the Consortium?" I asked in disbelief. "Wouldn't they come to the defense of one of their own?"

Scribe shook his head. "Once they found out they were harboring the Insurgents, they were outcast."

"What about my friends?"

Scribe and Menjaro exchanged glances. Menjaro looked at Vanth who studied the floor with his forehead against his staff. "You must tell him," he said slowly.

"As far as I know, Lianne and Kedge are with Vigil, regrouping on Sanctum. The good news is the Erudites have offered their support to what's left of the insurgency." Scribe licked his lips and tapped the helmet against his leg. "With that news though, I am sad to report Embeth is missing."

"Satou?" I asked with trepidation.

Scribe shook his head. "Vigil told me how fiercely he battled with the Ascended and it was his courage that allowed your friends to escape."

Tears burned the corners of my eyes but I closed them and willed them away. I knew deep down what news was coming before it came but I had no place for tears, not anymore. I kept them shut when Scribe continued.

"I'm sorry, Nathan. Satou was killed."

Suddenly I willed everyone in the room away. I called upon what Vanth had taught me. I focused on his words during day 21 of combat training: *You will never again fight on behalf of revenge. Revenge is an act of passion which is an emotion that needs to be controlled. Fight for vengeance. Vengeance is an act of justice.*

"Nathan, are you OK?" It was Vanth. For the first time since we met I sensed a bit of concern in his voice.

I opened my eyes and calmly looked around the room. Cantrell stared at me with his lips tight, as if he was bracing for an emotional explosion. Vanth studied me with his cloudy eyes. Grillick fixed me with a concerned look. He clenched and unclenched his fists rapidly as if he were squeezing an invisible stress ball. Menjaro looked at me evenly. Scribe tugged on his bandanna and blinked rapidly as if he were trying to keep dust out of his eyes. Despite the difference in expressions they all seemed to be waiting for one thing. My response.

"Nathan is gone," I replied icily.

Grillick formed a comical *O* with his lips. Menjaro's expression didn't change. Cantrell frowned. Scribe stopped tugging at the bandana. It wasn't until I glanced at Vanth that I knew my path had been laid before me. A small smile played at the corner of his lips in silent acknowledgement. It was time for me to take the first step and say the words.

"He was a boy, an explorer and the Cartographer." The words left my lips like molasses from a bottle, sliding slowly from my mouth. "That was before. Before they took everything from me." I locked my eyes on Vanth's and he nodded. "My name is Vengeance. I will destroy all of them."

Everyone exchanged unsure glances with each other, everyone except Vanth. He crossed his arms and smiled.

"Now you are ready."

A New Beginning

When Grillick's ship landed on Vaire unopposed I had to admit it caught me by surprise. When he told me there had been no onboard stealth capability I was positive Corvus would come at us with everything he had. Grillick simply smiled his dwarvish smile and pointed at me with his sausage fingers.

"You cannot even begin to contemplate my chicanery," he boasted, puffing his chest out like the world's ugliest peacock. "Failure to plan is a plan for failure!"

The ramp descended onto a sprawling sandy field with few trees nearby. They resembled palm trees but with thicker trunks, smaller trees and no coconuts. On the horizon I spotted foam white caps atop waves of sapphire. "I suppose I am now a firm believer in your chicanery," I conceded.

"The ocean beyond is the kingdom of the Hydrophants," Grillick explained, following my gaze.

"Hydrophants?"

Grillick paused. "Your friend Satou was a Hydrophant. They represent the aquatic species of Vaire."

The emotional pain stabbed my heart when the name was spoken. *Use your emotions as a tool to strike down your enemies*, Vanth's ghostly voice whispered from my mind.

Before we landed, Grillick handed me a suit which resembled an aqua-blue scuba diving wetsuit. When I asked what it was he responded with a diatribe of technical jargon that continued until I thought my ears would bleed. When he saw my confusion he changed his explanation so those of us who weren't billion-year-old scientists could understand. "It will protect you from the arid climate of the Badlands, otherwise known as the desert land of the Shreen."

"So how bad is the situation?" I asked.

Grillick led me off the ramp. He removed a square piece of glass no bigger than a credit card from his pocket and inserted it into a slot alongside the ramp. A three dimensional holographic image popped up about four feet from the ramp. The image showed an area of the desert that seemed to be some sort of oasis. Several of the strange palm-like trees were gathered in a semicircle around a dark blue pond no bigger than an average swimming pool. Around the water broken stones protruded from the ground like teeth. Several people were gathered around the pond. Two people sat on the stones as the others gathered around them. The entire image was bathed inside the bluish hue of the holographic projector giving it an eerie aquatic look, as if the entire scene were taking place under the ocean. I recognized Calypso and Corvus as two of the people standing. Several Scarlet Moon soldiers armed with rifles circled them. I recognized them from the bulky sashes that they wore around their waist, marked with the insignia of their group.

The two people seated before them were Hydrophants with their hands shackled behind their back. Standing behind them were two creatures which could only be Shreen. I had been briefed on their tribal history as well as their ferocity in battle but I never in my wildest dreams imagined their hideousness. Their grotesquely oversized claws clutched enormous battle axes which were at least as long as javelins. They rested them over their shoulders and listened to Corvus addressing the Hydrophants.

"I would love to hear what he was saying," I muttered.

Grillick held up his index finger. "Ask and ye shall receive." Next to the slot on the ramp was a switch which he pushed up like a dimmer switch. The holographic scene was soon accompanied by sound.

"You are forcing me to do this," Corvus stated to the nearest Hydrophant. "Your planet provides a strategic location to strike at Caelum. Your allegiance with the Consortium is just a ruse. I know you are upset with their actions of late. I can see through it, so why not join your forces with mine?"

The Hydrophant, slightly smaller than Satou and with shorter tentacles fixed his hard eyes on Corvus. "Because of what you did to our people," he replied icily. "Your 'allies' as you so eloquently refer to them are nothing but murderers and criminals. Vaire is proud. Vaire is strong. But Vaire will not align with you."

Calypso moved in between them. "Please," he urged. "You know me, Ajox! Vaire is critical to victory and I promise your planet will be spared in the upcoming battle. We will only use the planet as a flyover base. I promise no war will touch Vaire soil."

Ajox turned his head slowly. His eyes locked on Calypso's and he uttered a dry laugh. "Your promises are as empty as your soul, traitor."

Calypso turned and looked at Corvus with a frown. The image faded. "What happened?" I asked.

Grillick smacked the machine and cursed under his breath. "Infernal machine," he grumbled. "Remind me to liquidate the mechanic." He paused and scratched his head. "Delete that last remark. I'm the damn mechanic!" Suddenly restless, he rubbed his hands together. "This is much worse than I thought."

"What's wrong?" Seeing Grillick nervous made *me* nervous.

"Corvus managed to gain the trust of the Shreen. This is not good." He looked across the desert. "The meeting is taking place just over that dune." He pointed toward a hill approximately a quarter of a mile away. "You must stop them before Vaire falls."

"But you saw what happened. Ajox will never submit," I argued.

"Vaire will fall with or without his consent," Grillick explained. "His death will be no different from his submission. In the end Corvus will get what he desires."

Sergeant Cantrell exited the ship carrying several items. He described each as he handed them over to me. "Strap this on your wrist," he said and handed me a wide metal bracelet attached to a glove. The brace was forged from a thick metal which was bulky and awkward at first until my wrist could adjust to the weight. At the top of the bracelet there was a metal cavity where something no bigger than a pencil could fit inside. The glove had small, metal disks stitched into the fingers. "This item is called a *voltaic chain*." He attached it to my wrist and I proceeded to slip my hand into the glove. "The metal disks on the fingers are contacts," he explained. "Squeeze your hand so your fingers touch the palm."

I did as asked and a gray metallic chain erupted from the cavity and extended three feet in front of me before dropping to the ground. As soon as it hit the ground it became charged with electricity. The dull humming sound reminded me of power lines. "Whoa," was the only word I could manage as I flicked my wrist to the left and right. The chain moved like a snake along the ground. "Vanth never trained me on this."

"That's because he didn't want you killing yourself in the process," Grillick warned. "One incorrect move of the wrist and we will be replacing another appendage."

I stopped and opened my hands. The chain retracted into the bracelet. Cantrell handed me a round black cylinder about the size of an egg. It had a pull tab similar to a soda can except it was located on the side except the top. "Slide that into your belt loop there," he said, pointing to a loop near the belt buckle.

I slipped it in and made sure it sat snugly. "So what's this?" I asked once I secured it.

"To activate it all you need to do is pull the tab," he replied grimly. "But be careful, we call it the 'last resort'."

"Do I even want to know?" I grumbled.

"Basically, if you are going to use it then you are already dead," Grillick explained somberly. "Once you pull that tab you will have about five seconds to make your peace with whatever god you believe in."

I tapped it lightly with my index finger and swallowed. "Okay, I understand."

Cantrell glanced at Grillick with an expression that looked to be a mix of indigestion and irritation. "Are you sure you want me to give him this?" He held up a multi-colored cube with a small green button on top. It reminded me of the Rubik's Cube I had back on Earth, but about half the size.

Grillick nodded. "Yes. It could prove to be useful."

I took it from Cantrell and stuck it in another belt loop. "Please don't tell me this is a second 'last resort'. I might take that as a lack of confidence in my ability to complete the mission," I remarked dryly.

Grillick rubbed his stubby fingers together anxiously. "Let's just say it's a fail-safe in case you don't feel like dying." He quit rubbing his fingers together and fidgeted with his beard instead. He looked at the cube eagerly. "I just hope it works better than my Mechanical Gene Sequencer."

I glanced at him nervously. "What happened with that?"

Grillick looked as if he just ate something bad. "All I have to say is we are still looking for the remains of Test Subject number four. But that is neither here nor there. I can say with 97.4 percent accuracy that the cube will work as intended."

"This is the last," Cantrell muttered and held out a communicator no bigger than a deck of cards. "It works just like a cellular phone. Just push the yellow button on the side and talk to communicate with us. If you turn it sideways and adjust the dial on the bottom, it acts like a pair of binoculars. Its range is one thousand yards which should give you plenty of room to scout."

"Our scanners are not picking up any Shreen in the area with the exception of those on the other side of the dune," Grillick added. "You should be clear all the way to the oasis."

"What do I need to do once I get there?" I asked.

"Stay out of sight, whatever you do," Grillick urged. "Try to gather as much information as you can." He started up the ramp but turned before reaching the top. "If possible try to save Ajox just don't go getting yourself killed in the process."

"Easier said than done," I grumbled. Cantrell remained at the bottom of the ramp, studying me intently. "What?" I asked with minor irritation.

He held up his hand innocently. "I just wanted to give you some partin' words of wisdom, if you wanna call it that." He motioned toward the weapon strapped to my wrist. "That weapon will take down an Orgellian landshark. The Shreen, however, are a completely different foe." He folded his arms across his chest and stared past me toward the horizon. "It's believed that they fight even after death."

"Are you messing with me?" I asked, narrowing my eyes suspiciously.

He shook his head firmly. "No. Prior to coming under Grillick's employ I was a mercenary for hire. Back in those days I fought more people than I could count and killed more than I care to remember." He took a deep breath. "Anyway... without boring you with details, I had an assignment on Vaire. An expedition of researchers from Charr had been killed by the Shreen while trying to disable weapons which had been left behind. I was hired by the Hydrophants to go in and get the weapons back from the Shreen, who had confiscated the cache. I managed to sneak in unopposed and grab the case, but I didn't get out unnoticed. Two of them engaged me in combat. The only way I survived was one of them accidentally beheaded the other during the fight. While he was stunned at what he had done I shoved a frag grenade down the other's throat."

"Well, I'd say you escaped that battle pretty easily," I said, smiling broadly.

Cantrell scowled. He pulled his left pant leg out of his boot and rolled it up. A thick, angry scar ran from his ankle to his inner thigh. "This was done by the one who was beheaded. He had no goddamn head and still managed to shove his claw into my leg before he stopped moving completely. I nearly bled to death," he explained. "The only way I survived was by tearing off my shirt, tying off the wound and securing what was left of my shirt to the handle of the cache. I dragged it *and* my ass halfway to my ship. If it wasn't for my pilot spotting me laying half-dead in the desert, I wouldn't be here right now."

The smile fell from my face. "I'm sorry."

"Don't be sorry, be diligent," he shouted gruffly. "Absorb what I just said and maybe you will come out of this mission with all your limbs intact." He scowled at my right hand. "Well most of them."

I nodded and headed toward the dune before he stopped.

"One more thing," he said. "If you do find yourself backed into a corner with no way out, just remember that the 'last resort' is truly a last resort. You only get one chance to make a first mistake." He walked up the ramp and entered the ship.

Death is just a portal which leads to the next journey. Vanth taught me that during my first month of training, right after I almost died fighting four of his holograms. I scampered across the desert like a scorpion. As I approached the dune I pondered what I would do once I reached the oasis. There may never be another opportunity to eliminate Corvus. Stopping him would be a great step toward ending this entire conflict.

When I reached the dune I noticed it was actually made of stone, and much bigger than originally thought. The rocky outcropping rose about thirty meters high. Centuries of windblown sand eroded the surface enough where footholds pockmarked the angled surface which allowed for a much easier ascent.

When I reached the top I heard several voices below. Corvus and his troupe dotted the landscape below. I grabbed the binoculars for a closer look.

From my current position I was able to see the entire landscape. Shai's ship was off to the side, behind a group of trees, but he was nowhere to be seen. Behind the ship stood a smaller vessel which may have belonged to either Corvus or Calypso. It resembled an Explorer's League vessel which may have been commandeered during a raid. I also noted that one of the Shreen left, leaving one standing behind the Hydrophants. That would prove to be a godsend if I were forced to engage them.

I carefully made my way down the hill until I came to a large, round boulder sticking from the hill like an oversized zit. After propping myself against it I studied the scene through the binoculars. Calypso was still speaking with Ajox but I couldn't quite make out the words. There were only four Scarlet Moon soldiers standing behind him and Corvus. The rest must have returned to the ship. *Six Ascended and one Shreen*, I calculated. The odds weren't bad, but then I recalled Cantrell's story about the Shreen. I was torn between the chance to take out the leaders of the Ascended and fear of facing a Shreen warrior. *"Fear makes the enemy bigger than he is,"* Vanth whispered in my brain.

The Shreen's back faced me which would allow me an advantage. *When you face a situation where you are outnumbered, eliminate the biggest threat first.* I closed my hand and the electrified chain fell to the ground with a heavy clang. I winced, expecting the sound to alert the Shreen. He didn't move so I inched forward, dragging the chain behind me.

I weaved my way around the boulder but before I could pass a river of sand and rocks flowed past my feet. I turned around but it was too late. Something flat, hard and heavy slammed into my jaw knocking me down the hill. The world spun out of control. The sky gave way to the ground only to become sky again as

I rolled down the hill. The world eventually stopped spinning when I slammed into the soft earth many yards below.

"Wow, that's gonna leave a mark," I remarked before spitting out a mouthful of sand. I jumped to my feet as soon as I came to my senses. Fortunately the chains returned to the bracelet when my hand opened during the fall so I escaped serious injury but my face felt as if it had been hit by a bus. I looked up to see the second Shreen crawling down the hill. "Go big or go home I guess," I muttered.

"Nathan?" It was Calypso who spoke. I stepped sideways so I could see him but be able to keep an eye on the advancing Shreen. "What are you doing here?"

I closed my hand and he took a step back when the chain appeared. With a deep breath I locked on his eyes. *The eyes often betray a man's intentions*. The tone of my voice was even, just as Vanth taught. *Be the calm before the storm*. "I'm here to put an end to this."

"Get out of here, boy," Ajox growled. "Whatever suicidal task yer plannin' is sheer madness."

The Scarlet Moon soldiers raised their weapons. The Shreen standing behind the Hydrophants lowered his axe and took a menacing step forward. The other Shreen sidestepped his way down the hill, axe in hand.

"I gave you every chanced to join us," Corvus fumed. "I have no choice but to eliminate you from the equation."

"*Wait!*"

Shai exited the ship. In front of him stood a woman with a hood over her head and her hands bound in front of her. In his right hand was the same sword he used on Kedge. "Don't kill him yet," he purred. He poked the sword in the woman's back and led her down the ramp. "I want him to see this." They reached the bottom of the ramp and he pulled off the hood. Even though her head was lowered, I could see it was Deena.

I took a step toward him. The chain followed me, raising sparks as I pulled it across the rough sand. Before I could get close, Scarlet Moon soldiers blocked my path with their rifles raised. In my peripheral vision I saw that the Shreen had stopped their advance. Apparently they were more interested in seeing what would happen. "Let her go!" I growled.

Shai smiled broadly. It was the smile of the Cheshire Cat; toothy and loaded with mischief. "She missed you while you were gone." They stepped off the ramp and he poked her again with the sword, prodding her forward. "Go ahead dear tell him how much you missed him."

She looked up and the sun shined off her tear-stained face. She used her shoulder to wipe them away. With a final sniff she composed herself. She looked around before locking her eyes on mine. "It's true," she croaked. "I did miss you." Suddenly, she smiled.

Shai appeared amused by the show. He looked over and addressed the crowd. "See Corvus, I told you she would be pleased to see him again."

Corvus did not seem as amused as him. "Stop this stupidity, Shai. We have more important matters at hand."

He approached me and I raised the chain to strike. Before I could bring it down I felt something close around my throat. I dropped to one knee, confused. The closest person to me was Corvus but he was at least ten feet away. I clawed at my throat, trying to pry away hands that weren't there. Gasping I struggled with my throat while Corvus approached slowly with a smile.

"You have worn out your welcome, Cartographer," he sneered. "We will crush the Consortium. Your Insurgent friends will follow. The universe will belong to me!"

My legs gave way and I collapsed, struggling to draw breath. Fear took over until Vanth appeared before me like an illusion. A single word fell from his lips before he vanished: *Remember.* I closed my eyes and did as he commanded. *Fear is the strongest emotion of all. It feeds upon the concept of death, Nathan. If you refuse to fear death then you starve fear. Only then can you truly conquer it.* I was about to die. I needed to not fear it. I opened my eyes and willed myself to my feet.

Corvus' eyes widened with surprise. Once I overcame the fear, his psychokinetic ability was useless. *Is this what humans become in the future?* I remembered what Sam told me about the experiments using autistic children. Do I even want to be a part of an Earth like that? Horrified, I took a step toward him and raised the voltaic chain above my head.

"No, this is impossible," he gasped.

I heard a scream and looked in Shai's direction. The blade of his sword protruded from Deena's midsection. The distraction was enough for Corvus to knock me to my knees again. I felt the crushing weight of invisible hands around my throat. All of a sudden, everything moved in slow motion as I struggled to regain control. Deena fell to the ground while her lifeblood fell from Shai's sword in scarlet raindrops. Fury unlike any I had ever experienced before bubbled to the surface. I regained control and sprang to my feet, lashing out with the chain. My intended target was Corvus but an unfortunate Scarlet Moon soldier got between us. The chain snaked around his legs and I pulled him down. A loud hum filled the air as the electric charge fed on its prey. The soldier's bloodcurdling scream penetrated the otherwise silent oasis. The odor of cooked flesh filled my nostrils as the charge coursed through his body.

Before the other soldiers could fire on me, Corvus lunged. I felt cold metal touch my throat as he fell on me. He had a dagger in his hand and a madness in his eyes. "It's time for you to die," he growled through clenched teeth.

My hand fell to my waist and touched the 'last resort'. My finger found the tab. The Shreen moved in closer. They seemed entertained by the show. The remaining Scarlet Moon soldiers gathered around us as well. Apparently no one wanted to miss

Corvus cut my throat. I fingered the tab with the realization that I could take them all out with one simple flick of the wrist. *Death is just a doorway to another journey.* "I guess it's time to see if you were right Vanth," I whispered.

Before I could pull the tab I was showered in blood. Most of the coppery liquid fell into my mouth and I gagged. Corvus' eyes were wide saucers of surprise. A double-bladed knife was stuck through his throat. He gasped and tried to speak but the words formed bloody bubbles on his lips. The knife was pulled out in a spray of blood and he collapsed next to me. Calypso stood over us, clutching the murder weapon.

I wiped as much of the blood from my mouth as I could with the back of my hand. "What the hell?" I cried in surprise.

"You are probably wondering why I did that," Calypso mused while using Corvus' shirt to wipe the blood from his dagger.

Shai approached, sliding his sword into his belt. "It's done."

Calypso nodded and looked at the object I held in my hand. "What's that?"

I pressed the button on the cube and nothing happened. Calypso and Shai laughed. Shai waved his hands in the air, feigning surrender. "I give up," he mocked.

"Dammit, Grillick," I muttered. I turned it over in my hand. A word was written on the side; *THROW*! Shocked, I threw the cube to the ground where it split like an egg. Three metal legs folded outward from the center which caused the cube to flip over forming something similar to a camera tripod. Shai and Calypso took a step back when the cube collapsed on itself, revealing a fourteen inch barrel. Bullets flew. I ducked out of the way and so did Shai and Calypso. The Scarlet Moon soldiers weren't so lucky when the barrel pivoted in a 360 degree arc, cutting through them like wheat. The Hydrophants jumped into the pond, leaving one of the Shreen wide-open. He took several shots to the chest and stumbled backwards. The other Shreen managed to get his lobster claws in front of him, protecting his torso. His claws were so well armored that it was no more effective than it would have been had I been tossing M&M's at him. This did provide me with one important tactical advantage, however. Everyone had been so concerned with dodging bullets that they were no longer concerned about me. *STRIKE NOW.* Vanth's voice shouted at me from the back of my mind.

I closed my hand and the chain fell to the ground, crackling with blue fire. Shai was preoccupied, cowering on the ground with his face pressed into the sandy earth. The turret stopped firing and I struck. I ignored Calypso and wrapped the chain around his throat. His scream was ear-splitting. His eyes bulged to the point I thought they would simply pop from their sockets. Calypso jumped out of the way and ran for his ship. He threw one final horrified look our way before ducking into the ship. I pulled the chain with all my might. All of my hatred, all of my anger flowed through me. The muscle I packed on during training bulged from my biceps as I tugged harder. I didn't stop. Even when I heard the tearing sound I refused to stop. With a final pull, he gasped for his life. "DIE!" I growled before I fell backwards with a thud. The chain snapped back into place just as Shai's head rolled past.

Gunfire erupted behind me, but I didn't care. My rage had consumed me. I leapt on his head and pounded it repeatedly. I didn't stop when his eyes popped out of his sockets. I didn't stop when his nose was nothing more than shredded flesh. I didn't stop when Calypso flew past in Shai's ship. I didn't even stop when I heard my name.

"*Nathan!*"

I continued pounding as I thought of Satou, Deena, Wraith and my missing hand. More flesh tore from his skull, more bone splintered yet I continued pounding. Bone became embedded in the metal joints of my prosthetic hand yet I continued pounding. I pounded until someone grabbed my wrist. Chunks of flesh and bone fell from my knuckles.

"*Nathan!*" The voice shouted again.

I turned my fury on my newest attacker. Before I could land a single blow I looked into a familiar face filled with horror. I became convinced that the person must have been an apparition, because it was impossible to comprehend their existence at that time. I collapsed in their arms, overwhelmed from exhaustion. I looked up again and squinted against the sun's brightness, watching as the expression of horror softened into a warm smile. I never felt more relieved to see someone. It felt good to see her again.

Lianne.

THE AFTERMATH

The Shreen soon joined the Scarlet Moon in death. The shot-blocking Shreen ended up with a ragged, charred hole in his face for his trouble. His pal was on the ground not far from him, bloodied and lifeless. While surveying the carnage several winged beasts flew past me with their crude weapons clutched in their claws. They were escorted by Vayne and his merry band of "mini-Vayne" crewmembers, armed with hand cannons.

"It's the Quark!" I blurted.

Urlan approached with a bemused Vigil on his heels. Urlan bowed but with his oversized wings it made the gesture appear awkward. "We meet again," his gravelly voice cracked. When he spoke it sounded like an angry landslide.

"Look what we have here," Vigil crooned. A smile played at the corner of his lips. "When Vanth updated me on your progress I didn't believe it first." He surveyed the scene. "Now that I see what happened here, it appears I was wrong."

Lianne touched the side of my face. "Are you hurt?"

I wiped my face with the back of my hand and it came back sticky with blood. "It's his," I said, motioning to the corpse of Corvus. I slid my index finger along the base of my throat and winced. It too came back sticky with blood. "I'm afraid this is mine."

"Well at least you made it through the fight without someone trying to turn you into a cyborg," a voice growled behind me. Kedge stood behind me with his arms folded across his chest. "Yeah the gang's all here. Don't go getting all mushy on me."

I was pleased to see my old friends but my happiness was short-lived when I looked past them. Deena's body was being examined by One of Vayne's crewmembers.

"Get away from her," I screamed and ran to her. The crewmember jumped back with a look of alarm.

I cradled her head in my arms. Despite the desert heat she was cold to the touch. Where her face was once warm and vibrant it was now pale and lifeless. Her eyes looked blankly to the sky as if searching the heavens for an answer to the injustice of her murder. Although I felt a familiar burning at the corner of my eyes I refused to weep. Vanth spoke up from the recesses of my mind. *Do not weep for your friends in death, Nathan. They no longer bear the burdens life thrusts upon all her victims. Their soul's voyage to the afterlife is a voyage we all must face.*

"Except you, Vanth," I whispered. "Except for you and your *Timeless*." I pushed the thought aside as quickly as it came. I didn't need anger either. Anger was nothing more than a tool without a job, like a hammer without nails.

Lianne's hand fell on my shoulder. "I'm so sorry, Nathan."

I lowered my head and closed my eyes. "Calypso got away." I let the statement linger for a moment before continuing. "If you truly care, then help me destroy him."

Her hand fell from my shoulder. "I will," she responded firmly. She paused. "Don't forget about the Consortium too, Nathan. We must deal with them as well."

"By my calculations it is indeed a conundrum," a voice squeaked. I looked up from Deena's face to see Grillick approaching. "Oh I do so love conundrums. To solve the equation presented we will simply reflect our focus from one enemy to another."

Lianne glanced at him uncertainly. "Um, okay, so what does that mean?"

Grillick eyes filled with sadness when he looked at Deena's corpse. "It simply means our enemies remain the same. I have spoken with Ibune and she called for an assembly."

I laid Deena's head gently on the ground and I ran my fingers over her eyes, shutting them forever. When I slid my hand from behind her head, Lianne winced when she saw that my right hand was not what I had originally been born with. She remained silent on the subject, however.

"An assembly of what?" I asked. Exhaustion began to creep into my voice. I was emotionally as well as physically drained.

"For the first time in centuries we will have a formal gathering of the Timeless," Grillick explained. "We have been summoned and will meet aboard her ship."

"So what does this assembly mean?" asked Lianne.

"It means that this conflict veers dangerously close to something we are trying to avoid." Vigil explained enigmatically as he approached. "The Twelve are meeting in order to come to a consensus."

Vigil reached down and pick up the corpse of Deena. The care he put into it went against the assumptions I had made based on past interactions with him. He did it with the kindness of a father. When he looked at me his eyes were full of sympathy.

"We will take care of her." He walked towards Grillick's ship.

"Wait a minute," I exclaimed and started to follow them. "Where is he going with her?"

Grillick placed his hand on my arm. "We are born of the universe," he explained. "That is where we must return. She will be given the proper rite of passage to her next destination."

I watched as Vigil loaded her into the back of something Grillick referred to as an all-terrain skiff. The vehicle was nothing more than a Humvee with tank treads instead of tires. Sergeant Cantrell was behind the wheel. With a heavy heart I watched as they continued over the hill toward the ship.

"So what now?" I mumbled.

"The Timeless are coming," Grillick replied. "Let's go back to the Gordian Knot and wait for their arrival."

"The *what*?" I raised an eyebrow.

He threw me a bushy smile. "What? I forgot to tell you what she was called? It's the name of my ship. Just the process of naming her was a conundrum upon itself. But alas, that is a story for another day. Come, we have important work to do."

As we walked back to his ship we passed the turret. Grillick stopped and squatted next to it. "It worked! My Tri-Fold Inverted Plasma Turret worked!" He exclaimed as he flipped a switch underneath. The weapon folded into itself, reverting back to the cube. "Eureka!" He cried before shoving the cube into his pocket.

When we reached the entrance ramp we found Cantrell waiting with his arms crossed. On the far side of the ship, Vigil drove the skiff up a different ramp and out of view. An icy scowl was glued to his face when he saw Kedge. "I thought that was you. I didn't think I'd ever see you again."

Kedge met the scowl with one of his own. "It's been a long time, Cantrell. Which garbage scow have you crawled from?"

"It's good to see you haven't lost your sense of humor." Cantrell said before reaching into a scabbard attached to his belt. He withdrew a knife and I tensed. I relaxed slightly when he started picking at his fingernails with the blade. "So, where are all those mewling ladies you used to hang out with? You called them soldiers, I believe. I always thought they were more like prancing knuckle draggers."

There was a pistol strapped to Kedge's side. His hand rested on the handle. *This was a situation that was about to go south fast*, I worried. I had to diffuse it fast.

"How about we concentrate our efforts on locating our enemies instead of comparing the size of our jocks?" I stood between them.

Cantrell eyeballed me. Kedge breathed heavily behind me but remained silent. I breathed a sigh of relief when Cantrell nodded curtly and entered the ship. I hung back with Kedge.

"Why do I get the feeling that you have very few friends in the universe?" I turned to him with a smile.

"You may be right," he chuckled. "Cantrell is nothing more than a rented gun. He cares nothing about causes, only about filling his pockets." His tone softened. "Anyway enough about that. It's good to see you alive."

"It's good to be alive I suppose," I responded sourly.

Kedge laid a hand on my shoulder. "We will have plenty of time to talk later." He looked up the ramp and his expression turned somber. Vigil stood at the top of the ramp waiting for us.

"Ibune's ship has entered the planet's orbit." Vigil rubbed his cheek just under the triangle tattoo. He seemed jumpy. "We will be taking off soon to meet her."

"Are you OK?" I asked.

He stopped rubbing and nodded slowly. "Yeah." He turned abruptly and entered the ship.

Concerned, I turned to Kedge. "What the hell was that all about?"

Kedge's bionic eye hummed as he focused it on the doorway. He stared at it silently for a long time before answering. "I don't know. Let's go find out."

THE MEETING

Kedge left me when we reached Grog's. His large assortment of fine wines lured him away. He decided to hang back and do what he called "sample the stock".

"I thought you kicked the habit?" I asked, remembering his story of alcoholism.

He shrugged. "I have a feeling I'm going to need to be drunk by the time this meeting is over."

I didn't press further. He looked rattled and it took a lot to rattle him. I continued to my room and crawled into bed. I closed my eyes and thought about the upcoming meeting. Deep down I was excited to have the opportunity to meet the other ancient beings known as the Timeless, but a part of me feared the outcome of the meeting. I thought about all those I had met so far: *Grillick the Artificer, Vayne the Liberator, Vigil the Surveyor, Vanth the Adjudicator, Menjaro the Messenger, Scribe the Chronicler.* That was only half of them. I was curious to learn more about the first six, but I was even more interested to learn about the others. Before I could start forming grandiose assumptions about them, I fell asleep.

Shai haunted my dreams. The nightmare of his headless corpse chasing me through the darkened tunnel of Gorganna would have made Irving proud. I focused on the slim sliver of light ahead before realizing that I held his head in my hands. I dropped it in disgust and continued running. By the time I got to the end Shai had retrieved his head and placed it on his shoulder. He reached for me with his hungry mouth open wide. Rows of razor sharp teeth like a shark filled his gaping maw and he reached closer, as if he meant to swallow me whole.

A knock at the door woke me. Drops of cold sweat trickled down my back like icy fingers. I ran my hand through my soaked hair, moving it away from my eyes. I stumbled to the door like a drunken sailor and opened it to see Lianne standing on the other side.

Her face soured when she saw me. "Are you feeling okay?"

I motioned her inside. "I was just trying to take a nap before the big meeting. I'm almost positive I feel better than I look."

Lianne didn't seem to agree. "Sorry for waking you," she responded somberly. "We should be docking with Ibune's ship soon and I wanted to check on you and make sure everything was okay."

I rubbed the cobwebs of sleep from my eyes and laughed dryly. "Sure everything is okie dokie," I replied. "After discovering someone I considered a mentor had been killed by Shai, I received the opportunity to watch while he murdered another person I cared about before my eyes. This all coming before I proceeded to hammer his decapitated head into a pile of slush." I dropped my face into my hands. "Yeah I'm just peachy."

Lianne clucked sympathetically. "I'm sorry, Nathan. I wish everything could just go back to the way it was prior to Calypso's treachery. Maybe then my father would still be alive."

I looked into Lianne's eyes. They sparkled with tears at the mention of her father. "Me too," I muttered. I quickly moved to change the subject. The pain of Deena's death was still fresh and that was a wound I didn't feel like reopening. "I heard Embeth is missing. What happened?"

"When Satou discovered the Ascended had attacked Vaire, he grew furious. He commandeered a Defense Fleet ship and took off from Xajax with a crew of twenty. Embeth knew it was suicide so he tried to gather as many as he could against the advice of Vigil and took off after him." A flash of anger crossed her face. "None of the Timeless volunteered to join him. Vigil decided their time was better spent coming up with an effective strategy to attack Caelum. He felt the Ascended were a needless distraction."

"Well, we all saw how that turned out," I replied sourly.

"I don't want to hate them, Nathan," she said. "I realize we need them if we are to win this conflict. It's becoming hard, though."

I narrowed my eyes and locked on her gaze. "Don't hate them, Lianne. Hatred is an emotion better served in other ways."

She studied me for a long time. "What happened to you?"

I shrugged. "I guess you could say I had my eyes opened. Vanth taught me to control my emotions to better defend myself. He taught me what I needed to know to survive."

Several moments passed in silence. I used that time to pick at the remaining skull fragments embedded in my prosthetic hand while Lianne watched with a sour expression. Several months had passed since we last saw each other and I have changed since. It was almost as if we had to reintroduce ourselves to each other again, like complete strangers.

Lianne turned and looked toward the window. I followed her gaze to see a ship appear outside Vaire's orbit. It was the largest ship I had ever seen, dwarfing even the Astral Spirit. The hull of the ship formed a triangle. The front point glowed with a thousand small cylindrical lights of varying colors. Some were green while others were red. Some were even bright white which gave the ship a Christmas-like appeal. They blinked in conjunction with each other in some sort of signaling pattern. As we approached I could see that the hull had several metal plates which overlapped each other like scale, like a dragon. *A Christmas Dragon ship*, I mused.

"That is one hell of a ship," Lianne acknowledged.

I stood up and flexed my hand to make sure that the last remaining bits of Shai were gone. "It sure is. I bet this will be one hell of a meeting too."

Lianne offered a wry smile. "Let's go find out."

I opened the door to find Gard standing on the other side. He blinked his blue eyes rapidly before addressing us.

"*Oh, excuse me, Nathan, I was just about to knock. Your presence has been requested. Please follow me to the meeting location.*"

On the way we passed Grog's. He was busy smashing a small metal globe with a hammer. Unfortunately the tool didn't seem to have any affect. On his final swing the hammer missed and came down on his left thumb. "DAMN!" he shouted before sticking his wounded digit in his mouth. He tossed us a sour look as we passed. "Move along, this ain't no side show," he grumbled. He picked up the tool and continued hammering at the object.

When we reached the docking bridge connecting us to Ibune's ship I heard Grog cry out again. It seemed another finger had felt the wrath of the hammer. "Lessons are hard learned for some," Lianne muttered. She turned her attention to the bridge and sighed. "Well let's go meet these Timeless folks."

Gard stopped her. "*I'm sorry, Lianne. The Timeless will not allow anyone other than summoned parties into the meeting.*"

Lianne looked at Gard and pursed her lips. She appeared ready to rip his head off, but she backed off. "I'm not sure whether I should be insulted or relieved," she admitted.

I followed Gard through the bridge before coming to an elevator aboard her ship. We entered and the doors closed behind us. On the wall were buttons adorned with strange symbols. I didn't recognize most of them except for one. One of the buttons had a symbol of an ankh.

"The ankh again," I whispered. "What could it mean?"

"*Is something wrong?*"

"Um, no. Well, I mean, not really," I stuttered. "I was just surprised to see an ankh as one of these symbols."

"*What a coincidence*," he responded. "*That is where we must go.*" He pushed the button.

Three other symbols lit up before falling on the ankh. When the button illuminated the doors opened. We stepped out of the elevator and into a large circular room. The ceiling was domed and filled with stars, as if we just stepped into the world's largest observatory. A comet rocketed across the ceiling and I realized I was looking into real-time space, rather than an image. I marveled at the scene.

"Welcome, Nathan."

The voice broke my trance. A woman approached us. Behind her, In the middle of the room, there was an enormous circular table, black like obsidian, with sixteen high-back chairs positioned around it. Eleven people stood in front of eleven chairs. Some of the faces I recognized, others I did not. The slender woman standing before me was not much taller than me with long silver hair which seemed to flow endlessly over her shoulders, smooth bronze skin, full purple lips and a strange tattoo in the center of her forehead. It was made up of a sideways crescent with a large circle above it. The entire tattoo seemed to glow with a radiance of its own. She wore a silver tunic with many symbols embroidered in the fabric. I recognized them as the same ones that were inside the elevator. When she opened her arms wide to welcome me I noticed the ankhs etched on the wide metal bracelets encircling her wrists. I made a mental note to ask about the significance of the ankh.

"My name is Ibune," her voice was soft and melodic. Her words wrapped themselves around me, soothing me. All tension ebbed from my body and a calm peacefulness fell over me. "Come join us." She smiled and motioned me to the closest empty chair. "I will go around the room and introduce everyone."

There was a bronze plaque embedded in the rear of the chair. Carved into the metal were the words "Botha the Explorer". Ibune noticed I stared at the metal plate but said nothing.

The first introduction was Vigil who simply replied with his usual sour look. The second introduction was Grillick who was too busy scratching a screw out of his beard to acknowledge me. Third was Vanth who acknowledged me by a slow nod.

The fourth face was new to me. It was also the most fearsome. He wore a dark metal helmet which ended in a V, completely covering his nose and top half of his face. Sinister scarlet eyes locked on me from behind eyeholes carved from the metal. The lower half of his face was pale-blue with angry scars running along each cheek from lip to eye. He was at least seven feet tall and the ridged armor he wore covered his muscular physique well. To add to his ferocious looks were large blood-red wings which sprouted from his shoulders but were currently folded behind him.

"This is Moro the Exterminator," Ibune continued.

I was taken aback. I shuddered when I realized that he was the person responsible for Kale's assassination. I hoped I would never have to meet him in a dark alley. Ibune smiled warmly before continuing. She moved on to Vayne. He shrugged indifferently and waved his hand for her to move on. After him came Scribe. His expression remained a mystery behind the bandanna he wore.

The next person was another new face. A huge furry one. The next Timeless was a polar bear wearing a sumo mawashi made of metal. Two empty holsters were attached along each side. At first I thought he had antlers like an elk before realizing it was actually a helmet. His piercing azure eyes seemed to stare into my soul. I began to fidget with my foot underneath the table, tapping it incessantly. I wondered if he would leap across the table to sink his fangs into my neck. *Was he hungry*? *Was that his stomach growling*? My mind started to ask ridiculous questions in an effort to drive me batty.

"This is Arcturus the Navigator."

He growled and I remained rigid in my chair. I prepared myself to leap out of the way at his slightest hostile movement. Several long seconds passed while he studied me. Finally he smiled, revealing perfectly white teeth. He transformed from Mor'du to Yogi Bear in mere seconds. When he smiled he appeared as dangerous as a stuffed toy.

"That is nice set of teeth you have there," I chuckled nervously. "You must have one hell of a dentist."

His smile faded and he cocked his head inquisitively. I decided it would be best to lower my sarcasm level. My gaze instead fell to the empty holsters. "I think you are missing something there."

"Weapons are not allowed inside this chamber," Ibune explained. "This is a place for civilized discussion, not violence."

Ibune moved on to the next person who happened to be a Lianth-less Menjaro. Apparently gorilla mounts were not allowed inside the chamber either. Menjaro acknowledged me with a sly grin.

After passing two empty chairs, Ibune moved to the next in line. The next person had a canine face. Although I didn't know dog-face, I recognized him. Depictions of him were plastered in many of my high school history books. He was the spitting image of the ancient Egyptian god Anubis. He was as black as the table with the exception of his eyes which were two globes of pearly white filled with dots of blue. He wore the same crown and cloth tunic as the ancient pharaohs. The persona was complete down to the square, wiry beard attached to his chin.

"This is Horus the Advisor." Ibune moved behind him and smiled. He bowed but remained silent.

Ibune moved past another empty seat before coming to the second to last person in at the table. Moro may have looked evil but this person *radiated* it. The air around him seemed to yellow slightly, as if a sour gas oozed from his pores. Like Horus, he was completely dark-skinned with the exception of glowing yellow eyes which peered at me from behind a pale-green cowl.

He had a matching shawl draped across his shoulders as well as pants to match. Both seemed stitched together from some sort of animal skins. He wasn't very tall and despite his thin, lanky frame I knew better than to underestimate his strength. If his appearance didn't intimidate his enemies, the pole strapped to his back with a faded yellow skull dangling from it just might.

"This is Mortem the Destructor."

I raised an eyebrow. "The Destructor? That doesn't sound very appealing." As soon as the words left my mouth I wished I could take them back.

When he spoke it was raspy and distant, like a voice from the bowels of a grave. "It's not meant to be appealing *human.*" He spat out the last word.

Ibune dropped her hand on his shoulder and he relaxed. It seemed Ibune's calming influence worked on the Timeless as well as it did on me. "Let's move on."

She moved behind the last person and placed her hand on his lower back. If she wanted to reach his shoulder she would have had to climb on a step ladder because he had to stand nearly ten feet tall. His skin was emerald green with a barrel chest and arms as big as tree trunks. His bright red hair was unkempt and wild making it seem like his head was on fire. He shoved his thumbs into his wide leather gun belt (also empty) and fixed his fiery eyes upon me.

"And finally we have Lapiz the Protector."

He acknowledged me with a nod and Ibune took a seat. The others followed. She steepled her fingers underneath her chin and glanced at me. "It has been a long time since we have come together in this room." Her voice floated across the table like snow in a gentle breeze. I found myself hanging on every word, hungering for the next. "It has been even longer since we faced the threat of a war large enough to tear the universe asunder." She spoke to them as a mother figure just as Grillick had described. "I have summoned before us Nathan Chambers, human child from the planet Earth, located in the GX-743 galaxy. Some of you do not know him. Others have heard of him and a few have already interacted with him."

I looked around the room and noticed that the other Timeless hung on to each word as eagerly as I did. At the mention of my name a few murmurs sprang from the crowd. Not all of them had been pleasant. Unperturbed, Ibune continued. "All of you understand that he was a former member of the Consortium who held the title of Cartographer." A few more whispers passed through the group. "You are also aware that the Consortium is failing. It was once an organization that took pride in maintaining balance in the universe through exploration, knowledge and defense. At the time of its formation we agreed to remain in the background while continuing with our individual pursuits. We vowed to remain neutral and stay out of their conflicts as long as they did not threaten us directly. The time for inaction has passed. Meta's leadership is leading the organization down a dark path from which there is no recovery." She turned and looked at me before continuing. "The attack on Earth had been unprovoked and unwarranted. This goes against the very concept on which they were founded."

"That's what we get for empowering mortals with such a task," Mortem grumbled.

Ibune glared at him. He lowered his head and studied the floor. "We are mortal as well, lest you forget." She motioned to the empty chair next to him. "Or do you need a reminder?" Mortem remained silent and I noticed there was a metal plaque embedded in the seat. "Everything I just told you most of you already know. There is one thing, however, I have kept from everyone." All heads turned to her in anticipation. "Several years ago Kell, the previous Cartographer, stumbled across the true map of the universe on planet Andromeda 7. The map had been left behind carelessly by someone who shall remain nameless." Grillick lowered his head and muttered under his breath. "Once

Kell realized the map in his possession was not accurate he started his research at the Archives. At my direction Grillick worked with Kell in modifying the map to not only pinpoint wormhole locations but also design a device that would repair these wormholes."

"Transceivers!" I blurted. The word left my mouth before I could stop it. I looked around, embarrassed.

Ibune didn't seem to mind the interruption. Instead she nodded her acknowledgement. "The Consortium viewed the wormholes as convenient methods of travel either through space or time itself."

"But it was much worse than that," Vigil added.

"Correct," Grillick agreed. "The wormholes are rips in spacetime. If left unchecked they could lead to another universal breakdown."

"Another Big Bang, I suppose?" I asked.

"Precisely," Grillick replied. "Time is a river. Normal wormholes are like pebbles. They hardly affect the flow. Time holes, however, are like boulders. Depending on the size of the time hole, or boulder if you prefer, the flow of time will simply divert around it."

"But if the boulder is large enough, it could stop it," I finished.

Grillick brayed laughter. "See? I told you, Vigil. He's not as dumb as you think." Vigil waved his hand dismissively.

"If time is stopped, so is the universe," Ibune explained. "One cannot exist without the other."

"What does this have to do with me or the war with the Consortium?" I shook my head in confusion.

"Meta views the Ascended as a threat and treats the time holes as an enemy. Destroying a planet does not destroy the hole completely. That is an ineffective method of eradication. Despite this fact, Meta will continue to in his attempts to eliminate them. He does not have patience for the transceivers. In his zeal he will tear apart the universe." Ibune stiffened. Based on her somber expression, I realized she had taken the deterioration of the Consortium personally. There seemed to be more to her story, but I decided to not press that issue.

"What does this have to do with me?" I asked. "Shouldn't you be talking to someone leading an army? I'm just a kid with a robot." I glanced at Gard who lurked quietly in the corner flashing his eyes at us.

Ibune smiled. "You were brought here because of recommendations by your predecessor. I value Kell's input and the decision to bring you into this was not taken lightly, I assure you."

"Kell? I asked dubiously. "You brought me here on the recommendation of a dead man?"

Her smile didn't fade. She touched the table and a holographic screen appeared. Inside the screen was the metallic face of an android woman. When the woman spoke her voice was completely devoid of emotion. "*What is your command?*"

"Please summon our guest," Ibune commanded.

A door behind Vanth slid open like an elevator. A human male walked through the door carrying a book the size of a dictionary.

"*Sam!*"

Sam wandered over looking exhausted. It seemed he had aged ten years from the last time we spoke. "I'm sorry I couldn't tell you, Nathan. We had to see what Calypso had planned."

"What the—," I fumbled for words but failed to come up with a single coherent question. My mind was racing so I closed my eyes and breathed deeply before starting over. "How is this even possible?"

Ibune stood. "All will be explained in due time. It seems you two have a lot of catching up to do. As of right now we have a more important matter to discuss."

I leaned over to Sam and whispered in his ear. "What do you have to do with Kell?"

He smiled. "That's one thing we need to discuss," he whispered in return. Turning his attention to Ibune he nodded. "Yes, we do."

Ibune continued. "Solomon Corvus is dead. Calypso has taken control of his forces but as of yet we do not know what his next move is."

"We must strike now!" Vanth slammed his fist on the table. "We will never receive a more perfect chance to crush the Ascended and switch our attention to the Consortium."

"I disagree," Scribe chimed in. "I overheard what Meta was planning. He wants to rout the Ascended and destroy any planet containing time holes."

"That's insane," I said.

"I feel there may be a more sinister plot afoot," Horus interrupted.

All eyes turned to him. "Please enlighten us." Ibune folded her hands underneath her chin.

"Calypso's murder of Corvus was nothing more than a power grab," he insisted. He has been gaining power behind the scenes while all eyes were fixed on Corvus. I believe he may be attempting to establish some kind of universal empire. Perhaps even a twisted version of the Consortium. He has been gathering allies like flies to a corpse."

"It's true." It was Arcturus who spoke. "Word has spread that Consortium worlds are beginning to defect."

"I have heard these words first hand," Moro growled. "After slaughtering Kale I heard mutterings that of Umbra and Atrora have defected."

"That would be dire news indeed," Grillick squeaked. "The Umbrals were thought to be the strongest of the Consortium's allies."

"This really leaves us no choice." Vigil looked to Ibune for confirmation.

Ibune nodded slowly. She surveyed the room, looking long and hard at each one of them, including me. I swallowed hard, realizing that a decision was about to be made. Their faces were ancient masks of grimness.

"The Insurgents have been decimated by the attack on Vaire. I see no other option." She sighed heavily and paused before continuing. "Peace is no longer an option. I propose we fight alongside the Insurgents." She folded her hands in front of her and rested them on the table. "Cast your vote now."

Mortem was the first one to speak. He had a giddy look about him and I realized that war must have been right up his alley. "Aye!"

"Aye," said Vanth.

"Aye," Grillick squeaked.

Vigil looked down and muttered, "Aye."

"Aye!" Moro roared.

Vayne shook his head. He seemed undecided, as if he was torn between sacrificing himself for the greater good and holing up somewhere with his riches. In the end he choked out an "aye".

Horus also paused for a long time with a furrowed brow. He seemed deep in thought weighing the pros and cons. "Aye," he said after moments passed.

"Aye," Arcturus roared.

"Aye," said Scribe.

"Aye," Menjaro voted.

All eyes turned to the last vote, Lapiz. His closed fists sounded like thunder when he dropped them on the table. "I am the Protector. It is my job to do what must be done to prevent the undoing of the universe." He looked down and let out a heavy sigh. "Aye."

With unanimous consent, the war began.

EPILOGUE

Meta stood alone in the observation room aboard the Astral Spirit. He was busy pondering recent events. His ship along with the remaining Defense Fleet hovered near the Sloan asteroid belt preparing their counter attack on Vaire. When he first received the news that Vaire had fallen to the Ascended he was incredulous. That was until the first confirmed video footage rolled in. His face was grim as he tapped on the window and studied the stars.

"My precognition is failing," he muttered. The room offered a silent acknowledgement. *How could I have missed the attack on Vaire?* Not a single image of the attack came to him. He was losing his ability to foresee. If he lost that, command of the Consortium would surely follow. Command of the Consortium has been in his family for generations and he refused to lose it on his watch. A knock at the door interrupted his thoughts.

"Come in."

Hark-Kalech entered the room with Varooq in tow. They looked as grim as he felt. "The fleet is in place, sir," Hark-Kalech said.

Meta noticed that both were dressed for battle. Varooq had a rifle strapped to his back and a grenade belt fitted around his thick, hairy waist. Hark-Kalech wore a long slender dagger with a handle carved in the image of a daggerfish—the deadliest beast in the Caelum Sea. The weapon was a normal accessory for the senior officers of the Aquanauts. He also had a holstered hand cannon by his side and wore the angular, golden battle helmet of the Defense Fleet. Since Embeth's defection, he had been placed in charge of their defenses.

Varooq recognized Meta's expression of confusion. "I know it is not standard protocol for Council members to participate in combat, but we wanted to personally make sure Vaire is recovered," he explained.

"The soldiers' morale would improve significantly if we were to lead the invasion," Hark-Kalech added.

Meta nodded. He had been so worried lately about the defection of Consortium worlds that he had lost touch with the fleet. He turned to the window and folded his hands behind his back. "I agree."

Although they had been loyal Council members for as long as he could remember he refused to reveal his failing abilities. *No one must discover the truth*. Meta was determined to get to the root cause of the problem, but that was a battle for another day. There was a more important fight coming.

Varooq stepped forward. "I will lead four battle cruisers over the northern hemisphere of the planet."

"That part of the planet is comprised mostly of water," Hark-Kalech explained. "The Ascended forces are gathered along the southern hemisphere. They stray no further than the Shreen villages beside the beaches."

Meta turned. "What about the Shreen? They may be outnumbered but they are fierce warriors. Surely they could push back against the Ascended incursion?"

Varooq and Hark-Kalech exchanged glances. They were brief but Meta recognized the doubt in their eyes. If his Council members doubted his ability then doubt of his leadership will follow. He clenched his fists in agitation.

Hark-Kalech tugged at his left eyebrow which was a sign of apprehension. Meta recognized it. "We thought you were aware of the situation on Vaire. We apologize for not briefing you properly," he said slowly.

Whenever Hark-Kalech was restless like that something troubled him. Occasionally it had been Council matters, other times it had been matters of a personal nature. Was it the impeding battle that troubled him, or the fact that he recognized his leader had lost something of utmost importance? "What is wrong?" Meta asked.

It was Varooq who answered. "Calypso has somehow swayed the Shreen to join his cause."

That was a two-sided coin of bad news, Meta lamented. First, the Ascended have added a fierce fighting force to their growing numbers. Second, Meta should have seen this. The lack of clarity on the matter only further fortified his fears. He turned back to the window in silence.

Meta could see their reflection in the window. They were staring at each other uneasily. Why not? It was as clear as the Emerald Sea. Their leader had lost the ability which had guided the High Princes of the Consortium for centuries.

"This is ill news," Hark-Kalech said.

Varooq moved beside Meta and sighed. "I agree." His big arm fell across Meta's shoulders. "Do not worry, we will overcome this."

Varooq's arm was like a tree trunk bearing down across his shoulders. Meta found it difficult to simply nod his agreement. "It will be dealt with," Meta agreed. "How quickly can we mobilize against Vaire?"

Hark-Kalech moved behind him. Suddenly Varooq's arm closed around his head, shoving his face into the bigger man's fur coat of a chest. His air supply was cut off by the mass of Varooq's bicep. He wanted to cry out, but he couldn't breathe.

"This has been coming for a long time, *High Prince*," Hark-Kalech whispered in his ear. "Do not weep for the Consortium. Calypso will rebuild it and return it to its former glory."

Hark-Kalech's daggerfish blade plunged into Meta's back. Varooq let go and the blade twisted. A sound like paper tearing came from inside his chest. The pain of his heart rending sub-sided, soon giving way to the emotional pain of betrayal. "Ca-lypso!" Meta gasped. Dark blue slivers of blood fell from his lips.

Hark-Kalech tore the blade out and Meta fell to the ground. Blood bubbled from his lips when he rolled onto his back. Through dying eyes he studied his betrayers. Varooq looked on sadly but Hark-Kalech had a different look. It was the cold, emotionless look of an assassin. The treachery was complete. Calypso struck the first blow. Hark-Kalech struck the last.

"You will never take control of the Consortium," Meta gasped. "The Consortium will die with me."

Hark-Kalech snickered. "We are counting on it."

PREVIEW CHAPTER OF
BOOK 3 IN THE
CARTOGRAPHER SERIES

The boarding bridge attached to the ship. Once it locked into place the dock doors of the Astral Spirit lowered slowly. The interior lights from the ship illuminated a lone figure in the doorway. Hark-Kalech stood tall, ready to greet his visitor. It had been a long time since Calypso stepped foot aboard the Consortium flag ship and he smiled when he glanced at his former colleague of the Council of Five.

"Welcome aboard," Hark-Kalech beamed. "It's been a long time."

Calypso reached out and shook his hand. "It has indeed, my old friend. I assume by your warm reception that the task is done?"

"It is," Hark-Kalech let go of his hand. His smile faded when he saw the look of unease on Calypso's face. "Is something wrong?"

Calypso ran a hand through his flowing red hair and frowned when it came back moist with cold sweat. "It's the Insurgents. It seems they are not as disorganized as I originally had suspected. Our young Nathan seems to have a few tricks up his sleeve."

Hark-Kalech narrowed his eyes. "What do you mean?"

Calypso started to respond but he heard a noise coming from the docking bridge. It was as if someone dropped a coin on a metal surface. He looked back and saw nothing except the empty corridor of the bridge. The dimly lit hall was only visible on each end because of light coming from the open doors of their two ships.

"Calypso?" Hark-Kalech was looking at him with concern.

"Sorry, my nerves must be fried," he replied. "What I meant was that Nathan seems to have found new allies. The forces of Xajax have joined the scattered remains of Embeth's Defense Fleet. I assume after Corvus' failure on Vaire that the Hydrophants will not be far behind."

Hark-Kalech shrugged. "Once we merge the Consortium forces with the Ascended, Nathan can rally an entire galaxy to his cause and it will not make a difference."

"Perhaps you're right, but I prefer to take no chances," Calypso replied. He started down the hall but stopped when the hairs on his neck stood at attention. He suddenly felt colder for no reason at all. The temperature was a bit cool but nothing like the iciness that wrapped around him like a shroud. An overwhelming feeling of being watched overtook him, despite the fact they were alone in the hallway. He found his gaze drifting toward the bridge but the gloomy corridor remained empty. He shrugged it off as simple nerves.

"Shall we adjourn to the meeting room to discuss our next move?" Calypso asked.

Hark-Kalech swept his hand in an arc, motioning for Calypso to follow him. They entered an elevator that stood at the end of the hall. When Calypso turned around to wait for the elevator doors to close, he saw the docking bridge in the distance. A shadow passed before the open doorway and he froze. Squinting, he struggled to make out a shape in the gloom but the only thing he observed was the light wafting in from his ship. After several seconds passed he chalked it up to the light playing tricks on him.

When the elevator doors closed the shadowy figure dropped from the roof of the corridor. He landed softly, almost cat-like. His wings folded tightly against his back attracting the surrounding shadow to him like a magnet while he surveyed his surroundings. He crept toward the hallway while the shadows followed him as if they were his children. As he moved through the empty halls he marveled at his luck. No crowds made it easier for him to work. His primary objective was discretion. His mission was simple; *get in and get out unseen.* Calypso's skittish behavior amused him. The shadowy figure had been well briefed on Calypso's ability to sway his enemies with hypnotic charm and he took great joy in unnerving him.

He reached behind him and removed an eight-inch jagged steel blade out of the sheath. Its hilt had been carved into the shape of a scorpion, a gift from the desert nomads of Verillion 5. The blade was black, like the shadows. The little bit of light which did manage to penetrate the gloom reflected the deadliness of the ebony blade. It was coated with the essence of Moonweed, the most poisonous plant growing in the badlands of Epsilon Prime. His blade had one purpose and one purpose only—*assassination.* To him, murder was an art form and the only thing he was good at.

Moro smiled and drifted toward the elevator.

CPSIA information can be obtained
at www.ICGtesting.com
Printed in the USA
BVHW081022091120
592845BV00011B/746